Vietnam:
Green Hell Never Ends

Dale R. Lincoln

outskirts press

Vietnam: Green Hell Never Ends

v4.0

Outskirts Press, Inc.
http://www.outskirtspress.com

Paperback ISBN: 978-1-9772-5671-3
Hardback ISBN: 978-1-9772-5733-8

PRINTED IN THE UNITED STATES OF AMERICA

This book is about two complete strangers, Robert Dean Tomlin and Frederick (Butch) Philip (Pitbull) Price, who become the world's best friends. It tells about the adventures they had while in high school and the trails and tribulations while in the United Staes Marine Corps. They both went through the madness and heart ache of war with battles they fought together while in Vietnam. When ex-girlfriends and wives were easy forgotten. They stay best friends for ever, with equal parts irritation and cooperation.

This book is dedicated to:

To my wife Mieko for all her help with Okinawa

My world's best friends, Howard and Pat Price

To Robert Esslinger who is a Real United States Marine

To all the Marines of the United States Marine Corps
who were casualties of the Vietnam War.

Table of Contents

List of Notes and Illustations

Japanese Language

1-35 mongoose (マングース)
1-36 Minato (港区)
1-37 Sadao (サダオ)
1-38 Kiyo (きよ)
1-39 Father (父)
1-40 Mother (母)
1-41 Konnichiwa (こんにちは)
1-42 Thank You Very Much (ありがとうございました)

Vietnamese language

1-43 retreat (rút lui)
1-44 Who is found loving in the same field. Gay Neutral (Đồng Tính Luyến Ái)
1-45 no more (không còn, không còn)
1-46 they will kill me (họ sẽ giết tôi)
1-47 if I tell you (nếu tôi nói với bạn)
1-48 I will tell you (Tôi sẽ nói cho bạn biết)
1-49 Engineer Battalion (tiểu đoàn kỹ sư)
1-50 kill me (giết tôi)
1-51 I'am being cut to shreds (tôi đang bị cắt thành từng mảnh)
1-52 you blew off my nuts (anh đã thổi bay hạt của tôi)
1-53 retreat (rút lui, rút lui)
1-54 those frigging Marines (những thủy quân lục chiến chết tiệt)
1-55 I need a doctor (Tôi cần bác sĩ)
1-56 do not hurt me (đừng làm tổn thương tôi)
1-57 get that elephant off (đưa con voi đó ra khỏi)
1-58 I will tell you I can not breath (tôi sẽ nói với bạn rằng tôi không thể thở)
1-59 all Marines must died (tất cả thủy quân lục chiến phải chết)
1-60 kill all Amerians (giết tất cả người Mỹ)

CHAPTER ONE

The Football Game

It all started in 1964 when the Mayor of St. Louis Missouri, made a bet with the Mayor of Springfield, Illinois, over a high school football game. The Mayors were always making friendly wagers with each other over who was going to win St. Louis Cardinals or the Chicago Clubs baseball teams. Then, after a while, it was the St. Louis Cardinals and Chicago Bears who were going to win in football. The bets range from tickets to ball games or going to restaurants. Then one day Mayor of St Louis made a bet with Mayor of Springfield who had the best high school football team; Roosevelt High School in St. Louis, Missouri or Lanphier High School in Springfield, Illinois. The winner would receive a seven- course meal at the restaurant of his choice and with the icing on the cake, would have bragging rights over who had the best football team. Then each mayor had to give a little history of their schools.

Mayor of Springfield gave the following history of Lanphier High School. **(1-1)**

The name Lanphier was the last name of the family who owned the land on which our school sits. The first graduating class was in 1937. It is said that Lanphier means Land on Fire. The first change was the land that Lanphier now occupies. The area used to be a reservoir. It was part of a large park on the North end of Springfield. Many people would come and have picnics, go fishing, play sports, and take boats out on the reservoir. The reservoir aided in supplying water to the North side. Many were distraught to hear that Reservoir Park was being sold to the school district.

Construction of Lanphier High School was a project of the Work Progress Administration (WPA), a federal agency created during the Great Depression to provide paying jobs for unemployed workers. Most people would agree that the biggest changes for Lanphier have been expansion. The school has undergone a lot of construction. The biggest expansions of the school was Edison Junior High School. There was a walkway that connected the two schools. During the 60's the two buildings were combined to make the high school much larger. Some of the most recent modifications are the Commons Area, as well as a couple classrooms on the West end of the school. Because of these additions, the student body has increased in size as well.

One of the most difficult events Lanphier has ever faced was the Civil Rights Distribution in the late 60's. Black students were not treated as equals to white students. This caused major problems. Students of all races walked out of school because blacks were not allowed on the cheerleading squad. Students wanted their basic rights. It was probably Lanphier's darkest period in history. Lanphier High School has endured much in its existence, and there are still more developments to come. Many believe the stereotype that Lanphier is inferior to the other local high schools. Yet, all students who attend (and have attended) Lanphier have a strong pride for their school. The North Side Pride will live on forever.

Then Mayor of St. louis gave the following history of Roosevelt High School **(1-2)**
To relieve overcrowding at McKinley High School and Cleveland High School, the city's south side high schools for whites, the St. Louis Public Schools ordered the acquisition of property to construct a "New Southside High School" in 1922. Due to a lack of vacant land in the area, the Picker Cemetery (also known as Holy Ghost Cemetery) was acquired for the school's site, and evacuation of its graves began in October 1922. Most graves were relocated to mass graves in other cemeteries, although some remains were not relocated. During construction, neighbors reported dogs and children bringing home bones from the site, and workers reported finding jewelry and coffin handles while constructing the building. The building's cornerstone was laid on April 22, 1923, and the building was designed by R.M. Milligan at a cost of slightly less than $1.5 million.

The building opened to its first students on January 26, 1925, and it was officially named in honor Theodore Roosevelt. Most of its students and faculty transferred from McKinley High School, which was converted to a middle school from 1925 through 1932, and a smaller number of students transferred from Cleveland High School. Many school traditions and names relate to Roosevelt, such as its mascot (the Teddy Bear), its nickname (the Rough Riders), its original yearbook title (Bwana, in reference to Roosevelt's Swahili nickname), and its school colors and the melody of the school song are those of Harvard University, Roosevelt's alma mater.

From 1925 through the 1960s, Roosevelt served a predominantly white, ethnically German neighborhood, and due to school zoning, few black students attended after the integration of the St. Louis Public Schools in 1954. In the 1930s and 1940s, the Roosevelt boys' swim team won five state titles, and during the 1950s, students had a choice of seven musical instrumental groups. During the late 1970s, an increasing number of black students attended Roosevelt, although by the 1980–1981 school year, Roosevelt's student population remained nearly 70% white.

The big day was finally here. I thought about the football game all night, did not sleep very well. My brother Gene and Jimmy were telling me. "Robert you better go to sleep, you have to win that football game." In my mind I knew we had to win to save face for our Mayor, to give him bragging rights for the whole year. Gene and Jimmy were telling me: "we are behind you brother, just kick ass and take names." Then I finally went to sleep and I woke with the smell of my Mother's cooking. I could hear her telling me: " Robert get up wash and get dressed, your breakfast will be ready soon." As I walked down the stairs to the breakfast table, Mom had breakfast ready. She always makes a great meal; she had eggs, bacon, fried potatoes, pancakes, and milk. As I sat there eating, my Mom said: "eat up son you have to hammer that Roosevelt's Football Team. Your Dad and I will be rooting for you, just give it all, and that is all we can hope for." I looked at Mom and said: "Thanks Mom for the good breakfast and encouragement, see you after the game." As I started out the back door, I saw Robert Esslinger coming up the driveway. I said: "Hi Bob ready for the big football game." Bob said: " Sure I am, are we going to kick ass or what."

Bob was my friend since grade school; we did everything together fishing, hunting, swimming, water skiing, sports, you name it, we did it. The story that I always think of is, my Mom never fixed pasta. So one Thursday Bob had we stay for dinner and his Mon always fixed pasta on Thursdays. I sat there and ate with Bob's family and enjoyed a wonderful meal. Talking about my Mom who never fix pasta, Bob's Mom said: " Robert why don't you come over every Thursdays and have pasta with us." I was hooked, every Thursday I had pasta with the Esslinger's. It got to a point when Thursday rolled around; I didn't have to tell my Mom. She would say: "do not tell me, I know you are going to the Esslinger's for pasta."

One summer the crows were eating a lot of corn from farmers in Illinois. The Illinois Game Warrant put out a bounty of 10 cents for every crow head you brought to the Game Warrant's office. So Robert Esslinger, Danny Hinds, and I had a great idea to go hunting and kill crows and get the bounty of 10 cents for every crow's head. There a a giant corn field just south of Sangamon River, we would make this our base camp for the big crow kill. First we wounded a crow and tied his foot to a stake in the middle of the corn field; he would be our bait for the other crows trying to rescue him. As the crows started coming in to help the tether crow, we commence of popping every crow who was in our firing range. When it was all said and done, we had a gunnysack full of crow heads. The next day we went to the Game Warrant's office to collect our bounty. We took in the gunnysack to collect our bounty. The Warrant said: "How many crow head do you have." We said: "we do not know, but it has to be several hundred." The warrant said: " I am not counting them, so I will say it is 250 heads at 10 cent which come to $25.00 dollars." As we walked out of the office, Bob said: " we spend more for ammo." That night I told my Dad what happened at the game warrant's office. Dad said: "Son why don't you use your 22 rifle, shells are 50 cents a box of 50, where shotgun shells are $1.85 for 25. So that night I told

Bob and Danny, we are taking 22 rifles tomorrow. The next day we got up bright and early and headed for the corn field. We did the same thing staked out a crow for bait as the crows came in to help save him; we started shooting crows with the 22 rifles. By the end of the day we had three full gunnysacks of crow heads. As we were walking to the game warrant office, we saw a car hit and kill a fox. Danny said: "Hey boys there is 40 dollars right there, all we got to do is cut off his tail and ears. When we turn in the crow heads, we turn in the tail and ears for extra bounty." That day we walked away with about $38.00 dollars a piece. After we got home we made a pack; no more crow hunting.

The time my baby brother Kenny Ray died, he was only 11 months old. That morning I was playing with him , holding him up in the air; he would just laugh and laugh. I put him down and went to my girlfriend's house to play recorders and dance. Kathy and I had a good time listening and dancing to Elvis Presley's (Don't Be Cruel) and Johnny Cash's (Ring of Fire). We had lunch together; I kissed her goodbye and walked home. When I came through the back door, Gene and Jimmy were crying. I said: " what wrong." Jimmy said: " Kenny is dead." I said : " Hey you guys quit joking, that is not funny." Then Gene said: " yes Robert it is true, he bite into the electric cord of the radio and got electrocuted, and died on the way to the hospital." I just fell to my knees crying and thinking of my poor Kenny, he was so young. When Mom got home, she was a mess, tearing, just screaming down her face; Uncle Harvey was holding her up. I went over to Mom and I hugged her and said: "Mom I am so sorry." She pushed me away and said: "I just want to be alone" That was the first time in my life that the Mom ever rejected me. I was always a momma's boy, but that day I was nobody's boy. I told Mom: "I love you" and walked out of the house. I went right to Robert Esslinger's house and told them the bad news about Kenny. Bob's mom grabbed me and held me tight. She said. "Robert you know Kenny is in heaven with God now." I just stood there crying while Bob's Mom tried to comfort me. After about 15 minutes or so, I thank Mrs. Esslinger, went into the living room with Bob. Bob put his hand on my shoulder and said: "I am so sorry Robert, I do not know what I would do if I lost my little brother Harold." We talked for about an hour or two, then I went home. Mom was on the bed just crying her eyes out. She was a mess for about a week; she would not do anything; she ate very little, did not sleep much. She never ever got over losing her baby son Kenny. There has always been a special bond between Mother and Son, from the time they are born and until they are a hundred years old. I still tear up when I think about my baby brother Kenny and my Mom.

Then there was the time I had a hot date with Kathy for Saturday night. I did not do a certain chore and got grounded by my Dad. He said: call Kathy and tell her you are grounded, and you will not be going on a date." I said: "Dad I been planning this for weeks. He said: "Sorry son, you are grounded." I ran up the stairs madder, then a wet back hen. I had a plan. I changed into my good clothes, sneaked down the stairs and out the back door. Just as I had my hand on the door knob, I felt a hand on my shoulder. It was Dad. He said: " where in the hell do you think you going." I pushed Dad's hand off and said: " listen old man I am tired of you telling me what to do." I never finished my sentence because I never saw that right hook. I was on Mom's lap; she had a cold wash cloth on my forehead. She was yelling at my Dad: "why did you hit him that hard." My Dad yelled back: "I did not hit him hard." When I finally came to my senses, I realized I had made the biggest mistake of my life. I apologize to my Father and said: "Dad I am really sorry." From that day on I had a lot of respect for my Father; he was strict but always fair. I told Bob the next day and he said: " you are lucky your Dad did not kill you." Bob I have learned my lesson, as long as I live I will never stand against Dad ever. Bob Said: " if I ever did that to my Dad, I would not be talking to you right now."

At football practice that day we really went through the drills, our football coach was pushing us real hard. He kept saying: "if we do not win this game there will be hell to pay. Now go home gets some rest and eat a good protein meal, and be ready to stomp some ass at this football game." When I got home, I called Bob and said: "come by and we will walk to the high school for the game." I was laying on the bed resting when Mom said: "Robert dinner will be ready in about 45 minutes." I said: "OK Mom; I will be down after I rest." For about 45 minutes or so, I could hear Mom calling for dinner time. I got up, walked down the stairs and sat at the dinner table. Mom had fixed steak, potatoes, green beans, and her famous corn bread, with apple pie for dessert. As we talked my 8 year old sister Connie Sue said: "RobertI hope you win tonight." I turned to Connie and said: "Thanks Sis." Then Dad said: " I just hope you give them Roosevelt boys a good shellacking and send them back to St. Louis with their tails between their legs." Then Gene and Jimmy said: "make that double for us." Then Mom said: "make that triple for me." When I was helping Mom with the dishes, Bob came by. I told Bob I would be in a minute or two. Then I said: " I will see everybody at the game." Bob and I walked to High School to get ready for the big game. We got to the locker room; our football coach said: "listen up, get dressed, do your warm ups, and we have to win this game tonight for our mayor."

It was time to go to the field. We were really nervous with the, have to win hanging over our heads. . Bob and I played on the Offense, I played Left Tackle, and Bob played Right Tackle. The Quarter Back came up to us and said: "Robert and Bob you better protect my ass tonight. With out me a snowball in hell has a better chance to win." The captains from both teams were on the field for the coin toss. We won with heads and took the south end goal. When we were in the huddle, the quarterback said: "we are doing a draw play, Robert and Bob keep them damn big defensive ends away from my ass." The referee blew the whistle, and now it was do or die. This big defensive end from Roosevelt, who was 6 feet 4 inches tall, and weighed about 280 pounds, hit me like a ton of rocks. My ass was going straight to the ground. Just as our quarterback moves back as if to pass the ball and then hands the ball off to a running back. He also was hit very hard by the giant defensive end. When we got back to the huddle, the quarterback unloaded on me like a double barrel shot gun. He said: "Robert you have to stopped that monster, or we both will be killed." I said: Mike, when you hand the ball off, I will hit him from the left side and Bob can hit him from the right side." Mike looked at me and said: "this better work, I am not taking another ass beating." The play call was Blue 70; then Blue right, 70, left Red 60. When the quarterback says Blue 70, before the ball is snapped. That's when the quarterback yells Blue 70, as a cadence to tell the center when to snap the football. When he says Red 60, it lets the offense know he is ready to start the play. When Mike yelled Red 60 Bob and I hit that damn defensive end from Roosevelt with every ounce of power in our bodies; that poor son-of bitch hit the ground like an elephant getting hit with a .620 caliber bullet. He just lay there moaning and groaning, and asking for help. When they took him off the field and he never returned to the game. When we got back to the huddle, Mike said: " Robert and Bob thank you, now I do not have to worry about getting my ass kick all over this field."

While Bob and I were on the side lines resting, while our Defensive was playing, we noticed a running back from Roosevelt who was racking up a lot of yards. Bob and I kept checking on this running back, who was number 49. Bob turned to me and said: " look at charging Rhino run, no body can stop him." I said: " we better stopped him or we will lose this game. Bob and I just sat there thinking who in the hell is this guy number 49 with the name of Price, what a power house of a running back. The game was getting down to the wire the score was 27 to 27 with 3 minutes to go. Our coach was telling us we cannot get a touch down on this team, we will have to go with a field goal. Then he said; " Let the clock run down to 20 seconds, then we will kick the field goal. He then said:" We only kick when we are trying to score points without getting a touchdown. We did have to make this field goal to win." We had the ball on the 50 yard line with about 40 seconds left on the play clock. The coach called for a time out, as we ran for the side line to get the final play. The coach said: : we need 20 more yards to give our kicker a chance. This is the play: "Mike this a draw play and make damn sure you hand the ball to the running back, because with this running play, we have a chance. Now the coach is addressing the running back, "when you receive the ball runs toward the sideline and then up field." Mike said: "got you coach" When we got back to the huddle, Mike said: " Robert and Bob I need the protection to get the ball off." The play call was Yellow 50; then Yellow left 50, right; Green 60. Mike called for the signal. and handed the ball to our running back; he hesitated for a second, then took off like his ass was on fire. He was chunking up the yards, 5, 9, 11, 13, 17, when they stopped him; he gained 22 yards. The coach yelled: "time out" Our kicker had to make a 43 yard field goal. Now it is down to the wire; it is do or die. The long snapper is looking through his legs and the holder has his hands clenched pre-snap. The holder then shoots his hands open and the ball is snapped. As the kicker's foot hits the football, every body is holding his breath as the football is heading towards the goal posts. The ball is tumbling over and over; it is getting closer and close; it seems like it was taking forever. Then the ball goes through the goal post, and we win by 3 points. Our coach and team just went nuts, everybody grabbing each other, jumping up and down, screaming, cheering, and we are all very happy that we won. We shook hands with the losing team, Roosevelt High School. Number 49 came up to me and shook my hand and said: " great game, man you are one hell of a Left Tackle." I shook his hand and said: " no you are one hell of a running back." When we got back to the locker room, the coach was all smiles and really happy. Then he said: "boys I am so proud of you tonight, what a hell of a game, we fought tooth and nail but we came out on the top. I know our mayor is really gloating and giving it to the Mayor of St. Louis." Then he thanked us all personally, told us to take a shower, go home to celebrate and get our rest. Bob and I were the last ones to shower and get dressed.

As we walked out of the locker room onto the field, we noticed our opponent number 49, standing by himself. I said: "hey what's up" He turned to me and said: "I missed my bus back to St. Louis." So I said come home with me. I just live about 6 blocks from school. I will talk to my Dad and Mom about you staying at our house for tonight. Then my Dad can drive you home Saturday morning." Then I said: " by the way I am Robert Tomlin and this is Robert Esslinger." Then old number 49 said: " I am Butch Price, would it be possible I could call my Dad and Mom when I get to your house." I said: " sure thing" That was the beginning of a long-lasting friendship between two complete strangers that lasted a life time. I talked to Dad and Mom about Butch staying at our house for the night and Dad would drive him home the next morning. Butch asked to use the phone to call his Dad and Mom and tell them what happened about missing the bus. He said: " I met this football player from Lanphier High School name Robert Tomlin that he and his family offer to help him. He insure them that everything was ok and he would be home the next morning. Dad said: " We can leave about 8 o'clock in the morning and you will be home by 10 o'clock." So that night I slept with my brother Jimmy and gave Butch my bed. We lay there and talked about the game before going to sleep. I woke the next morning with the smell of Mom's cooking. We walked down the stairs to the breakfast table and sat down for a wonderful feast. Mom was singing right along to Don Gibson's "Sea of Heartbreak" as she made biscuits and gravy, eggs, bacon, toast, and waffles. Butch turned to me and said: "Your Mom and Dad likes country music also." I said: "yes and my Dad likes Hank Williams and Eddie Arnold. When ever they would leave, I would turn the radio station to good old Rock N Roll, then when I hear the car pull in the driveway, I put the station back to country." My Dad would say: " how can you listed to that Rock N Roll crap." As Butch was eating he said: " Mrs.Tomlin you are just a good cook as my Mom. Everything is really good and I thank You." My Mom turned to Butch and said: "you are welcome and Thank You Butch for that wonderful comment." My Mom said: " Oh by the way Butch is not your first name, are you a junior with your Dad's first name." Butch said: " No Mrs Tomlin my real name is Frederick Philip Price." Then my Mom looked kind of puzzled and said: " Where did you get the name Butch." Then Butch said: "It is kind of embarrassing." My Mom said: " We all adults here nothing to be embarrassed about." So Butch said: " well here goes when I was a little boy I always walk around with a hardon and my Dad though it was funny." So one day my Dad told my Mom, you know it is a chip off the old block and I am going to call him Butch Pitbull. So, Mrs Tomlin, that's how I got the name Butch." We finish breakfast; I help Mom with the dishes. Then we loaded into Dad's car to go to St. Louis.

On the way to St. Louis we talked about anything and everything. When we got to Butch's house, Butch said: "come in and meet my Dad and Mom." Dad and I walked in, greeted Butch's parents. Butch's Mom said: " it was really nice you took good care of our son." Dad said: " that is ok I am sure you would do the same for our son." Then Butch showed his room while our Dads were talking about being in the United States Navy. How both were at the battle of Midway in World War II. We stayed a few hours and Dad said: "well son its time to head home." As we shook hands and said our goodbyes, Butch and I exchanged phone numbers and said: "call me". We both said we would, and Dad and I walked out to get in the car to head home. The next day I called Butch about spending the week end in Springfield, and he said: " only if you well spend the following week end in St. Louis." I said" " I would." Then we talked about taking the Greyhound Bus to and from St. Louis to Springfield. Then I said: "my girl friend Kathy had a sister name Rose Ann." I told Butch I would call her the next day or two to see if Rose Ann wanted to go out with you. Butch said: " that would be great, cause my girl friend Helen and I are not getting alone right now. She is so damn bossy and her Dad is a real dick and really does not like me." Then I said: " good timing I hope you and Rose Ann hit it off."

CHAPTER TWO

Kicking around in Springfield and St. Louis

The next weekend we pick up Butch at the Greyhound Bus Station in Springfield. As we were walking to the car, my Dad said: " what you boys got planned for this week end." I said: I think we go to the movies, Gabatoni's, and meet Kathy and her sister Rose Ann. My Dad said: " that sound like fun, but do not get into any trouble." I told Butch we could take my old 1950 Chevy that I had been working on. I said: "I brought the car for $70.00 dollars with a bad main bearing." Dad said: " take it easy when you drive and next spring we will rebuild the engine." Well, old Robert blew it the first night I had the car out. I was at a stop light on 9th and North Grand. When this 55 Chevy pulled by side me and started revving up his engine, I dropped my transmission down in first gear and was waiting for the light to change. The light was on red, then yellow, then green; I popped the clutch, pushed the gas pedal to the floor, then when I shifted to second gear the engine was really hammering. I knew right then and there my ass was grass and my Dad was the power mow. Just before I got home I shut the engine off and coasted in the alley to our back yard. When I walked into the living room to tell Dad I was home. He looked up with a big grin on his face and said: : "I don't why you turn off the engine, I heard you coming two blocks away." I said: " I am sorry Dad, I know you told me to drive it easy." Then Dad said: Just leave it parked in the back and next spring we will put in a used engine." That spring we pick up a GMC truck motor, 292 cubic inches. We clean up the engine and rebuild it from the ground up. We put in new rings, bearings, gaskets, valves, rocker arms, push rods. waist pins for the pistons; I was none with the rebuild, it cost me about $150.00 dollars. I painted the engine GMC red, just left it on the engine stand while I cleaned up and painted under the hood. I cleaned up the fire wall, the inner fenders, and painted them the same color as the car's dark blue.

I was looking in the paper one day and came across this ad which read, selling all my car stuff, moving to California. I called the guy on the phone, he said: "he had a lot car parts for chevy and ford ." So I asked him, did he have anything for a 292 GMC, then said: " I do." I got to his address and rushed right over to his house. When I got there he said: "the parts our in the basement," I went downstairs. I could not believe my eyes, right in front of me was a Offhauser high compression head with large intake and exhaust valves; Offenhauser cast aluminum valve cover, three carb manifold with three strongberg 97 carbs, progressive linkage, split exhaust manifold, high lift cam, and a floor shift kit. I asked him what he wanted for the car parts. He looked at me and said: "fifty dollars." I could get my billfold out of my pants fast enough. I paid him, got a receipt, loaded the parts in my trunk, and headed home. When I got there I took my Dad out to the car, opened the trunk and showed him, he just stood there in a maze and said: "what did you pay for all of this". When I told him fifty dollars, he nearly fell over. He just looked at me and said: " son looks like you and I are building you a hot rod."

Dad and I started putting on all the hot rod parts to the engine. First we install the cam, then Dad said: " Son we are going to figure out the best way to get this cam to preform, 1. With short duration cams with relatively high valve lift can provide excellent responsiveness, great torque, and good power. 2. With performance cams increase the duration and timing of the valve openings during the engine stroke, increasing horsepower and making your car accelerate more quickly. My dad was a genius when it came to car engines, if I knew half of what he knew I would be happy. So inclusion we went with the performance cam, I wanted quicker acceleration coming off the line. Then we put on the head, three carb manifold, split exhaust manifold, strongberg 97 carbs, hooked up the progressive linkage. Then Dad said: "We will wait for Bob Ferman electronic ignition system, then we can set the rocker arms and adjust the valve before we fire the engine;" Then, Dad said: "We can measure for the length for your exhaust pipes and mufflers. Then we can go to the muffler shop to pick up the pipes and mufflers." Then I think we are going to have a major problem with installing that Saginaw 3-speed overdrive." Dad said: " we will go with the 3:55 rear end gear, that will give performance and speed.

Dad was right that Saginaw 3-speed overdrive was a real bitch to set-up and get running. Then Bob Ferman came up with a great idea with disc brakes; Dad and I got Chrysler Imperial Crown disc brakes from the junk yard to work on the chevy. The first day we fired up the old Chevy, as soon as Dad turned on the key and that baby just fired right up, my Dad had the biggest smile on his face. The car sounded and ran really well. There were a lot of V-8s that could not beat that old six-cylinder. Then I told Butch enough, talking about the old Chevy, let go in the house and clean up and pick up the girls..

We got to Kathy and Rose Ann's house about 4:00 PM, we got out of the car and walked to the front door. I rang the door bell, and Kathy came to the door and said: "Hi Robert" Then I introduced her to Butch and said: "I guess we will be going to the movies at the Orpheum Theater to see Lawrence of Arabia, then have pizza at Gabatoni's. The Orpheum Theater in the 100 block of North Fifth Street was Springfield's preeminent movie palace from 1927 to 1965. It was demolished to make way for expansion by the Illinois National Bank. The theater, with a spectacular Art Deco interior, seated more than 2,700 people for films, vaudeville and theatrical performances of all sorts. Total estimated construction cost was $2 million in 1927. The Barton Theater Organ alone cost $50,000. **(1-3)**

Gabatonis was founded by Johnny Lynn and his wife Rosemary, back in 1951. After completing his service in the United States Marine Corps, Johnny Lynn decided to take his love of food and share it with the community in which he lived. They had their first location at 300 Washington Street in Springfield, Illinois, and stayed there for eight years. In 1959, they moved their beloved family-owned pizzeria to their present location on 300 Laurel Street, where they still make the freshest, most delicious pizza 24 hours a day 7 days a week. **(1-4)**

Kathy invited us in, then we waited for Rose Ann to get ready so that we could go. Kathy"s Dad and Mom came into the living room where we were seated. Kathy's Dad said: " Hi Robert, how was your day." I said: " just find SIR" Then I introduced Butch to Bill and Susan Nelson. Bill like me better than Susan; I think she held that against me because my Dad was a coal miner. Then Bill ask Butch: "What does your Dad do" Butch answer back with: " well Mr. Nelson my Dad is retired United States Navy, and works for barge system on the Mississippi River." So then Bill said: " oh your Dad is not home much." Then, Butch said: "no he is home every night causes he work out of St. Louis." As Butch was telling them about his family, he said: "I have 9 brothers and sisters, but my Mom keeps us in line, matter of fact she is the hub, that keeps our family wheel together." Then Susan said: " my your Mother is a busy woman cooking and cleaning with 10 children." Then Butch said: "Well Mrs. Nelson we all pitch in and help, believe me she keeps all of us in line." By that time Rose Ann entered the living room and said: "I am ready" I introduced her to Butch; they shook hands in some idle conversation. Then I could see old Rose Ann eyes light up when she saw Butch, and you know, that's funny, his old eyes light up too.

Rose Ann was about 5 feet 8 inches tall, and weighed about 120 pounds. Red hair, green eyes and a figure that would not quit. Then there was Kathy; she was about 5 feet 10 inches tall, and weighed about 135. She also had red hair and green eyes just like her Mother. Her skin was smooth as silk and her legs went all the way up to her neck. Then I said we better get going, this is a long movie. Bill and Susan almost spoke at the same time: "make sure, the girls are home at 11:00 PM." I turned and said: "do not worry they will be home on time." We walked out, got in the car and drove off to the Orpheum Theater.

As soon as we got in the car, Old Butch had his arm around Rose Ann and both were in deep, conversation. I could tell right away they really like each other. Then Kathy said: "Your friend Butch is a very handsome and my sister really likes him." We parked on Fifth Street close to the theater, and as we were walking, Butch and Rose Ann were holding hands like they had known each other for years. I walk up to the ticket box and purchase four tickets at a $1.00 apiece; tickets were usually 69 cents but higher for a premier movie. I got the tickets, we all went inside, then of course everybody had to have refreshments. So while at the refreshment stand, I ordered 4 popcorns, 4 cokes, and 2 boxes of Good & Plenties that came to a total of $1.50 one dollar and 50 cents. I handed out the goodies, and as I gave Butch his refreshment, he said: "Robert I will buy the pizza." I said to myself, thank goodness I did not have much cash left. We went into the theater, the usher took us to our seats; we all got settled and were talking before the movie. Then, before, you know, the movie Lawrence of Arabia started, Kathy and I really got into the movie. Not Rose Ann and Butch. They were hugging and kissing like two minks in the heat. The movie was 3 hours and 48 minutes long, then half way through the movie they had an intermission. The girls got up to use the bathroom and

Butch and I just sat there and talked. The movie ended about 8:30 PM, so that left us with about 2 and half hours to eat and get the girls back home by 11:00 PM. We all walked out of the movie theater, got in the car and drove off to Gabatonis on Laurel Street. On the way we were talking about how good the movie was, Butch and Rose Ann were talking about how much they liked the movie, but to tell the truth Romeo and Juliet probably only saw half the movie.

We pulled into the parking lot of Gabatonis, parked the car. Butch helped Rose Ann out of the back seat, then in the corner of my eye I saw he gave Rose Ann a little squeeze on her behind. We walked into the restaurant, got seated. The waitress gave us the menus. I suggested we all slit a large pepperoni with mushrooms, green pepper, onions, and black olives. Then we all agreed and ordered 4 cokes to drink. The total cost was $2.75 two dollars and 75 cents. While we were waiting for the pizza, Rose Ann asked: " Butch are you coming to Springfiedl next week?" Butch answered back with, no. Robert is coming to St. Louis next week, but I will be back in two weeks. Then Rose Ann grabbed his hand and said: " Make sure you call me" then she handed him her phone number. Kathy looked at me and said: " what do think of these two love birds." I said: "Kathy I though I was fast, but old Butch beats me." Then Kathy had a big smile and said: "fast is not the word, you good looking man." We ate our pizza and talked for a while.

Johnny Lynn came up to the table and asked: "how was the pizza" We all agreed it was very good. I asked him about the Marine Corp. He just smiled and said: "you boys thinking about joining the Marines. Let me tell you one thing the Marines are very tough and proud, and always remember once a Marine always a Marine." He thanked us for coming in and having a great night and walked away to go to other tables. Then I looked up and saw the clock; it was 10:30 PM. I said: " we better go to get you home I do not want your Mom and Dad mad at me. Butch paid the bill handed the waitress a 75 cent tip, thanked her and we all walked to the car. We got to Kathy and Rose Ann's house at 10:50 PM, we were cutting it close we had 10 minutes to spare. Butch gave Rose Ann a long kiss goodbye and I kissed Kathy goodbye, we walked them to the door. Then Rose Ann whisper in Butch's ear make sure you call me. Kathy said call me Robert, we kiss them on the cheeks. They went into the house and Butch I walked back, got in the car and drove off. On the way home Butch was really excited about Rose Ann, he was talking up a storm about how good looking and geat she was. Then said: "Robert we have to go out with them in two weeks. I am crazy about that girl." Sunday afternoon we drove Butch to the Greyhouse Station so he could get a bus back to St. Louis; the round trip ticket was around $8.00 dollars. Butch said: " Thank You Mr. Tomlin and see you in about two weeks." My dad told Butch: " you are welcome take care and have a safe trip home." As Butch was getting on the bus, he yelled back: "see you next week Robert". It would be my turn next week to take the Greyhound Bus to and from St. Louis. Well, the week went by real fast, the next thing I knew Dad was driving me to the Greyhound Bus Station so I could go to St. Louis. Dad walked me do the Bus Station; we shook hands and Dad said: "Son be good and do not get into any trouble, we do not want your Mom to worry, I will pick you up Sunday afternoon." I said: "ok Dad see you Sunday and tell Mon not to worry I will be ok." I got on the bus heading for St. Louis on Highway 55. It took about two hours to get there, so I took a little nap.

When the bus pulled into the St. Louis Bus Terminal, I could see Butch and Dad waiting for me. I said: " Hi to Mr. Price and Butch." Then Mr. Price said: " I got you and Butch tickets for the St.Louis Cardinals at Sportsman's Park III Saturday night, they are playing the Chicago Clubs." I said: " Thanks a lot Mr. Price, now I get to see Stan the Man." We got in the car and headed for Butch's house. As we pulled into the driveway, one of Butch's brothers said: " hey its Robert from Springfield, looks like some us will be bunking together tonight." I said hi to everyone, then Butch's Mom came out and asked: " Robert do you want a nice cold glass of lemon-aid." I said: "I sure do Mrs. Price." Butch and I goof around until dinner, then we heard the famous call come and get it. We all pile around the dining table and what a feast, fried chicken, mashed potatoes, (Butch calls them taters) gravy, green beans, okea, and man, can Mrs. Price make a mean apple pie for dessert. After dinner I helped with the dishes, then we got ready for the baseball game. Mr. Price drove us to the ball park and said:"boys I will pick you up after the game."

Butch and I walked to the front gate and gave our tickets to the usher, then we found our seats. I was looking at the baseball program of the players and their positions. For the St. Louis Cardinals the Catcher was Gene Oliver, First base was Bill White, Second Base was Julian Javier, Short stop was Julio Gotay, Third base was Ken Boyer, Left field was Stan Musical, Center field was Curt Flood, right Field was Charlie James, and Pitcher was Bob Gibson. For the Chicago Clubs the catcher was Dick Bertell, First base was Ernie Banks, Second base was Ken Hubbs, Short Stop was Andre Rodgers, Third Base was Ron Santo, Left Field was Billy Williams, Center Field was Lou Brock, Right Field was George Altman, and Pitcher was Dick Ellsworth. Then Butch turned to me and said: " can you believe Stan is 41 years old and they are paying him $55,000.00 dollars a year to play baseball."I said to Butch: "but he is one hell of a baseball player and he is my favorite." Then, Butch said: "how come you are not a fan of the Chicago Clubs since you live in Illinois." I said: "I just like the St. Louis Cardinals for baseball and Chicago Bears for football." Butch said: "at lease we have same baseball team in common." These smart asses college students from University of Evansville in Evansville, Illinois were listening in on our conversation; this one student turned to Butch and said: " I bet you $10.00 dollars the Clubs will kick the Cardinals ass tonight." Butch said: "I will take that bet." In the fifth inning the Cubs were ahead 5 to 3, and I could see Butch squirting a little bit about the $10.00 dollar bet. I assure him Bob Gibson is not going to let us down. In the seventh inning, St. Louis was at bat. Julio Gotary was on second base and Ken Boyer was on first base, who was coming up to bat, you guessed it, Stan (The Man) Musical. First pitch is ball, second pitch Stan hits a foul ball, third pitch is a ball, fourth pitch foul ball, now two balls and two strikes against Stan. Old Dick Ellsworth getting ready with the fifth pitch, and I told Butch going to be a curve ball. We are in suspence because we can not see the ball in his glove, now Dick Ellsworth winds up and hurls the ball right at Stan Musical, who is as cool as a cucumber, steps back a little, then swings that mighty bat. Stan hits that ball with all his might and the ball goes up in a 90-degree arch and starts to climb higher and higher, then the ball heads for center field. Lou Brock is running his ass off trying to get to the ball; just as Lou Brock goes up against the wall to catch the ball, it misses his glove only by inches, the ball goes over the center wall. The crowd goes nuts; Butch and I are jumping up and down yelling Stan the Man, Stan the Man. Now we are ahead 6 to 5 and that's how the game ended. St. Louis 6; Chicago Clubs 5.

Butch asked the student from Evanville for his money. The student who gave no name, said: "I do not have it" Then he pulled out his wallet to show Butch it was empty;, then Butch grabbed the wallet to check to see if it was empty. Then all hell broke loose, there were about seven of them to two of us Butch and I. Fists were flying; students were screaming and yelling we will kill you, son-of bitches. But Butch and I held and stood our ground. Three guys were on Butch just beating the shit out of him. I ran down, grabbed one bastard, and hit him right between the eyes; he fell back and dropped like a rock and did not move. By that time Butch had recovered and became this damn fighting machine. I saw him hit a student so hard, teeth were flying out of his mouth. I saw him punch another student so damn hard, it looked like his face just collapsed under Butch's fist. Another student grabbed Butch from behind and was ready to put the hay maker on Butch's head. I grab the son-of-bitch, turn him around and give him the old Tomlin special, two quick jabs to the face, then the right under cut that my Dad taught me. I think I broke his jaw, because I felt his face crumble under my fist. That was three down and four to go. So Butch, and I were standing side by side waiting for the other four to make their move. Then one student said: " lets go I am not getting my ass kicked by these two belligerent cocksuckers."

So they left and the fight was over. Butch looked at me and said: : do we look like we"ve been through the saw mill." I said: "worst you have a black eye and a swollen ear and I got a bloodly nose and cut lip." But damn Butch, we kicked ass. When Mr. Price picked us up, he said: "were you boys prize fighters tonight". Butch said: "no Dad just a miss under standing about a bet on the baseball game." Though all that turmoil and fighting Butch never got his 10 bucks. We went back to Butch's house to clean up and went to bed. Got up the next morning and Mrs Price fixed a great breakfast, eggs, sausage, hash browns, and pancakes. I told Mrs. Price, thank you for a wonderful breakfast and help with the dishes. When upstairs to rest before they took me to the Greyhound Bus Station. After we got to the bus station I told Mr. Price, thank you again for the baseball tickets. Then I told Butch I would see you next week, then I reminded him of the hot date with Rose Ann. He grabbed my arm and said: " Robert do you think my face will be heal by then." I said: "yes pretty boy your face should be heal by then." I got on the bus and headed for Springfield. When Dad picked me up at the bus station and saw my face, he said: " looks like somebody had a mis understanding, I hope it was not you and Butch." I said: "no dad some jackasses would not pay their bet at the ball game." Then, Dad said: " did they finally pay." I said: " no but Butch and I kick their asses." Dad had a big smile on his face, then laughed a little and said: " like I have always told you do not go looking for a fight, but if you are backed into a corner always come out swinging."

So the next week end Butch came up from St .Louis and we made plans to take Kathy and Rose Ann to the movies at the Phantheon Theater to see Battle Cry, a 1955 movie with Tab Hunter. Both Kathy and Rose Ann. thought he was a dream boat. We made plans to see the movie then go to A&W Root Beer to get hamburgers and root beers. Pick Butch up at bus station, on the way to my house, we were talking about the movie Battle Cry about the Marine Corp in the pacific in World war II. Butch Said: " you know Robert I have seen the movie a couple of times but I want to see it again." I answer back: " I really want to see it again." Then my Dad said: : do not get any funny ideas about joining the Marines, you know you are going to the Navy." Then Dad went on with his pitch about the Navy and said: "all our family members were in the Navy, except your cousin Eddie who was in the Marines." Then Dad had a sad tone in his voice and said: "Eddie just turn 18 years old when was killed in Korea, my brother Ike really never got over loosing his son." Then Dad had a stern tone in his voice and said: " That my son is the main reason you will join the Navy." Then I said: "I know Dad" Butch said: "you know Mr. Tomlin my Dad feels the same way, because he was a Navy man." My Dad said: " enough of the Navy talk, lets talk about something else." So on the way home we talked about any and everything.

We got to my house then Butch said: "Robert can I use your phone, I want to call Rose Ann." I said: "sure when you get done talking, do not hang because I want to talk to Kathy." Butch said: " you got it Big Robert." Butch got on that phone and I did not think he was ever going to get off. Then finally he handed me the phone and said: "Kathy on the phone." I was telling Kathy we had plans to go to the Phantheon Theater to see Battle Cry, which was about a 2 and a half hour movie, then go to A&W Root Beer after the movies. She said: "ok I will tell Mom and Dad of our plans, then you know what my Mom is going to say: "be home at 11:00 PM." Then I said: I hope one day I can keep you out all night." Then she came back with, you know, that will never happen with my Mom. So I said: "good by and see you this afternoon," then I hung up. Butch and I went outside and messed around with the car and just waited until it was time to pick up Kathy and Rose Ann. Just before we left Mom said: " Oh Robert Esslinger called you the other day, asking for you; I told him you and Butch had plans this week end." That was kind odd ever since I started running around with Butch Price, Bob and I went our different ways. I figure he did not want the competition for my friendship with Butch. Bob started to run around with Bill Moody and Robert Kidd.

Oh, that Bill Moody was a character, he was funny, joked around a lot, and was the life of a party, and was a hell of a drummer. We worked at the Senate Theater as ushers. I remember one Saturday Bill came down from the balcony and said: " Robert you have to come up to the mezzanine to the phone booth, it looks like a man is having a fit in there." So I run upstairs and there is a man in the phone booth with the phone against his ear, he is twitching back and forth, he has all kinds of odd expressions on his face, he looks like he was in a lot of pain. So I walked up to the phone booth to see if I could help, I looked in, to my surprise there was a woman on the floor giving his guy a blowjob. I signal Bill to come over and look. When Bill looked in, he started laughing like a wild man. The man heard Bill laughing; the man got the girl up, and they both left the phone booth. Bill and I never laugh so hard in our lives. Another time Bill had these 4 black kids leave the theater because they would not stop talking while the movie was going on. So Old Bill escorted them out of the theater, and as they were leaving, one black kid said: " we want our money back." Bill said: "no way you just lost your money, besides you should have shut up when I told you to be quit." Then, he said: "we are going to wait for you till after the show lets out then we are going to stomp your ass." Bill said: " and who's army." The second black kid said: " we do not need an army cause we are going to kick your ass up and down the street." Bill said: " move on" and went back into the theater. The theater was letting out and Bill walked to the front and looked out. To his surprise, the 4 black kids were waiting for him. Bill came running up to me and said: "Robert what am going to do, they will kick my ass." I said: "let me talk to the manager Mr. Rice." So I went up the stairs and talked to Mr. Rice and told him what had happened. Mr Rice said: "they are outside waiting for Bill to get off." I said: "yes SIR and they looked like they might hurt Bill. Then Mr. Rice said: " Will give you 4 theater passes to the Strand Theater for them to see the next show, and that should smooth things over." Mr Rice wrote out 4 theater passes, handed them to me, and said: "tell the kids the next movie is on us." I took the passes, when outside and explained to the kids. I said: " you know Bill was just doing his job and for the misunderstanding here are four movie passes to the Strand Theater." the one black kid said: " thanks, you just save your buddy from a good ass kicking." They took the passes and moved on. I went back into the theater and Bill said: " thanks Robert for saving my ass."

Then there Robert Kidd the golf pro from high school. He had a 1952 Chevy that had a real bad front seal that was leaking oil like a sieve. That damn engine was using about two quarts of oil every day. Bob would buy the refine oil at 25 cents a quart and put it in his car. One night we were going to a dance in Decatur, which is about 40 miles from Springfiedl. We just got to Riverton, which is about 16 miles from Springfield, when all of a sudden his old engine started, knocking. I said: " Bob did you put oil in the car before we left." He turned to me and said: " oh shit Robert I forgot to put in the oil." About that time that old engine just exploded, a damn piston came through the hood, and the car came to a squeaching stop. As I got out of the car, I could see bits of glowing parts from the engine all over the highway. I cuss Bob all the way back to Springfield as we had to walk 16 miles back home.

Then one time Bob and I were walking back from batting practice; I was carrying about 3 bats in my right hand. When Jim Cronkin kicks the bats and one flew up and hit me in my head. I turned around and said: " what the hell is your problem." Then Jim said: "Asshole you are my problem and what are you going to do about it." I was boiling mad and I grabbed him and Bob stepped in between us. Bob said: "not on the school grounds meet him at Steincoolers Grocery Store after school." When school was out and Bob and I were walking to Steincoolers, just before we got there, we could see that half the school was there, in the back parking lot waiting for the big fight. I got to the parking lot and there was Jim Cronkin spouting off how he was going to kiss my ass and make me eat dirt. So Jim and I were in the middle with students around us. Robert Kidd said: "when I drop my arm come out fighting." Bob dropped his arm and Jim took a big swing at me: he just caught the very top of my temple. I jumped back and gave him two quit jabs to his face and a left cross on the side of his face. You could hear him moan as he stepped back. Then he came at me with his arms swinging like a windmill; he hit me a couple of times in the chest and arm. I just stepped back and unloaded a right upper cut right under his chin. The force was so strong that when my fist hit him under his chin, it knocked out 2 of his teeth. Blood was pouring out of his mouth and he said: " Tomlin I am going to kill you." He came straight at me with his fists flying all over the place. I hit him right in the bread basket with a hard right punch, then I hit him in the face with my left. By now he looked like a chopped hamburger; blood was pouring out everywhere, students were yelling to finish him off Robert. Then he grabbed me and held me with both arms to tie me up, and then that bastard head-butted me, split my forehead wide over, and then I was bleeding like a stuck hog. I stepped back to gain my composure, then I just did a threw rapid body punches every where on his body, after about hitting him several times, he kept saying: "uncle Robert uncle." Then I felt this hand on my shoulder and a voice: " ok Rocky Marciano junior the fight is over." It was a Springfield Police Officer telling me to get in the squad car and wait for him. Old man Steincooler called the police. As Bob and I were walking to the police car, Bob said: " your Dad is going to kill you." When the police got to his car, he said: " what was the fight all about." I explained to him what had happened at school earlier and that Jim was going to kick my butt. The police officer took the report and said: "I'll take you and your friend home."

As the police car was pulling in our driveway Mom and Dad and the Browners from next door were sitting on the porch, drinking coffee. The police officer gets out of the car and says: " Mr and Mrs. Tomlin I am bringing home Rocky Marciano junior who was fighting at Steincooler's. But do not worry he is not into any trouble, I just brought home before he killed the kid he was fighting. You have have a nice day:, then he looked at my Dad and said: " Do not be to hard on Rocky." My Dad started laughing and said: " I won't" I went inside and cleaned up, came back out and explained everything to Mom and Dad. Then Dad and I drove Robert Kidd home. As Bob was getting out of the car, I said: "thanks Bob for being there for me." Bob turned around and said: " anytime Robert." Then he went into his house Dad and I drove home.

The movie started at 5:30 PM, so Butch and I got to Kathy and Rose Ann's house around 4:45 PM. I parked the car in the driveway and Butch and I walked up to the house to meet their parents. We rang the doorbell; Kathy came to the door in this beautiful floral pink and white dress with high heel shoes; to me she was a living doll. I kissed her on her cheek and said: " Hi good looking what you got cooking."She said: " be quiet Mom is going to hear you." Then Butch said: " Hi Kathy where is Rose Ann." Kathy answered back with, you know, she is up the stairs getting ready. Walk into the living room and we say hello to Mr. And Mrs Nelson. Mrs. Nelson asked if we wanted anything to drink; we both said no at the same time. Then I started counting, 1 coke, 2 cokes, 3 cokes, 4 cokes, then Butch said stop. Mrs Nelson said: " what was that all about." I said: " Well Mrs. Nelson if you say the same word at the same time with someone, you count how may cokes they own you until they say stop. So now Butch owns me 4 cokes." Then Mrs. Nelson said: " you kids think of the craziest things to do to amuse yourselfs." By that time Rose Ann came down and said: " guess what I am ready to go." Then, just like clock work, Mr. And Mrs. Nelson said: " remember the girls have to be home by 11:00 PM." We got to the Phantheon Theater. I bought the tickets at 50 cents each; we all walked in; I went to the freshmen stand; I ordered 4 popcorn, 4 cokes, and 2 boxes of Good & Plenty at the cost of $1.10 (one dollar and 10 cents). Butch said: " Robert I will pay for the A&W." The usher shows us to our seats; we talk some before the movie starts. I, though old Butch and Rose Ann would be lovely dovely while the movie was on, but I was wrong. Butch and Rose Ann just held hands, because Butch was ready watching and getting into the Battle Cry movie. After the movie we walked back to the car and headed for A&W Root Beer down North Grand. As we were driving Butch said: "you know Robert just screw the Navy I am going to join the Marine Corp. I answer back with: " Me too Butch, you know we can join on the buddy system." Then I went on with our conversation by saying: the next time the Marine Recruiter comes to school I am going to talk to him." Butch said: " Me Too." Then Kathy and Rose Ann got all teary eyes. Kathy said: " Robert I will never see you again." Then Rose Ann told Butch the same thing. I turned to Kathy and said: "I will write to you and you will wait for me won't you." Kathy with tears running down her face, said: " of cource I will, no mattet how long it takes." I gave her a big hug and kiss and said: " you will always be my girl." Then Rose Ann started on Butch and she said: "you will write me, and I promose I will wait for you." Butch grabbed Rose Ann with a big hug and kiss and said: "you do not have to worry I will write and you will always be my girl." After a few minutes every body was back to normal; we were laughing and carrying on. We pulled into A&W, got parked, and I pushed the button on the speaker to tell them we were ready to order. A tall skinny girl came flying out on her roller skates to our car to take our order. She was smacking her chewing gum and said: "what can I get you." I said: go ahead; Kathy and Rose Ann." Kathy ordered a mustard hotdog, fried fries, and a root beer. Rose Ann ordered a hamburger, fried fries, and a root beer. Then I said: "ok Butch ordered 2 hamburgers, fried fries, and a root beer. By the time it got to me to order, the waitrest was really smacking on that gum. I said: "I have 2 mustard dogs, fried fries, and a root beer. Then, the waitress said: " will that be all." I said: "yes and whats our total. She said: "I will have your total in a minute." Then she repeats our order back to us. She said: "3 dogs with mustard, 3 hamburger, 4 fries, and 4 root beers, that comes to a total of $4.20 dollars and 20 cents. Butch handed her $5.25 dollars and 25 cents and told her to keep the change. She said: "Thank You and your food will be out soon." We ate our food and talked and laughed a lot. Drove over to South Grand to Washington Park to make out. As we were hugging and kissing, Kathy let out a scream and said: oh my God it is 10:40 PM." I rev up that old engine dropped that baby in first gear and the tires were smoking as we left the park. We got home by 10:55 PM, boy was that ever close. We said our goodbyes, and Butch and I went home. On the way home Butch kept talking about the buddy system in the Marines. He said: "just think Robert you and I will be station together." I said: "I know damn sure we will be in war together." Then I told Butch: " lets not tell our parents until we al sure thats what we want to do. I do not want to worry my Mom and I am for sure you do not want to worry your Mom." So Butch and I made plans for next week, we were going to seek over to Gaslight Square in St. Louis, with out telling our parents.

Next week was my turn to take the bus to St. Louis. Dad drove me to the bus station and told me he would pick me up Sunday afternoon. You know, I knew my Dad always had a sixth sense about us kids if they were going to get into any trouble. The main reason, I thought, was that, he was the seventh son of a seventh son. My Dad put his hand on my shoulder and said: "son promise me you will not get into any trouble." right then and there, I knew that Dad had figured out what Butch and I had planned. So I turned to my Dad and said: "Dad do not worry, I promise I will not get into any trouble." I got out of the car, walked towards the bus station, turned around and waved my Dad off. Got on the bus and headed to see Butch in St. Louis. Got to the bus station in St; Louis; Butch and Mr. Price were waiting for me.

When I got in the car, Mr. Price asked: "what you boys got plans for tonight." Butch answered back with: "oh Dad Robert and I are going to the Fox Theatre tonight." Mr. Price did not know that Butch and I were pretended to go to the movies and that we had about a mile to walk to Gaslight Square from the Fox Theater. Butch had been telling me about Gaslight Square for weeks, like he would say: " you know Robert there is more pussy in Gaslight Square then you can shake a stick at." Then he would go on about how beautiful the women were running around half naked. I could not wait to go to see if he was telling the truth. Mrs Price fixed a nice dinner; we all sat around the dining room table talking and laughing. I told Butch, I will help you with the dishes so that we could get going. Butch's brother drove us to the Fox Theater, so that our plan would work. Before we got into the car Butch told his Dad and Mom goodbye and see them later. Butch's brother drove us to the Fox Theater and told Butch: " Butch if Dad ever finds out about your little scheme of you going to Gaslight Square, he will skin you alive." Then Butch said: "I just hope Dad never finds out." Then his brother said: "how you and Robert getting home." Butch said: " we plan on taking the bus home." Then his brother said: " Butch do not get home late and please do not get into any troule, or Dad will have my ass too." Butch said: "ok brother, Robert and I will see you later." As soon as Butch and I got out of the car, we started walking towards Gaslight Square. Butch remember we have to get around the doorman at O'Connell's Pub because that where all the hot women are at. We have to make some kind of attraction so that we can seek in."

The doorman or (bouncer) was arguing with two drunks about coming in. While he was paying attention to them, Butch and I slipped past him, right into the club. Once in side we found a table close to the stage and waitless took our order of 2 cokes and we waited for the show. This band came out with a female singer; she was singing old Elvis Presley tunes. Then she started singing Teddy Bear; I started singing right along with her and she heard me. She came over to the edge of the stage and said: "you want to join me in a Elvis song." I said: " yes I do" she said: "then come on stag and join me." Before I got on stag, she made an annoucement, coming on stag to join me in a song is a young Elvis Presley. I was really nervous, my legs were knocking together when I went up on stage to join her. Butch was yelling: "go Elvis go." I got on stage, then she asked me my name and I said: "Robert Dean Tomlin". She said: " ok Robert we are going to do Don't Be cruel, do you know the song." I said: "Yes, I know it by heart. So the band started playing; I started singing and really getting into it; I was shaking my legs and rotating my hips, and moving around the stage while I was singing. The women in the audience were screaming and carried on. Butch kept shouting go Elvis go. When I finished I went back to the table with Butch .

While we were watching the rest of the show, a woman in a tight fitted yellow dress came up and said: "what you boys got planned for tonight." Then she said: "may I join you", she set down, and she had the biggest tits I ever saw. We were talking about the show, and asked if we came here alot, Butch and I said:" No, this was our first time." Then she asked the big question: " How old are you guys." We said 17, her eyes lit up like candles, then she said: "you boys mind if I drive you home." We both said: "no" Then she said:" lets go; I will drive you home, the car is in the back." When we got to the car she open the front door of that Cadilac, sat on the edge of the seat, hike up her dress pulled down the top of her dress; she had the largest tits with nipples as large as my thumb, spread, her legs wide open, with no under pants on, and that hairy beaver staring us right in our faces. She said:"Who is going to be the first one to ride old Momma." Butch and I looked at each other and both of us said: " no Thank You" and we were scooting to the front of the building. Oh, she was pissed, she called us every cuss word there was. She was yelling: "I knew you were a couple of bozos you are young, dumb, and full of cum, and ungreatful little bastards, that could of have best ride and pussy in your life, now you wasted my time for nothing." Then Butch said: " Lets get the hell out of here and I am glad we did not screw that bitch." We ran to the front of O'Connell's Pub; we left Gaslight Square, caught a bus for Butch 's house. On the bus Butch and I were talking about the woman in the yellow dress. Butch said: "Robert I do believe that woman would have screw us to death." Then I was joking and said: "but it would a hell of a way to died with those tits in your face." Butch was telling me a story about a girl, he was romping her one night, " she was telling at me that I was killing her and I said: "You want to stop" then she said: " no go ahead and kill me." We both laughed so hard, even the bus driver was laughing. The bus driver said: " boys it never chances, from the time they think about sex until its time for you to died." We got to Butch's house, went right to bed and went to sleep. When we got up the next morning, Butch was telling his brother about the incident at Gaslight Square with that woman in a yellow dress. His brother said: "was she look looking, you and Robert ought be happy nothing happen, you could have got the clap, or Syphilis. Then Butch said: " She was a looker with the biggest tits you ever saw." We had breakfast, then we just messed around the rest of the day, until it was time for me to go to the bus station. Butch and his Dad took me to the bus station. I told Mr. Price Thank You and told Butch, I would see him next week. I took a nap on the bus going back to Springfield. Just like clock work, Dad was waiting for me at the bus station. I got in the car and Dad asked how my weekend was. I said: "it was ok and I am glad to be home." I wanted to tell Dad about the incident at Gas Light Square, then decided to quit while I was ahead.

CHAPTER THREE

Getting Ready for Boot Camp

Butch and I went to the Marine Recruiter Station to enlist in the United Staes Marine Corp. After Gunnery Sergeant Charles W. Wilson came to Lanphier High School in Springfield, Illinois. He talked about the requirements for physical and mental tests and that the Marine Corp only wanted the best. He also mention the The Buddy System, which you can join with your friend, the Marine Corp guarnteed two years of service together, that is going to boot camp and station together for two whole years. Then, he said: " we have the DEP (Delayed Entry Program) when you pick the date to join the United Staes Marine Corp." I said: "can we join in September 1966, that way we will have the whole summer with our families." Gunnery Sergeant Charles W. Wilson said: " he could make the arrangement for the DEP." I told the Gunnery Sergeant that my friend Butch Philip Price lives in St. Louis Missouri. He said: " that is ok the Marines can make arrangements to bus me to St. Louis or Butch to Springfield, that way we leave together to go to boot camp in San Diego." Gunnery Sergeant Harold W. Brown went to Roosevelt High School in St. Louis, Missouri and told Butch the same thing about the Marine Corp. He told Butch to get together with your friend Robert and pick a date when you wanted to enlist and go to boot camp togethter. I called Butch that night and gave him the good news. Then I told him about DEP (Delayed Entry Program) where we could wait until summer was over and spend time with our families, then join the Marines. Then I told Butch the hard part was going to be telling my Dad and Mom, but I am going to tell them as soon as I hung up the phone and Butch said the same thing about telling his Dad and Mom.

Dad and Mom were in the living room watching TV. I said: "Dad and Mom have something I want to tell you." My Dad said: "what that son", I was really nervous and I just said it out: "I want to join the Marine Corp." To my surprise, my Dad got up, went over and shook my hand, and gave me a big hug. Then he added, you know, we are at war and for sure you will go to Vietnam. I still wish that you had joined the Navy like your brothers Gene and Jimmy. Make me a promise son, that you will be careful and please come back home. Then my Mom with tears in her eyes, said: "you are so young at 18 to be going to war." Mom came over to me and gave me a big hug and kissed me on my cheek, while she was holding my hand; she said: "promise me that you will come back." While I was holding her hand, a great memory took me back a couple of years when I went to my first prom; I came home from school so excited that I was taking Kathy Nelson to the school prom on Saturday night. Mom was going with me to pick out my tux from Hubb Clothiers; she even helped me clean up my car. That Saturday night I came down the stairs with my tux on and I was having trouble hooking the cummerbund belt; Mom reached around and hooked it for me.

She straightened my bow tie and called Dad. She said: "Dad just looked at this handsome devil," then she said: "some lucky lady is going to prom with our son." She gave me a big hug and kissed my cheek; Dad came in and shook my hand and reminded me to be a perfect gentleman and not to stay out late. Now her little boy is going off to war. I made a promise to my parents that night that I would not take any unnecessary risks and I would try my damndest to come home to them.

I called Butch the next morning and his parents did about the same as mine. His dad said: "he wish he would of join the Navy and told him it was a hell of a lot easlier to sleep in a hammock than a dirty old muddly fox hole." He said his Mom was crying and had him make a promise that he would come home. So I said to him over the phone: "I was going to the Recruiter Station today to take my phyisical and mental tests today". Then, Butch said: "He was going to do the same at the Recruiter Station in St.. Louis today. We hung up and wish each other good luck and I headed out the door. I jumped in the old Chevy and headed down town, when I found a parking space; I put coins in the metor and went inside.

In the Recruiter Office, a big old Marine greeted me at the door and said: "can I help you." I said: "yes I am here to see Gunnery Sergeant Charles S. Wilson." Then I told him I am here to take my physical and mental tests today. The Marine Sergeant said: "right this way", then he took me over to Gunnery Sergeant Wilson. He said: "Gunnery your recruit is here", Gunnery Wilson signaled, for me to come over to his desk. Gunnery Wilson said: "we will do the phyisical first that way we will not waste your and my time if you do not pass. He took me into the back room and told me to stripe off every thing but your shorts. Then he added, the doctor will be in soon; I just stood there waiting for the doctor; finally the doctor came in and introduced himself and told me what the physical consist of. First we are going to check your heart, lungs, liver, kidneys, and so on. So if you would pee in this bottle, I will take some blood for you. I will check you for a rupture, check your prostate, your feet, toes, hands and fingers. I think this doctor got the pleasure of ramming his finger up my scrotum and telling me to cough. Then comes the good part, the old magical finger right up your ass hole to check your prostate " I swear both of his hands were on my shoulders" when he rammed my ass hole. The doctor gave me a clean bill of health and said welcome to the Marine Corp son. He told me to get dressed and go into the next room for the mental exam. I got dressed and went into the next room where another doctor was going to evaluate your mental health. The doctor told me to take a seat and he was going to ask me some questions. The first question was: "do ever feel like hurting your self or other around you," I said: "no never." Question two: "do you hate your Mom and Dad" and I said: " no, I love my Mom and Dad, my Dad is strick but he has always be fair." Question 3: "if you have to kill to defend your self what would you do," I answer: " if it was a matter of life and death and I had to protect myself, and it would be the matter of kill or be killed. Question 4: "if you are ever in a situation where you can only save your Mom and Dad who would you save", I said this is really hard, I said: "my Mom has always been there for me and my Dad has always been there for me too, I know I could not live with myself if I save just my Mom or Dad, there would not be any hesitation, I think all of us would died together." question 5: "if you found a large sum of money what would do," I said: " I would turn it over to the local police station."

Then, the doctor said: " that is all the questions I have, now its time to take the written exam." He explained that, the exam is to test your physically, mentally, legally, morally, and financially and mechanically abilities. The test consists of multiple choice and written answers. I remember this one question was to adjust a carburetor you would need A. hammer, B. pair of pliers; C. monkey wrench, D. screw driver. But over all I scored a 96 mental and written exams. The Gunnery Sergeant said: "I will get every thing set for you and Butch can go into the Marine Corp on the Buddy System." I called Butch that night, he said he got a 95 on his tests, and the recruiter was setting everything up for him to come to Springfield, and we could leave together from there. So I asked Dad and Mom if Butch could spend a few days at our house until we left for San Diego, and they said: "it was ok." Then Mom said: "I like Butch he his a nice gentleman," then Dad said: "looks like we are not working on cars this weekend." I said: "No; Butch and I will be saying our goodbyes to Kathy and Rose Ann before we head off to boot camp. We are just going out to eat and go to the movies.:

Dad always gave good advice; you boys be good and don't get into any trouble and please do not drink and drive. Son you and Butch, please keep your dicks in your pants because I once was a young man. Then he went on: "you know them sex hormones can drive you crazy and make you do stupid things. Son please be home before midnight, so I will not have to worry about you and Butch ." I called Butch and told him the good news. The next morning we pickup Butch at the Greyhound Bus Station in Springfield at 11th and South Grand. When Dad and I pulled into the bus station, Butch was standing in front waiting for us. Butch threw his stuff in the back seat and said: "Good Morning Mr. Tomlin and Robert." My Dad said: "please Butch call me Gene," then Butch said: "in a funny way Robert do you want me to call you Mr. Tomlin." I said: "Butch do not be funny, then I said: " "Hey Mom is going to fix us breakfast.".

On the way home we talked about sports, about Butch's Dad, Mom, brothers, and sisters. As we pulled into our driveway, and soon as I got out of the car I could smell Mom's cooking. When Butch went in he said: "Good Morning Mrs. Tomlin," Mom turned and said: "Good morning to you Butch ." Mom fixed a nice breakfast of eggs, ham, potatoes, and toast with orange juice and coffee. Butch gave my Mom a nice comment by saying the food smells so good. Butch told my Mom she was a good cook, just like his Mom. We got up the next morning at 7:00 AM, then I said: " Go Marines" then. Butch said: "right back at you buddy." Then Butch reminded me to call Kathy and Rose Ann that were picking them up. Then, Mom said:" What plans do you have for today's boys." I said: "we were going to run over and see Kathy and Rose Ann Nelson." We all talked and laughed about the present and the past. I told Mom that Butch and I would clean up and do the dishes. I wash the dishes while Butch cleans the table and hands me the dishes, then Butch said: " he would dry." After kitchen details Butch and I said said goodbye to my Dad and Mom, and we headed out the door to go to Kathy and Rose Ann's house

On the way over to Kathy and Rose Ann's house, I was thinking the first time I saw Kathy was at Thomas Jefferson Junior High. I was walking down the hall way to put up my books in my locker; she was getting something out of her locker. When she looked up, I thought she was the most beautiful thing I ever saw, her green eyes and red hair. My heart just melted into my chest. I walked right over and introduced my self. I said: "my name is RobertTomlin" she said: "my name is Katherine Nelson but my friends call me Kathy. I said: "oh what a beautiful name that is my Mother name spelled with a C but her sisters and brothers call her Katty." Kathy and I hit it off right away; we were going to lunch and sock hops together. I would walk her home and carry her books. When we started dating her, Mom did not think much of me since she found out that my Dad was a coal miner. Mrs Nelson wanted her daughter in the future to marry a doctor, lawyer, highly business person. Her Mom thought it was just a fling between us and it would die out soon. But in secret between us, Kathy loves me and I love her. Her Dad, on the other hand, like me, he always said: "it makes no difference what you do for a living, if someone loves you that all that counts." My Dad was the same way he always said: "a hard days of work make a good day of pay." I remember my first date with Kathy; we were going to go out and eat and go to the movies.

When we pulled into the driveway at Kathy's house, the girls came running out to greet us. Kathy gave me a big kiss and hug and Rose Ann did the same to Butch . We all went into the house; both Butch and I said: "Good Morning Mrs.Nelson," she turned around and said: "oh hi boys what are your plans for today." Mrs Nelson was very over-protective of her daughters. She was always concerned about who they were going to date, about their families, what kind of work did Fathers did and etc. When I first started dating Kathy, her Mom ranked me over the coals, what my in tensions were with her daughter; what my Dad did for a living. When I told her my Dad was a coal miner. I thought she was going to flip out, then she asked me, are you going to be a coal miner, to which I replied with no. I am going to be a mechanical engineer. Kathy and I had problems with her Mom for a long time after that. Then Butch started to date Rose Ann's Kathy sister. Mrs Nelson ranked him over the coals. The only thing that saved old Butch's ass was that his Dad was in the Navy. Butch and I told Mrs Nelson we were taking the girls to eat and the movies. Then she said you boys have my daughters home before 11:00 PM. I said: "we would" and she said: "ok Robert I will be holding you to that," we said our goodbyes and walked out the door. We jumped in the old 1950 Chevy and headed for Burgun Park to relax and talk about our future together. When we got to the park we found a nice shade tree and started our conversation about Butch and I joining the Marine Corp, and if the girls was going to wait for us. We talked for hours about out in tensions and the future with Kathy and Rose Ann.

We said we would promise to write to them every day while we were away. We must have talked for a couple of hours when Rose Ann said she was hungry, so we headed for Steak'n'Shake on South Grand Street for burgers and fries. We had a nice lunch and talked some more, then the girls popped the question if we wait for you, do you have in tensions to marry us? Then Kathy and Rose Ann hit us with the big question if you do not, then while you are gone we will date other men. Butch and I sat there in shock. we were we being railroaded into marriage. Then Butch and I answer at the same time by saying: " we really can promise you that because anything can happen." I told Kathy: "that I loved her and wish she would wait for me." Butch told Rose Ann the same thing. Then I said: "lets not count our chicken before they hatch, lets us be cool and see what happen." We finished our lunch and headed for Phantheon Theater on Norh Grand to watch Ben Hur. I saw Ben Hur so many times as a usher at the Senate Theater, we were only going there for us to make out and not watch the movie. I noticed Butch and Rose Ann were making out also. That movie was 3 and a half hours long. I still think Kathy and Rose Ann had mixed feelings about waiting for us, so I said to myself what the hell lets just live for today. After the movies we went to Gabatoni's Pizza, we split a large pepperoni and had cokes; after we ate we talked and danced and had a good time. I looked up at the clock; it was 10:30 PM. I said we better go or Mrs Nelson will skin Butch and I alive. We all laughed and headed for the door. As I was leaving I told Mr. Lynn, Butch and I were joining the Marine Corp because I knew he was a Marine. He kind of laughed and said watch out for those drill sergeants; they can be real mean. It was 9:50 PM when we pulled into the drive way of Kathy and Rose Ann House. The girls got out and gave us a big kiss and hug and said: "see you guys tommrow." Then, Kathy said: "come by in the morning and we can all go to church." I said: "ok" and headed home.

When Butch and I got up Sunday morning Butch said: "Robert I did not bring a tie," I said:" Just use one of mine." We got dressed and headed down stairs Dad, Mom, brothers Gene and Jim, my sister Connie were waiting at the table for us. Mom makes the comment that looks like you boys are going to church. I said: "you are right Mom, Butch and I are going with the Nelson family to church this morning". We had our breakfast talked about old times, my brother Jimmy said: "how come you knuckle heads did not join the Navy." Then Butch came back with a smart ass answer:" because we want to be the few and proud of the United States Marine Corp." Then, my brother Gene said: "you will not be so proud with your asses shot off." We all laughed and started the old BS'ing again. Then my Dad makes this comment: "this is all fine and dandy, but we have to defend our county to the very end. I know when I was in the Battle of Midway, I saw stuff no man should ever have to see. Son just promise you will be careful and watch out for each other. Kick that Viet Cong's ass all the way to China and get the war over and come back home early."

We said our good-byes and headed for Nelson's house. I parked my car in front because I knew we all would be riding to church in Nelson's sedan. As Butch and I were walking up to the front door, the Nelson family was coming out. Butch and I said: "good morning Mr and Mrs Nelson, Kathy and Rose Ann and they all said good morning and we all got in the family sedan and headed for church. When we got to church the sermon was the same old thing the pastor was laying it down real heavy about fire and brimstone, then he went on if you let your guard down the Devil will get you. Then he added, only God can save your soul from the Devil. I am not a very religious man, but I still believe in God and Jesus ever since I was a little boy. After church we all headed back to the Nelson's house; when we arrived Mrs Nelson said: "come on in I will fix lunch." Then I asked Mrs Nelson if I could use their phone so that I could call my Mom and tell her Butch and I would not be home for lunch. We were having lunch at Nelson's house. After lunch Butch and I told Mrs Nelson we would do the dishes. After we finished doing the dishes, we all went into the living room and talked about the weather, sports, and our future plans. We asked Kathy and Rose Ann if they wanted to ride to Lake Springfield; they both said yes. Then Mrs Nelson said for the girls to be home before 11:00 PM. We all got in the car and headed for the lake. After driving for a few minutes I told every body I wanted to stop by Bill Moody's house and tell him good-bye. I always felt sorry for Bill Moody ever since his dad killed himself. One day when Bill was a sophomore in high school, he came home from school and called out to his Dad with no answer. Bill looked over the whole house and went down to the basement; there was his Dad hanging in the basement. His Dad stepped off a coal bucket and hung himself. Bill took it pretty hard; after that I tried to comfort Old Bill the best way I knew how. I can say one thing about Bill he was one hell of a drummer, and he was self-taught. When I got to Bill's house I rang the door bell; he came to the door and said: "what do I own the pleasure" and laughed. I told him I would be joining the Marine Corp. He gave me a big hug and shook my hand and wished me luck and said: "good-bye." Got back in the car and headed for the lake.

Kathy and I were making out like two tigers in the heat. I tried my damndest to get her pants, I even went as low as promising her the moon, she pushing my hand away and saying no because her Mom would kill her if she had sex before marriage. So we just kissed and held each other tight and held hands. Butch was not having any luck with Rose Ann, she told him the same thing, that her Mom would kill her if she had sex before marriage. So we all just talked and the time went by real fast. It was time to take the girls home; we got to their house about 10:30 PM; we all kissed good-bye for the last time, for which Butch and I did know until the 13 week of boot camp. We both got the "Dear John" letters at the same time. Kathy letter she wrote she had met this guy in college and that her Mom approved of him. She went on to say how sorry she was and in a way she still loved me. The thing that hurt me the most was her returning my friendship ring. I remember the day I brought that ring at Forever Jewals on the 10th block of North Fifth Steet in Springfield. I walked in one day and ask the owner if I could look at the friendship rings. He asked me is this for someone special and I said my girl friend who means the world to me. He took over to the ring counter and showed off the rings. I saw this bright green emerald that was the same color as Kathy's eyes. I asked the jeweler what the price was. He said it was $90.00 dollars, but for you, young man, I will sell to you for $55.00 dollars. I told him all I had was $20.00 dollars and could I put it down, and for him to hold the ring for me. He said yes, but you have to pay it off before the end of the month because we are having inventory at that time. I gave him my name, address, and phone number; handed him the $20.00 dollars; he gave me a receipt with the balance due by the end of the month, and I walked out. I paid the ring off in time and gave it to Kathy on our third date; she had tears in her eyes when I gave her the ring and she promise me she would cherish it for ever. As I finished the letter I had a small tear in my eye and was thinking what a fairly tale this romance was. That was the last letter I ever received from her and never saw her again. When I was in the jungles of Vietnam, I would think about what our lives would have been like if we were together. Poor Butch got the same from Rose Ann and she met this nice guy in college and her Mom approved of him. The was the last letter he ever received from Rose Ann, and he never saw her again. The only bad thing about Butch, he really took it hard, he started to drink real heavy, plus he was depressed over the break-up. I thought he would go crazy. If it was not for the Drill Sergeant that straighting him out, he would have, been kicked out of the Marine Corp. If that would have happened his Dad would have kicked his ass all the way back to San Diego. I'll have to say, when it is all said and done with this incident of breaking up with Rose Ann Nelson, Butch Philip Price turned out to be the best Marine I ever served with.

CHAPTER FOUR

Marine Corps Recruit Depot San Diego

When Butch and I got up that morning on the 15 Sepemteber, 1966, we had this funny feeling, about this was our last day as civilians. Butch was all excited and telling me: "just think Robert tomorrow we are going to be Marines." Our bus was going to leave right at noon from Springfiedl, Illinois, to San Diego, California, to our boot camp at the MCRD (Marine Corps Recruit Depot, San Diego). Our Marine recruiters pull some stings into getting us to have boot camp at San Diego and not Parris Island, South Carolina. Gunnery Sergeant Harold W. Brown said: " Since you and Butch are friends and are in the Buddy System, and since Jefferson City, Missouri is west of the Mississippi River, that why we are sending you to San Diego. When I talked to Gunnery Sergeant Charles W. Wilson he told me how the Buddy System works in the Marine Corp. He said: "The buddy program is designed so that people who enlist in the Marine Corps together from the same area can get sent to recruit training at the same time and be in the same platoon. Going through the transformation into United States Marines together is the next step in their friendship. Then said: " We make an exception to the rule since Butch enlisted in Missouri and you in Illinois, but only because you are friends.

Mom was calling us for breakfast, so Butch and I went downstairs for our last civilian breakfast. Dad looks up from drinking his coffee and says: " are you boys ready for the thrill of your lifes by running, exercising, marching, rifle range, and combat training. You have to remember the Drill Instructors will make your life a missable hell for the next 11 weeks." Then dad went on with this good advice: They are there trying to break you, because if you break in Boot Camp, you are gone before you get to the battlefield and break down, that way you will not be killed and everybody around you get killed." I said: "do not worry Dad I will make it." We all sat around the breakfast table and talked about any and everything. Butch and I helped with the dishes, then went outside to see my old Chevy. Jimmy said: " he would start it and drive it once in while so she would be running when I got home. Then Gene said: I will keep it clean for you Robert." I could see in my Mom's eyes she was really sad and I knew she did not want me to go. Then, before you knew it was time to go to the bus station to head for SanDiego. Butch 's Dad and Mon were driving up from St. Louis to see us off. When we arrive at the bus station Mr. amd Mrs. Price were waiting for us, as we got out of the car, they were walking towards us. Butch's Mom came up and gave Butch a big hug and kissed him on his cheek. She had tears running down her face as she was holding

Butch 's hand real tight. Butch was saying: " I am going to miss you Mom and Dad. Then Mr Price said: " just remember son they will dish out alot of shit, but be strong and take and handle everything they throw at you. Remember look after yourself and Robert and take care of each other.: Butch said: " I will Dad" Then Butch 's Dad gave him a big hug and they shook hands and Butch got on the bus. Then Mrs Price pulled me over to the side and said: " Robert promise me that you will look after Frederick Philip (Butch) and that you will take care of each other in peace and combat. Promise that you make sure Frederick comes home no matter what happens." I gave a big hug to Mrs. Price and said: " Do not worry I will look after Frederick (Butch) I promise I will bring him home." I kissed my Mom and sister Connie goodbye and told them that I loved them. I hugged my Dad and brothers Gene and Jimmy and shook their hands. Dad said: "son take care of your self and you and Butch cover each other backs and look out for each other." I said: "I will" walked over and got on the bus. As the bus pulled out of the station I could see my Mom, sister Connie and Mrs. Price were crying and waving their handkerchiefs goodbye. Butch turned to me and said: "it is kind of sad to see our Moms cry." Butch told me later that my Mom had him promise, to watch after me and make sure that I got home. Then I was thinking I sure hoped I could keep the promise I made to Mrs. Price. I knew I would do everything in my power to keep that promise and that both of us would be coming home.

Butch and I were on that bus for about 51 hours traveling to San Diego; we stopped several times to drop and and pick up packages and passengers; every time we stopped we stretched our legs and ate. We went from Springield, Illinois, to Springfield, Missouri, which is about 300 hundred miles, and stopped;to dropped off packages and get packages. When from Springfiedl, Missouri to Okahoma City, Okahoma, which is about 280 miles. Okahoma City, Okahoma City, Okahoma to Amarillo, Texas, which is about 250 miles. Amarillo, Texas, to Las Cruces, New Mexico, which is about 400 hundred miles. Las Cruces, New Mexico to Tucson. Arizona. which is about 270 miles. Tucson, Arizona, to Yuma, Arizona, which is about 230 miles. Yuma, Arizona, to San Diego, California, which is about 170 miles. Then finally the bus was going through the gates of Marine Corps Recruit Depot San Diego. Marine Corp boot camp was 11 weeks and was cut to 8 weeks when the Vietnam War started and broken down and completed in five phases **(1-5)**

Forming and processing of Marine boot camp is the toughest phase as recruits adapt from civilian habits to rigorous Marine Corps standards. During forming and processing, which covers the first week of boot camp, you will be issued your gear and uniforms and learn hygiene, regulations and medical evaluations You will also learn Marine Corps history, rank structure, chain of command, and code of conduct. **(A)**

Basic training, classroom time and drill of Marine basic training involves an initial physical fitness test, or PT (Physical Training), during which the recruit will need to run three miles within 30 minutes, with the goal being 18 minutes, along with the sit-ups and pull-up are requirements. **(B)**

Marksmanship , which involves rifle instruction and the rifle range qualification.

Here, recruits must achieve a shooting score of 190 to 250 points with the M-14 service rifle. The rifle range is critical because every Marine must be able to qualify with the M-14 rifle to pass through boot camp. The three levels of marksmanship in the Marine Corps are Marksman, Sharpshooter and Expert. **(C)**

Mess and maintenance, a period in the boot camp program when recruits worked in chow halls and did maintenance jobs. **(D)**

Advanced training, combat training and inspection During this phase, recruits demonstrate their new skills before earning the title of Marine and graduating from boot camp. This phase involves the final PT, knowledge test, drill marching competition between platoons, exercise in which recruits take part in various obstacle courses; team exercises, outdoor survival drills, day and night combat movement courses, and a 10-mile hike to and from the wilderness site. They are awarded the title of Marine and given their eagle, globe and anchor emblems. After a week of administrative processing, the Marines have their graduation ceremony where they are officially dismissed from boot camp. **(E)**

When the bus stopped Butch and I were sleeping, then we heard this sonic boom, what the "FUCK" are you ladies doing. Butch and I woke up and saw this mean-looking Marine Drill Instructor with a bulldog face who was on the bus harping orders at us. He said: " ladies I am Drill Instructor SSgt Robert Johnson and this is my assistants Drill Instructor SSgt John Jackson and Drill Instructor SSgt Gary Tibetts for the next 8 weeks, you little boys will become men. Now get the fuck off this bus and get into formation." As every body piled out of the bus and got in some kind of formation, we looked like a bunch of lost sheep. He started again: "I am going to train you dumbnuts into rigorous team building, weapons training and disciplinary tactics, and if you fuckheads thing you can handle it, then step forward. If not I will personnely escorts your asses out the gate ." Every one step forward move instead we just stood there wondering what the hell was going to be next. Then Drill Instructor SSgt Robert Johnson said: " A bout face, foward march" our platoon headed for the barracks; some guys could not march worth a damn. Drill Instructor SSgt Robert Johnson was yelling: "if you ladies do not get into step, my foot will be up your ass." He called halt in front of our barracks. He called at ease, then said: "you ladies will march into the barracks in a single file and stand by a rack.". When we all got inside, standing by our racks. Then the shit hit the fan. Drill Instructor SSgt Robert Johnson started. I will show you how to make a rack the Marine way. When you are finished I will. I come by for inspection and I will drop a quarter on that blanket and if it does not bounce, you are going to be doing push-ups until your fucking arms fall off. Do I make myself perfectly clear ladies. We all said: "SIR yes SIR"

The next day, about 4:00 am, Drill Instructor SSgt Robert Johnson came in the barracles, beating a night stick on a garbage can lid. He was yelling: "ladies get your asses out of bed, brush your teeth, shave, shower, and dress you have 5 minutes to get into formation outside." We were running around like monkeys trying to screw a beach ball Some recruits had tooth paste running out of their mouths; some had shaving cream dripping off their faces, and while others were half dry from taking a shower. As we lined up in formation, Drill Instructor SSgt Robert Johnson called us to attention. And said: " I am impressed you had 30 seconds to spare."

Then, in a very stern voice, he laid down the law. He said: As you can see ladies, you are still in your civilian clothes. The first thing we are going to do is eat breakfast at the chow hall, now remember when you sit down at the table, you have 3minutes to eat. If you are not finished in 3 minutes, get up from the table; throw away any remaining food go outside and get information. Then we go to the barber shop and you ladies will have your hair done. At the barber shop the barbers were saying: " now how do you want your hair cut." One recruit from South Dakota said: " just take a little off the top, back, and sides." He got a buzz job like the rest of us, right down to the skin. Then Drill Instructor SSgt Robert Johnson said: " you ladies will get a hair cut every week." After the barber shop we will march over to the reception station. There, we were given our initial clothing issue, which included BDU's (Battle Dress Uniforns), dress uniforms, boots, black shoes called low quarters, belts, hats, coats, and even towels, socks, and underwear. Then we all marched back to the barracks, where we took off our civilian clothes and shoes; put them in a cardboard box, and mailed them to our home address. Everybody changed from civilian clothes to military uniforms. Then one recruit from New Mexico asked the drill instructor: "why do we have to mail our civilian clothes back home." Drill Instructor SSgt Robert Johnson looked him straight in the eyes and said: "well dumbnuts, for you pussies will not be going AWOL (absent without official leave) and to seek out of camp." Drill Instructor SSgt Robert Johnson said: " Did you ladies notice a footlocker at the front of your bed, I am going to show you how to keep and maintain your footlockers.

Then, he said: "now listen up everybody gather around Tomlin's footlocker." Then he said: "Tomlin open your footlocker." So I opened the foot locker and stood there. Then the drill instructor said: "there is lock with two keys you will keep one key on your person at all times and the other key goes to me. God help you if you loose your key." Then he was saying the locker has two compartments, the bottom compartment is for your clothes, shoes and boots, and the top compartment is movable and this compartment you will have your grooming supplies, tooth brush and paste, shaving mug and soap or shaving cream, razor, comb, hair brush, belt, stamps, stationary, eye glasses, and a small amount of cash. Then, in a very stern voice, he said: "if you are caught as a barracks thief, you will receive a Hollywood beating from your fellow recruits." Then a recruit from Iowa asked: "SIR what is a Hollywood beating SIR." Drill Instructor SSgt Robert Johnson said: A Hoolywood beating is a bar of soap in a sock, and your fellow recruits hammer on you, and the soap in the sock does not leave any marks plus it hurts like hell." Then he when on: "Now tommorow we are marching over to the Marine exchanges (NEX), store for you to buy brand new grooming supplies to put in your footloacker to be shown at inspection and they will be use for display only. Your other grooming supplies you use everyday will be stored in a shaving bag." Then one recruit from Arizona said: "but SIR I do not hav enough money to buy new grooming supplies." Drill Instructor said: " that is ok I will keep a running tab for thoses who not have enough money and you can pay me back on your first paydate." Then the Drill Instructor showed us how to fold our clothes where they would not show wrinkles and how to pack and display our foot lockers. Now you ladies will have the rest of the day off to write letters home and get this barracks in shape. Then he said:" Dismiss, and be ready for a real ass kicking tommorow." Butch and I wrote letters back home to our Dads and Moms and to Kathy and Rose Ann, then helped clean the barracks. Then we hit the racks because we knew from now on our asses would be going through the winger.

The next morning we were up at 4:00 AM running 3miles, going through the parell bars, and on the last rung we had to do 3 pull-ups. Then on to Push ups, Sit ups, Running in place, and the damn Monkey Rolls: which is the recruit rolls toward one of the recruits on the side, who must jump up and over, continue rolling into the next guy, who jumps up and over, and the whole dreadful process is repeated until the Drill Instructor yells stops, Crabs Crawls: which is the recruits must put their hands on the ground, butt in the air and proceed across the field in this position. running in place, and the Gauntlet, which is: several recruits, are placed in a row, and the Drill instructor picks one recruit who must try to maneuver through them, all while being pummeled repeatedly. Every day was just pure hell and torture, but I have to say one thing: " Those Marine Instructors make and create a real mean lean fighting machine. They weed out the weak and keep the strong. That is way the Marine Corp has one of the best fighting infantry in the world." The first four weeks of Phase I were the toughest as a recruit, you had to adapt from civilian habits to rigorous Marine Corps standards. We learned about Marine Corps history, rank structure, chain of command and code of conduct, and the three core values of the Marine Corps, which are Honor, Courage, and Commitment.

After our resistance-training exercises, we had our 3 minute breakfast and got back into formation to march to the Marine Exchange (NEX), store. Drill Instructor, SSgt Robert Johnson called us attention and started explaining to us what we needed to buy at the exchanges store and then the boom came down.When he said: "Ladies make this perfectly clear, if you buy anything other then what you are to get I will make you sit down and you will be eating it. Do you understand." Everybody shouted back:"SIR yes SIR." Then, he said: "who in this company can sing." Butch answered with: "Tomlin can sing like Elvis." Drill Instructor SSgt Robert Johnson said: "Fuck Elvis" Tomlin I am going to teach you a Jody Call and it goes like this: "Your left, Your left, Your left right left, My back aches, My belts too tight, I don't know but I've been told, Eskimo Pussy is mighty cold, Sound off 1, 2, Sound off 3, 4" So we sang that cadence all the way to exchanges store, when we got to front of the store. Drill Instructor called: "halt and stand at ease." Then, he said: : four recruits at a time in the store and only buy the stuff you need and get back into formation." These two recruits from Texas brought the stuff they needed and snicker candy bars. When Drill Instructor SSgt Robert Johnson saw those two bozos eating those snickers bar, he called them front and center and said: "I said: "only buy what you need, now these two fuck ups brought candy. Now these two screw balls is going to eat the candy with wrappers and all." As the two recruits were eating the candy and choking down the candy wrappers. Drill Instructor SSgt Robert Johnson said: " When I tell you knuckleheads maybe next time you will listed, now get the fuck back in rank."

In the class room I learn a lot about the Marine Corp History **(1-6)** It all started on November 10, 1775,the Second Continental Congress meeting in Philadelphia, passed a resolution stating that "two Battalions of Marines be raised" for service as landing forces with the fleet. The Marine Corps was established as the Marine Corps on 11 July 1798. Marines saw action in the quasi-war with France,landed in Santo Domingo, and took part in many operations against the Barbary pirates along theShores of Tripoli. Marines took part in numerous naval operations during the War of 1812. During the Mexican War (1846-1848), Marines seized enemy seaports on both the Gulf and Pacific coasts.

A battalion of Marines joined General Winfield Scott's army at Pueblo and fought all the way to the "Halls of Montezuma," Mexico City. Marines also served ashore and afloat in the Civil War (1861-1865).

Following the Spanish-American War (1898), in which Marines performed with valor in Cuba, Puerto Rico, Guam, and the Philippines, the Corps entered an era of expansion and professional development. saw active service in the Philippine Insurrection (1899-1902), and the Boxer Rebellion in China (1900). and in numerous other nations, including Nicaragua, Panama, Cuba, Mexico, and Haiti.

In World War I, the Marine Corps distinguished itself on the battlefields of France as the 4th Marine Brigade earned the title of "Devil Dogs" for heroic action during 1918 at Belleau Wood, Soissons, St. Michiel, Blanc Mont, and in the final Meuse-Argonne offensive.

During the two decades before World War II, the Marine Corps began to develop in earnest the doctrine, equipment, and organization needed for amphibious warfare. The success of this effort was proven first on Guadalcanal, then on Bougainville, Tarawa, New Britain, Kwajalein, Eniwetok, Saipan, Guam, Tinian, Peleliu, Iwo Jima, and Okinawa. By the end of the war in 1945, the Marine Corps had grown to include six divisions, five air wings, and supporting troops. Its strength in World War II peaked at 485,113. The war cost the Marines nearly 87,000 dead and wounded, and 82 Marines had earned the Medal of Honor.

Landing at Inchon, Korea ,in September 1950, Marines proved that the doctrine of amphibious assault was still viable and necessary. After the recapture of Seoul, the Marines advanced to the Chosin Reservoir only to see the Chinese Communists enter the war. After years of offensives, counter-offensives, seemingly endless trench warfare, and occupation duty, the last Marine ground troops were withdrawn in March 1955. More than 25,000 Marines were killed or wounded during the Korean War.

In July 1958, a brigade-size force landed in Lebanon to restore order. During the Cuban Missile Crisis in October 1962.

Then we taught the Marine Corp Code of Conduct which has six articles **(1-7)** Which are as follows:

Article I: I am an American, fighting in the forces which guard my country and our way of life.

Article II: I will never surrender of my own free will.

Article III: If I am captured I will continue to resist by all means available.

Article IV: If I become a prisoner of war, I will keep faith with my fellow prisoners. I will give no information or take part in any action which might be harmful to my comrades. If I am senior, I will take command.

Article V: When questioned, should I become a prisoner of war, I am required to give name, rank, service number and date of birth. I will evade answering further questions to the utmost of my ability.

Article VI: I will never forget that I am an American, fighting for freedom, responsible for my actions, and dedicated to the principles which made my country free. I will trust in my God and in the United States of America.

Drill Instructor SSgt Robert Johnson makes Butch and I Squad Leaders of San Diego MCRD, C(Charlie) Company 1st Battalion (red), Platoon 117, I was Squad one and Butch was Squad two. Our job was to help the recruits in our squad through training and help guide them. The down side of a squad leader, if a recruit in your squad screws up, that means Drill Instructor SSgt Robert Johnson and Drill Instructor SSgt John Jackson is coming down on your ass. I remember one time in the middle of our barracks we had what we called no mans lands, you could walk there if you had socks over your boots. One day this jerk-off from Nebraska walked in the middle with no socks on his boots; he had suffs marks everywhere on that floor. When Drill Instructor SSgt Robert Johnson saw this and called out in the loudest voice ever: "Tomlin and Price to my office ASAP (As Soon As Possible)." We ran there as fast as we could; when we hit his doorway; we both announced Tomln and Price, reporting SIR. Then he hit us with every cuss word you could think of. Then he said: "who has Wilson in his squad, that dickwad just fuck up my barracks floor." Then I stepped forward and said " SIR Wilson is in my squad." He looked straight in my face with his fingers poking in my chest and saying: "Tomlin you better get the recruit straighten out, or your ass is grass and I am the power mow. Do I make myself perfecting clear, now get the fuck out my face correct that recruit right now." I said: SIR yes SIR perfecting clear." I did about face and when looking for Wilson. When I found Wilson, Katty bar the doors, I came down on him so hard about the floor, he just stood there not saying a word. I told him: "you will strip all the wax off the black tile floor, and you will spit shine the floor with black boot polish and I do not give a fuck if it takes you all night." Wilson worked all night on that floor; when he got finished you could actually see your face on the floor. Drill Instructor SSgt Robert Johnson was really happy and said: "from now on, this floor will always look like this. Or there will be hell to paid." All the recruits said: "SIR yes SIR'." But the nice perk of a Squad Leader you make a PFC (Private First Class) rank after boot camp. We started to see the light at the end of the tunnel when week four was almost over.

Now it was time for the second fours weeks with rifle range; Manual of Arms, Bayonet Training, pugil sticks, gas chamber, Physical Fitness Test, and hand grenades. Our first day in Phase 2 we are standing in formation when Drill Instructor SSgt Robert Johnson picks out a recruit to show the procedure on how to hold his rifle. The recruit had an M-14 rifle and DI took the rifle and demonstrated the stance, holding the rifle, and timing. Then the DI handed the rifle to the recruit and said: "stand straight, head right, shoulders square, stomach in, chest out, heels close, toes turned out a little. Then the DI said: "This is the way a Marine holds a rifle, on the left shoulder, forefinger and thumb to the side of the stock; the other three holding the butt. Next comes the timing: "each motion to be done on a count of one, two". The DI said: we will all practice this procedure on the rifle." As we were all practicing how to hold the rifle the Marine Corp way, the DI was going around checking on the recruits to see if we were doing it right. All day long we held them rifles until the platoon had it right. Finally, Drill Instructor SSgt Robert Johnson said: "Dismissed and get ready for chow and tomorrow ladies we will start drill exercises. We marched to the chow hall to have our 3 minutes dinner, then back to the barracks for rest and relaxation. As we were getting ready to hit the racks, then the shit hit the fan a recruit from Texas called a recruit from Kansas a "a fucking nigger" then the recruit from Kansas called him a fucking Mexican, and now the fight was on. Here were these two in their skivies, with fists flying, and blood was pouring everywhere. Punches were being thrown left and right, and about that time Drill Instructor SSgt Robert Johnson walked into the barracks. In his frog-like voice he said: "what the fuck is going on" I said: "SIR Jose Rodriguez called William Jackson a fucking nigger and William Jackson called him a fucking Mexican and the fight started SIR." The Drill Instructor said: "both to my office right now" Rodriguez told the DI he could fuck myself and let him finish the fight. The DI turned to me and said: "Tomlin hold my Compaign Hat and took off his rank and handed it to me. Then he said: "Rodriguez and I are taking a trip to the back of the barracks." Rodriguez followed the DI out of the barracks. About 5 minutes later the DI walked back in and said: "take this sorry ass to the Medical Dispensary and tell them, he fell down some stairs." The DI turned to me and said: "hand me my Compaign Hat and rank and I will deal with this fucking mess in the morning."

The next morning after **PT** (Physical Training), **PTT** (Physical Training Test), and breakfast, we were training for **Drill and Cermony**. Drill Instructor SSgt Robert Johnson lowers the boom about racial calling. Then said: "the next time I hear any more racial remarks about any recruit in my platoon. I will have you do so many push-ups and you better learn to speak Chinese, because you will be pushing your ass all the way to China." Then he said in his frog voice, do I make myself perfectly clear. We all said: "SIR yes SIR." Then the DI called us to attention and we started our drill training. Then said: "You will need to know the following drill terms." Then he started telling us the definitions first there is **Element:** This is an individual, squad, section, platoon, company, or larger unit formed as part of the next higher unit. **Formation:** This is an arrangement of the unit's elements in a prescribed manner such as a line Formation, in which the elements are side-by-side, and column formation, in which the elements are one behind the other. In a platoon column, the members of each squad are one behind the other, with the squads abreast. **Front:** This is a space from one side to the other side of a formation, and includes the right and left elements.

Then Drill Instructor SSgt Robert Johnson and Drill Instructor SSgt John Jackson started with training and information on the Purpose of Drill and Purpose of Formations. Drill Instructor SSgt Robert Johnson gave us the following information on the Purpose of Drill. 1. Move units from one place to another in a standard, orderly manner. 2. Provide simple formations from which combat formations may be readily assumed. 3. Teach discipline by instilling habits of precision and automatic response to orders. 4. Increase the confidence of junior officers and noncommissioned officers through the exercise of command, by the giving of proper commands, and by the control of drilling troops. 5. Give troops an opportunity to handle individual weapons. Drill Instructor SSgt John Jackson gave us the following information on the Purpose of Formations. 1. To build unit cohesion and esprit de corps by recognizing Marines during awards and promotion ceremonies. 2. To maintain continuous accountability and control of personnel. 3. To provide frequent opportunities to observe the appearance and readiness of the uniforms, arms, and equipment of the individual Marine. 4. To keep the individual Marine informed by providing the means to pass the word. 5. To develop command presence in unit leaders. 6. To instill and maintain high standards of military bearing and appearance in units and in the individual Marine.

Hour after hour day after day, our DI's were yelling and giving out commands starting with Stationary Movements: Attraction, Parade Rest, Stand at Ease, At Ease, Rest, Face to the Flank, Face to the Rear, and Hand Salute. Then it started all over again with Marching: 30-Inch Step, Change Step, Rest movement (30-inch step), Half Step (15-inch step), Halt, Marching in Place, 15-inch Step (Right/left), 15-inch Step (backward), 30-inch Step (Double Time). Then came the Manual of Arms with the M14 Rifle: order Arms, Port Arms, Present Arms, Inspection Arms, Right Shoulder Arms, Left Shoulder Arms, Sling Arms, Salute at Sling Arms, Order arms at Sling Arms, Port Arms at Sling arms, Inspection Arms at Sling Arms. At first our platoon looked like a bunch of monkeys fucking a beach ball. We were so disoriented and disorganized, running into each other while we tried to march, we could not get our weapon movements right. The Di's kept on our asses until we were a well-oiled maching and manual arms machine. After a day of marching and drilling, I remember one day that Drill Instructor SSgt Robert Johnson was telling Drill Instructor SSgt John Jackson: " John I think we are going to have a bunch of fine Marines when we are done."

One day after Manual of Arms we were marching back to the barracks; Drill Instructor SSgt RobertJohnson came running out, yelling at the top of his lungs. Recruit Wilson front and center, then the shit hit the fan. Drill Instructor SSgt Robert

Johnson said: " why in the fuck did you leave your footlocker unsecured." Wilson said in a mouse like voice: "I forgot to lock it SIR" Then Drill Instructor SSgt Robert Johnson said: " you forgot to lock it, you go in that squardbay and bring your footlocker outside and you will be doing Manual of Arms." Wilson said: "SIR yes SIR." Wilson ran inside to the squardbay got his foot locker and came back out. The DI said: "Wilson that footlocker is going to be your rifle and you are going to do the Manual of Arms." Drill Instructor SSgt Robert Johnson said: "Right Shoulder Arms." Wilson picks up his foot locker and puts it on his right should. I was thinking that poor son-of-bitch moving that 90 pound foot locker compared to a 9 pound rifle. The DI kept hammering out orders for Left Should Arms, Port Arms, Present Arms, Inspection Arms, after a hour or so of Manual of Arms, then finally the DI said: "Wilson take that fucking footlocker back to squardbay and get square away and back to formation." Wilson Said: "SIR yes SIR" He ran in and back out and got in formation before the DI said another word. Then the DI said: "If I ever catch another foot locker unsecured, all of you dumbnuts will be doing Manual of Arms with your footlockers. Do I make myself clear." The whole platoon yelled at their top of their lungs: "SIR yes SIR" Then Drill Instructor SSgt Robert Johnson said: " If I do not get the Honor Platoon of the Cycle because some dumbdick did not secured his footlocker. I will run your sorry asses ten miles every day, and forget about your arms, because your arms will be gone from doing pushups Now do I make myself perfectly clear." The whole platoon said: SIR yes SIR." Then we all march off to the chow hall.

Then there was the Sand Pit, conveniently located right next to the parade deck, where you do your exercises in. You do pushups, sit-ups, mountain climbers, side straddle hops, or hold a plank while screaming at the top of your lungs. Usually you are screaming at the number of reps completed. Drill Instructor SSgt Robert Johnson screaming at the top of his lungs: "If you fuck heads drop that plank, I will drop knick your asses, do you hear me." We would all say: "SIR yes SIR" As we kept up and down, right shoulder, left shoulder with the plank while running in place. Then them damn dreaded Sand Fleas (they are parasitic crustaceans which are found in sandy areas) that suck your blood like a mini vampire. I do not know who is worse a Sand Flea in California or a Chigger in Illinois. I remember as a kid on a hot summer night laying in the grass with my shirt off. I got up the next morning and my back looked like a war zone; I had hundred of Chigger bites and I was try to scratch my back and going nuts. My Mom heard me screaming and ran to my room and said: " I told you not to take off your shirt and lay in that grass." She got the calamine lotion and started rubbing me down; I can not explain what relief I felt as she rubbed the lotion on my back. I said: Thank You Mom, you saved the day." She just smiled and said: " Do not be so hard headed and listen to me next time."

The next day was Marksmanship we went to the firing range Drill Instructor SSgt Robert Johnson took half of the platoon with squads 1 and 2. Drill Instructor SSgt John Jackson took the other half with squads 3 and 4. Then Drill Instructor SSgt Robert Johnson said: "Remember what you were taught in class room." Then he went over some of the fine points of firing a rifle. He said: " Just remember recruits from the start of dry-firing your weapons, or snapping in, you have learned proper weapons handling, how to clean and maintain your weapon. But the most important four safety rules." Then he said: " Tomlin rule number one." I snapped back with:" Treat every weapon as if it were loaded SIR." Drill Instructor SSgt Robert Johnson said: "Very good Tomlin" Then he said: "Price rule number two." Butch snapped back with: " keep your finger straight and off the trigger until you intend to fire SIR." Drill Instructor SSgt Robert Johnson said: "Very good Price" Then he called out a couple other recruits for rule three, which is "never point your weapon at anything you don't intend to shoot" and rule four "keep your weapon on safe until you intend to fire." Then Drill Instructor SSgt Robert Johnson said: "You recruits will be shooting at targets that are 200, 300 and 500 yards away from the prone, sitting, kneeling and standing positions. Just remember the Marine Corps is the only branch wherethe recruits will be shooting from distances of 500 yards away." Then the DI said: " Are there any deadeyes in group of recruits. Then he called out our names, one at a time, to the firing line. As I was in the prone position, getting ready to fire. Drill Instructor SSgt Robert Johnson said: "Tomlin remember your breathing just before you fire hold your breath, trigger control squeeze that trigger like you are milking a cow gently squeezing that udder, zero your rifle on target, and fire at will." I commence firing my 10 rounds at the target 200 yards away. I received the signal, all ten shots were bullseyes. Drill Instructor SSgt Robert Johnson turned to the Range Officer and said: "SIR I think we have a Buffalo Bill on our hands." The Range officer said: "SSgt Johnson that was mighty good shooting for a new recruit." Then it was Price's turn; he fired off ten rounds, which were all in the bullseye. Drill Instructor SSgt Robert Johnson said: " I'll be damned another Buffalo Bill on my hands"

That whole week for every bullseye I got, Butch would do the same. Our DI was really impressed with our markmanship on the rifle range. Every weapon I became a Expert on, Butch was right behind me becoming an Expert with the M14 Rifle (select-fire battle rifle), M60 Machine Gun (general-purpose machine gun), M1911 pistol (single-action, semi-automatic, Caliber.45), M72 Law (Light Anti-Tank Weapon), and Hand Genades. Drill Instructor SSgt Robert Johnson said: " Is there any weapon that you can not fire and make Expert." I was being a smart ass and said: " SIR a sling shot."

Then Drill Instructor SSgt Robert Johnson Said: "Tomlin you are on the defense end of Pugil Sticks, and no one in your squad gets past you, and let me repeat no one in your squad get pass you. If one recruit gets through, heaven help you. " I said: " SIR yes SIR." I took up my position on the back side of the Pugil Course as a defensive end. I was standing at the exit of the course when the first recruit tried to get through. He came charging at me at full blast, with his Pugil Stick waving like a wind mill. His first blow was to the side of my head; I countered with two quick blows to his stomach and the side of his head. The last blow back him up and he came charging at me again; this time he wacked me on my right knee and I nearly dropped to the ground. I gather my strength and did a side step and wack him on the left side of his head and a quick turn around with a harder wack on his right side of his head. He went down like a ton of rocks. Then I heard Drill Instructor SSgt Robert Johnson said: Get that dickwad out of there and yell next. This recruit was playing it safe; he was keeping himself at a safe distance trying to wear me out by swinging the Pugil Stick back and forth at me. Then all of a sudden he charged at me full blast swinging that Pugil Stick like a propeller blade on an airplane. I side-stepped and caught him with two hard blows, one on the side of his head and the other on his back. He went down with blood just pouring out of his mouth. Again, Drill Instructor SSgt Robert Johnson said: get that fucking dumbnuts out of there and yell next. But he was a little tricky this time he sent two recruits straight at me. As I was preparing to make my stance, both recruits caught me on the side of my head with two hard punches from the Pugil Sticks. Blood was pouring out of my nose like a water fall. I gather my composure, did a side step to the right, and then to the left, and I open up with a whirling wind mill action, and catch both recruits with numerous blows to the face and head. Blood was spurting out of their faces as both went down. Again, Drill Instructor SSgt Robert Johnson said: " get those two DFB's (Dick For Brains) out of their and yelled next" I was starting to get real tired and my arms felt like iron weights. Now this recruit was really cautious; he was moving real slow, which gave me time to catch my breath and rest before the next battle. As my last opponent came creeping up, I did not waste any time; I hit with three rapid punches that put him right to the ground. Again, Drill Instructor SSgt Robert Johnson said: this time in a loud voice :get that ass wipe out of there, can anybody in Tomlin"s squad take that swinging Pugil Machine. I knocked out every body in my squad and not one got through my defense line. Drill Instructor SSgt Robert Johnson said: "Tomlin you are one tuff Son-of-bitch, now get yourself to the Medical Dispensary and get your face taken care of." I said: "SIR yes SIR" I found after I got back to the barracks that Butch did the same. Price held his ground and knocked out all his squad members from getting through his defense line.

Then we had the famous Gas Chamber Drill. A gas chamber is a room that has a controlled concentration of CS (orto-chlorobenzylidene-malononitrile) gas, more commonly known as tear gas. As our platoon was in formation, getting ready to go through the Gas Chamber. Drill Instructor SSgt Robert Johnson said: You will put on your gas masks and your whole squad will walk into this smallroom. I will touch your shoulder and ask you to lift your mask and state your name, rank and serial number. Take in a couple of deep breaths, then you will Don and Clear your gas mask and walk out." Then he went on with as you are exiting the gas chamber, your eyes will fill with water, and the mucous will fill your lungs and face. The best treatment is air. Immediately upon exiting the gas chamber, you should open your eyes. This will seem like a hard task under the circumstances, but keeping your eyes open in fresh air will allow any discomfort to dissipate very quickly. I cannot emphasize enough to not touch your eyes.

As me and my squad walked into the gas chamber there was Drill Instructor SSgt Robert Johnson without a mask on with a few tears running down his face, walking around touching recruit on their shoulders They would, crying in pain and agony, shouting out, with their names, ranks, and serial numbers. Bob Jackson from Idaho did not Don and Clear his gas mask properly. He was crying, gaging and taking in deep breaths of the tear gas. When he finally got on his gas mask he started to throw up inside his gas mask, you could see vomit slowly rising up in his clear eye pieces of the mask. Drill Instructor SSgt Robert Johnson said: " Tomlin take this recruit out and get him square away,." I grabbed recruit Jackson"s arm and led him out of the gas chamber. When we got outside, I ripped off his mask, laid him on his side and cleared his airway. He was still having difficult breathing, so I cleared his airway again and gave him mouth-to mouth resuscition. He started throwing up again; he got everything out of his airway and started breathing again. The next thing I knew I started throwing up from that smell of volmit. By that time Drill Instructor SSgt Robert Johnson was outside checking on his recruits and making sure everything was under control. He said: "Tomlin, fast thinking, you just saved this recruit's life. Even if we do not make the Honor Platoon of the Cycle. I will personlly give you a three day pass with a buddy of your choice to stay in San Diego."

Then we had an instant on the hand grenade range if it had not been for Drill Instructor SSgt Robert Johnson's fast thinking and quickness, several recruits would have been killed or seriously injured. At our hand grenade class. we learned how dangerous this weapon really is. We practice throwing dumbing hand grenades to get used to the weigh and how far we could throw them. Drill Instructor SSgt Robert Johnson and Drill Instructor SSgt John Jackson taught the hand grenade class. Drill Instructor SSgt Robert Johnson said: "Before you use a grenade, first you want to have a really good idea where you want to throw it, because things are about to happen real fast. Grasp the grenade tightly in your hand, with particular care to grip the lever hard against the body. Next, remove both the steel safety pin this is attached to a pull ring and safety clip. Removing the pin releases the spring-tensioned lever, and you will notice the grenade is noticeably harder to hold." Then Drill Instructor SSgt John Jackson took over the class and said: "At this point the grenade is ready to be thrown. Once thrown, the spring will force the lever to pop off, initiating the fuze. The grenade's fuze will "cook" for four or five seconds, and then the grenade will go boom." Then they both said: "remember the live grenade can be thrown 30 to 35 meters by an average Marine. It has a casualty radius of 15 meters, a fatality radius of 5 meters and its detonation delay is from 4 to 5.5 seconds."

Then came the big day of throwing a real live grenade. They divided us in to our squads; we went over the safety and procedures. When they call your name, you step into the throwing bunker; the DI hands you a live grenade; you put it into your chest. The DI gives instructions at what target you are throwing at. Then the DI gives the command: " Pull pin" and you throw it at your target and get down quickly. As I heard the explodsion I could hear Drill Instructor SSgt Robert Johnson saying: " Tomlin Bullseye"Then the DI called out Jake Smith from Oregon. We all called him Jake the Snake because he was so damn skinny and terrified of everything. Drill Instructor SSgt Robert Johnson went over the safety and procedures with recruit Smith. The DI handed him the grenade and right away Smith got scared and really nervous. The DI gave the command: "Pull Pin." Smith pulled the pin and dropped the hand grenade down on the bunker floor. Drill Instructor SSgt Robert Johnson with his quickness, grabbed the hand grenade and yelled everybody down and threw the hand grenade into the sump hole inthe middle of the bunker and threw his body over Smith's body. The hand grenade blew up without any injuries to the DI's or recruits. When Drill Instructor SSgt Robert Johnson pick himself up off of Smith. He asked Smith if he was ok. Then Smith said: " I am ok SIR." That's when all hell broke loose; the DI called Smith every cuss word in the book . Then he said: " Smith see that pine tree" Smith answered with SIR; yes SIR. Then Drill Instructor SSgt Robert Johnson said: "You fucking DFB, you climb half way up that tree, perch yourself on a limb and you say I am Dick For Brains and I will never put my Drill Instructors and fellow recruits in danger again. You keep repeating that over and over again until I tell you to Stop." Smith said: SIR yes SIR." Then Drill Instructor SSgt Robert Johnson was yelling at the top of his lungs: " move out you fucking dumbnuts and climb that fucking tree."

Another time we were on exercise in combat training on infantry movement and position against the enemy. This recruit was to throw a white Phosphorous Grenade to give a screen against the enemy. Drill Instructor SSgt Robert Johnson always told us: " The M15 was initially intended to be a screening weapon, a tool designed to cover troop movements or disrupt enemy fire. However, you have to remember, the bursting design coupled with the emitted white phosphorous is burning at over 2,700 degrees. This grenade made the an effective weapon against enemy infantry. The bursting radius of the grenade is about 17 meters with the white phosphorous having a burn time of approximately sixty seconds. Anyone within the 17 meter radius would have to be covered or run the risk of being hit by the many white phosphorous particles in the air. If any white phosphorous comes in contact with your skin make damn sure you doused in water to avoid further combustion. Well this recruit from another company was to throw M15 Grenade on signal when our compay was to advance through the woods. He threw the white Phosphorous Grenade and just stood there because he like the pattern of the white phosphorous was giving off and forgot to run back 17 or more meters. I can still hear him screaming as the particles was hitting all over his body. Drill Instructor SSgt Robert Johnson was yelling: Squad 1 and 2 run as fast as you can, and take your canteens and doused him with water. We all ran as fast as we could and started pouring water on that poor burning bastard, he was getting some relief, but he was in a lot of pain and agony. As the medics were carry him away he looked like he was stuck with several branding irons over his whole body. On his left hand the white phosphorous burn a hole all the way through. Drill Instructor SSgt Robert Johnson said: " That poor son-of-bitch, I kind feel sorry for the kid."

One day we were standing inspection for the Battalion Commander, who made a surprise visit to inspect the companies. Just before the Battalion Commander got to our company for inspection. A recruit in squad 4 kick the back of squad 3 boots. The recruit in squad 3 turns around and hits the recruit in squad 4 right in the face. Right away Drill Instructor SSgt Robert Johnson had our company under control, called us to attention, and got us squared away before the Battalion Commander made his inspection with our company. The Battalion Commander told Drill Instructor SSgt Robert Johnson: " Drill Instructor this is the best recruits I have inspected in a long time, they are well despline and in great phycial shape." Drill Instructor SSgt Robert Johnson said: 'Thank You SIR these recruits will make good Marines." When the Battalion Commander left the parade grounds. Drill Instructor SSgt Robert Johnson called out the two recruits from squads 3 and 4. He gave the comand front and center. When the two recruits were standing at attention in front of the DI. Drill Instructor SSgt Robert Johnson lower the boom on the two recruits. He said: " You two fuck ups", I want you to hold each other hands and look at each other and said: " I love you and the other one will say I love you too, then both will say and we will never fight each other again while in formation. Then you both skip up and down the parade the field while holding hands, and repeating every thing I told you. Now move out, you two dickwads." For four hours those two skip up and down the parade field like two little kids. All you could hear was I love you, I love you too, and we will never fight again while in formation.

Oh, that dreaded 20 mile tactical march in which you carry 90-plus additional pounds of field gear. M14 Rifle with fullMagazine and cleaning equipment 13 pounds, 200 rounds of 7.62 ammo 10 pounds, two hand grenades 2 pounds; canteen of water 4.5 pounds; backpack 45 pound;, gas mask 3.5 pounds, bayonet under 1 pound, steel pot helmet 4 pounds, Flak Jacket 15 pounds, web belt, combat boots, flash light, and c-rations. C-ration, that is, a meal you can not refuse with one canned meat; one canned fruit, bread; a desert, four-pack of cigarettes, matches, chewing gum, toilet paper, coffee, cream, sugar, salt, and a spoon. I always gave my cigarettes to Butch for this can of peanut butter. I had my own personal P38 can opener. I could open a can of peanut butter faster than you could say: "peanut butter." Well, that P38 is another story one day Drill Instructor SSgt Robert Johnson called for an inspection with our dog tags out. He walked up to me and said: " Tomlin what the fuck do you have around your neck." I said: "SIR I have my dog tags, key to my foor locker and my P 38 SIR." The Drill Instructor said: " when I turn around that fucking P38 better be out of my sight, you got me Tomlin." I said SIR yes SIR." I took off that P38 faster then BlueJay eating a Junebug on a hot August night, and stuck it in my pocket. When the DI turned around and saw the P38 gone, he said: "Now Tomlin you pass inspection." I was thinking about what would be the best way to keep my P38, so I came up with this great idea I Super Glued a leather pocket in the top of my right boot and tucked the P38 in there. Every time we had C-rations, I would reach in the top of my right boot, pull out my P38, and start opening the cans of food. This way I did not have to wait until other recruits were finished using the P38.

After walking ten or so miles, Drill Instructor SSgt Robert Johnson called out Halt, take a rest, and smoking lamps are lit if you have them. While Butch and I were setting, he lit up a cigarette and started smoking. Drill Instructor SSgt Robert Johnson said: " smoking lamp is out and get ready to move out." Butch squeeze the end of his cigarette off and put the butt in his back pocket. We were called to Attention, then forward march. As we were marching along, Drill Instructor SSgt Robert Johnson said: "Tomlin Jody Call the Crawdad Song." I started out with You get a line and I'll get a pole babe You get a line and I'll get a pole babe You get a line and I'll get a pole An' I'll meet you down by the crawdad hole go to your left your right and left. Then I started the verse all over again, then I noticed Butch was jumping around grabbing his ass and doing the Hooha-Booha dance. Drill Instructor SSgt Robert Johnson said:"Price what the fuck is your problem." Then Butch said: "SIR my ass is on fire." Now he is really jumping around. I ran over and took out my canteen and started pouring water on Butch 's back pocket. After the fire was put out, Butch turn to me said: " thanks Robert." Then Drill Instructor SSgt Robert Johnson hit him with both barrels: "Price get down and knock out fifty"

In the four weeks of Boot Camp our Drill Instructor SSgt Robert Johnson called out Pvt Tomlin and Pvt Price to front and center. We ran up and stood at attention, rendered a salute, and said Pvt Tomlin and Pvt. Price were reporting SIR. Then SSgt Johnson let us have it with both barrels " You two dumbnuts really fuck up this time. On the infantry combat exercise this morining, too start with you let a fellow Marine down, when Pvt Jackson was running up the hill and twisted his ankle you two dumbnuts just left him there. Just rememeber you two fuck heads "NEVER" let me repeat myself "NEVER" leave a fallen Marine dead or a live. Now for the next fuckup, you two DFBS (Dick For Brains) commit. On the infantry practice with the machine gun, you two dumb dicks had a center position you were to sweep 90 degrees right flank, then 90 degrees left flank, but no you two fuck faces were concerned on center and left flank positions, and left, the right flank of Marines exposed to the enemy. You two fuckups have to work as a team, if it is one or twenty marines, we always work as a team as if we were only one Marine. If I ever see you fuck up again, I will personally pop out your eye balls and skull, fuck you in your eye sockets. Do I make myself clear, we both stood at attention and yelled SIR, yes SIR we rendered a salute. Drill Instructor SSgt Johnson said you are dismissed, get back in formation. Then came the sonic boom, as SSgt Johnson gave us the famous China; again, he dismissed the rest of the platoon. Drill Instructor SSgt Johnson said: " Tomlin and Price you are going to be doing push ups until your fucking arms come off or you push your self all the way to China. Now give me 80 or until I tell you to stop. We both said: "SIR, yes SIR;" Butch and I dropped to the deck and started pushing them out with One Drill Instructor, two Drill Instructor, and so on until we hit 80. Then Drill Instructor SSgt Johnson said: "Now you are dismissed and get the fuck out of my sight."

Four more weeks and boot camp is over and Butch and I were really surprise that we were building muscle and getting stronger every day. When I would write home and tell Dad and Mom about Butch and I and how hard it was to be coming a Marine. Then I would tell Dad about how right he was about me joining the Navy. I would tell Mom not to worry I am fine and doing OK, and eating very well, then I would send her pictures of me and Butch. Then I remember what my Dad told me: "Son its is an all mind game, they want to break you to see if you would crack under pressure. Because if you break while in combat you will be killed and everybody around you will be killed." You know, Dad was right and he should know. He was in World War II in the Battle of Midway. He never talked about the sad and heart break of the war; only the good and fun times. I always felt he did not talk about the war, because he did not want to hash up old memories of the terrible things that happen in war. I know in my heart my Father was a proud man, he always took good care of his family, if you were down and out he would give the shirt off his back to you, he was strick, but always fair.

On Sunday morning we were in formation right after breakfast in front of the chow hall. Drill Instructor SSgt Robert Johnson said: "You know this Mess and Maintenance week. Tomlin and Price you have the mess hall Monday, Tuesday, and Wednesday, and Maintenance in the Motor Pool on Thursday, Friday and Saturday. Then he annouced the remaining names for Chow Hall and Maintenance for the week. Monday morning Butch and I reported for duty at the chow hall to SSgt. Robinson. As we came through the back door and said: " We are reporting for duty SIR." SSgt. Robinson said: " Knock off that bullshit I am an NCO not a drill instructor. He when on with go to the back room where you will find potaoes and onions. One of you will peel potatoes or onions and put them in the two big steel pots, then you will switch off this afternoon." Butch and I walked back to the small room, that was the biggest pots I ever saw in my life. I told Butch I will peel onions this morning and potatoes this afternoon. I started on the 50 pound bags of onions and Butch started on the 100 pound bag of potatoes. After about 5 minutes of peeling onions, I had tears running down my face like a water fall. Howad was laughing his ass off as I tried wiping the tears away. Then I said: " Ok potatoe boy wait until its your turn to peel onions." Then Butch stopped laughing, and was peeling those potatoes like a mad man. SSgt. Robinson came back in about 2 hours to check on our process. He said: " Great job boys I will send you some stawberry shortcake at lunch time. Then I told him my stawberry shortcake story. I said: "Drill Instructor SSgt Robert Johnson told us no deserts while in bootcamp, so our second week we had strawberry shortcake, which is my favorite dessert. So I got the strawberry shortcake to return to my table. Drill Instructor SSgt Robert Johnson saw me; he yelled: "Tomlin don't you dare take a bite and throw in the trash can, then knock out 50." As I was walking over to put the cake in the garbage can.I thought I was going to cry for throwing the strawberry shortcake away. SSgt. Robinson said: " do not worry boys when I bring you the stawberry shortcake, you can eat in the back room, and I will keep a look out for Drill Instructor Johnson." Butch and I kept peeling those onions and potatoes until lunch time. We finished our chow and headed back to the kitchen to start peeling. Just as we started peeling, SSgt. Robinson brought us the strawberry shortcakes. I savor every bite of that strawberry shortcakeand even licked the bowl. Butch said: " I just hope Drill Instructor SSgt Robert Johnson doesn't finds out or we are going to have hell to pay with them damn pushups, and my arms are ready, killing me from all this peeling." Finally, our KP (Kitchen Patrol) was over; we had our dinner and headed back to the barracks. When we got to the barracks we took our showers and hit the rack.

Tuesday morning started all over again, we reported for duty at the chow hall. Ssgt. Robinson has us making gallons of orange juice and breaking eggs for the cooks for they could make scrambled eggs for the troops. For lunch SSgt.Robinson snuck us a slice of apple pie. Now Butch was really getting nervous about having desert, thinking

Drill Instructor SSgt Robert Johnson would catch us. In the afternoon Butch make orange juice and I cracked the eggs. We finished our KP , we had our dinner and straight back to the barracks. As we were walking in the the door, Drill Instructor SSgt Robert Johnson yelled at us. He said: "Tomlin and Price I need to talk to you." Then Butch started flipping out and saying: " Robert he knows about the desert and our asses are cooked." I said: "no he just wants to talk to us." When Drill Instructor SSgt Robert Johnson approached us we stood at a attention. He said: at ease, and I got the report from SSgt.Robinson that you two recruits are the best workers he has had in a long time. He said: "maybe on your last day of KP, I might consider you two having a small desert." We both said: SIR Thank you SIR." The Drill Instructor said: " hit the showers and rack and finsh your KP tomorrow." We both said: "SIR yes SIR."

Wednesday morning we reported for duty at the chow hall. Then SSgt. Robinson said: " well boys how did meeting go with your Drill Instructor, I pull in a good word for you." We both said: "Thanks Ssgt.Robinson, and he might lets us have a small desert." SSgt.Robinson said: " I can tell that Drill Instructor Johnson really likes you boys, he told me you are the best recruits he has trained in a long time. Sorry to say you going to be on garbage detail today. You will have to get the food garbage cans together for our local pig farmer this morning. Just much sure before you take out the garbage cans to his truck that is food only. Because he does not want any paper products or sweet potatoes that could cause digestive issues with his pigs." Butch and I spent the whole morning making sure there wasn't any paper products or sweet potatoes in the garbage cans. Then we started taking the garbage cans to the loading dock. It was a good thing we had a two- wheel dolly; those cans had to weigh over 250 pounds. Just as we were taking out the last garbage can to the loading dock, the pig truck was pulling up. The driver of the truck said: " I'll back up the truck then I will unload the clean cans, then we can load the garbage cans." Butch and I took the clean garbage cans inside and started to load the garbage cans on his truck. Butch and I were asking him about his pig farm. He begins with: "he raised Berkshire Pigs that is one of the oldest heritage breeds of hogs. Originally from the Berk area in England, the Berkshires are a popular choice for meat production and possess an easy-going personality. They have a 600-pound average market weight is easily obtained with foraging. They love Marine food specially water melon rinds, mashed potatoes and gravy, and meat loaf." When we loaded the last garbage can on the truck. Mr. Browner was telling about his favorite pig named Herman. He said: " When Herman was born, he was the cutest little pig you ever saw in your life, he was pink and smooth as a baby's behind. As soon as Herman saw me, he took to me like a duck takes to water, he follow me every where I went." Then Mr. Browner was so happy about talking about Herman. He said: "he taught Herman how to sing, sit up, shake hands, roll over and play dead. You know Herman smarter then any dog I know of. By the time we loaded Mr. Browner's truck and talked to him about the pigs our workday was over. Drill Instructor SSgt Robert Johnson caught up to us before we got to the barracks. He said: Tomlin and Price, you are at the Motor Transportation tomorrow, report to GySgt James Hendson." We said: "SIR yes

SIR." We hit the showers and the rack.

The next morning we did our PT, ate breakfast and headed for the motor transport. We reported toGySgt Hendson for duty. He got us squared away on what our duties were and gave us clean coveralls. As I was changing the oil on a M151 utiillty jeep, I just got the drain plug back in, and Battalion Commander LTC Joseph Braxston pulled up in is 1962 red Corvette. He got out, walked into the shop and said: "recruit where is GySgt Hendson." I said: "I will get him SIR." I went to the shop office and told GySgt Hendson that the Battalion Commander wanted him. He dropped all his paper work and ran out to greet the Battalion Commander. He said: " SIR what can I help you with." LTC Braxston said: " Gunny my Vette is running a little rough do you have any one who could look at it." GySgt Hendson said: " SIR I'll have someone on it right away." About that time there was a honking of a horn. LTC Braxston said: " that is my wife picking me up, spare no cost I will pay for everything. and I will be back this afternoon." GySgt Hendson said: " do not worry SIR we will have your car running when you get back." As LTC Braxston got into his wife's car. GySgt Hendson said: "does anyone know a fucking thing about a corvette." I said: " I do GySgt Hendson." GySgt Hendson said: " get the fuck over here and fix the LTC's car." I pulled the vette into the shop and it was running rough, and the car would hesitate when you stepped on the gas. Then GySgt Hendson said: " Tomlin if you fuck up LTC's vette, when he has my ass, I am going to have your ass." I said: " do not worry GySgt Hendson I got

us covered." GySgt Hendson said: "Price finsh up on the M151 utiillty jeep, while Tomlin works on the LTC's corvette." I popped the hood on the vette and saw the problem right away, the vacuum hose to the distributor had a crack in it and was not letting the distributor advance the timing. It is going to be a full tune up on the LTC's vette with new spark plugs, wiring, distributor cap, points, rotor, and condenser. Then I will sat the timing and adjust his carburetor. GySgt Hendson said: I will send Cpl Smith to Advance Auto Parts to get the stuff." I said: Make sure the parts are for a 1962 Vette, 327 with 250 horse, with vacuum advance, with tach drive and a 4-barrel carburetor." I took out all the old parts and replaced them with the new ones, set the timing, and adjusted the Carburetor. Then I started it up, that baby was purring like a kitten. When LTC Braxston picks up his car and starts it up and gives it a little gas. He turned it off and walked over to GySgt Hendson and said: :Gunny, who worked on my car."GySgt Hendson said: " Recruit Tomlin did SIR." LTC Braxston said: Get him over here, my car has never ran that good." I reported to LTC Braxston, stood at attention and said: "Recruit Tomlin reporting SIR." LTC Braxston said: "recruit I am going to talk to your Drill Instructor, about the hell of a job you did on my car, it has never ran this good." I said: "Thank You SIR." I did about face and went back to work. LTC was telling GySgt Hendson about his wife's car, a 1962 chevy Impala that was not running very well and he would drop off tomorrow. Butch and I took off our coveralls, got cleaned up, and started to the chow hall. GySgt Hendson said: "Price you will be working on the LTC's wife car and Tomlin you will be changing oil and greasing vehicles tomorrow. We both said: " Yes GySgt Hendson and started walking towards the chow hall.

The next morning we did our PT, ate breakfast and headed for the motor transport. As Butch and I changed into our coveralls and walked into the shop to report for duty, the 1962 Impala was in the shop already. Butch popped the hood and called me over. He said: " can you believe this shit Robert a 409 with 409 horse and a 4-speed transmission that LTC's wife must be a real hot rodder." Butch told GySgt Hendson what parts he needed. I went back to work changing oil and greasing vehicles. Cpl Smith went to Advance Auto Parts to get the needed parts for Butch. Butch was in pig heaven working on that 409. You could hear him fire it up, give it some gas and shut it down. Butch worked his ass off adjusting them two four barrels. He told me at lunch time those two carburetors were so fucked up, I think somebody with all thumbs made the adjustments. Butch installed all the new parts and started adjusting the carburetors. He worked on those carburetors all day, adjusting this and adjusting that. He finally came up with a solution, then he had the game plan. He found the primarys of the secondary carb [frontcarb] were opening when the rear carb was not opening, this kept all 8 barrels from being fully open at full throttle. He had a hell of a time setting the linkage up for the progressive linkage to work property. He would make an adjustment, then start the car say a few cuss words turnoff the car and start adjusting again. While I was changing oil, all them jeeps, Butch just kept his nose to the grid stone with the carburetors adjustments. Then Butch yelled at me: "Robert with these adjustments, I am going to have this old Chevy running like a stripped ass ape." Then the master went to work by setting all 4 idle screws at 2 turns from lightly seated, (it means he did not break the tip off the idle mixture needle by tightening it into the seat.). He makes sure that the idle screws are both adjusted the same. He installed a vacuum gauge as well as a tach, adjust the idle screws; he turned them inward for the highest vacuum; this makes the highest rpm at an idle. He hooks up the vacuum line for the vacuum advance to the drivers side vacuum port on the rear carb. He got in the car rev that baby up a couple of times, you could hear that old engine had lots of power. He shut it off and cleaned up the car and drove outside and parked it. He told GySgt Hendson the job was finished and that the car was running good. By that time I had just finished my last oil change. Mrs. Braxston came to pick up the car; GySgt Hendson handed her the keys; she walked out and got in and started the car. She came back in the the biggest smile on her face and said: " Tell the recruits they did a great job and the car runs great. She walked back out got in started it up, drop it in first gear and lay a strip of rubber all the way out of the gate. GySgt Hendson told Butch you are one hell of a carburetor man. Then he said: " Clean up early and take the rest of the day off." We walked to chow hall, had our dinner, went back to the barracks, cleaned up, and wrote letters home.

Saturday morning was our last day at maintenance work, we did our PT, ate breakfast and headed for the motor transport. When we got to the motor motor transport. Butch and I changed into our coveralls and walked into the shop to report for duty. As we were walking into the shop, LTC Braxston and his wife and GySgt Hendson were standing there. Butch and I said: Godd morning SIR, Mrs. Braxston, and GySgt Hendson. LTC Braxston said: " Tomlin and Price you did just a good job on fixing our cars, and GySgt Hendson said you are hard workers. We have decided to give an easy job today, just hang around the shop until 1600, then after today you both can go back to regular duty. Butch and I said: Thank you SIR, Mrs. Braxston, and GySgt Hendson. We did about face and went to the break room (Oasis) just to rest, drink coffee and talked about the old times. We stay in there until it was chow time. We were talking about our pugil stick fighting to get ready for Bayonet training and how we got our asses beat to no end. How Drill Instructor SSgt Robert Johnson kept yelling at us: " if you go down and let those recruits go through the defensive line, my foot will be so far up your ass with pain that you will pray for hemorrhoids." Drill Instructor SSgt Robert Johnson would say: " Maintaining good footing is the importance of footwork as you stabbed a worn-out tire you become more efficient." My favorite that Drill Instructor SSgt Robert Johnson would say about bayonets was: " Sure, without the real threat of danger, the point may be missed by some, but it's important nonetheless. If you and your unit are in a situration with making a last-ditch effort to stop the enemy and all you have is your bayonet, many of you may die. But when you know for certain that you and your brothers will charge into death head-on with the hopes of gutting at least that one, last son-of-bitch." Butch and I laughed and joked around and talking about how far we came in boot camp. Thinking in the next couple of weeks, we will take our finial PT Test, knowledge test, drill marching competition between platoons, exercise in which we take part in various obstacle courses, team exercises, outdoor survival drills, day and night combat movement courses, and our graduation ceremony. By that time when everything was soaking in our brains, it was time to go to chow. Butch and I were sitting in the chow hall talking about how we had to get back to work on the events coming up in two weeks. I told Butch we both have to pass, if we plan on staying together. Butch said: " do not worry Robert I am passing boot camp come hell or high water." I said: " Well brother I am with you all the way, we will be Marines." We finished eating and headed backto the barracks. Drill Instructor SSgt Robert Johnson stopped us and said: " I got high comments from everybody that you pulled duty with. LTC Braxston really though, you are going to be good Marines and he has a great surprise for both of you after graduation. But starting Monday next week, be prepared to work your asses off and have your squads in good shape. If we do not make Honor Platoon of the cycle, you forget about LTC Braxston, big surpise. Tomlin and Price, your asses will be mine." We said: SIR yes SIR." 4:00 AM came early Monday morning as we jumped out of our racks, shower, dressed and ran outside for our PT and that famous 5 mile run. After chow we were called into formation, then Drill Instructor SSgt Robert Johnson said: " all your ladies will given a strength test, you will do 3 pull-ups, 30 push ups, 40 sit-ups and a 1.5-mile run in 12 minutes. If you pussies fail you will have hell to pay with special training from Drill Instructor SSgt John Jackson. We were divided into our squads, squard 4 two recuites failed. Squad 3 one recruit failed. Then it was squad 2, everybody passed. Squad 1 everybody passed. Drill Instructor SSgt Robert Johnson said: "everybody that passed, formed a formation here; all others form a formation over there." Then Drill Instructor SSgt Robert Johnson said: "Now while Drill Instructor SSgt John Jackson is working with the pussies that failed. Drill

Instructor SSgt Gary Tibetts and myself we will be working with you on your marching and weapon drills." We marched and handled those rifles until I thought I was going to be dropped. We though Drill Instructor SSgt Robert Johnson was giving us extra rough treatment, and all he was doing was preparing us to be Marines and to graduate from boot camp. Then Drill Instructor SSgt Robert Johnson would say: " you think your ladies had it rough in boot camp, just wait until you get to School of Infantry West at Camp Pendleton, boot camp is a picnic where you are going." Since Butch and I took infantry, we would have to do another 8 weeks of training in ITB (Infantry Training Battalion) at Camp Pendleton.

The last three weeks of boot camp were the toughest and roughest. We did more PT, rifle and marching drills than any possible civilian could think of. But I will be the first one to admit Drill Instructor SSgt Robert Johnson was turning Butch and I into real Marines that are **Real Lean Mean Fighting Machines**. Butch and I excel in everything that we were trained for. We both fire expert on the rifle, hand grenade, pistol, and machine gun range. We even had a shoot-off one day, to see who was the best shot. They gave us 80 rounds of 7.62 and had targets at 200. 300, 400, 500, and some at 600 yards. Butch fired 80 rounds and hit every target, then I fired 80 rounds and hit every target. The Drill Instructors could not believe it; they would say: " we got two Buffalo Bills and its a tie." Besides Butch and I, there were six other Marines that fired experts. I will have to say all that hard work paid off. We were graded as a whole on six different events, including Initial drill, Final drill, a written test in Marine Corps knowledge, rifle range scores, and the physical and combat fitness tests. San Diego MCRD, C (Charlie) Company 1st Battalion (red), Platoon 117 made **Honor Platoon of the Cycle**. Drill Instructor SSgt Robert Johnson kept his promise; he gave the whole platoon a 3 day pass in San Diego. He said: "Friday morning you can skipped PT have your breakfast and catch the bus to San Diego for your three day pass. Monday morning you better be in formation at 0600 and every swinging dick will be in fornation. Do I make myself clear." We all said: "SIR yes SIR" He called us to attention, then said: "dismissed and have a fun week-end." We all ran into the barracks, packed a small seabag, went to sleep and waited for Friday morning

There was four us in our small group going to San diego. John Lewis from Dubois, Iowa, Ben Stevenson from Grand Island, Nebraska, Butch Price from St. Louis, Missouri, and Robert Tomlin from Springfield, Illinois. We took our seabags to chow hall after breakfast, we all ran down to the bus stationto catch a bus to down town San Diego. As we were climbing on the bus, Butch said: "before I have a beer I am going to get a big fat juicy hamburger at A & W Root Beer with a large order of frieds and a big mug of root beer." I looked at Butch and said: " I am with you brother, that hamburger and mugof root beer sounds real good." Then John who was in our group, said: We spent three nights in the Gaslamp Quarters at The Grand Horton on 311 Island Avenue for $17.00 dollars a night for a total of$34.00 dollars, we can split it four ways at $8.50 dollars and 50 cents each. I said: "that sounds good,because I have fifty bucks" In our group every body had fifty bucks and we were going to paint the town red. When we got to the hotels and checked in. Butch asks the hotel clerk where the best hamburger was from the hotel. The clerk said: " There is a little place right down the street called Mom & Pop's Restaurant, and they have the bet hamburgers in the world." Then he just jaw- on about the history of the hotel that it opened in 1880. Wyatt Earp had a room there, and that he was an active businessman in addition to a gambler, and was engaged in a variety of real estate ventures including the land boom of the mid 1880's. He said: "Earp leased four saloons and gambling halls in San Diego, the most famous was his Oyster Bar located in the Louis Bank of Commerce on Fifth Avenue. Earp was a gambler in the San Diego City in 1887 and among his other winnings, he won a race horse." We said: " Thank You". We went to our room, which had two queen size beds, so that we would be able to bunk two to a bed. John said: " I am not sleeping with a fellow Marine, I called down and asked for two roll aways." I said I would call the front desk and request two roll away. When I was talking to the front desk, the clerk said: " We normally charge one dollar per roll away, but since you are in the Marine Corp we will dropped the charges. They brought the bed up away and put them in the room. Then we flipped to see who got the queen beds and surprisely Butch and I both won. Then Butch said: " it is only fair that Robert and I get the roll aways tomorrow night." We put our seabags in the room and headed for the restaurant.

We had to walk only a couple of blocks to find the restaurant; we all went in and ordered hamburgers. Butch told the waitress he wanted the biggest hamburger they had with a large order of fries and a large root beer. The owner of the restaurant said: "you boys must be from boot camp, you are so young looking and you are still green behind your ears." I said: " how did you know SIR, you got that right we graduate from boot camp next week." Then the owner, whose name was Mario, said: " I remember Marine boot camp, it was hell to pay if you mess with your Drill Instructor." Then Ben said:" It is still like that SIR." Mario said: " I remember our Drill Instructor who was always poking his finger in your chest and asking you if you wanted to fly. He was one mean son-of-bitch and tuff as nails. But in a way I was glad he was like that, it help me to get through World War II to come home to my family. So I say thank God for the Drill Instructors." Then we all said: "Thank God for the Drill Instructors." We finished our meal and sat around talking about boot camp and could not wait to get home. We told Mario a great meal and we had a nice conversation about the Marine Corps, and walked out to check out the town.

John said: " lets shoot a game of pool before we hit the bars." Butch said:" Great idea Robert and I will be a team against John and Ben." Then Ben said: ' I smell a rat I think we are being set up." We found a pool hall only a few blocks from the restaurant, we all walked in to get a table. I went to the counter and asked the clerk for the pool balls and rack. He said: " that would be 75 cents an hour for the table."I gave him a dollar and a half and took the ball and rack to the table. Butch racked them up, and we flipped to see who was coming to break. It had to be our lucky day, but Butch and I won again. John was getting pissed and said: " do you guys ever loose." In a smart ass way, I said; " sometines we do." Then we all just laughed and started shooting pool. Then about 6 or 7 Squids came in to play pool; they were acting like they were real tough when they saw us. This E-5 Petty Officer Second Class, came up to me and said: " you fucking boots just out of boot camp" I said:' No SIR, we graduate nextweek."Then he said: " hay fuck face I am a NCO (Non Commission Offier) and I worked for a living and do not call me SIR. I said: " Sorry, we are so use of calling our Drill Instructors SIR." Then he said the wrong thing with if your fucking Drill Instructors were here, I would kick his ass and send him back home with his tail between his legs. I said: "That would be the day." Then the fists started flying, Marines had Navy fist in their face and Navy had Marine fist in their face. The clerk yells at us if you do not stop I am going to call the SP (Shore Patrol). We all stopped and got the hell out of there, the Marines went one way and the Navy went the other way. That all we needed to end up in the brig, Drill Instructor, SSgt Robert Johnson would have had our hides; plus we would be doing push-ups until we were very old men.

Butch said: " let get a drink" I said: "no more fighting and we do not want to wind in jail and have Drill Instructor SSgt Robert Johnson getting us out. Or we can kiss our Marine careers good-bye." Soas we were walking down the street we saw this bar called the Blue Dragon, so we stopped and walked inand right away walked right back out. We could tell there was a bunch of guys just waiting to fight at the drop of a hat. Then, John said: " lets find a quite place where we can just drink, talk and relax without fighting our way out. So we walked a few more blocks and found this nice little neighborhood bar where locals hang out and enjoy themselves. As soon as we walked in this eldly lady who name was Sarah setting at the bar shouted out in a real loud voice" the Marines have landed." She ran over and gave us a big hug and said: "you boys sit over at that table I am going to buy you a drink. Then she said: " What are you drinking." We all said: " Bud" She brought our drinks to our table and pulled up a chair and started talking about her husband, who was in the Marine Corp. She said: " you know my husband Tony was the sweetest man you ever want to know, and he was a real Marine and the toughest son-of-bitch that walked on two legs. We were only married six months when I got the telegram that he was killed on Iwo Jima in World War II. I told myself I just could not live without my Tony, and my Father help me make it through that living hell." So every Marine I see today, I just have to buy him a drink in memory of Tony. We all made a toast clicked our beer bottle together and said: "here is to Tony" Sarah had a big smile on her face with a small tear coming down her cheek and said: "Thank You boys, keep safe and keep out of harm's way." Then she got up and went back to the bar. Butch Said: " what a sweet old gal and sad about her husband." We sat around talking and listening to songs on the juke box by Roy Orbison - Oh, Pretty Women, The Beatles - I want to hold your hand, The Animals - House of the Rising sun, Johnny Rivers – Memphis, Tennessee, and The Righteous Brothers - You've lost that lovin feelin' then I started thing about Kathy. We sat there serval hours, just talking about old times, family and what we were going to do after boot camp and combat training. We finished our drinks and said our farewell to the people in the bar and headed back to the hotel.

The next morning we got up early, took our turns taking showers, shaving, and bushing our teeth. We went down stairs for breakfast. I told the guys I was really hungry and I ordered a big breakfast, three eggs, bacon, toast, orange juice, coffee, and a waffle for a mere $1.45 one dollar and 45 cents. Everybody else got similar breakfasts. We sat around talking and I said: " can you believe its been 30 minutes and we are still eating. Without some Drill Instructor yelling: " Ladies, you have 30 seconds to eat." We just sat there enjoying the peace and quiet and idle conversation. Then, Ben said:" lets go to the beach today and look at all the pretty women in their bathing suits." So I said: " lets walk we can use the exercise." After breakfast we started walking towards the beach. Butch saw all those beauties in their bathing suits and said: " Robert it was well worth the walk" I just knew he was thinking of Rose Ann. We kicked around the beach for a couple of hours, then headed back to the hotel. Then John said: " I am going to the Palace Bar tonight in the hotel, I am sure Earp drink his famous Red Eye whiskey in there." When we got to the hotel we went to our room to freshen up and get ready for dinner. After dinner we all went to the Palace Bar for drinks. John was asking the bartender for the same drink that Earp used to drink there. The bartender scatch his head and said: " you want ice cream" John said: " hell no I do not want ice cream, I want the whiskey Earp use to drink." Then he bartender said: " No, the great Wyatt Earp, as macho as they come, never let liquor touch his lips. But he did have a vice: his love of ice cream." John said: " just give all of us a Bud." As were sitting around talking about the morning would be here before you know and we all would be headed back to boot camp. John said: "can you believe that pussy Earp did not drink, but love ice cream." We all had a big laugh and called it night, cause we all knew the morning would be here fast. We would have to be back at boot camp to get ready for graduation.

The bus pulled through the gate at boot camp at 0530; we had a half hour to get ready and be in formation for Drill Instructor SSgt Robert Johnson inspection. All the squad leaders called their squad at Attention as Drill Instructor SSgt Robert Johnson was walking to the front of the platoon. He said:" I am very happy that all you ladies made it back to boot camp. The next several days you are going to be very busy getting your uniforms, boots, and shoes, spit shine and polish. When we are on the parade field for pass and review on your graduation day, I want to see the best looking Marines in all the Marine Corps. Do you hear me." We all said: "SIR yes SIR". Then he said: " I can not hear you." Then, at the very top of our lungs, we said: "SIR yes SIR" I swear I saw his Campaign Hat move a little on his head when we all said: "SIR yes SIR" He called us to Attention and said: " get your uniforms square away and make me proud on that parade field Friday." Then, he said: "dismissed and make sure you use a lot of elbow grease." Drill Instructor SSgt John Jackson and Drill Instructor SSgt Gary Tibetts started drilling us on our marching for pass and review for graduation. We marched for about three hours, when Drill Instructor SSgt John Jackson said: " I am in total surprise, you ladies have your marching down to a tee and "**BAMCIS**" you are ready. Then he called us to Attention and said: " dismissed go back to the barracks get it square away and start using them elbows." We all said: "SIR yes SIR." We went back to the barracks, we all pitched in, got the barracks squared away from top to bottom. Had our foot lockers ready for in spection, spit and polish our boots and shoes. We got our uniforms ready for graduation on Wednesday. We got special permission from Drill Instructor SSgt John Jackson to take our uniforms to the cleaners on base to have then clean and press. He said: " I do not want to see one wrinkle any where on your uniforms." Butch and I took extra time polishing the brass and spit shinning our shoes. When I was putting the finial shine on my shoes, Drill Instructor SSgt John Jackson walked by and picked up one of my shoes. He said: " Tomlin this is the best shoe shine I ever saw, I can see the color of my eyes in your shoe. You and Price go around and get the rest of the platoon square away on getting their shoes shine." I said: "SIR yes SIR" For the rest of the night we were showing the recruits in our platoon how to shine their shoes. Then one recruit asked me what my secret was for just a great shine.

So Butch and I had all the recruits get in a circle; we had them heat their black shoe polish to where it just melted. Spread a medium-thick layer of polish over the portion of the shoe to be spit shined. Allow it to dry for five to 10 minutes. Wrap a soft, clean cloth around your index finger so that it is smooth (no wrinkles). You can also use a cotton ball. Dip your finger or the cotton ball into a container of water. The cloth/cotton should be wet, but not dripping. Buff the dried polish (using a circular motion) with the wet cloth/cotton ball, until the wax starts to become shiny. Still, using the damp rag on your finger, apply a fine layer of polish in a circular motion and keep on rubbing lightly until a hazy shine develops. Using the damp cloth, or cotton ball, keep applying thin coats of wax, then spit on the polish buffing with a small circular motion. When the shoe is highly glossed, use a clean dry soft cloth to give it a final buff. Then I said: " when you are finish your shoes or boots will look like glass. Remember take your time, do a small section at a time, and have patience do not rush." Butch and I helped the recruits that were having trouble getting the super shine on their shoes. But it pays off in theend on our graduation pass and review our platoon look like we were wearing glass shoes. As I was laying in bed that night, I was thinking about my Dad and Butch's Dad who served in the United States Navy to help keep The United Staes of America safe and to keep our freedom. Then I thought about all those draft dodgers and war protestors who were against all the military for going to war. I know some of those assholes had Dads, Grandfathers, Brothers, Uncles, and cousins that served in some branch of the military during the war. What a let down for their relatives that gave their live and who became a casualty of war to keep them free. Those who so call I have rights to protest, should be ashame of themselves, that their relatives who died or suffered from the wars; that those assholes could be safe to have a better life and to keep their freedom. Them bastards should live in Russia, China, North Korea, and Middle East and find out what kind of freedom they would have. Then to top it all off years later, you have these so-called I have my rights not to stand when the National Anthem is playing. That still burns my ass just thinking of all the veterans that sacrificed their lives and who got wounded with disabilities to have then son-of-bitches set while the National Anthem is being played. I just thank God we still have people who care enough to stand and honor our United States Flag. Old glory has waved through a lot of wars the Untied States has fought in; and the great star and strips are still waving even though she has been weathered, tore, shot, and burnt; and may she wave on forever. So as a veteran, I salute the Untied Staes Flag with pride and honor, and I pray and hope the next generation does the same

Then came the big day we were graduating from boot camp on 15 October, 1966. Drill InstructorSSgt Robert Johnson said:" I will give you a final inspection of your uniforms before we get to the parade field." As we were standing in formation in front of our barracks with our uniforms which consists of our peaked cap (called a barracks cover) a green coat, green trousers with a khaki web belt, a khaki long-sleeve button-up shirt, a khaki tie, tie clasp, and black shoes. waiting for the final inspection. Drill Instructor SSgt Robert Johnson said: " I will check the caps, coats, shirts and trousers. Drill Instructor SSgt John Jackson will check belts, ties, and tie clasps. Drill Instructor SSgt Gary Tibetts will check shoes and socks." He called us at attention and the inspection began. Drill Instructor SSgt Robert Johnson when he got to me, he said: " Tomlin you are one hell of a square leader recruit, see me in my office after graduation." Then he told Price the same thing. He called for parade rest and he made his final speech. He said: "All you recruits look real sharp today, when you make your finial pass ande same. review everybody is going to be impressed. Then he stepped back and said: "I am really going to miss this group of recruits, you have to be the best recruits us Drill Instructors have trained in a long time. Just remember when you are on that battlefield , never leave a fellow Marine dead or alive, you bring them home." We all stood at attention and said: "SIR yes SIR" Then we marched down to the parade field to our final graduation from boot camp. As we were marching to the parade field we could hear the United Staes Marine Band playing the The Marines' Hymn. Then I saw the United States Flag; I got a warm feeling all over knowing it was an honor to serve our country and protect against all domestic and foreign enemies. My Dad and Butch's Dad served in the United States Navy in World War II so that the Untied Staes of America could keep its freedom.

As our platoon was the last platoon to pass the viewing stand, with all the officers and Commanding Officer of the Marine Corps Recruit Depots watched as we passed. Then came the famous command of EYES RIGHT everyone except those on the right flank turned their heads smartly 45 degrees in the direction of the command right. The command Ready, FRONT is used to return your head and eyes forward. It is given to the left or right foot that strikes the ground. With the command FRONT, you return your head and eyes smartly to the front. As the last recruit passed the viewing stand, we knew it was over. We just graduated from boot camp and we woud be receiving the Eagle, Globe and Anchor and becoming a Marine. As we marched back to the barracks, halt was called, then attention, stand at ease, and finally dismissed. Then Drill Instructor SSgt Robert Johnson called out Tomlin and Price to my office. Butch and I ran to Drill Instructor SSgt Robert Johnson's office and said: " Tomlin and Price reporting SIR." SSgt Robert Johnson said: " Stand at ease." then said: " have great news for both of you. First you are gettign a 10 day furlough to go home. After you ten day furlow report to Camp Pendleton for infantry training, You both should have been promoted to E-2 Pivate First Class. But since you shown outstanding leadership and excel in all weapons, and discipline your men as true Marines. BattalionCommander LTC Joseph Braxston, Drill Instructor SSgt John Jackson, Drill Instructor SSgt Gary Tibetts, and myself all agreed that you were great squad leaders and you should be promoted to E-3 Lance Corporal. I asked Battalion Commander LTC Joseph Braxston if I could personally pin your strips and Eagle, Globe and Anchor. Drill Instructor SSgt Robert Johnson pinned my strips and Eagle, Globe and Anchor on first while I stood at attenntion. After he was finsihed, he rendered a salute and said: " thank you SIR" Then he told me, to stand at ease and walked over to Price. Butch stood attention while Drill Instructor SSgt Robert Johnson pinned on his strips and Eagle, Globe and Anchor. He render a salute and said: "thank you SIR" then he shook ours hands and said: " it is a great honor to shake the hands of fellow Marines Then Drill Instructor SSgt Robert Johnson said: "I have more great news; I sign both of you for Mountain Warfare Training close to Leadville, Colorado, and Jungle Training Okinawa, Japan." SSgt Robert Johnson said: "You better say your goodbyes to your squads, get packed cause you have a train to catch to go home." Then he looked kind of sad and said: "Just remember, when you are on that battlefield, look out and protect each other and give cover to the blind sides of your fellow Marines We gave our final salute, did about face, and walked into the highbay to pack and say our final goodbyes.

It took for ever for the train from San Diego, California, to Springfiedl, Illinois; it hit every whistle stop to drop or pick up passengers and packages. I got plenty of much needed rest from the lack of sleep in boot camp. The food was excellent on the train and I ate like a pig. We had a layover in Chicago and had to catch a different train to Springfield. We were on our last leg, about 35 miles from Springfield, and we were getting anxious to see Dads and Moms. Butch's Dad and Mom were picking him up in Springfiedl and they were driving back to St. Louis. As the train pulled into the depot we could see our Dads and Moms through the window of the train. My Mom and my sister Connie were waving their arms as the train came to a complete stop. I jumped up and grabbed my duffle bag and ran to meet them. Butch was right behind me as we exited the train. I ran over and shook my Dad's hand and gave a big hug to Mom and Connie. Mom had tears in your eyes and said: " Robert I am just glad you are home." I said: " me too Mom I have a ten day furlough." Both families greeted each other and said their goodbyes. I told Butch I would call him in a couple of days. On the way home in the car. Mom said: " What the first thing you are going to do get a beer." Then Dad said: "No he going to get a girl." I said: " No as soon as I get home, I am going to the bath room and sit on the toilet and take a dump with out 45 guys looking at me. Then I am going to take a shower by myself without 45 guys that are all press together and you are wondering who's dick is pressing into your leg. Second day I am going to have a beer and girl. We all laughed and through it was funny. But over all it was wonder to be home to hang out with my brothers Gene and Jimmy. We talked about old time and all stuff and troubles we did and got into.

We were laying in bed talking one night talking about the older days and all the crap we did and got into. Jimmy said: "remember that one summer day in August where we were driving my old 55 Mercury out in the county going real fast." I said: I was in the middle; Gene was riding shotgun and I was holding doors in case they flew open while we were taking them curves about 90 miles an hour. We were laughing and carrying on and were not worried about the danger we were in or could have been killed." Jimmy said: "Remember my car was behind Dad's car and he had to go to work. Dad yelled at me to move the car, so I went down stairs and the car would not start. So I yelled at you and Gene to help me push it back. While we were pushing back that old 55 Mercury, the tie rod snapped the front tires just went into the fenders. Gene said: " we just stood their our faces were white as ghosts. Then Dad said what wrong with you boys. Then we all said: "We can move the car; the tie rod broke." Dad said: " it back far enough I can get out." He got in his old 55 Ford and drove off to work. Jimmy said: " Boys just think what would happen to us on the last curve we went around going about 80 miles an hour." All three of us were shaking and thinking we would not be here today. They would be picking up the three Tomlin boys in baskets.

Then Gene said: " Remember them damn mosquitos on Sangamon River." So Gene, Jimmy and I were going fishing on Sangamon River for catfish. Mom fixed us mustard and bologna sandwiches, oatmeal raisin cookies, and we took a bag of marshmallows to roast on a fire. We loaded every thing into Jimmy's car and headed for Sangamon River. We parked the car on top of a hill and walked down to the river. We threw our lines in and waited for the catfish to strike. It was getting close to noon and we decided to eat and roast them marshmallows. We just finished eating, and had the fire going to roast our marshmallows. Then, Gene said: "do you hear that sound, it sounds just like a giant buzz saw." We looked up and saw a couple of hundred thousand mosquitos coming right at us. Jimmy said: "lets jump into the river." Then out of no where, there was a couple of thousand Purple Martins diving right into the middle of those mosquitos. They were eating mosquitos faster than you could have said jack rabbit. I remember this one Purple Martin that was kind of thin, but after five or so minutes he was fat as an elephant. He was so fat he could not fly, cause he ate so many mosquitos. He just hopped on the ground still eating them damn mosquitos and getting bigger and bigger. After about 15 minutes, we got a few mosquitos bites, but we roasted our marshmallows, and pulled our lines in. We walked up the hill and got in the car to go home. Then we just sat in that car and thought how lucky we were for the Purtle Martins. Gene said: "thank goodness for the Purple Martins or those mosquitos would have sucked us dry."

Then I said: "Oh how about the time I got drunk when I was 15" Our cousin Mary Joe was having a birthday party, so she invited Gene, Jimmy, and I for her party. We got to her house around 6 PM, knocked on the door and heard this voice come in. As we walked in, Mary Joe said: "cousins grabbed yourself a beer." So I grabbed a quart of Reisch beer, which was about 12.5 percent alcohol, and started drinking. Jimmy yelled at me and said: "Robert take it easy or you will be drunk on your ass." I said: " I do not feel a thing" and grabbed another quart and drank it down. Then all of a sudden it hit me like a ton of rocks I was drunk on my ass. Gene and Jimmy were helping me home and keeping me from falling down. Jimmy said: "Gene and I will go through the front door and you come through the back door and go up stairs right away. Gene and I will tell Dad you had to much cake and ice cream and you do not feel good so you went right to bed." As I got to my bed and lay down, the bed and room were spinning around real fast. Then I had to take a piss, but I did not want to go down stairs cause Dad might see me. So I opened the side window and started pissing out the screen window. But I was pissing out on the side of the house where Dad was watching TV. Then I had this strange feeling somebody was standing behind me. Then I heard Dad's voice: "Robert I will talked to you in the morning" Oh no Dad caught me and I knew my goose was cooked. I could not sleep thinking about what Dad was going to do to me. As I went down stairs for breakfast, Dad was setting up at the table drinking his coffee. He looked up and said: " Son I hope you learn your lesson about drinking." I said: "I have Dad" From that day on I have never taken another drink. Gene, Jimmy, and I just laughed about some of our siturations that we got into. I could see some tears in their eyes when they said: "Robert just come back home after the war."

Butch and I talked on the phone a couple of times; we both decided just to stay home and be close to the families since we knew we would be going off to war. I really enjoy staying at home with Dad, Mom, Gene, Jimmy, and Connie. We talked a lot, had good times visiting family and friends. I worked on my car and told Jimmy to keep it running after I left cause I did not know how long I would be gone. Then stupid me tried calling Kathy to see if she wanted to get something to eat and talk about old times. That was a mistake; she was to be involved with a new boyfriend and did not have the time. I am sure, her Mother was so happy that she did not have anything to do with me. I found out years later her so-called boyfriend turned out to be gay. I bet you, her Mother is wishing that she did not get between Kathy and I. Well, you know, in the long run somethings just work out better. The time went by real fast and the next thing I knew I was packing my duffle bag and getting ready to catch a train to San Diego. Butch's Dad and Mon drove him to the Springfield Train Depot. As we said our goodbyes, I told my Dad, Mom, Gene, Jimmy, and Connie not to worry that I would be home again. Butch told his Dad, Mom, brothers, and sisters that he would be home again. As the train pulled out headed for Chicago, we could see our Moms and sisters were crying and waving their arms off. Butch turned to me and said: " Robert promise me that you will cover my ass so that I can come home again." I said: " I will and promise me you will cover my ass in battle so that I can come home again." We both just laughed and sat back and rested while the train was moving on down the tracks. I told Butch some of the stuff my brother and I pulled some boners as teenagers.

Then Butch was telling me about his little brother, who was Daddy, little boy that told his Dad everything that Butch did wrong. One day he squeals on Butch about some trouble Butch got into. So after Butch's Dad gave him the one, two, three and grounded him for a week. Butch was thinking how could I get even with his little rat. So the next day Butch was drinking a Bush beer and walking down the street with his little brother. Butch said: "hey little brother do you want a beer." His little brother answered: " does this mean we are friends again" and said: "yes I will have beer." So Butch shoved him in the bushes and said: " have a bush." His brother was furious and said: " I am telling Dad." Butch said: " tell Dad and I will really beat your ass." Then, Butch said: " my younger brother and I never got alone after that we were always fighting. Then was the time my younger sister and I were going to run away from home. I do not know what we were thinking, we did not have any money, no place to stay, and no food to eat. We went down the street about a mile or so to this old empty house and was going to lay low there. Then we got hungry and decided to go home. We did not know Dad and Mom were looking for us. So we were racing to get back home and I felled down and my sisiter pass me and ran in the house first. Our Dad was madder then a wet back hen and grabbed my sister and started thumping on her head. By the time I got to the house, he was wore out from thumping my sister, he just tapped me a couple of times. My sister to this day said: " I wish that you ran into the house first. We just sat back and laughed about the good old days. The time went by real fast and the next thing you knew, we changed trains in Chicago and headed for Camp Pendleton in San Diego for infantry training.

CHAPTER FIVE

Marine Infantry Training Camp Pendleton

When Butch and I arrived at Camp Pendleton on 26 October, 1966 for four weeks of infantry training, we though it would be a piece of cake compared to boot camp. We found out real fast this was not a cake walk. The Drill Instructors were twice as disci-pline and hard core as the Drill Instructors in boot camp. GySgt Gerald Stevenson first day at Camp Pendleton, laid down the law about being in Marine Infantry Training. Drill Instructor GySgt Gerald Stevenson said: " This Infantry Training is to train and qualify Marines in entry level infantry military occupational specialties to provide the Operating Forces and Marine Forces Reserve with Marines capable of conducting ex-peditionary combat operations." Drill Instructor GySgt Gerald Stevenson did not take a breath and said: " this training course will develops you Marines into infantry men, who can fight, survive, and win in a combat situation. The first two weeks you will learn common skills to make you a infantry man. You will receive instruction in com-bat marksmanship, use of grenades, identifying and countering improvised explosive devices, convoy operations, you will learn tactical formations, land navigation, and pa-trolling. Then as a Marine you will receive instruction specific to your infantry MOS, regarding machine guns, mortars, reconnaissance.. I will run your asses into physical conditioning and physical training, conditioning marches, and sustainment training in hand to hand combat." Then he said, do I make myself clear on what is a Marine in-fantryman." We all stood attention and shouted at the top of our lungs, "SIR yes SIR" He turned to his assistance Drill Instructor SSgt Wayne Boseworth, and said: "get these pussies ready for a five mile run." In less than an hour of being in our new company, we were going to do a five mile run. Drill Instructor, GySgt Gerald Stevenson said: " I will be given a class on the M14 rifle after your run and you will know the M14 rifle inside and outside." Drill Instructor SSgt Wayne Boseworth called us to at attention, with right face, forward, double time march. As we were running on pavement, we did a quick left turn straight up this hill and Drill Instructor SSgt Wayne Boseworth was saying: "ok ladies step it up we have a hill to climb. After the run I through we would get a rest, but I was wrong straight to the class room to learn about the M14 rifle.

As we walked into the class room there was a table with an M14 completing torn down. Drill Instructor GySgt Gerald Stevenson was standing there with an M14 in his hands. He said: This rifle will save your live in a combat situation and your fellow Marines who are around you. This weapon will be treated with respect, so keep it clean and always in good working condition. When you finish with this course, you will know every part and how they worked on the M14 rifle. On your final test you will be blind-folded, and when the instructor hands you a part, you will identify and tell what the part is and the operation of the part." So everybody was handed a M14 rifle, then Drill Instructor GySgt Gerald Stevenson started to tell us the various names and parts. He said we will start at the rear of the rifle, with the top part of the stock being called the Heel of Butt, and the bottom being called Toe of Butt. Moving forward you have the Lower Sling Swivel, Trigger and Trigger Guard, Rear Site, Magazine, Operating Rod Bolt, Upper Hand Guard, Upper Sling Swivel With Retaining Band, Front Site, and Bayonet Lug. Then he started tearing down the rifle and naming the major groups. He said: " here are the major groups and assemblies first is the Firing Mechanism, Gun shoulder stock assembly, Operating rod and Connector group, Bolt assembly, and Barrel and receiver group. Then is a very stern voice he said: "Start tearing down your rifles and lay all parts in front of you." After two days of tearing down and reassembly of the M14, the next day we will be given the test. The night before Butch and I quizzed each other on the major groups and assembly parts of the M14 rifle. As we were in the class room with our M14 waiting for the instructors to give us the test. Drill Instructor GySgt Gerald Stevenson came up to me and said: " Tomlin show me the Bolt assembly, then tear it down and name each part and the main funcation of that part." I said: "SIR yes SIR" I took out the bolt assembly and torn it down and started to name each different part and how they work. First I said: "the main part is the bolt, it has an extractor, with a extractor plunger and spring, with a bolt roller, and bolt roller retainer." I performed the following operation 1.Separate the base and cover. Bolt disassembly you disassemble the bolt using the GI multi-tool. 2. Put the smiley face cutout portion of the multi tool over the ejector and place the screwdriver blade portion of the tool directly under the extractor. I told the Drill instructor you can use your P38 if you do not have a screw driver handy. 3. Push in and compress the ejector. 4. Continue pressing and rotating the tool clockwise. This should push the extractor up and out of the detent position. 5.The extractor can now be removed and the ejector and spring can be removed. 6. The firing pin can now be removed. The Drill Instructor said: "very good Tomlin now reassembly and have the weapon operational." I put the bolt assembly back in the rifle and handed it to the Drill Instructor. He took the rifle and checked to make sure it was operational; as he handed the M14 back to me he had a sight grin on his face. Then said: "Tomlin this is he kind of action needed on the battlefield and you passed with flying colors."

Then he walked over to Butch and said: "Price show me the Operating rod and connector group then tear it down and name each part and the main funcation of that part." Butch said: "SIR yes SIR" Butch took out the operating rod and said:" The main part is the Connector Rod Assembly, Connector spring; Connector Plunger, Connector Rod body; Operating rod; Operating rod spring. And Operating rod spring guide. 1. Place the barrel and receiver group on a flat surface, sights down, muzzle to the left; put a magazine clip to support the receiver to prevent stress or damage to the rear sight. With your left hand, pull towards the muzzle on the operating rod spring to relieve pressure on the connector lock. With your forefinger or a small flat blade screwdriver, pull the connector lock toward you. Butch told the Drill instructor you can use your P38 if you do not have a screw driver handy. 2. Allow the operating rod spring to slowly expand, disconnect and remove the operating rod spring guide by pulling upwards. Remove and separate the operating rod. 3. Removing the Operating Rod Turn the barrel and receiver group so the sights are up and the muzzle is pointing away from you. Pull back on the operating rod handle until the guide lug on its inside surface is aligned with the dis-assembly notch on the right side of the receiver. Rotate the operating rod downward and outward, then pull it to the rear, disengaging it from the operating rod guide. The Drill Instructor said: "very good Price now reassembly and have the weapon operational." Butch put the operating rod and connector group back in the rifle and handed it to the Drill Instructor. He took the rifle and checked to make sure it was operational. Then he said: "Price you are just like Tomlin you know this rifle inside and out. You are the kind of Marine that will help end this war."

After day after day of physical conditioning and physical training, our platoon was really shaping up into a real fighting Marines. Then one day after crawling under barbwire several times with a 50-caliber machine firing real bullets over our heads, trying to beat our previous time. First we would go through the low crawling on our stomachs, then go through again on our backs. Drill Instructors yelling and screaming orders and instructions at us, you Dick Heads, are not going to make it. But that just makes us push harder and harder. Then Drill Instructor GySgt Gerald Stevenson called halt and got us into formation. I can tell you we were a sight for sore eyes; we looked like wet mudding rats standing in formation with mud dripping off of us everywhere. Then Drill Instructor GySgt Gerald Stevenson said " I could not be more prouded of a bunch of Marines since I have been a Drill Instructor in Infantry Training. I pushed you Marines to the limit and you took it and stood tall and give yourself a pad on your back. Then he screamed at the top of his lungs **"BAMCIS",** and said dismiss go back to the barracks, get cleaned up and take a must- needed rest. Oh, one more thing in the Mess Hall you can haveone desert." We all said: "SIR yes SIR", then we all screamed at the top of our lungs with "Semper Fidelis" We were so hyped up, we doubled time back to barracks to clean up and go have chow.Then Drill Instructor GySgt Gerald Stevenson said: "tommorrow we will go to the hand grenade class.

We got up the next morning at 0400, did our PT and ran 5 miles, then went to the mess hall. After breakfast we double time to the Hand Grenade class room. Drill Instructor GySgt Gerald Stevenson was at the head of the classroom and said: "When you are finish with this class, you will know the proper way to throw a hand grenade, know what is the best way to throw a hand grenade, how to pick your target, know all parts and components of the hand grenade. Drill Instructor SSgt Wayne Boseworth amd myself will give you a hands on test in the class room. After you pass the test in class room we will go to the hand grenade range, you will given a test on your throwing skills, and put in different situations as if you were in combat." The drill instructors gave us training grenades containing no explosive charge or chemical; these are for grenade throwing practice, .and to handle and look over as he names the components. Drill Instructor GySgt Gerald Stevenson said: " A GRENADE is a hollow ball, cylinder, or cube, made of metal or other material, which is filled with some explosive, and burst by means of a fuse, or on impact when it falls among an enemy. The Body is hollow filled with TNT charge, and above the charge is the primer, stroker spring, and striker, then you have the power train, then the iginter or detonator. Moving to the outside of the grenade you have the lug which the safely handle or lever is attached, under the lug is the fuse, then too the right of fuse is the safely pin and pull ring. This is a very deadly weapon in the wrong hands, make damn sure you have a target before you throw."

Then Drill Instructor SSgt Wayne Boseworth gave us the effins and a dimastaration on the proper throwing of a hand grenade and how it works and explodes. Drill Instructor SSgt Wayne Boseworth said: "**1.** Holding the grenade in the throwing hand, thumb over the safety lever, pull the safety pin (pull force of 10-35 pounds). **2.** When the grenade is thrown (safety lever released), a spring throws off the safety lever and rotates the striker into the primer. **3.** The primer contains material like the head of a match. When struck by the striker, it ignites and sets fire to the fuze, or powder train. The fuze burns at a controlled rate, providing a time delay (usu 4-5 seconds). When the flame of the fuze reaches the detonator or igniter, it causes action on the filler. **4.** A detonator is similar to a small blasting cap. Very sensitive to heat, when the fuze burns into it, it causes the grenade to explode. **5.** An igniter is a cap that burns rapidly. It basically sets fire to the filler causing a rapidly expanding gas which bursts the container.

Drill Instructor GySgt Gerald Stevenson had several hand grenades in front of him on a table in the class room. He said: " Hand Grenade in broken down into 5 groups. **Group 1** is Offensive grenades . Contain an explosive charge filler of flaked TNT in a body with sheet metal ends and pressed fiber sides. Designed for demolition effect and to stun the enemy in enclosed places. **Group 2** is Fragmentation grenades. Contain an explosive charge in a metal body, designed to break into fragments upon the charge exploding. They have a killing radius of 5 to 10 yards, and fragments are dangerous up to 50 yards. Normally thrown less than 35 yards, that means 'duck' until they explode, and the time delay after pulling the safety pin was from 4.0 - 4.8 seconds. Remember do not be a fucking John Wayne and throw your body on one. For the simple reason it will kill you and every body within 15 feet. **Group 3** is Chemical grenades Designed to produce a toxic or irritating effect, a casualty effect, a screening or signal smoke, an incendiary action, or some combination. Some of these grenades, as with the TH M14 thermite (bottom center, and enlarged bottom left without fuze), come with metal straps which prevent rolling, and an M200A1 igniting fuse with only about 2 seconds of delay after safety lever release. Baseball-type tear gas grenades (bottom right) are special issue for riot control, using a CN filler. **Group 4** is Practice grenades. Contain a reduced charge for safe use in training. **Group 5** is Training grenades . Containing no explosive charge or chemical, these are for grenade throwing practice.

Drill Instructor SSgt Wayne Boseworth said: "Remember on the battlefield you got to ask yourself this How long does it take to cook a hand grenade? The answer is somewhere between 3-5 seconds. You can "cook" the hand grenade by igniting the fuse and then wait two seconds so once the hand grenade is thrown, it can't be picked up and thrown back at you. So cook the hand grenade before you throw, or the enemy could throw back at you and blow your ass off. Everybody in our class passed the hands-on and written test with flying colors. I scored a 98, and Butch scored a 98, and we miss the same questions on chemical hand grenades, the color and marking. We wrote down our answer with the old ammunition color-coding system; the white phosphorous grenade is light gray with a single yellow band and yellow markings. We should have used the newer standard color-coding system, which is light green with a single yellow band and light red markings. The drill instructors cut us some slack, saying we were in the ball park about the phosphorous grenades and we should remember the right color combination. Butch and I said: "SIR yes SIR"

The next day would be the real test when we went to the hand grenade range. We got out of the rack at 0400, took a shower, shaved, and brushed our teeth, and got dressed. We did our PT ran our five miles, went to the mess hall, had our chow. We were marching to the hand grenade range singing "Around her neck she worn a yellow ribbon." we were all feeling good and ready to get our qualification with the hand grenades. When we got to the range we put in rifle squads and each squad was given different orders as if we were in a combat situration. The Rangemaster Instructor had the course laid out for each squad. Drill Instructor GySgt Gerald Stevenson and Drill Instructor SSgt Wayne Boseworth said: " Follow the instructions of the Rangemaster Instructor you all will do just fine. But on the other hand if you fuck up and do not pass your asses will be in our hands. You will pay dearly with pain and misery and I will run you until yours legs fall off. Do I make myself clear. We all stood at attention and said: "SIR yes SIR"

Before we started our training sessions, the Rangemaster Instructor said: " throwing positions are used for uniformity and control and to familiarize personnel with the proper manner of throwing grenades from positions commonly used in combat. Care must be taken not to overemphasize throwing positions in training; for in combat, the soldier's throwing position will be dictated by the amount of available cover, the range to the target, and the type and location of the target." Then he pointed to me and said: "Tomlin what is the best hand grenade throwing position and why?' I said: Standing SIR it is the most desirable and natural position from which to throw grenades." The Rangemaster Instructor said: " outstanding Tomlin you hit the nail right on the head." Then he turned to Butch and said: "Price can you throw grenade a graeter distance at a Prone position and why?" Butch said: "no SIR standing you can have a greater distance then lying on your stomach, but on the other hand you minimize your exposure to the enemy if he is firing at you." The Rangemaster Instructor said: " lets give another outstanding to Price for that great answer." The Rangemaster Instructor said: " Lewis why would you use the Kneeling position in throwing a grenade and why?" Lewis said:' SIR if you have a low wall or shallow ditch for cover to protect yourself, this would be the best throwing position, but this reduces the throwing distance." The Rangemaster Instructor said: "another outstanding answer can we bat a thousand with the next question." The Rangemaster Instructor said: "Stevenson what the advanaish of Prone over

Kneeling." Stevenson said: "SIR kneeling can be use when the soldier is in the open and he can throw the grenade farther, but the prone mimimize his expossure to enemy firing at him." The Rangemaster Instructor said: " what an outstanding group of Marines, we did bat a thousand today."Then said: "there will be four rifle squads. Each rifle squad will have 13 men with one Squad Leader, 3Fire team Leaders, 3 Automatic riflemen, 3 assistant automatic riflemen, and 3 riflemen. The Squad Leader will have an M-14 rifle with a bayonet knife. Fire Team Leaders will have M-79 Grenade Lauchers and M60 Machine Gun with Ka-Bar knife. Assistant Automatic Rifleman will have M-14 rifles and bayonet knife Rifleman will have M-14 rifle and bayonet knife."

The Rangemaster Instructor said: " Tomlin you have Squad number 1, Price Squad number 2, Lewis you have Squad number 3 and Stevenson you have Squad number 4. When you go out on the course each squad will put in a different combat situation, you will be graded as indidvuds and as the team on how well you perform under combat. Remember if you fired marksmen, sharpshooter, or expert on the rifle range you have to fire the same on this combat course to keep your qualification." Then he said: "Tomlin's Fire Team mission is to locate, close with, and destroy the enemy by fire and maneuver, or repel the enemy's assault by fire and close combat. Your mission consists of offensive and defensive elements." Now move out, you are on course 3A." The Rangemaster Instructor said: " Price's Fire Team is to locate and set up a primeter around a known enemy base camp and take out the enemy camp. Then give Tomlin assistance if he calls you. Now move out, you are on course 3B. Then he said: " Lewis's Fire Squad to set up an observation on a well-known enemy camp, and if they start to move you are to lay down fire power to keep them from moving. If you need help call on Price's Fire Squad. Now move out, you are on course 3C. Then Rangemaster Instructor said: " Stevemson"s Fire Team will set up and observe an enemy motar group and knock them out before they begin firing on Squad one, two, or three. If you need help call on Tomlin's squad. Now move out, you are on course 3-D. All missions went according to plan and were successful with high scores. Every Fire Team member kept the same shooting medal that they qualified on the rifle range. The Rangemaster Instructor said: All you Marines did very well, and I will put in the report to be given to your Combat Instructors.

We learn to fire and operate several weapons on different weapon ranges. We were put through several combat situations in our Combat Training at Camp Pendleton. One morning after our PT, five mile run, and chow. Drill Instructor GySgt Gerald Stevenson called us in formation and said: " In a couple of days you will be graduating from Combat Training, some will go to your MOS (Military Occupation Code) training and other into special training." Then he said: " Tomlin and Price see me after formation." We said: " SIR yes SIR" When formation was dismissed we reported to Drill Instructor GySgt Gerald Stevenson. We came to attention, gave a salute, and said: " Tomlin and Price reporting SIR." Drill Instructor GySgt Gerald Stevenson said: "stand at ease, you know you two are going directing to Mountain Warfare

Training in Colorado and that you will be going to Jungle Training in Okinawa, Japan." We said: "SIR yes SIR" Then he said: " I have all your paper work and packets ready for you on the day of your graduation. I have trained a lot of Marines in my time, and you two are high on my list. It has been an honor and a privilege to train and call you fellow Marines." He we stood attention, he shook our hands, then we rendered a salute and said: "No SIR the honor has been all ours to serve with an outstanding and a special Marine that we will never forget." We did about face and started to walk back to the barracks to rest and get ready for chow. When Drill Instructor GySgt Gerald Stevenson said: " Assistant Commandant of the Marine Corps call me and asked about Tomlin and Price and was looking over your records and make this comment. He said: " With their performance in bootcamp and infantry training had been nothing but excellent and outstanding. You can tell them they will be promoted to E-4 corporal after they pass their Mountain Warfare Training." Drill Instructor GySgt Gerald Stevenson said: "all my years in the Marine Corps I have never seen anyone move up in rank so fast. I put your corrupal strips in your packets, cause I know you two will graduate high in your class." We stood at attention rendering a salute and said: "thank you SIR then we did about face and walked to get chow. After chow we went back to the barracks

Butch and I started talking about and listed what makes a good Marine. **1.** The Marines expect every member to possess the ability to fight in combat. **2.** That all Marines are riflemen. **3.** The training program's design gives Marines an overview of combat skills. **4.** Marksmanship with various weapons. **5.** Marines know navigation, and other warfare fundamental skills. Then, Butch said: "after we graduate on 11 November, 1966 we have to proof our weigh in salt on becoming outstanding Marines."I said: "just make our parents proud, and be the best Marines that we can be."

That night Butch and I packed our duffle bags; we had our orders and train tickets. We graduated the next day, said our good byes; we got a cab to the train station to go to Colorado for our Mountain Warfare Training. We got to the train station and got on the train and got seated. We took out our E-4 strips from our packets and pulled them in our shaving bag for save keeping. If we got the promotion, we were going to sew them on. We were both tired and lay back to take a nap.. The conductor came by and said: " are th Marines goin g to eat" We both said: yes SIR." Then the conductor said: " just straight a couple of cars up and we are having a wonderful dinner of Lobster Newburg for $3.85, Fried tender chicken for $3.60. Baked smoked ham hawaiian for $3.45, or Sirloin steak broiled over charcoal for $5.25. Both Butch and I said: "Get the steaks ready." We walked up to the dining car to have our feast. We sat down at the dining table, and placed our order. Butch ordered Garden Spinach and hash brown potatoes with his steak. I ordered buttered snap beans and baked potatoes. We got a garden salad with thousand island dressing, mixed olives and carrot sticks. For desert Butch got strawberry ice cream with old fashioned rice pudding. I got hot gingerbread with sherry whipped cream and vanilla ice cream. We walked back to the sleeper car, then before you knew it the train was pulling into Union Station Denver, Colorado.. It took about 21 hours to get to Denver from San Diego. We got off the train to catch another train to Leadville, Colorado. We were not waiting very long when we heard the next train to Leadville was loading now. Then it took another 6 to 8 hours from Denver to the Marine Base Camp in Leadville, Colorado.

CHAPTER SIX

Mountain Warfare Training

On 13 November, 1966, as the train pulled into Leadville, we saw two Marines waiting in a M151 Jeep to pick us up. As we got closer we could see one was an E-5 Sergeant and the other E-6 Staff Sergeant. Butch and I saluted and said:" SIR reporting for duty." We both handed our orders and packets to the E-6. Our Mountain Warfare Insructor was Ssgt Joseph Peterson, he said: " been waiting for you to take you to base camp and tommrrow morning you can start your training." the driver Sergeant Ben Woodson said: " you know you boys are going to freeze your asses off , it get real cold in these mountains." Then Warfare Insructor SSgt Joseph Peterson said: "do you know how to ski." We both said: "no SIR" Then he said: " well you both are in for a real treat." We drove to the gate of the base camp and got stopped by the guard who asked for our identification; we were cleared and were driven to our Quonset hut. Then Warfare Instructor Ssgt Joseph Peterson said: : Run and PT at 0400 and chow at 05:30, get your rest and will see you in the morning. Butch and I said: "SIR yes SIR." We got into the hut, found a couple of empty racks, unpacked our stuff and put them in the foot lockers and locked them up. Then we hit the rack cause 0400 was coming real early.

Butch and I got up about 03:30, hit the showers, got dressed, and went outside and got into formation. Warfare Insructor SSgt Joseph Peterson said: " At attention, right face, forward march, and double time", then we began running down this long path in the mountains. We could see snow around us and you could feel the cold wind in your face as we ran. After our run we did PT with situps, pushups, pullups, hand over hand bars, and going up the rope. After PT we went to breakfast, had steak, eggs and potatoes. After breakfast, Warfare Insructor SSgt Joseph Peterson said:" see in my office to go over your training and teach you how to ski." After breakfast Butch and I walked over to Warfare Insructor office. We knock on the door and wait for the command to enter. Butch and I stood at attention, rendered a salute, and said: Tomlin and Price, reporting SIR." The Warfare Insructor said: "stand ease." Then he said: " Mountain Training in Leadville is just experiment in high attitude training for Mountain Warfare Training. You are the first group of so called Marine Guinea Pigs to see if this program for four weeks works in higher attitude. So give it your all the Marine way for this program to work and be successful." Tomorrow you both will start on the ski slope where you will be taught you how to snow ski. Take note, if you can not learn to snow ski in three days, you will automatically flunk out of Mountain Warfare Training and be deployed to Jungle Training Okinawa, Japan. He said: "Your training will be as follows All personnel will be require specialized training in technical climbing, military mountaineering, snow mobility, field craft, survival, CASEVAC (casuality evacuation), navigation, use of pack animals and high angle marksmanship. You will use and be graded on treatment of high altitude and cold weather illness and injuries, and casualty transport in a snow covered mountainous environment." Then Butch said: "SIR pack animals." Warfare Insructor said: "yes pack animals, you have have a three days of training on pack animals" Then, he said: "go down to supply depot and the quartermaster will issue the gear you will need." We came to attention, rendered a salute, did about face and walked out. Then we headed for the supply depot to get our gear. We got to the supply depot and walked in. The quartermaster looked up from his desk and said: " looks like we have new recruits to issue gear too. Come over here to the counter and get your gear." We got wool and cotton socks; we got two sets of boots; sleeping bag, winter tent with bivouac sack, 2 canteens; First aid kit, fleece top and bottom. Windproof fleece, winter coat, field tarp, poncho liner, five finger gloves with inserts, black leather gloves, wool mittens, 2 towels, 5 washcloths, personal compass, maps, pens, and protractor, knife with multi-tool, sunglasses, chap stick, 2 combination locks, flashlight, and special back pack to carry our gear. . Then he took us to the next room to get snow shoes, skies, boots, and ski poles. Then, he said: " if you break or bust any of the snow shoes or ski equipment , you will be buying them." Butch and I loaded up and headed back to the Quonset hut. By the time we got square away, it was lunch time. Then we found out years later when you did the Mountain Warfare Training, you were issued all kinds of winter gear and light clothing to keep warm and cozy in the coldest temperatures.

We walked over to the mess hall, had a great meal of steak, potatoes, vegetables and fresh fruit. Warfare Insructor SSgt Joseph Peterson sat at our table and said: " After chow come to my office and we will go over your training program." We both said: "yes SIR" we finished eating and walked with the Warfare Insructor back to his office. Went we got inside, he had laid out our training program. He said: " first thing we will teach you to ski, and how to maneuver on skies. There is a skiing test you have to pass to be able to graduate Mountain Warfare Training. This will be your training program **1.** You will have to do winter survival in the mountains for one week. **2.** You will have to go on a comabt mission in the snow. **3.** You must be qualified with a rifle and grenades in the snow. As Marines you will have to be able to employ weapons and conduct tactics with the skills and fundamentals we teach them here. **4.** During the day, you will traveled long distances up to 50 kilometers, and at night you will coordinated battle skills while on the same challenging terrain. The exercise involved a simulated call for fire from artillery, movement to an enemy base, proper reconnaissance of an enemy position at night and live-fire and maneuver and firing on targets. **5.** Then there is the last test with the pack animals. To take supplies, weapons and ammuniction to a base camp under fire. When you get to the base camp you are to pick up and give first aid to the wounded and bring them back. As you both can see you have a lot of work to do in a short peroid of time. So tommorrow morning bright and early be on the ski slope to start your training." We stood attention, rendered a salute and said: "see you in the morning SIR." We did about face and walked back to our Quonset hut to get ready for our ski lessons in the morning.

The next morning came early as we finished our 5 mile run and PT, had breakfast at the mess hall. Walked over to the ski slope to start our snow ski training. We never snow ski, but Butch and I water ski a lot. Our Ski Instructor Ssgt John West said: " I see here you both water ski a lot, that is good, that means you have a good balance." Then I said: "SIR is water sking is about the same as snow skiing." The Ski Instructor said: " The biggest difference is, in water skiing on water as you go through the course, you fight to stay wide so you are early for the turn. But in Snow skiing through a course, you to try and stay as narrow as you can, and ski straight down the fall line on purpose. In snow skiing your base and edges make contact with snow while in water skiing, the skis are traversing through water. The best rule of thumb always look down at your skis to make sure they are always pointed in the right direction." I was the first one to go down the slope. I snapped my ski boots in the ski bindings and started out real slow; I though I was doing real good until my ass hit the ground. Butch was laughing so hard and said: " Robert you looked like a grenade going off with all that snow flying up when your ass hit the ground." I got up and started out again; I got about ten or so feet, and down I went again. After my ass hit the ground several more times, I started to get the feel of the skis and I was actually moving on the snow with the skis with out falling down. The instructor told me to take a couple more runs then rest and it was Butch's turn. Butch did the same thing I did, now it was time for his ass to be hitting the ground. After several turns down the slope, he was actually snow skiing. The instructor said: " ski a few more hours and practice some small turn and stops, and fall down and get yourself up using your skis and ski poles. Then you are finsih for today and see you back here in the morning." As the Instructor skis off, Butch and I practice the excises of turning, stopping and falling down. We went back down to the holding area, took off our skis, and walked back to the Quonset hut. The next morning after our 5 mile run and PT had breakfast and headed back to the ski slope for more practice and punishment. We skied down from the holding area to our ski instructor who was waiting for us. As we ski up to him he said: " I am impressed you guys took to snow skis like a duck takes to water. Now get ready for some real snow skiing." He took off down the slope like a banshee out of hell; he had a rooster tail of snow that was so damn high you could not believe. it. Butch looked at me and said: "Robert do you thing we will be able to ski like that." I said: "yes with a lot of practice, we should be able to ski better in no time." Then, before you knew it, the ski instructor was back on the hill and said: " now are you ready for some fast turn and stops." Butch and I practice all day on turns, stops, and going up and down the ski slopes. On our last run down and up the slope, the ski instructor said: " you guys do not need any more ski lessons, I will tell Warfare Insructor Ssgt Joseph Peterson that you both passed the snow skiing and report to him in the morning.

The next morning after our 5 mile run and PT, we sat at the same breakfast table with Warfare Insructor SSgt Joseph Peterson. He said: after breakfast we can start our training in the class room." So after breakfast Butch and I walked over to the Mountain Warfare Training class room. We walked in and found desks next to each orher. We had 25 students in our November class of 1966. Just as we all got settled in, Warfare

Insructor Ssgt Joseph Peterson walked in and said: "Good Morning Class the next few days will be discussing and demonstrating the use of fire arms in cold weather." Since the M14 rifle will be your main weapon while on patrol, combat, or during firing exercise. **1.** Just remember as the mercury dives below zero, actions can seize, powders and primers cease to operate effectively and wood can splinter. **2.** The cold does, however, affect the external ballistics of a fired round. **3.** Cold air is more dense than warm air, creating more resistance to a bullet passing through it, and more force pushing the bullet off course in a crosswind. **4.** So when we go to the firing range you will be put in different weather conditions and have obstacle to over-come before you fire." Then he said: "You were told to study your handbook on cold weather shooting before you came to class. He said: :Tomlin I just need a simple yes or no to the following question: When firing a weapon in cold winds and snow is it too great to be overcome?" I said: "no SIR" Warfare Insructor said: " very good Tomlin looks like to read the handbook. Then he said: "Price another simple yes or no answer, can harsh environments offer different ways to mechanically prevent or hinder the progress of the shooter.? Butch said: "yes SIR." Butch thought he was off the hook, but the Warfare Insructor came back with this question, why? Butch said: " SIR if you did not properly prepare your weapon before you fired then you would have a mechanically failure." The Warfare Insructor said: " very good Price it looks like you studty the handbook." We work all day on the fundamentals of cold weather shooting and operation of fire arms in cold weather. Study what happens when a weapon seizes from mechanical failure because of rain, snow, and it too cold outside.

Warfare Instructor SSgt Joseph Peterson gave us all a bottle of his special weapons lubricant, which he made from a formula of various oils. I call JPS (Joseph Peterson Special) to keep our weapons well lubed no matter the condition of the weapon or weather. This JPS lube is good in high temperatures and minus 55 below zero." Then he said: "With out a good working weapon in combat, you are a sitting duck in the water. This JPS lube will keep your weapons operating no matter what temperature." Before the class was dismissed Warfare Insructor Ssgt Joseph Peterson said: " one last thing to remember, Cold winds and snow are not too great to be overcome. While harsh environments can offer different ways to mechanically prevent or hinder the progress of the shooter, frozen weather need not be a deterrent to a fun day of shooting. So long as a few simple precautions are taken and a little extra maintenance performed, even the coldest temperatures will not take away from finding that perfect shot. Get your rest and finish reading your handbooks, there could be more question tommow and a written test." We all walked out of the classroom and headed for the mess hall. Butch and I had a good supper, after supper, we sat and talked about the class we had today. Then, Butch said: " you know they will throw in a monkey wrench when we are on the firing line, to see how we handle that situreation." I said I know they will, but we have to pass this course to get our E4 strips and stay in the Buddy System, then we can go to Jungle Training Okinawa, Japan. Butch said: " That all fine and dandy, but you know the the next stop after Jungle Training Okinawa, Japan, is Vietnam. Where we will be in the real fighting and getting our asses shot off. We talked for awhile longer, then headed back to Quonset hut; we hit the rack and finished reading our handbook; then we went to sleep.

The next few days of class room was the fundamentals of rock climbing, over-the-snow mobility and alpine movement. We were taught the proper way to move through snow, how to climb a rock formation, and different movements in the alpine area. Then we we taught how to pitch a tent in the snow, set up our sleeping bag, out back pack, and always keep our feet and boots dry. When our class was over, Warfare Insructor SSgt Joseph Peterson said: " tommorrow we will be going to the weapon's range to get our qualification on rifle and grenades. You must pass this test to be able to move on to rock climbing." Butch and I went to the mess hall for super, ate and headed back to the Quonset hut. We wanted to be rested and in a good mental state of mind and sharp for the weapon's range the next day. By 0400 we were up and running our 5 miles and doing PT, before going to breakfast. After we ate, we lined up in formation and marched off to the weapon's range.

Weapon Range Instructor SSgt Jerry Harris gave us a class on safely, and what was exspected of us so that we could make qualification on the rifle and hand grenades. He said: "you were taught the fundamentals of throwing hand grenades in boot camp and combat training. But it is a little different throwing in cold weather." Then, he said: "remember you will throwing the hand grenade without a glove on, for the simple reason you must be able to feel the grenade in your bare hand and put the pin with a bare finger. Then he looked right at me and said: 'Tomlin when trowing a hand grenade what is minimize exposure time to the enemy?' I said: " SIR no more than 3 seconds." The Weapon Range Instructor said: "very good Tomlin." Then he said: "Price why do you use the overhand method when throwing a hand grenade?' Butch said: " SIR that the grenade arcs, landing on or near the target." The Weapon Range Instructor said: "very good Price." The Weapon Range Instructor said: " Jackson why do you allow the motion of the throwing arm to continue naturally once the grenade is released?" Jackson said: "SIR follow-through improves distance and accuracy and lessens the strain on the throwing arm." So the instructors let us practice the necessary throws that are used in combat, such as the underhand and sidearm throws with practice grenades. The Weapon Range Instructor said: " but they must throw live fragmentation grenades overhand in a training environment to pass this course." We practiced for several hours throwing grenades, then went to lunch. While we were in formation waiting to march to the mess hall. The Weapon Range Instructor said: :after lunch we will be on the rifle range." We had lunch and marched back to the weapons range. When we arrived the Weapon Range Instructor said: " it is very cold and windy today, now we will see if you Buffalo Bills make qualification with the M-14 rifle."

I put tape on the end of my barrel to keep the bore dry before it was time for me to shoot. I cleaned and lubricated my M-14 with my special JPS lube while I was waiting on the firing line. I was checking the temperature and wind direction while waiting. The target was 250 yards towards the North from me; then I noticed a strong cross-wind blowing from the East. To make the adjustment I had to put my front side about 2 inches off center to allow for the cross wind. With the strong cross wind this would allow the bullet to be pushed straight into the target. The Weapon Range Instructor said: " Tomlin its your turn to fire, I want you to put 6 rounds in bullseye for qualification." I said:"Sir yes SIR" Finally it was my turn to fire; I got in the prone position, put the rifle butt tight into my shoulder, aligned the front sight about 2 inches from center, and started firing. The first round bullseye, second round bullseye, third, fourth, fifth and sixth rounds all bullseyes. The Weapon Range Instructor said: " Price its your turn to fire" Butch did the same as me; all six rounds were bull's-eyes. The Weapon Range Instructor said: "looks like Buffalo Bills are back. Then we went to the hand grenade range Butch and I made qualification by making perfect scores. The Weapon Range Instructor said:" Tomorrow it will be rock climbing, get your rest and have a good meal with lots of protein because you will need all your strength for rock climbing."

The next morning we ran our 5 mile run, did our PT, went to the mess hall for breakfast. After breakfast got into formation and march over to our rock climbing class room. Just as we got seated our Rock Climbing Instructor SSgt William Bean was handing us paper work and a small hand book on rock climbing. He said: "Where we fight, (the mountains) are everywhere, and all the possible conflicts in the future are going to be in mountainous terrain. In the past, the mountains haven't been our strong suit and with this course your skills will overcoming the obstacle of the steep earth and the height, bringing the fight back to being even and we aren't restricted by the terrain." Then he said: this Mountain Warfare Training in Leadville, Colorado, in the future training ground for future Marines to train for mountain warfare. If you graduate from this training program and everything goes as planned, then Marines will be able to fight on land , air, sea, and mountains." Then, he said: "in front of every desk is a back pack with everthing you will need to climb a mountain." He had his assistant going over the inventory and what items we had and what their use was". SSgt William Moody, Rock Climbing Instructor Assistant, had us dump out our back packs, then he went over each item. He said: " **1.** Quickdraws is a piece of climbing equipment used by rock and ice climbers to allow the climbing rope to run freely through protection such as a bolt anchors or other traditional gear while leading. **2.** Carabiners a coupling link with a safety closure, used by rock climbers. Just remember you'll still need a good locking biner for belaying and rappelling and the wise climber has a half dozen or so more at their beck and call to use as anchors, for setting top ropes and who knows what else. Carabiners are the duct tape of the climbing world. **3.** Climbing boots, You won't get far without a great pair of rock climbing boots. They define the relationship between you and the rock surface. **4.** A Harness, all the quickdraws, carabiners, altimeter watches and climbing shoes on the planet won't do you much good if you don't have some way to catch yourself in the event you lose your handhold or footing. That's where the harness comes in. The harness fits around your waist and your upper legs and attaches you firmly to the rope via a robust locking carabiner. The harness then distributes the forces that are brought to bear in the event of a fall. **5.** Rope, Some of the things you'll want to keep in mind when selecting a climbing rope include the four factors **A.** The weight **B.** The length **C.** Dynamic vs static **D.** Weight capacity. **6.** Rock climber Helmet, a helmet isn't going to save you if you're free climbing and fall from a great height. But it might just prevent your head from being split open by a rock tumbling down from above. Rock Climbing Instructor said: " For the next couple of days in the class room we will be teaching some fundamentals and basic rock climbing. The third day we will be doing hands-on with real rock climbing."

The second day of class he started asking direct questions of us. He said: "Price what is the difference between a Dynamic vs static rope and why?" Butch said: " SIR Dynamic and static ropes usually have their own distinct purposes. Dynamic rope is better for activities that carry a risk of falling, such as climbing, while static rope is a better choice for haul lines or activities requiring more controlled ascents and descents like rescue operations or rappelling." The Rock Climbing Instructor said: " Damn good answer Price, looks like you studing the handbook. He said: "Tomlin, why is the length of the rope important and why?" I said: "SIR The length is determined by the climb or climbs you plan on tackling. Most climbing ropes are either 50, to 100 meters in length. If you only need 50 meters do not bring a 100 meter rope cause you're be lugging around a lot of extra weight when you are climbing a shorter distance." Rock Climbing Instructor Ssgt William Bean said:" Tomlin you gave a great answer." Then he said: "Jackson why is your Rock Climbing Helmit important?' Jackson said: :SIR Because even during a short fall you may wind up getting turned around and have your head make contact with the rock face and the Helmit will protect your face from injury," Rock Climbing Instructor said: " very good Jackson" Then, he said: " you are dismissed from class be ready to climb rocks tomorrow"

We all left the class room and headed for the mess hall.

The next morning we all march to a rock face part of a mountain to start our climbing qualification. As we were marching up we could see the Rock Climbing Instructor and his assistant was waiting for us. We came to a halt and stood at attention. The Rock Climbing Instructor said: "stand at eaase.: Then he gave us our training for today. He said: : you will be divided into groups of two, your team will have a specific rock face to ascend or climb, and when you reach the top, you will find a plastic tube with an test paper inside. You are to answer the test question and descend or rappel down from where you started from and hand your test paper to the assiatant. Lucky for us Butch and I got pair together as we walked to face rock to strat our test. I remember looking up and thinking this face rock is 300 hundred feet stright up. The Rock Climbing Instructor said: " Tomlin go up about 100 feet and position yourself, giving a tug on your dynamic rope to signal Price to start his ascend. When Price get close the the 100 feet, you will ascend to two hundred feet and give Price a tug on the rope. When Price gets close to the two hundred feet, you ascend to the top at 300 hundred feet. When you reach the top, you will tug on the rope and Price will ascend to the top. When both of you are on the top of the rock face, find the plastic tube with the test, answer the questions. Tomlin, you will descend down to 100 hundred feet, then tug on the rope; then Price will descend to 100 hundred feet. Just repeat everything going down, just like going up. Butch and I answered all the questions, which was everything we were taught in the class room. I remember one question that had to be answered in three parts. Part one the most important thing about your helmet? Butch and I wrote down this answer: a rock climbing helmet protects you as well as everyone else in your climbing party. Part Two why do you want a Chalk Bag And Chalk? Butch and I wrote down this answer: Chalk dries up any moisture on your hands, thereby allowing you to get a nice secure hold. Part Three how Important is a Harness? Butch and I wrote down this answer: if you are climbing with a buddy and he slips and falls, you can hold on to is harness to keep him from falling without injury himself. When we finished the test, I descended to 100 hundred feet, tugged on the rope, and Butch started his descend. As I waited on the ground for Butch to descend his last 100 hundred feet. When Butch was on the ground we handed the test to the assistant and waited in formation until all the climbers were on the ground. We all march back to base camp. The Rock Climbing Instructor said: "Tomorrow come to the class room for your scores and you are dismissed." Butch and I went to the mess hall and ate like two starving dogs. We finished our meal and went back to our Quonset hut to get ready for our test results. As we were waiting in the class room, the Rock Climbing Instructor said: " Tomlin and Price finish at the top of their class. You have two legs left to finsih this course, one week of winter survival and Pack Animals. Tomorrow after breakfast be in your Winter Survival Class at 0700. As you leave get your survival handbook and study it before class.

Butch and I got our hand books and went back to our Quonset hut to rest and study for Winter Survival Class. Got up the next morning, ran our 5 miles, did PT, and had breakfast. March over to the Winter Survival Class room. As soon as we got seated, the Winter Survival Instructor Ssgt Joseph Braxton was giving out special note books. He said: " In this class the training emphasizes development of both individual and unit mountain skills with primary emphasis on enhancing overall combat capability. Marines at the Center are also involved in testing cold weather clothing, equipment, human performance, rough terrain vehicles, and developing doctrine and concepts to enhance the Corps' ability to fight and win in mountain and cold weather environments. Physically demanding, the course is conducted in an inherently dangerous environment with an emphasis on safety, individual survival, cold weather bivouacs to survive the Winter. Snow accumulation can be 6 to 8 feet. Further, severe storms can deposit as much as four feet in a 12 hour period. Annual temperatures range from -20 degrees. The best way to Survival Course is you have to work as a team." He went over what the objective was for the Winter Survival Course. Then, he said: "the class room will take about a week to

Butch and I got our hand books and went back to our Quonset hut to rest and study for Winter Survival Class. Got up the next morning, ran our 5 miles, did PT, and had breakfast. March over to the Winter Survival Class room. As soon as we got seated, the Winter Survival Instructor Ssgt Joseph Braxton was giving out special note books. He said: " In this class the training emphasizes development of both individual and unit mountain skills with primary emphasis on enhancing overall combat capability. Marines at the Center are also involved in testing cold weather clothing, equipment, human performance, rough terrain vehicles, and developing doctrine and concepts to enhance the Corps' ability to fight and win in mountain and cold weather environments. Physically demanding, the course is conducted in an inherently dangerous environment with an emphasis on safety, individual survival, cold weather bivouacs to survive the Winter. Snow accumulation can be 6 to 8 feet. Further, severe storms can deposit as much as four feet in a 12 hour period. Annual temperatures range from -20 degrees. The best way to Survival Course is you have to work as a team." He went over what the objective was for the Winter Survival Course. Then, he said: "the class room will take about a week to cover the following **1.** Requirements for survival **2.** Survival kit **3.** Water Procurement **4.** Expedient Shelters & Fires **5.** CoreValues & Mountain Leadership Challehges **6.** Signaling & Recovery **7.** Survival Navigation **8.** Traps & Snares **9.** Uses of Game **10.** Survival Fishing **11.** Field Expedient Tools, Weapons, and Equipment **12.** Expedient Snowshoes **13.** Winter Tracking **14.** Survival Medicine **15.** Weather **16.** Intro to Evasion **17.** Avalanche and Ice Hazards" he said: " there is a total of 17 chapters we have to cover. I will cover some chapters and my assiatant will cover the other chapters. After each chapter we will have hands on and a written exam. The lowest score you have to pass this Winter Survival Class is 80."

Butch and I found out this was not going to be an easy class to take; you had to read and study a lot. Then they gave you hands-on with different procedures, and methods to survive the winter in the mountains in a combat situration. I still can remember our Winter Survival Instructor saying: " to survive the winter in the mountains, there is no short cuts to take for survival, all short cuts usally end up that you are dead or you wish you were dead." We were in our class for three days when the Winter Survival Instructor and his assistant started asking questions. Winter Survival Instructor said: " Tomlin if your team member is seriously injury how would you signal for help?" I said: "SIR I would make a big X out of wood or tree branches to make it visable from the air. This is visual international distress signal to ask for aid. Then I would protect and wait next to the team member until help came." The instructor said: " is the only way to signal help?" I said: "no SIR but this the safest way to signal without giving your position away to the enemy. You could use a pyotechnics, but the down fall on a smoke grenade you have to build a platform or your grenade will sink in the snow and the snow will absorb all the smoke. You could use your flashlight with three dots, three dashes, and three dots as a SOS distress call." The Winter Survival Instructor said: " very good Tomlin, it looks like you are going to pass this course." The Winter Survival Instructor said: " Price if you set up a snare to catch a rabbit what kind of bait would you use?" Butch said: " SIR the best thing I would use is Tomlin's peanut butter." Then the instructor scratched his head and said: " What the hell is Tomlin's peanut butter." Butch said: " I guess I could explain myself SIR. SIR since Tomlin loves peanut butter, he always carry a small tins with him. That what I would use as bait to lure the rabbit into my snare." The instructor just stood back and laughed his ass off and said: " you learn something new every day, now I know what Tomlin's peanut butter is. Price that is a good answer, no I will said a good damn answer."

The next day in class the Winter Survival Assiatant said: " Jackson how would you skin a small animaland why would you throw away the skin?" Jackson said:' SIR Small game can be skinned like large game or it can be cased. Casing a hide means to pull the entire skin off the carcass from the rear forward, with cuts made only around the feet of the animal and from the back legs to the tail." Then, he said: " no SIR do not throw the skin away, the skin to be made into mittens, bags, and other holding devices." The Winter Survival Assiatant said: " very good Jackson, that was a great answer." As our week was coming to an end, we were to have our written exam the next day. The next day we ran our 5 miles, did PT, had our breakfast and marched to our class room. We all got seated, as the Winter Survival Instuctor and his Assistant were handing out the exams. He said: " you have two hours to complete and hand in your exams. Tomorrow morning come back to the class room to get your exam scores and get your supplies and equipment you will need for your one week of Winter Survival in the mountains. That night Butch and I packed our back packs, got our snow shoes and skis ready. The next day Butch and I drew weapons with our back packs and equipment, went to the class room for our test scores.

Butch got a 90 over all test score; I got a 92 over all test score. When in the class room, the Winter Survival Instructor said: " you will taken to a designated place in the mountains, you have to follow a course we have laid out for your team. You have checked points you have to check in and report to everyday. You will be given two days of food with two canteens of drinking water and a key to unlock the check-in box. The rest of the five days you will have to find water and forage for food by hunting or fishing. The weather will be really cold with lots of snow. Keep your feet dry and stay warm. Always watch out for Avalanche and Ice Hazards You will walk a total of 50 kilometers to your final check-in. Good luck remember, if you get into trouble or someone gets injury send up a survival signal for recovery."

The next day they loaded us into the trucks and took us to our isolated start point. As we unloaded the truck with our gear, Winter Survival Instructor said: " you were given a key and map where to go and where the check points for each day. Make sure you check in everyday, cause if you miss a check point you will fail the Winter Survival Course. On day one Butch and I got out map to see where our first check point was. The snow was really deep so Butch and I strapped on the snow shoes to make it a lot easier to walk in the deep snow. Butch said: " Damn Robert it is really cold this morning." I said: "let find the first check point and set up camp for tonight." We walked about 10 klicks when we spotted the first check point. It was a cover box with paper inside that we had to sign in,; we both signed in with the date, time, and our names. Then there was a pull tag we had to pull to keep with us and turn it in at the final check point. As we were leaving there were new instructions for the second check-in. The old check in was we had to walk 15 clicks to the next check point. The new check-in was changed. we had to ski 12 klicks down a narrow slope to the next check-in. We got out the map to check what are new direction was. We set up camp and started early the next morning.

On day two Butch and I took off the snowshoes, put on our ski boots and skis, and started cross county to find the narrow slope. We check our map and headed in the right direction to find the narrow slope. We got about another 2 klicks and there is the slope right in front of us. We both skied down at a normal pace and found the second check point box. We unlock the box sign in with the date, time, and our names, then we pull the tag and find no new instructions. We went another 1 or 2 klicks and saw this open spot that was surrounded by pine trees and decided to camp for the night. While I prepared the ground to pitch the tent and got the sleeping bags ready for tonight. Butch was making a fire to put on coffee and broke out the C-Rats (C-Rations). Then Butch said: "Robert Turkey or Ham, I got your cigarettes for my tin of peanut butter." I yelled back Ham and said: "what kind of fruit and dessert." Butch said: "peaches and ginger cake." I whip out my old P38 and start opening the cans of food. We ate our C-Rats drank our coffee, and turned in for the night. I can remember it was really cold that night; the pine trees kept the wind down, with the help of the tent. The sleeping bags kept us warn, and we were nice and cozy.

On day three we got up the next morning and had breakfast of cans, eggs, potatoes, and bacon. Butch makes sure we had coffee for the whole week by making weaker cups of coffee. We got out the map to find the direction for the third check point. As we were going over the map we noticed there was a slight elevation change; we were at about 9,500 hundred feet and on the map it was about 10,500 feet to the third check point. I looked at Butch and said: " well brother looks like we will be climbing to day." Butch said: " I hope it is a gradual climb or its going to be a bitch with this extra weigh." I said: " after we make the climb hope we can find a good spot to set up camp." We started out to find the rock formation we had to climb. We went about 4 klicks and right in front of us was that damn rock formation. To me it looked like it went straight up, but as we got closer the slope kind of angled off and it was not straight up. We got our climbing gear on and I started first. I climbed up about 100 feet or so. I jerk the rope to signal Butch to start his climb. On the second leg I could see a nice flat spot so I yelled down to Butch and said: "we can rest here it is nice and flat." When Butch made the second leg we both drank some water and rested. As we we look up we notice the top just rounded off. I said: "we can camp there tonight." So I started the last leg up the mountain, when I got there it was flat and a good place to camp. I jerked the rope to signal Butch to start his final climb. When Butch got to the top we both kind of laughed and said we made it. I prepared the ground and pitched the tent and got the sleeping bags ready. Butch made a fire put on the coffee, and said:" Robert, last supper meal, we have one breakfast meal left of the C-Rats." We sat around the fire, drank our coffee ate our C-Rats talked about finishing this Winter Survival Course and finding check-in number four.

On day four the next morning came early, we were up and packed, had our coffee and the last of the C-Rats. We took out the map to get the direction of the next check point. According to the map, we had to go down the back side of this mountain to find a small stream by a wooded area for the fourth check point. I told Butch we could get water there and maybe do some fishing to have lunch or supper. Butch said: " I can set up a snare and maybe catch a rabbit for supper." We made our way down the mountain and the ground was not too uneven, so we could not walk with out a lot of effort or problems. Just as we finished coming down the mountain we could see the wooded area straight right in front of us. As we got closer we could see the little steam and the water was crystal clear. To the right of the stream was the check-in box. We unlock the box sign in with the date, time, and our names, then we pull the tag and did not find any instructions. I took the canteens to fill them with water when I noticed there was trout in the water. After I filled the canteens, I dropped in the Globaline tablets to make sure the water would be safe to drink. I took out my fish hook and line; I found a good strong tree limb to use as a pole. I tied the line to the tree limb and put on the hook. For bait I roll up a ball of peanut butter and put it on the hook. I threw in the line and waited, and it was about a minute or two when I got a strike. I set the hook and pulled in the fish. It was about a 3 pound rainbow trout. I gutted and cleaned him right there, and used his eyeballs for my next bait. I threw in the line and the next thing you knew I hooked another rainbow trout, a little smaller then the first one. I gutted him and cleaned him; we had our supper for tonight and tomorrow.. I yelled at Butch and said: "brother we well be eating good tonight"

I took my pancho and wrapped the second trout in snow and ice to keep him fresh. I found a good camp site by a brunch of pine trees. I pitched the test and set up our sleeping bags. By the time I walked out of the tent Butch had the fire going and the pan hot to fry the fish. We ate good that night with a cup of coffee, trout, can of mixed vegetables and fruit. We sat there after supper and looked at our map to see what direction we had to go to find the number 5 check point. We found check point 5 on the map; it was about 15 klicks from where we were. Butch said: "Robert I think I will set a snare, I seen some large rabbit tracks when I was getting fire wood. I think is a snowshoe rabbit" I said: "I know you are going to use peanut butter for bait." Butch just laughed, worked on his snare for about a half hour. He was going to use wire that way the animal could not chew through it. He made the noose about 4 to 51/2 inches and was going to make the ground clearance 1 ½ to 3 inches. Then he left camp to setup his trap with the fencing method. He would put the loop at one end with the peanut butter bait in the middle. He would take thick branches and place them on both sides to make a path of fencing to the loop. The rabbit would smell the peanut butter and hop in the middle of the man-made fence. When he bends down to get the bait, the snare wire will slip around his neck. Then, when he tried to pull his head out, the snare would tighten around his neck, and the harder he pulled, he would strangle himself to death. Butch came back and said: " we will know in the morning if we get a rabbit."

On day 5 Butch was up by 0400 to check on his snare. He came running back yelling Robert, we have for breakfast I got a big rabbit. When he got back to camp. I could see he snared a big fat snowshoe. Right away Butch skinned and cleaned him and cut the carcass in half. We had the front half for breakfast and he put the back half of the rabbit in with the fish. We had our cup of coffee and rabbit for breakfast. I took down the tent and packed everything away and we set out to find check point 5. We had 20 klicks to walk to check point 5. We were walking in this wooded area and the snow was getting deep. We stopped and strapped on the snowshoes and started walking towards check point 5. Walking in snowshoes slows down our process and it seems like it would take forever to get any where. Just as we finished the last part of the deep snow there was a clearing right in front of us with very little snow. We stopped, took off the snowshoes and started walking towards the clearing. Then out of the blue there was check point 5. We unlock the lock on the box, sign in with the date, time, and our names, then we pull the tag and find instructions. The instructions read as follows: you have two days to check point 6. Right away we looked at the map to find check point 6. To our surprise it was a 60 klicks of a hike to check point 6. According to the map, the terrain looked like it was going to be rough to travel. Butch said: "Robert fish or rabbit for dinner." I said: " fish we will save the rabbit for dinner tomorrow." I pitch the tent and set up the sleeping bags. Butch got the fire started and cooking the fish. After supper, I said: " we better start early in the morning because we only have two days to get to check point 6." Butch set up another snare and caught another rabbit.

On day 6 we got up early at 0500, had rabbit for breakfast, broke camp and started on our last leg to check point 6. We started out with no problems; we got about 10 klicks as we went up and down valleys of terrain. We were really slow going up and we had to be caution going down by not moving to fast and not losing our balance. On day 6 we fought this clearing in the trees and decided to stop and camp for the night. We made about 30 or so klicks and we were dog tired walking up and down with all that weight we had to carry. I put up the tent and got the sleeping bags put down. Butch had the fire going and frying the rabbit. We sat at the camp fire almost to tired to eat; we drank our coffee and Butch had a cigarette and I had a cigar. We talked for a few minutes and hit the rack. I said: "Butch come hell or high water we have to made check point 6 without being late." Butch said: "do not worry brother we will make it.

On day 7 this was our final leg and we had to make it. We got up at 0500, had breakfast, broke camp, and started out to find check point 6. We looked at the map again and it looked like we had about 25 klicks to go. We were all happy and singing as we started our last leg. Butch said: "Robert sing She worn a Yellow Ribbon." We were both singing and moving right along and a good steady pace. Then all of a sudden all hell broke loose right in front of us was a ridge about 100 feet straight down. This was the only way to check point 6. We did not have time to regroup and find another way. I told Butch I would rappel first and he could send down the back packs one at a time and then he could rappel. I started my decent down slow inch by inch, was being careful not to fall. I got about half way and yelled back at Butch and said: "Be careful there is some rocks with sharp edges." Butch yelled back: Ok Robert I will be on the watch out." Finally I got to the bottom and jerked on the rope to signal Butch to lower the back packs. When I got the last back pack, I jerked the rope again to signal Butch to start his decend. I could see Butch was being careful descending down the ridge. When he got to the bottom he said "Robert we make it and lets get going." Then Butch pulled the side of the rope that was knotted at the top and the rope fell freely down to us. We gathered up the rope and pulled on our back packs and started walking towards check point 6. As we were walking, we started singing to keep our spirits up. We knew in the back of our minds we had to make it to check point 6 because we had to graduate this course. We walked about 20 or so klicks when Butch let out a yell and said: "Robert straight ahead I can see the check in box." Down from the check-in box was the base camp. We double time to the box; we unlock the box sign in with the date, time, and our names, then we pull the last tag. We headed for camp thinking we are going to get real food, take a shower, and sleep in a real bed tonight. We make it to the commander's tent, and knock on the door. The commander said: "enter" Butch and I stood at attention and rendered a salute and said: "Tomlin and Price reporting after our final day of Winter Survival SIR." The commander said: "stand ease, you Marines make it in record time. Go get clean up and get some chow and I will talk to you later." We stood back at attention, rendered a salute, and said: "Thnk you SIR." We did about face and headed to our assigned tent.

We found the tent stowed our equipment away, took a very long hot shower, got dressed and headed to the chow tent. Just before we got to the mess tent we could smell the aroma of the food cooking. Butch said: " just let me eat a good cook meal, that I do not have to cook." We sat down and had steak, potatoes, salad, mixed vegetables and I even had apple pie with ice cream. We just sat there enjoying every bite. The command came up to our table and said: "tomorrow our supply truck is going back to Leadville at 0700 to get supplies you can hitch a ride back with the truck." We said: "Thank You SIR, we will be ready to go. The next morning we got up at 0500 packed out stuff and headed for the mess tent. We had our breakfast and went to the supply truck, threw our gear in back and waited for the driver. We pulled out right at 0700 heading for Leadville. We were stopped at the front gate by the guard who asked for our identification cards. We were cleared the truck went to the supply depot where we got off and walked to our commander to report in. We knocked on his door and he said enter.Butch and I stood at attenuation, render a salute, and said: Tomlin and Price, reporting back for duty SIR." The commander said: "stand at ease, you Marines make that Winter Survival in recorder time. Your last leg of this course will be the Pack Animals. I said: " Yes SIR" Then he said: " it will only be a six day course with two days in the classroom and four days with the pack animals. You will start your classroom at 0700 tomorrow and you are dismissed." Butch and I stood at attention render salute and said: "SIR yes SIR" Did about face and walked out. Just as we were about to leave, the commander said: "you will need these hand books." Butch and I turned around and got the hand books on pack animals. We both said: "Thank You SIR." Butch and

I walked back to our Quonset hut to rest and read our hand books.

The next morning came early, we ran our 5 miles, did PT and had breakfast and headed to our class room for pack animals. The Animal Packing Instructor Ssgt Philip Barlow was waiting for us as we enter the class room. He said: "the purose of this Animal Packing Course is designed to aid Marine Corps units in alternative methods for transporting crew served weapons, ammunition, supplies, and wounded personnel to and from areas inaccessible to mechanized and air mobile transportation. The course subjects include introduction to animal packing, anatomy of pack animals, animal packing techniques, casualty evacuation techniques, animal first aid, and bivouac considerations." The Animal Packing Assistance Ssgt Ron Nelson said: The normal course is a month long, but this class will be the short version with the fundamentals of working with and packing the animals." The Animal Packing Instructor said: " we will have two days of class work and four days of hands on and working with the animals which will be mules. Tomlin and Price you will be asigined to Rosie who is our best mule. As you work with her you will find she is a character and a half." Then he said: Tomlin if a pack animal weigh is 1,400 hundred pounds, which is the maximum weigh they can carry.?" I said: " SIR they can carry about 30 percent of their weigh or 420 hundred and twenty pounds." The Animal Packing Instructor said: " well I can see somebody read the handbook." Then he said: " Price what is the most important about a mule and why?" Butch said: "SIR trust is the most important to have with your mule, because if you loose the trust of your mule, you have a 90 to 95 percent chance of not getting it back," The Animal Packing Instructor said: "Jackson why are pack animals needed for the mountains." Jackson said: " SIR for trips down the rugged trails through forests and mountains, performing tasks in rugged areas that can't be reached through any other means of transportation." He said: " looks like this class read the handbook. We will go over the techniques and fundamentals of pack animals in the next couple of days. Then we will be doing hands-on with the animals and then you will be given a test. On packing the animal and carry supplies to a designated area in the mountains for a score. You have to score an 80 to pass this course. This will be the last course in Mountain Warfare Training, then some of you will be going to Vietnam while others will be going to other destinations." The classroom lasted about two days and on the last day we had a written exam. The Animal Packing Instructor said: " great news everybody passed and tomorrow you will meet and work with your pack anaimal the mule."

I have a lot of dogs and work with horses and farm animals, pigs, chickens, ducks, turkeys, cows, but I have never worked with a mule. The next morning we were up at 0500, ran our 5 miles, did PT and had breakfast. Our class marched over to the animal stables to meet and learn about our mule. As we marched up to the stable, the Animal Packing Instructor and his Assistance was waiting for us. As we came to a halt and stood at attention. The Animal Packing Instructor said: "stand at ease" Then he said: "Tomlin and Price your pack animal is a mule name Rosie. Treat her with respect and while she is in your care, make damn sure you take care of her." Tomlin and Price stepped forward. I will intro duce you to Rosie." As Butch and I moved closer to meet

Rosie, her ears went straight up along with her tail. Then she started prancing around and started to Hee Haw like crazy. The Animal Packing Instructor could not believe it and said: " in all my years working with mules this is the first time I ever saw a mule take to two perfect strangers like a duck takes to water." Right away Roise started to nudge us with her nose and push us back; then she would just Hee Haw and prance around. The Animal Packing Instructor said "you Marines are in luck Rosue likes you right away and she will be easy to work with." Then, Butch said: " why did Rosie nudge us like that." The Animal Packing Instructor said: "That is Rosie's way of making friends. Rosie is saying: "I wanna be your friend!" Then, he said: "that is rare for her, it takes awhile before she warms up to any body."

The Animal Packing Instructor said: "you will be working around a 1,400-pound animal. We give you a lot of time with the mules so that when you take them to the field portion of this course you will be very familiar with this animal." So Butch and I spent a couple of days with Rosie the mule to get familiar with this 1,400 hundred pound animal. I found out real quick she loved sugar cubes; you could hide them in your shirt pocket and she would find them and then she would let out a big Hee Haw cause she was so happy. The Animal Packing Instructor said: " Tomlin or Price do you smoke cigars or chew tobacco." I said: SIR I smoke cigars." So I found out the hard way Rosie loves to chew tobacco, one day I had a couple of cigars in my shirt pocket. Rosie came up and took out a cigar out of my pocket and started chewing it. I asked the Animal Packing Instructor about Rosie chewing tobacco. He said: "The man that sold us Rosie taught her how to chew tobacco, but remember always give her a sugar cube first before giving her tobacco. Butch and I started to have a real good relationship with Rosie, she was as smart as a whip and always follow comands. In the hands on we learn how to pack Rosie and distribute the weigh evenly where she was in perfect balance while she walk up and down the mountains.

The Animal Packing Instructor said: " feed and water is essential for a pack aniamal to work hard and keep fit and Mules are very easy keepers." Butch and I learn that the Marines buy special pellets to feed the mules. These pellets include grains, corn, wheat bran, cottonseed meal, and oats. These types of pellets are necessary for hard working animals. If the animal is not fed enough grain, he will first burn body fat for energy and then burn muscular tissue and this will result in a thin and less effective working mule. After working a couple of days and knowing about Rosie, we were given a hands-on test. We had to pack her with various supplies and had to water and feed her. We had to take off the packs and rub her down. The Animal Packing Instructor said: " Tomlin and Price go behind the stable and out of sight." So Butch and I walked behind the stable and waited. Within 5 or so minutes the Animal Packing Instructor called us back. He said: "now walk Rosie around." As Rosie was walking I noticed she was limping real bad. I brought her to a halt and started lifting and looking at her hooves. I looked at the front hooves and Butch was looking at her rear hooves. Rosie did not move; she just stoodand waited until we were finished. When we pick up the front and rear hooves and we look at the bottoms. We wanted to see an almost round shape on the front and rear hooves. The frog should be wide at the back of the hoof, and when the mule or donkey steps down heel first, they should touch the ground with the frog. This contact is critical to stimulating good blood flow. The frog should take up about 2/3 of the length of the hoof and about ½ of the width at the back. If it is smaller than that, contact with the ground will not be sufficient. We learn in class about the hooves on the mules. The frog should be wide at the back of the hoof, and when the mule or donkey steps down heel first, they should touch the ground with the frog. This contact is critical to stimulating good blood flow. Then I notice a small rock right in the middle of her frog. I carefully took out the rock without any damage to her frog. As soon as I removed the rock, she let out a long hee-haw and started prancing around like a kid in a candy store. The Animal Packing Instructor said: " Tomlin and Price you are ready for your supply trip for tomorrow." We both said: "SIR yes SIR." Then, he said: " go back to your Quonset hut get some rest you will start at 0600 you have to pack ammuntion, weapons, and medical supply and pick up a wounded Marine and bring him back." Butch and I walked Rosie down to the farrier to make sure her hooves were good for the animal pack test. The farrier looked at her hooves and said: " her hooves are perfect and she is fit as a fiddle to make the trip. I said: "Thank you." Butch and I walked her back to the stable, got her water and fed her for tomorrow's big trip.

Butch and I went to the mess hall and ate our chow and went back to our Quonset hut to get our rest. We got up at 0500, packed our back packs and headed for the stable. When we got to the stable our supplies with instructions were waiting for us. I got Rosie out of the stall, gave her water and fed her and got ready to be packed. Butch said: "Robert we have 1,000 thousand rounds of M14 ammo, 10 M14 rifles, and 150 hundred and fifty pounds of medical supplies to pack. We got the pack on Rosie back hitch it down and make sure iy was not to tight. We put a can of ammo on the left and right sides. We did the same with the rifles 5 on the left and 5 on the right, and put the medical supplies right in the middle. We had our map and instruction where to go and pick up the wounded Marine which was about 30 klicks. A good healthly mule loaded down can travel between 20 and 25 miles a day We told the Animal Packing Instructor we were loaded and ready to go. Then we said: " SIR see you went, we get back. Then, he said: " you have to be back with the wounded Marine by 0700 on Saturday morning to pass the test." We both said: " SIR we will see you Saturday at 0700." Then Butch, Rosie and I headed out to the Marine Base Camp to deliver our supplies and pick up the wounded Marine.

On day one I was leading Rosie in the front and Butch was bringing up the rear. I thought when we started out our trip to the Marine Base Camp would be a piece of cake. Boy was I wrong about 5 or so klicks in our travel we hit rough terrain lots of rocks and up and down valleys. The best thing about Rosie, she was sure footed more so than a mountain goat. The reason she was so sure-footed, she could see her back feet and that is why she had no problem walking in the mountain terrain. We had gone about 10 klicks when Rosie pulled real hard on the reins and almost pulled my arm off. She stopped dead in her tracks and would not move. I walked back to her and said: " Rosie what wrong." She just shook her head and would not move. Then I looked out towards the front of us, about 75 feet away, was a large Mountain Lion in a pine tree. I hand signal for Butch to come forward. When Butch got up to me, he said: "Robert what wrong." I said: " get your rifle ready there is a Mountaion Lion about 75 feet in front of us." We both took our rifles off our backs and locked and loaded a 20-round magazine. I told Butch I would fire from the right and he could fire from the left. As soon as we had our rifle butts in on our shoulders the Mountain Lion jumped out of the tree. I fired, hitting him in the right eye and Butch fired, hitting him in the left eye. Those two rounds took off half of his head and he was dead before he hit the ground. Rosie was as cool as a cucumber and did not move when Butch and I were firing on the Mountain Lion. After we killed the Mountain Lion I told Butch lets take a rest. I walked up to Rosie and gave her 2 sugar cubes for saving our lives. We rested for about 15 minutes and started our trip again. I was smoking a cigar. Butch was smoking a cigarette, and Rosie was chewing tobacco. We were moving along at a good pace singing, smoking, and chewing. We stopped about 10 klicks from the Marine Base Camp to rest and eat. I wash Rosie's mouth out with water to get rid of the tobacco before she eats and drinks water. Then I took off both ammo cans and rifles to let her rest in comfort. Then I fed her and gave her water. Butch broke out the C-Rats so we sat down, ate and rested for about an hour. I put the ammo cans and rifles on Rosie's back and we headed to the Marine Base Camp. We were about 1 or 2 klicks away and spotted the Marine Base Camp. But Rosie spotted long before that, she had been there so many times. We reported to the commander, stood at attention, rendered a salute, and said: SIR Tomlin and Price reporting for duty. He said: " drop off your supplies to the depot tent and take your mule to the stable. Go to your tent and get ready for supper and I will talk to you later and now you are dismissed." We stood at attention, rendered a salute and said: "SIR yes SIR." did about face and headed for the supply depot. We unloaded the supplies and headed for the stable. We got Rosie in the stable. I took off her pack and blanket, rubbed her down, and checked her hooves.Butch gave her water and food and we headed for our tent. We cleaned up and waited for chow. While in the mess tent the commander set down with us told us that we were to pick up corporal Jones and take him back to our Marine Base Camp in Leadville to our field hospital. We said: " SIR yes SIR." He said: "be at our field hospital by 0700 and be ready to move out." We said: "Sir we will be ready at 0700." The commander got up and left and Butch and I finished our supper.

On day 2 we woke up by 0500, had our breakfast, walked over to the stable to get Rosie ready. We gave her water and fed her and I checked her hooves. They had made a special aparejo pack to carry a stretcher for the wounded with little shock absorbers on each corner to make the ride back as smooth as possible. Butch and I figure the total weigh for Rosie would be about 3 hundred and 90 ninety pounds. We secure the special aparejo pack and head for the field hospital tent. When we arrived at the field hospital tent, a nurse greeted us and helped us load the patient on Rosie. I asked the corporal if he was comfortable and he said: " yes he was." We said: ' Thank You and good bye and headed back to Leadville about 30 klicks away. I never once told Rosie or led her to which way to go. She knew that trail like the back of her hoof. We got about

15 klicks and stop to rest, water, and feed the mule. We took down corporal Jones to give Rosie a break while she water and ate. Butch broke out the C-Rats and asked the corporal if he wanted antthing to eat. He said: " just a can of beans and peaches." So we sat, ate and rested for about an hour. We got corporal Jones's stretcher back on the special aparejo pack and headed for Leadville. We were about 2 or 3 klicks from our base camp when old Rosie started to Hee Haw like nobody's business. We found out later she was telling the other mules she was coming home. We dropped the corporal off at the field hospital tent. Took Rosie to the stable, took off her special aparejo pack and rubbed her down. Gave her water and feed, and I checked her hooves. Then Butch and I went to the commander's tent to report in. As we stood at attention and rendered a salute and said: "SIR Tomlin and Price reporting back to duty." He said: " stand at ease. With you two Marines are outstanding and preform your assignments flawless and make it back in recorder time without further injury to the wounded Marine. Now go clean up get your rest and have chow and report back here tomorrow morning at 0700. You are dismissed." We stood at attention, rendered a salute and said: "SIR yes SIR. Did about face and walked back to our Quonset hut.

After graduation on 14 December, 1966, the next morning on Thursday reported back to the commander. As we walked into his office, all the instructors were there and shouted Devildogs, Devildogs, you are promoted to E-4s Corporals. The commander said: " I want to personally shake your hands for being top notch Marines. For my appreciation I giving you a four day pass to the city of Leadville starting on Friday and report back to base on Tuesday before you have to report for Jungle Training Okinawa, Japan. Then went in to detail, a train to Union Station Denver and a cab to Buckley Air Force Base in Aurora. The you will fly from Buckley Air Force Base to San Francisco on a C-130. You will fly MATS (Military Air Transport Service) from San Francisco to Kadena Air Force Base in Okinawa. From Kadena Air Force Base to Camp Gonsalves is a U.S. Marine Corps jungle warfare training area located in northern Okinawa, Japan, across the villages of Kunigami and Higashi. Then the commander said dismissed and go have some fun and relaxation. We stood at attention render a salute and said; " Thank You SIR." did about face, walked back to our Quonset hut, packed our bags to to get ready for a wild weekend.

Manhattan Bar (Known as The Hat) Butch and I had four days off for outstanding training in Winter Training at the top of our class from our Commander and Mountain Warfare Training Instructor with direct orders be in camp at 0700 Tuesday morning clean shave, proper uniform and be ready to go to Buckley Air Force Base. The first place we stopped at Leadville was the Manhattan Bar known to the locals as The Hat. Just as we walked in the door we noticed these two red heads sitting at the bar. Butch walked over and interduce himself; Corporal Frederick (Butch) Philip Price, then he turned around and said: "this is my brother from another Mother Corporal Robert Dean Tomlin." I said: "hi what are your names" the red head closer to me said: "my name is Lucille Mary Watson and this is my sister Therma Louise Watson." Then, without skipping a heart beat, I said: "what a petty name you both have." They looked at me and laughed, then Lucille said: "you guys are kind of cute are you in town long."

Butch said: "just for four days then we have to back to camp." Then I said: "does this place have good food." Then, Therma said: "only the best hamburgers in the whole town." I said: " would you ladies like to join Butch and I for dinner." They both said: "why not", so we proceeded to get a table for four. The jude box was playing Roy Orbison's "Oh Pretty Woman" I asked Lucille to dance she jumped up and we hit the dance floor; we were shakin and rockin and ready cutting up the rug on that dance floor; she looked at me and said: " you dance just like Elvis Presley."I told Lucille, to put on "Don't be Cruel" I will show you Elvis; she went right over to the jukebox and pushed C-17, then the Elvis show began. I was shaking my legs and dancing all over the dance floor; women were screaming and shouting go Elvis go. Between Butch, Lucille. and Therma I do not know who was laughing the loudest. Then one of the customers put on Don Gibson's "I Can't Stop Loving You", I grabbed Lucille held her tight and started slow dancing; our bodies were so close you could not get a feather between us. This old hard corp Marine just melted in her arms as we danced across the floor like we were on ice skates. I was holding her tight, with her breast tight against my chest, and she was kissing me on the cheek. I looked at Butch and Therma; they were doing the same thing, dancing slowly and hold each other tight. Butch gave me the thumbs up. We had a few more drinks, did a lot of dancing, talking about our childhood and school. Then, out of the blue, Lucille asked us if we wanted to spend the weekend with them. I said: "we did not have a car", then the girls said: "thats ok we have a jeep and our place is nor far from here."

So we finished our drinks and headed out the door to their jeep, got in and started driving to their place. As we got close to their house we could see it was an older house, once we got inside the place was very clean and organized. Lucille said: "do you want a drink" and Butch and I said: "a beer if you have one", so we had a Coor's beer. Then Lucille said: "Robert I bet you are tired lets go to my room", Butch and Therma stay in the living room. When we got to her bedroom, and she started taking off her clothes I was horny, then a 3 pecker billy-goat, there she stood with just her black panties and bra; my dick was so hard a cat could not scratch it. She grabbed me, I grabbed her and we made hot passion love that was the first sex I had in about six months. She had those long legs wrapped around my body like a snake. I was pumping her so fast and hard, you though I was a "human machine gun". A lot of people think Elvis had swivel hips, but that night I was the king of swivel hips; I was pumping her so fast I heard her say you are killing me, then I said: "do you want me to stop," then she said: "no just go ahead and kill me. I swear I heard her knee caps pop as we were going at each other like wild animals. As we were catching breaths, I could hear Therma moaning and groaning, old Butch as giving her the old Marine push ups, I know he was trying to push his ass all the way to China, I can still hear old SSgt Robert Johnson our Senior Drill Instructor yelling: "you dumb nuts you are going to give me push ups until your ass reaches China." I think Butch was doing the push-ups on Therma until his ass did reach China. As Lucilla lay there while we were holding each other in our arms, she said: "you and Butch can stay the weekend. I fix breakfast in the morning then we can go skiing, the powder is really good this time of the year." Then I said: "sounds like a good plan, now that I know how to ski.: She look right in my eyes and said: "I, though my old boy friend, was a good lover, but you got him beat you are just a sex machine who never gets tired." I felt like I was sleeping in her arms and slept like a baby. I could smell the coffee and the food cooking. I got up, took a quick shower and went down stairs; I told the girls I was so hungry I could eat the ass out of a skunk. They thought it was really funny and laughed out loud. Lucille and Therma fix Butch and I eggs, bacon, and toast with orange juice and coffee to drink. We all sat around the kitchen table, ate our breakfast and talked. I said: " Butch and I would clean up and do the dishes." The girls said: "ok then we will get ready then we all can go skiing." The girls came down with all their ski clothes; Lucille said: "I will put the skies on the jeep" and I said: "I will help her." After putting the skies on the jeep, we jumped in and headed for the slopes.

They had a place to ski that was away from the ski crowd, kind, of a private area on the mountain; the only bad thing was you had to hike up this steep slope to get there. Butch and I were used to physical work because that's all we did in the Marine Corp, when we reach the top Lucilla make a bet who could get down the slope the fastest. As we waited for the signal to start, she looked at me and said: "I am going to kick your ass." Then, Lucille said: "on your mark get set go," we all shot down the slope about the same time. Then Lucille and Therma shot out in from of Butch and I like they had rockets strapped to their butts. Butch and I tried our damndest to keep up with them, but it was to no avail; they were way in front. Butch and I were weaving in and out of those damn pine trees. I thought for sure we were going to hit one. Lucille and Therma were shooting down that slope just like the pros. At bottom of the run I said: "man you girls are fast", then Lucille said: "we have been sking since we were 3 years old and we love to ski." Then she went on; our Mom and Dad taught us how to ski. They both love the snow that one reason why we moved to the mountains, skiing in the winter, fishing in the summer, and horse back riding in the fall. We did a couple more runs and headed back to the house. Lucille was telling me about her Dad when he skied he got such a rush, you though he was on drugs. My Dad love the snow because he knew he would be skiing. Then she told me her Dad and Mom brought Lucille and Therma's a house in Leadville to live in because they love the snow so much. Then she looked at me and said: "promise you will write to me." I told her I would, but you have to remember I am Unitd States Marine True and Red, White, and Blue, and I will always stand up for my country and defend her even if it cost me my life.

When we got back to the house, Lucille and Therma fixed us a nice supper with steak, baked potato, vegetables, and salad. As we were eating and talking, the girls said: "we can watch football on Sunday. The Broncos are playing the New York Jets, yum-yum Joe Namath, my kind of quarterback, but over all we still love the Denver Broncos." We all went to bed that night and the sex party started all over again. Then Lucilla said: "I want to see you again." I said: "I would love to see you again but Butch and I am leaving to go to Jungle Training Okinawa, Japan next week, but I can write to you." We kept talking for awhile, then we fell to sleep in each other's arms. Got up the next morning, the girls were upfixing us breakfast again. We sat around the breakfast table eating and talking, then Butch said: "Robert Therma is going to write to me when we leave to go back to Japan". I told Butch Lucille wasis going to write to me. Then Therma said hey, its about time for the game, as we sat around and while watching the game on TV, we were laughing joking, eating popcorn and drinking beer. That day the Denver Broncos got slaughtered by the New York Jets 45 to 10. The girls were sad that the Broncos lost, but they fixed us a nice going away dinner, Italian pasta and the works with bread, salad, and a nicebottle of red Mastroberardino Aglianico. Then Lucille said: " I brought Elvis Presley's album A Touch Of Gold with the song Wear My Ring Around Your Neck would you wear my ring around your neck." I said: "I would love too but in the Marine Corps I would be out of uniform so I can not." She said: "Thats ok I'll just put my arms around your neck." We already enjoyed our last night together, got up bright and early to head back to camp, we packed our bags and got ready to leave. Lucilla and Therma said: "they would drive us back to camp, as we were riding back to our Mountain Warfare Training Camp, the girls remind Butch and I to make sure we write them. When we arrive at the front gate of the camp, Butch and I got out grab our bags and gave Lucella and Therma a lot of kisses and said our goodbys. I was thinking was I in love or just lust, I gave Lucille a long good by kiss and ask her to write to me. When Butch and I got back to Okinawa, Japan we wrote to Lucille and Therma, we were receiving letters from them every week. Then we got a letter once a month after Butch and I went to Vietnam and then they just stop writing. I figure she must of went back to her old boyfriend. I was still thinking of the warm feeling I had with her naked body press against mine, but it did not make any difference because we never saw them again.

CHAPTER SEVEN

Jungle Training Okinawa, Japan

Butch and I got on the Colorado & Southern Railrod in Leadville to go to Union Station in Denver, Colorado. The train pulled into Union Station; we got off and got our gear. We were about to hail down a cab to Buckley Air Force Base in Aurora. When these two Air Force MPs (Military Police) pulled up in a jeep. One Sergeant said: " Tomlin and Price" We both said; "yes" Then he said: "hop in we are taking you to Buckley Air Force Base to catch a C-130 to Travis Air Force Base near San Francisco. Butch and I threw our gear in the back of the jeer and we headed for Buckley. When we arrive at Buckley we had to clear the Security Police then we proceeded to the air strip where a C-130 was waiting for us. The flight officer got us on the plane and had our gear loaded. Then he said: " It will be bumping in flight and really loud with a lot of noise. Put on your field jacket, it could be a little cool and put in ear plugs to drown out the noise." We said: " Thank You SIR" We got on the plane and waited for take-off. All I remember is how cold it was inside, the seats were not comfortable, and that noise coming from the engines was unbearable. Finally, after about 3 hours in the air, the plane was landing at Travis Air Force Base. After we got our gear, we were directed to the MATS Terminal for a flight to Kadena Air Force Base in Okinawa. We went to the counter to be checked in, gave them our orders, and had our gear taken, to be stowed on the flight. We only had to wait a few minutes when they called our fight number. Butch and I boarded the plane, found our seats, and waited for take-off. We were really happy with this flight; it was just like a commercial flight. We had comfortable seats, no noise coming from the engines, and a stewardess serving us food and drinks. It was about an 11 hour flight to Okinawa, Japan. Butch and I just rested, relaxed, and talked about the good old times. Finally, the plane was touching down at Kadena Air Force Base in Okinawa. We got off the plane and got our gear and waited for our ride. Two Marine corporals pulled up in a jeep and said: "Tomlin and Price we are here to take you to Camp Gonsalves for your jungle warfare training. Butch and I threw our gear in the back of the jeep and we drove off to Camp Gonsalves which was about a 20 mile drive. We stopped at the gate to show Our ID's and orders. We were direct to the commander office to report in.

As Butch and I walked to the commander's office, we stopped at his doorway and knocked. The commander said: "enter" Butch and I stood at attention, rendered a salute, and said: "Tomlin and Price reporting for duty SIR." The command said: " stand at ease." Then he said: " what was exspected of us for Jungle Warfare and this was hard course to complete. You have good Marine Instructors here, that will push you to your limits but in the end you will become the world's best jungle fighters." Go to your Quonset hut, get square away and get some chow and be in the Jungle Warfare class room by 0700. Pick up your Jungle Warfare handbook on the way out. Butch and I stood at attention, rendered a salute and said: "Thank You SIR" did about face, walked out and grabbed a handbook and headed for our Quonset hut. We found our quarters, unpacked, and made up our racks and waited for chow. The next morning our Squard Leader said: "Tomlin and Price you will just run 3 miles today and half of the PT for about a week until you get acclimated to the heat and humidity. Just remember be on the look out for those damn insects and snakes." After PT we went to the mess hall, had breakfast and marched over to our Jungle Warfare classroom. Butch said: "Brother I through the humidity was bad in Missouri, it is a piece of cake compared to this place." I said: " Illinois humidity would be a vacation to this hot place."

As we walked into the classroom, our Jungle Warfare Instructor SSgt William Beckford, was seated at his desk. Jungle Warfare Instructor SSgt William Beckford said: "I want every Marine find a seat."Then he said: "ln jungle warfare the soldier fights two enemies: man and nature. Of the two, nature is often the more formidable. Troops newly arriving in tropical jungle areas experience a climate to which they are not accustomed and are exposed to diseases with which they are not familiar. These conditions impose a special responsibility on all commanders; they must assure themselves that their troops are adjusted to tropical climates and that the health and combat effectiveness of the command will ensure the execution of the assigned mission under tropical jungle conditions." Jungle Warfare Instructor SSgt William Beckford said: "my assistant and I will be teaching fundemetals and the in and out of Jungle Warfare with **1.** Hygiene and Sanitary **2.** Acclimation **3.** Physical Conditioning **4.** Insect- and Animal-Borne Diseases **5.** Water-borne Diseases **6.** Intestinal Infections. **7.** Special Tropical or Exotic Diseases **8.** Fungus Diseases of the Skin and Hair. **9.** Venomous Snakes and Snake-bite Remedies. **10.** Clothing and Equipment **11.** Sleeping **12.** Food **13.** Cooking Utensils. **14.** Medical Care. **15.** Expedients." Then, he said: " we will spending about a week in class room and another week with hands on, then about 3 weeks in the jungle, any questions. You are dismissed for today, so read your handbooks, get your rest from the jet lack and be in class tomorrow at 0700 to be ready to work.

The next morning Butch and I were up bt 0500, ran our 3 miles and did our PT and went to the mess hall for breakfast, then we marched to Jungle Warfare classroom. We walked in and took our seats. Jungle Warfare Instructor SSgt William Beckford said: "One jungle is rather much like another, and the soldier who learns to live and fight in a Okinawa forest will be able to do the same in the jungles of South Vietnam or Central America or northern Borneo. You do not have to eat snake if you do not want too, there are other food sources you can eat." As part of training, Marines can eat only what they kill or pick from the vegetation." Then Jungle Warfare Instructor SSgt William Beckford said: "This was a good opportunity for you Marines to pick up some different skills. This is training not normally trained in infantry. The last part of the training will be a seven-day basic jungle survival course. Following its conclusion, the Marines will be tested on there skills during a evaluation at the training center." Jungle Warfare Instructor SSgt William Beckford said: "You have to have a 80 score to pass and he added if you pass or not you still will be deployed to Vietnam." Mind over matter is the key to coming out of a desolate jungle situation alive, said Jungle Warfare Instructor SSgt William Beckford. Then, he said: "we teach troops to focus on equipment they should carry a cigarette lighter to build a fire and and a knife to make a dagger or spear for hunting." Sitting on the table in front of the class were several glass jars containing various snakes (mostly venomous). As the glass jars were passed around, the instructors said these are some of the threats to be aware of as we conduct your training in the jungle. Butch and I started to put things into perspective. I said: "Butch with those damn snakes we are not the king of the jungle."

Jungle Warfare Instructor Assistant Ssgt John Worth said: "During jungle warfare training, navigation becomes exponentially tougher when working under a double canopy jungle. This means due to the canopy of trees blocking out the sun you must be confident at using a map and compass. A machete or kukri becomes more useful than smaller belt knives to allow you to cut through the thick vegetation, dispatch snakes for food, and for other various survival tasks. ." Jungle Warfare Instructor SSgt William Beckford said: " Let me make myself perfittly clear another stupid piece of Marine Corps gear to ditch during jungle warfare training is the boot blouses. All those accomplish is holding water inside your pant legs. Depending on your unit's SOP (Standard Operating Procedure) you may or may not be able to go without these. Lastly, we learned quickly how important it was to have multiple pairs of socks to change into. If you don't attempt to keep your feet dry and taken care of, consider yourself a casualty of the jungle.

Jungle Warfare Instructor Assistant Ssgt John Worth said: "Tomlin what is the procedure to follow if a Marine gets bitten by a habu?' I said: SIR do not attempt to make an incision or suck out the venom. Instead, keep the victim calm; elevate, immobilize and wrap a cloth firmly around the bite area; and immediately seek medical attention. Jungle Warfare Instructor Assistant Ssgt John Worth said: "Outstanding answer Tomlin." Then Jungle Warfare Instructor SSgt William Beckford said: "Price the seas surrounding Okinawa also are home to many dangerous creatures. Why should you avoid that little cute blue-ringed octopus and why? Price said: " SIR commonly found in rocky shallow pools of water, is about golf ball-sized but its venom can shut down the lungs and kill an adult in minutes, and there is no known antivenom." Jungle Warfare Instructor SSgt William Beckford said: " Another outstanding answer Price. If you and Tomlin keep up the good work and do good in jungle survival I will give you two a three day pass in Okinawa." Then with that, SSgt William Beckford said: " class dismissed be back in classroom at 0700 tomorrow." We march over to the mess hall, had supper, and march back to our Quonset hut and study our handbooks and hit the racks. We got up at 0400, ran our 3 miles and did our PT. We came back to the Quonset hut cleaned up, went to breakfast and marched to our classroom.

In the classroom we got the scoop on all the dangers and precautions in the jungle on what to do or not to do. One day in class a Marine asks Jungle Warfare Instructor why would we need a whistle, would that not let the enemy know your position."

Jungle Warfare Instructor SSgt William Beckford said: "As silly as it seems, having an emergency whistle on your person can be a lifesaver. Give you example during a nighttime patrol, you have a Marine step out onto the lower canopy thinking it was the ground and fell quite a ways. The only way you would be able to locate him was to follow the sound he was making with his whistle." Then Jungle Warfare Instructor Assistant Ssgt John Worth said: " speaking of nighttime ops in the jungle; having a good pair of leather gloves is a must. Some of the plants and vegetation have extremely sharp edges on them as you guys are falling you are trying to grab onto things to stop your fall and tearing your hands to shreds."

The class went on for another 3 days with discussions and written exams. Marines are encouraged to use their imagination, from finding rocks and old coffee cans, to building traps to catch small edible animals, to wrapping plastic bags around the leaves to soak up precipitation for drinking water. The Marines also learned to navigate without a compass, tell time using the sun, set up shelter out of harms way, and distinguish between edible and poisonous plants. Jungle Warfare Instructor SSgt William Beckford stressed the importance of readiness and knowing how to properly prepare and cook an animal. The fun part for me was hands-on for the simple reason I learn faster and never forget with hands on. Like my Dad always said: " you can tell somebody what to do, but they will never learn to do it until they get hands on." Jungle Warfare Instructor Assistant Ssgt John Worth said: " This is about killing and preserving animals so you can eat. If I want chicken you usually go to KFC, there will be no KFC in this jungle."

We were taught to read a map and use a compass. One day for practice they took us out in the jungle and we had 2 hours to get back where we started. Butch and I make it back in an hour and a half. These two Marines we had to set up a search party to find them; they were really lost. Jungle Warfare Instructor SSgt William Beckford chewed their ass to no end. He said: "if you two were in a combat, they would be putting you in body bags. I suggest you learn the map and compass reading in the next couple of days or you two will be funked out." To my surprise, they passed the course with flying colors. Jungle Warfare Instructor SSgt William Beckford said: "Monday you will start your one week jungle survival, you will be paired with a buddy. I just ask one thing do not be a Macho Marine if you get into danger or badly hurt just ask for help. We will send somebody to rescue you, to give you aid or get you out of danger." We all said: "SIR yes SIR" Jungle Warfare Instructor SSgt William Beckford said: "class dismissed, go back to your huts, get your rest because you will need it, and study those handbooks. Without a dought you will not get much rest or good meals in that jungle." We all marched back to the Quonset hut, cracked the books, and waited for chow. The next morning Butch and I had to run 5 miles and do a hundred percent PT. We asked each other questions about Jungle Warfare until we were blue in the face. In our minds we planned, how in the hell we were going to survive that jungle for a whole week. I said: " remember Butch we felt the same way about Mountain survival and we make it. Then Butch said: " Robert the moutains were cold and we kept warm. This damn jungle is hot as hell and no way to keep cool. Now we have to worry about venomous snakes and insects with no food to eat. Then I said: "Butch it is not going to be a picnic when we get to Vietnam, and most likely it will be worst by us getting killed." Butch said: " I promise your Mom I will bring you home no matter what." I said: "I promise your Mom I will bring you home."

Monday morning they loaded us into the trucks, to take us us to the drop point to start our one week of Jungle Survival. When we got to the drop point, we all got off the trucks and paired up with our buddies. A Staff Sergeant Said: " you have to make it back to Ckeck Point Charlie in a week, if not you will funk this course. Now would it be nice before you go to Vietnam that you passed. Now move out." As Butch and I moved from the truck into the jungle, I knew it was do or die. We took out the map to get our bearings and what direction we should go. We were taught to obtain, especially with care or effort, water, build shelters using tree limbs, and trap and skin games. The rugged terrain, stifling humidity and a complicated irregular network of passages or paths in which it is difficult to find one's way through thick brush and trees were unfamiliar conditions for us. Butch and I went into the wild Tuesday to learn to survive in the jungle. We were armed with knives, a cigarette lighter to start fires, cords and ponchos. We had two canteen of water, a small pot fork and spoon.

First day, after 18 hours without food, Butch spotted an Amami rabbit which is black (アマミノクロウサギ 奄美野黒兔) **(1-9)** hiding under a bush. Butch took a gamble and threw his knife and stuck that rabbit right in the neck. Butch was jumping up and down with joy and said: "Robert how does rabbit stew sound." I answer back with something about as tasty as a New York strip steak. Butch and I skinned the rabbit, that was to be our only meal for the day. But it was not the first time we had ever killed our dinner. Butch finished cleaning the rabbit and since he did not want to cut it in half, he put the skinless black rabbit into broth and cooked it over an open fire. Butch said: "Robert we will have meat with our soup." I said: "sounds good to me, I am so damn hungry." I told Butch we have to make do with what we have. Cause when we are deployed in Vietnam and you could have the best gear and still go down, it comes down to the basics and that will keep you alive. Butch looked at me and said: "I hear you brother." I said: "Butch we have to have the mind-set and the will to survive." Butch said: " Robert if we don't have that mind-set we won't survive. So shut the fuck up and lets eat."

After we ate, we made a temporary shelter by cutting tree limbs and bush so that we could sleep. We put down some grass to make the ground a little softer and covered up with the ponchos to keep warm. The second day we were up at 0600 and hungry as hell; I told Butch lets go out and forge for food. I walked out about a mile from our camp site and found blueberries (ブルーベリー) **(1-10)** and Cloudberries (クラウドベリーエクスプ) **(1-11)**; I filled my helmet liner with all the blue and cloudberries to the top. As I was walking back to our camp, I smelled something cooking. Butch found some Okinawa Shallot (沖縄ラッキョウ) **(1-12)**, Goya (ゴヤ) **(1-13)**, and Papaya (パパイヤ) **(1-14)** and was cooking up us some vegetable soup. I walked in and Butch said: "Robert soup will be done in about 15 minutes." I said: " good I got us a mess of berries we can eat." Eating the soup was a little bitter, but anything taste good when you are hungry. After eating the berries, it kind of washed the bitter taste away. We broke camp and headed out in the direction from the reading of our map. We went about 9 or 10 klicks, it was about 2 0r 3 in the afternoon. When Butch said: "do you hear that strange noise. It sounded like a pig to me who was calling for another pig."

After further invest cation we saw it was a little black pig or Wild Pig (野生の豚) **(1-15)** was separated from the other drove of pigs. He weighed about 30 0r 40 pounds. The first thing Butch said: "Robert we have to catch that pig. He will make a meal that will last us for a couple of days." It was a sight to see Butch and I trying to catch that pig. We look like two monkeys tying to fuck a beach ball. We never laugh so hard in our lives. I was laughing so much, I had tears in my eyes. We would go one way, the pig would go the other way. I grabbed him once, but he kicked loose with his hind legs. I told Butch you go from the left side and I will go from the right side. We saw him in a clearing, and charged him at the same time. I grabbed a hind leg and Butch grabbed a front leg. When Butch was holding down the pig, I pulled out my knife and slit his throat. He was squealing and blood everywhere, then he just went calm. Butch said: "Robert I will clean and dress him out. You gether fire wood and build a good fire, and we are eating good tonight." I built a nice fire and told Butch I saw a little steam when I was searching for wood. I will go and fill the canteen while you cook our supper. Walking back I could smell that pig cooking and as I went closer it smelled ever better. When I got to our camp site, Butch Said: " Robert we are having cooked pig smother in Okinawa Shallots with Papaya and Goya on the side. We sat around the fire and talked about the good old times and waitied until the pig was done. Butch took his knife amd made a little slit in the meat and said: "about another 15 minutes before our big feast." That night we ate that pig like two pigs. We went to bed that night with full stomachs and went to sleep right away.

On the third day the next morning we were up by 0600, had pig for breakfast, broke camp, and headed out in the direction according to the map. It was hotter then hell in that jungle and I was sweating like a pig. You know, a funny thing, pigs do not actually sweat, it is an old saying a person will say when they are hot and sweating. Butch said: "Robert " lets stop and rest and take a couple of small drinks of water." We found this down tree to sit and rest, boy was it hot. I told Butch, with this damn heat and humanity I would take Illinois anytime. Then Butch said: "give me old Missouri anytime, to compared to this hell hole." After we rested and drank our water, we headed out in the right direction so that we would make it to check point Charlie on time. I can say one thing while in that jungle, you sure hear a lot of strange noises. Butch said: "Robert some of those damn sounds just puts me on edge. You don't know if it is friend or foe." I said: " with some of them sounds, I hope it is friend." We kept walking, then we found a nice clearing to set up camp. I went for fire wood so Butch could cook. After I dropped off the fire wood, I grabbed the canteens and went to look for water. I went out about 1 or 2 klicks and found this little steam. The water was crystal clear, so I filled the canteens and headed back to camp. As I was getting closer, I could smell Butch's cooking. I said: "something smell real good." Butch makes this funny comment: " well tonight we are having roast of pig with all the fixings." I said: "ok master chef give me the works." We ate our supper and sat around and talked about the family and going home one of these days. We turned in and went right to sleep.

On the fourth day we got up at 0600, had pig for breakfast, broke camp, and headed hopefully in the right direction. Butch said: "Robert just 3 more days and we should be at check point Charlie." I told Butch if the jungles are like this in Vietnam I can see it will not be any picnic." Then Butch said: In this jungle we can walk in peace, but in that jungle the enemy will be firing at us." We just kept walking and checking the map every now and then to see if we were headed in the right direction. We walked for about 9 or 10 klicks when Butch said: " Robert I am getting hunrgy and I need water." I said: " there a clearing right in front of us and we can stop there." We still had some pig, berries, and vegetables left, but this would be our last meal until we hunted or found something else to eat. I told Butch to start the fire and I would find water. I walked about 3 or 4 hundred feet when I heard water running. I followed the sound and found a clear stream with clear running water. I filled the canteens and as I was walking back I saw a family of mongooses running, trying to catch birds. When I got back to camp, I told Butch about the mongooses. Butch said: "after we have supper I will go and try to trap a couple mongooses for breakfast and lunch" Then I said: " I found a big plastic bottle maybe we can make a trap out of it, too catch a mongoose." Butch said: "does it have a lid." I said: " it should does. While we were eating I told Butch save a piece of that pork we can use that for bait." So Butch and I figured out a way to trap the mongoose in the plastic bottle. We took the elastic and string out of one of the poncho's to put on the lid to use as a rubber band. We put an elastic hinge on the lid to close when the mongoose trips the bar going in after the pork bait. The elastic over the lid would keep in place, so the mongoose could not get out. We put a hole in the top of the plastic bottle to stick him with a pointed stick to kill the mongoose while he was in the bottle. Butch set up a trip bar make from a stick with an elastic attached to the lead. When the mongoose went in the plastic bottle to get the bait, he would trip the bar and the lid would slam shut and he would be trapped.

On the fifth day we got up at 0600, then Butch and I went for water. On the way I showed Butch where the mongoose were chasing the birds and he went to set up the trap. I went the other way to get water. When I got to the water stream, I filled the canteens and headed back to our camp site. Butch was really clever about sitting up, he trap he use the fence method with a narrow path to the bait. He covered the fence with fresh cut branches from a tree and left the path open to the plastic bottle. After I got back to the camp site, Butch came in about a half hour later. Butch said: "Robert I set the trap and we can go back in a few hours. I said: "I wonder what mongoose taste like." Butch said; "I bet it taste like raccoon." Then I said: " what ever it taste like at lease it will be food." I told Butch you can check the trap, I will go and forge for some food. I walked about 2 or 3 klicks and spotted the biggest bunch of Cloudberries I ever saw. I filled my hat and inside of my shirt. Then I walked back to our camp site on the way back I spotted some Okinawa Shallot and Goya growing wild. I took the berries back to camp and put the berries in my poncho. Went back to get the Okinawa Shallots and Goya. I pulled several dozen of Okinawa Shallot out of the ground. Then I picked several dozen Goya and put them in my helmet liner. As I was walking back to camp, I saw Butch skinning the mongoose, which weighed about 2 and ¾ to 3 pounds. Butch cleaned him and had him roast on an open fire while I had the Okinawa Shallots and Goya boiling. I asked Butch, was it hard skinning and cleaning the mongoose. Butch said: " Robert it is exactly the same as cleaning a squirrel." We were a little caution about eating the mongoose, but once we bite in, it really tasted pretty damn good. That day we had a wonderful meal of mongoose, Okinawa Shallots, Goya and Cloudberries for desert. We started to clean up and move out. When Butch said: " I am going to trap a couple more Mongoose, those babies are better then squirrel." I said: " Butch go ahead I will finish cleaning up and pack up while you go trapping." I was just finishing rolling up the ponchos when Butch came back with two mongooses. He skins and cleans one while I skin and clean the other one. We wrapped them in banana leaves and put them in the ponchos and started walking towards the Charlie Check Point.

We walked about 10 or 12 klicks and found this nice spot under a Fukugi tree (福木の木) **(1-16)**. I told Butch to start dinner and I would get wood and water. I gathered up a bunch of wood for Butch and then took the canteens to look for water. I walked out about 3 or 4 Klicks and found a clear water hole. Just as I was filling the last canteen I heard a pig squeal. I turned around and there was a little pig, about 20 or so pounds caught up in the vines; the more he struggled the vines became tighter. I walked over and cut his throat and let him bleed out. I cut him loose from the vines and carried him back to our camp. I could smell that mongoose cooking as I approached camp. I yelled out: "Butch we have food for the next couple of days I just killed a pig." Butch popped up and said: "what did you kill." I said: "a pig he was caught in some vines and it was and easy kill." Butch was all excited and said: I found some duck eggs; now we can have pork and eggs for breakfast." We had our supper of mongoose and some berries, and sat around the fire and talked about old times and went to bed.

On the sixth day we were up by 0600 while Butch fixed breakfast I went to get fresh water. As I was walking back to camp I could smell the amora of the cooking pig. My mouth was watering and I was hungry to eat. There is nothing better than eggs and roasted pig for breakfast. After breakfast Butch was looking at the map and said: "You know Robert we are not that far from Check Point Charlie." I said: "man that is great I need to take a shower those whore baths are not cutting for me. I am satrted to smell like a goat." Butch looked up and said: " you know it brother." According to the map, we were only about 20 or 25 klicks away from Check Point Charlie. I told Butch if we push it, we can make it today and be a day early. Butch said: "lets clean and pack up and head out. I want a hot shower and regular chow." So we cleaned, packed up and headed out towards Check Point Charlie. It was really hot that day and the humidity was higher than normal. We were sweating like pigs while walking through that jungle that day. I told Butch lets slow down we will kill ourselves trying to get to Check Point Charlie. Our canteens were running low and told Butch we had to fill the water or we were done. Just as we got out of the jungle in a small clearing we found this clear water hole. I stuck my face down in the water and started drinking like a mad man. Butch did the same thing while I filled the canteens. We rested for about a half hour and started walking again. We must have walked about 20 klicks when we spotted Check Point Charlie. As we walked through the check point, a sergeant of the arms said: "report to the commander tent." We walked up to the commander tent, stood attenuation rendered a salute, and said: Tomlin and Price, reporting for duty SIR." The commander said: " said stand at ease." You two Marines made it in recorded time, a matter of fact, you were one whole day early. For that achievement I am giving you a 3 day pass in the city of Okinawa. Go clean up and get square away and have some good chow in the mess tent." Then he said: "sergeant show these Marines to there tent where they can clean up and point them to the mess tent." The sergeant said: "Yes SIR." We stood attenuation render a salute and said: "thnak you SIR." The commander said: " you are dismissed." We did about face and followed the sergeant out of the commander's tent.

We got to our tent and that shower never felt so good. I wash off 6 days of dirt and sweat from walking in that damn jungle. They brought our uniforms and boots from Camp Gonsalves. We cleaned up, shaved, got dressed, and went to the mess tent. As we were going through the mess line, that was the biggest steak I ever saw. I got a double helping of potatoes, gravy, vegetables, and lemon cake. I was drinking ice tea like there was no tomorrow. A sergeant came by and make this comment: You boys are eating like two starved dogs." After we were finished eating, we sat in the mess tent and talked about how we made it. Then I said: "Butch I am going to sleep like a baby in that cot tonight." I had no longer than got to sleep when a sergeant came into our tent yelling come on sweathearts, it was time for PT. We jumped out of the racks, took a quick shower and shave, got dressed and went outside to get in formation. We ran our 5 miles, did our PT and came back to out tent cleaned up again and went to chow. After chow the commander talked to us and said: "tomorrow at 0700 you will be driven back to Camp Gonsalves and start your 3 day pass. We stood attenuation render a salute and said: "Think You SIR." The commander said: "go back to your tent and rest until the truck pick you up. You are dismissed." We rendered another salute, did about face and walked back to our tent. We went back to our tent to get more sleep for the simple reason we did not sleep very well while we were in the jungle. Butch and I were up by 0500, got dressed and packed when to the mess tent, and waited for the truck. The truck was on time at 0700, we got loaded and started heading back to Camp Gonsalves. We had to drive about 30 miles back to our base camp. As we were driving I said: "Butch they had us walking in a big circle for our survival week in the jungle." Butch said: "you know Robert we did not know we were walking in a circle because nothing in that jungle looks the same." On 15 January, 1967, as we stopped at the gate sergeant of the guard said: " Tomlin and Price see the commander right away."

The truck stopped; we got off and went directly to the commander's office. We knocked on the door; The commander said: "enter." Butch and I stood attenuation rendered a salute, and said: Tomlin and Price, reporting for duty SIR." The commander said: "stand at ease, on the Jungle Survival Week you two Marines did an outstanding job. Thats why I agree with commander Maj. William Lowe about giving you a 3 day pass in Naha, Okinawa. But after looking at your records with your great process as Marines in the United States Marine Corps, I am giving you a 5 day pass in Naha. You will both be transferred to Vietnam after your 5 day pass. Your orders will be cut and you will be with 3rd Battalion, 7th Marines embarked on board the amphibious ships Iwo Jima(LPH-2), Talledega(APA 208), and Point Defiance(LSD 31) in Okinawa and departed for Vietnam. I wish you the best for your endevers and watch each others backs. You are dismissed." We stood, stood attenuation render a salute, and said: "Thank yoy SIR ." did about face and walked out of the commander's office. Just as we hit the door way, the commander said: " I almost forgot SSgt William Beckford wants to see you." We walked over to Jungle Warfare Instructor SSgt William Beckford's office. We knock on his door. The instructor said: "enter," Butch and I stood attenuation rendering a salute, and said: "Tomlin and Price reporting as requested SIR." The Insrtuctor said: "tell me about that black rabbit." When we told Jungle Warfare Instructor SSgt William Beckford about the black rabbit. He said: " you two Marine are damn lucky because that rabbit is a dark-furred rabbit which is only found in Amami Ōshima and Toku-no-Shima, two small islands between southern Kyūshū and Okinawa in Kagoshima a district under the government of but actually closer to Okinawa in Japan. I would give my left nut to find out how in the hell that black rabbit got to Okinawa." I said: " we were real hungry and he was real tastely SIR." The instructor said: "the commander said to give you a jeep to use on your 5 day pass. in Naha. Here is your orders for the jeep to pick up at the motor pool." Then, he said: " have fun and stay out of trouble and you are dismissed." We stood attenuation, rendering a salute, and said: " Thank you SIR." did about face and walked to the motor pool. When we got to the motor pool we handed the orders to the motor sergeant. He said: "just a minute some one will bring the jeep around." A corporal who came driving up in a brand new jeep stopped and handed me the keys. He said: "please corporals bring back in good condition or it will be my ass." I said: "do not worry corporal it will be like new when we bring it back." Butch said: "Robert hand me the keys I am driving." We drove back to out Quonset hut packed our bags and drove off to Naha. We had reservations at a Mom and Pa motel in Asahibashiekimae-Naha at the rate of $5.00 dollars a night.

As Butch and I were driving down the Okinawa Expressway, we were just passed Kadena Air Force Base when we noticed these two little cute Japanese girls in short shorts hitch-hiking. We waved and they waved back and we drove to our motel. We check in and Mr. Takahashi shows us to our room. In broken English, he said: " nice sushi restaurant down the street to eat." We got in the room, unpacked and sat around and talked about what we were going to do. Then Butch said: "beer, women, and song and I do not care in what order." I said: "got you brother, let try that sushi restaurant." We walked down to the restaurant and got seated. The waitress came by and took our order. Butch said: " bring us two bottle of beer." She said: " will Kirin Ichiban be ok." Butch said: " that will be fine." When she went to get the beer Butch and I looked over the menu. Butch said: "Robert did you ever have sushi before." I said: "what we ate in the jungle sushi will be a feast." Butch and I ate like pigs; we had all kinds of sushi tuna

(鮪) **(1-17)**, crab roll (カニロール) **(1-18)**, octopus (蛸) **(1-19)**, squid roll (イカロール) **(1-20)**, vegetable roll (野菜ロール) **(1-21)**, yellow tail (ハマチ) **(1-22)**, and miso soup (味噌汁) **(1-23)**. After dinner Butch said: " Robert I have have never had Sushi before but I have to admit that sushi was real good." Then I said: " how about that beer it was real good too." I total bill for food and beer for both of us was around $13.00 dollars and we gave the waitress a $3.00 dollars tip. We were full to the gills as we walked back to the motel. Butch said: "Robert that is really eating compared to that damn jungle food." I said: "we better enjoy while we can cause when we go to the Vietnam Jungle that food and heat will be the **Green Hell Never Ends**."

The next morning Butch and I drove to the PX on Kadena Air Force Base to get a hair cut and Fonseca Cuban cigars. As we were headed on the Express Highway there were those two young, good-looking Japanese girls in their short shorts. Butch Said: "Robert pull over lets pick them up." I pulled off the highway and waved our arms in a motion to have then come to the jeep. They came running up giggling and speaking Japanese with hello (こんにちは) **(1-24)** and Thank You (ありがとうございました) **(1-25)**. As they got in the back of the jeep I said: " my name is Robert and this is Butch." The one in red shorts was about 4 feet 11 inches tall; weighed about 100 pounds soak and wet, with dark black hair and beautiful brown eyes, and was speaking in broking English. She said: " my name is Mieko and my friend is Keiko." Then they started laughing and speaking in Japanese in which Butch and I did not understand a single word they were saying. Then Mieko spoke in broken English, saying: "we want to go to A&W Root Beer to get fried chicken."I said: " is it near the air force base." Then Keiko said in broken English, it is real close to the air force base." We were getting close to the air force base when Butch said: " Robert A&W straight ahead." We pulled in and found a parking space then blinked our head lights for service. A young Japanese girl came out to the car to take our order. She spoke perfect English and said: " may I take your order." I said: let the girls order first." In Japanese, Mieko said: "she would order for her and Keiko 2 fried chicken dinner with french fries and a root beers." Butch said: 2 Bar-B-Ques and french fries and a large root beer. I said: 2 hot dogs and french fries and a large root beer. Then I asked the waitress, could you please ask the girls how old they were. She said: "yes I can do that." She spoke in Japanese and asked Mieko and Keiko how old they were. Mieko and Keiko answer with seventeen years old (17歳) **(1-26)**. Then the waitress said: "they are 17 years old ." I said: "Thank you." I looked at Butch and said: " well old buddy they are too young for us and it looks like jail bait. We well just try to talk to them and have a good time and pay for their meals and take them back to the Express Highway." We actually had a good time talking, laughing and joking around with Mieko and Keiko. We finished eating Butch and I paid for the meals, which came to a total of $3.34 cents. We gave the waitress $4.00 dollars and told her to keep the change. We took Mieko and Keiko by the highway and drove on toward Kadena Air Force Base. Then Butch said: "stop Mieko is saying something." Mieko said: Thank You (ありがとうございました) **(1-27)** and if we come by tomorrow, her and Keiko would take us to a Haba (幅) **(1-28)** and Mongoose (ングース) **(1-29)** fight. We said:

" we will pick you up tomorrow at the same place." We could hear Mieko and Keiko say: "we were so cute and good looking." They were giggling and laughing as they walked off. I told Butch the girls are too young, its not worth screwing up our military career and going to the brig for. Then Butch said: " I hear the Marine jailers are rough and tough on new Marine prisoners."

As we were driving down the Express Highway we could see Mieko and Kieko waiting for us. We pulled over and they jumped in the back of the jeep. Mieko in broken English was trying to tell me which way to go. Mieko said: "when you get pass the Kadena Air Force Base take road to the the right which will take you to Tamashiro Village where Keiko and I live." Then, she said: " the snake and mongoose fight will begin at noon." As we pulled into the village there must have been two thousand villagers standing around in a big circle; they were all waiting for the big snake and mongoose to fight. Then Asahi (朝日) **(1-30)** Okinawan from their village walked up to us and spoke in perfect English and said: " サキシマハブ(Sakishima habu) **(1-31)** is a venomous pitviper species endemic to Japan in the southern Ryukyu Islands. The Sakishima habu comes from The Sakishima Islands (先島諸島, Sakishima-shotō) **(1-32)** are an archipelago located at the southernmost end of the Japanese Archipelago. They are part of the Ryukyu Islands and include the Miyako Islands and the Yaeyama Islands." Then said: "This Okinawan Haruto (ハルト) **(1-33)** has a Sakishima habu he called 王様 (The King) **(1-34)** because in five years he has never lost to a マングース (mongoose) **(1-35)**. So Haruto would take The King to varoius islands in around Okinawa and make bets that his snake would win. There was a Okinawan Minato (港区) **(1-36)** from Tamashiro Village on the island of Okinawa that a had a small skinny mongoose name 貴重 (Precious) who also has never lost to habu. All the villagers from the all the islands are getting sick and tired of The King (haba) winning." Then Asahi said: " see the two men standing over there with a large brown bag they are taking bets and giving 30 to 1 odds on the mongoose." I said: " Asahi thank you for the information. Who would you bet on?" Asahi said: " at those kind of odds take the mongoose. Mieko took my hand to meet her Father Sadao (サダオ) **(1-37)** and Mother Kiyo (きよ) **(1-38)**. As we were walking up to meet her parents, if their eyes could kill I would be dead by now. Mieko spoke in Japanese and said: "Father (父) **(1-39)** and Mother (母) **(1-40)** this is Robert. Her father bows and says: "Konnichiwa (こんにちは) **(1-41)** Robert-san" But I could see in her Father's eyes he was not to please with me. I bow and say: " Konnichiwa" to her Father and Mother. I could see her mother was giving me the evil eye also cause I was holding Mieko's hand. Then Mieko told me to go over there and see the man who was taking bets. So Butch and I walked over to the man with a big money bag accepting bets and giving 30 to 1 odds on the mongoose. Butch bet $10.00 dollars for him self and $5.00 dollars for Keiko for the mongoose. I bet $10.00 for myself and $5.00 dollars for Mieko on the mongoose. Butch gave the $5.00 dollar betting slip to Keiko and I gave the $5.00 betting slip to Mieko. Then it was time for the big snake and mongoose fight; all the villagers let out a big cheer as the mongoose (Precious) entered the center of the ring. Then, when the haba (The King) entered the ring, not many villagers were cheering.

The mayor of the village was the ring master and said in Japanese to bring the haba and mongoose to the center of the ring. Then, he said: " on my command release the animals to begin the fight." The mayor said: "release the animals." Haruto released the haba and Minato released the mongoose right away the haba went crawling towards the mongoose. As soon as the haba was within 3 feet of the mongoose, he curled up and make a strike at the mongoose. Just as haba (The King) stuck at the mongoose (Precious) did a quick step to the right and the snake missed. Butch said: "Robert that mongoose is quick as lightning, we would never trap her." The haba coils back and waits for another chance for a quick kill. Then the mongoose started moving, very slowly around the snake. You could see the snake's head moving with the mongoose, waiting for the right opportunity to sank its fangs into the skinny mongoose's body. Then the haba rears up again, calculating the distance and time when to strike again. But the mongoose had already figured out the distance and time when to stay out of striking distance. The haba crawled forward about 4 or so feet and waited to see what the mongoose was going to do. I said: "Butch that mongoose is one clever son-of-bitch and thats why he has won so many fights with a haba." When the haba came forward, the mongoose circled to the left, which put the sun right into the eyes of the haba. Then all of a sudden the haba figured out the trap. He would be blinded by the sun and could not see the mongoose. Precious would be sinking his teeth into him. So the haba circles back to the right to keep out of the sun. All the mean time Asahi is getting nervous and yelling at the snake "kill, kill, kill." Butch said: "Robert old Asahi is worry about all that money he has to pay out if that haba is killed by the mongoose." Minato was very calm and talking softly in Japanese to the mongoose, telling him to take his time and be careful. Then the mongoose surprise everybody by just laying down with out moving in the middle of the ring. But you could see his eyes following every move the snake was making. I said: "Butch that sly fox is setting the trap for the snake." Once the snake saw the mongoose laying down, he went crawling right towards him. Then the mongoose ears perked up and you could see the muscles in that skinny body tightening up. As the snake got closer, you could see that the mongoose had his right front and hind legs on its paws. The snake coils up and makes the final strike to the left of the mongoose. Just as the haba head was on the left side of the mongoose, he pivet on his right front and rear pads and sunk his teeth right into the haba neck. That mongoose was shaking him so hard with his teeth sunk so deeply into the snake's neck, and blood was pouring out everywhere. When the mongoose let go of his deadly grip, the snake was dead. All most of the villagers let out a big yell; the snake is dead. You could see poor Asahi just sink to the ground without saying a word and thinking of all the money he had lost.

So Butch, Mieko, Kieko and I walked over to collect our money. We all handed in our betting slips Butch and I got $300.00 dollars each and Mieko and Keiko got $150.00 dollars each. Mieko and Keiko walked right over to their parents and handed them a $100.00 each and kept $50.00 each for their selfs. I told Butch that it is really admirable to hand their parents the most money. Mieko Father saw me and he bow with a smile on his face and said: " Thank You Very Much (ありがとうございま

した) **(1-42)** he bow again and both families left. That was the last time Butch and I never saw Mieko and Keiko again. We found out years later Mieko married a sailor who was in the United States Navy and Keiko married a airman who was in the United States Air Force. Butch and I jumped in the jeep and headed back to our motel. Butch and I had only a few days left on out pass, so we made the best of it. We went sight seeing all over Okinawa we visit Gyokusendo Cave, we Drove at the underwater ruins of Yonaguni, went whale watching, tried the local food, we visit Shuri Castle, explore the local villages on Taketomi, and took in the views at Akajima Island. Our 5 day pass was up and we ran out of time on slight seeing, then we had to report back to base camp and get ready to be shipped to Vietnam.

The next morning Butch and I reported back to camp to the Base Commander. We knocked on his office door, and he said: "enter." We stood attenuation rendered a salute, and said: "Tomlin amd Price reporting for duty SIR." The commander said: " stand at ease, you will go to the armory and supply depot to draw weapons and your equipment. You will board the amphibious ships tomorrow morning at 0500 heading for Vietnam. Go at God's speed and look out and take care of your fellow Marines and each other. You are dismissed." Butch and I stood back attenuation, rendering a salute and said: " we will SIR." Did about face and walked to the armory and supply depot. We went to the supply depot first as we walked in, a sergeant said: "you Marines here for your Vietnam gear." We both said: "yes'. He said step this way and get your gear." First we were handed the M1967 USMC Combat Field Pack designed specially for the Vietnam conditions. Canvas rotted in the jungle, and weighed more, especially when wet- the M1967 Nylon did not have any of these problems. Then we got Helmet – 5 lb., Boots – 2 lb., Poncho and liner 3 lb., Entrenching tool (shovel) – 5 lb., M1967 USMC M14 Magazine Pouch – 1 lb., Machete – 3lb, Sandbags (empty) – 4 lb., 3-4 days C-rations 6 lb., 1 1/2 gal. Water – 12 lbs. Then Butch said: "do we get a tent." The sergeant shouted back no fucking tents; they only rot in that jungle, if you need cover, use your poncho." We gathered up our equipment and headed for the armory. When we got to the armory this tuff bull dog face staff sergeant said: :if you do not have your fucking orders, you will not be drawing any weapons." We said: "we have our orders." Butch and I handed our orders to the staff sergeant. The staff sergeant handed us a M14 rifle – 9.2 lbs., and read and recorded the serial number. Then, he said: " if you loose or destroy your rifle it will cost you $104.00 dollars for the replacement. I suggest you bring it back in good condition." We received 8 20-round detachable box magazines with 7.62×51mm (.308 Winchester) ammo. -12 lbs., 2 Frag grenades – 2 lb., 2 Smoke grenades – 3 lb., 1 claymore mine – 3.5 lb. When Butch and I walked out of the armory we had to carry about 85 or 90 pounds of equipment and weapons. As we walked out we were directed to the holding area for tomorrow's departure to Vietnam. That night Butch and I talked about our good old times in high school and our other adventures. Then Butch said: "I promise your mom I would bring you home no matter what." I told Butch I promised your Mon I would bring you home. I said: " we better hit the rack, we have an early start in the morning.

Then all of a sudden this booming voice was yelling rise and shine its time to go.

Butch and I jumped out of the rack, got our gear and weapons, and when outside to get in formation. As we were standing in formation, a Marine officer LTC. Paul Stevens said: " I will be your commander for your deployment and while you are in Vietnam. Your First Sergent is 1stSg Roger L. Lewis, you may damn sure you follow the chain of command, if you have a problem you talk to him first. Do I make myself clear." We all said as loud as we could be with "SIR yes SIR.' Then LTC Paul Stevens said: " We are going to try something new. The old composition of the Rifle Squad, the squad is composed of 13 men: a sergeant (squad leader) and three fire teams of four men each. Each fire team consists of a corporal for each fire team. We will be making a slight change with composition of the Rifle Squad The squad is composed of 17 men: a sergeant (squad leader) and four fire teams of four men each. Each fire team consists of a corporal for each fire team. We will be adding the M79 grenade launcher with each fire team. You will be the 3rd Battalion, 7th Marines embarked on board the amphibious ship Iwo Jima (LPH-2); This ship will carry a squadron of 24 Marine helicopters plus a Battalion Landing Team of 1500 Marines with companies from India, Kilo, Lima, Mike, and November. So after this formation all corporals report to 1stSg Roger L. Lewis for further instruction." The First Sergeant said: "Attenuation then dismissed." Then all the corporals reported to the First Sergeant. 1stSg Roger L. Lewis said: " I will call your name to what assign Rifle Team and fire team you will be in charge of." The first sergeant started calling out names to who was assigned to what company, squad, and rifle team. Then 1stSg Roger L. Lewis called my name Tomlin you will be in Lima Company, 1st Squad, and 1st Fire team. Then he broke it down Squad Leader is Ssgt Henry Watson, Fire Team Leader is Corporal Robert Dean Tomlin, with Automatic Rifleman and Assistant Automatic Rifleman, M79 Grenade Launcher, and 12 Rifleman. Then he calls Price, you will be Lima Company, 2nd Squad, and 1st Fire team. Your Squad Leader is Ssgt William Houser, Fire Team Leader is Corporal Frederick (Butch) Philip Price; with Automatic Rifleman and Assistant Automatic Rifleman, M79 Grenade Launcher, and 12 Rifleman. He finished calling the names for all 5 companies who were going to be deployed to Vietnam in the morning. Then 1stSg Roger L. Lewis said: " Marines will be broading the Iwo Jima (LPH-2) at 0500 in the morning, so have your gear packed and weapon ready to move out. Get your rest and have a good meal cause it might be a long time for your next good meal. You know our motto you do not leave any Marine behind dead or alive. Remember look out for each other and cover each others backs." He called everybody at attention, then dismissed. Butch and I walked to the Quonset hut.

In our minds we were thinking now this will be the real thing; no excuse, they will be shooting real bullets and live explosives will be hurled at us. I told Butch I will always have your back covered when we are in combat. Then Butch said: " Brother when we are in battle you can count on me to cover your back." We finished packing our gear and cleaned our rifles and made sure they were operational

before our big trip to Vietnam. We checked our equipment and took inventory of everything. Butch said: "remember brother my peanut butter for your cigareetes." I said: " as long as I get to smoke my cigars that will make be happy." It seemed like no sooner did our heads hit the pillows when 1stSg Roger L. Lewis said: " out of your racks grab your gear and weapons and load on the truck to the docks." Butch and I jumped up, got dressed, grabbed our gear and weapons, and got loaded on the trucks. On the way to the ship Butch said: brother, I am really getting nervous about this trip to Vietnam and I hope I just get to see my family again." I told Butch you were nervous; I am more nervous than a long tail cat in a room full of rockin chairs. That broke the ice; every body on that truck was busting a gut. Then the truck stopped; everybody got off and marched to the gang plank. LTC. Paul Stevens was the first one on board; he stopped, saluted and said; "permission to come aboard SIR." The officer of the ship said: "permission granted come aboard." Every Marine in the 3rd Battalion, the 7th Marines, marched single file and asked permission to come aboard the ship. We were shown to our quarters as the ship was pulling away and heading for Vietnam. We left the dock at 0700 on Monday morning with a sailing distance of around 1,450 miles. It took us about 2 ½ days to get to vietnam. To me it seemed like I was on the ship forever; Butch and I killed time with PT, lubing our rifles with JPS (Joseph Peterson Special) to keep our weapons well lubed, and writing letters home. LTC Paul Stevens gave classes on what to expect with the customs of the Vietnamese, the country and terrain of vietnam. 1stSg Roger L. Lewis gave classes on the Viet Cong on their tactics, boobie traps, and their style of fighting. Then, he said: "these little bastards are tricky and can pop up any where or when you lease where to expect them. Always be on your toes when you are in the jungle, these little devils know the jungle like the back of their hand. Then on the third day somebody yelled I see land. The Iwo Jima (LPstop H-2) dock at Cam Ranh Bay in Vietnam. LTC. Paul Stevens was the first one off , he stopped, saluted and asked: "Permission to come ashore. SIR." The officer on the ship said: "permission granted to go ashore." Every Marine in the 3rd Battalion, 7th Marines, marched single file. They stopped, saluted and asked: "permission to go ashore."

CHAPTER EIGHT

Vietnam War

Operation Green Hell

The Operation Green Hell was fought between September – October 1966. Since the People's Army of Vietnam clearly did not want to keep within certain limits and confines by the Demilitarized Zone, they were crossing the DMZ on a regular basic. The Operation Green Hell was to push the PAVN forces back across the Demilitarized Zone (DMZ) and keep them there with a build-up of United Staes Marines. .

Key United States Commanders
LTC Joseph Muller USMC
LTC Joseph Benkly USMC
2ndLt Harry Wilson USMC
1stSg Roger L. Lewis USMC
GySgt Russell Owens USMC
Ssgt Henry Watson USMC
Ssgt William Houser USMC
Cpl Robert Dean Tomlin USMC
Cpl Frederick (Butch) Philip Price USMC

Key North Vietnam Commanders
Colonel Pham Chi PAVN

Cpl Robert Dean Tomlin and Cpl Frederick (Butch) Philip Price were transfer to the 3rd Battalion, 9th Marines of 500 hundred troops were being send to Tomahawk Base to give the Marines station there, a break and some relief from fighting so they could take some R&R (rest and recreation). The distance from Cam Ranh Bay to the Tomahawk Base Marine Base was over 400 hundred miles, so we had to fly in the CH-53 helicopters. So Lima Company, 1st, 2nd, and 3rd squads got loaded in the first helicopter, as we were lifting off other helicopters was right behind us. Butch and I looked down and could believe how dense that jungle was. I said: " Butch how in the hell can you see anything in that jungle." Then, 1stSg Roger L. Lewis said: "do not worry Marines you will get use to it. Make damn sure your weapons are well lubes and operational. When we hit the ground you just might be firing." It took us about 2 ½ hours of flying time to reach Tomahawk Marine Base. As we were making our last leg, everything looked real quite down there. A Marine was waving us in to land on the helicopter pad. Just as the CH-53 touched down, the First Sergeant was shouting out orders: "move out at double time." As soon as our boots hit, the ground, we were rolling to the holding area. The Marines station there were yelling in loud cheers and singing The Marine Hymn. They were so damn happy to get some relief from every day fighting.

1stSg Roger L. Lewis called us at attention and said: "the Base Commander LTC Joseph Muller has a few words he wants to say." LTC Joseph Muller said: "Marines you are in a different environment that you are not used too. Remember the PAVN are ruthless killers and will not hesitate to kill you then chopped you up in smallpieces. Always be on the look out for snipers and booty traps. Most important to remember is the "rule of three" A corporal has a three-person fire team; a sergeant has a squad of three fire teams; a lieutenant and a staff sergeant have a platoon of three squads. Get square away, go to chop, and get some rest. You are dismissed." We all said: "SIR yes SIR." 1stSg Roger L. Lewis march us right over to the living quarters to get square away. Then, he said: " after chop line up in formation, LTC Joseph Muller will be giving our new mission asignment." He marched us to the Base Commander Tent, he call "Halt and stand at ease. He reported to the base commander and said: " 1stSg Roger L. Lewis reporting for duty SIR, with 500 hundred ready and fresh Marines to fight SIR." The base commander said: " stand at ease and get your men square away, bring yourself and all squad leaders to my tent for a briefing." 1stSg Roger L. Lewis said: "yes SIR, called us at attention, forward march and took us to our living quarters. When we arrive he called us at attention then stand at ease. Then he said: "Get square away, and all squad leaders be in front of the commander's tent in 10 minutes, and you are dismissed." When Butch and I got to our living quarters there were wooden barracks (hootches) on cots. The hootches were open bays, covered with sand bags around the outsides. Or we could live in tents. Butch and I took the tent with 10 other Marines. We found a couple of empty racks and stored our gear away.

This would be the first combat mission for Butch and I. We did not get much sleep that night thinking what the hell, we would be firing real bullets at the enemy and they would be firing real bullets back at us. We rolled out of the sack the next morning, did our PT and headed for the mess tent. On the way we looked at all the hills, trees, and bush. Butch said: " Robert look at all that green trees and bush everywhere, you know them frigging PAVN are hiding, just waiting to shoot our asses off." A Marine sergeant over heard our conversation and made this comment: "yes the Green Hell Never Ends, those frigging PAVN are everywhere and we will never kill all those little bastards and to tell the truth we will be lucky to win this war. But what really burns my ass, it is not a 3 foot flame but those damn Russian, Chinese, and North Korea sticking their noses in this war. " We told the sergeant: " you can say that again." Then we went to the mess tent to have chow. While we were eating 1stSg Lewis came by and said: " be ready to move out in the morning we will be going on patrol." After eating, we went back to our tent to get our weapons and equipment squared away. 1stSg Roger L. Lewis said: "here are your assignments, 1st Squad Leader Ssgt Henry Watson with Cpl Robert Dean Tomlin the 1st Squad Rifle Team Leader, 2nd Squad Leader Ssgt William Houser with Cpl Frederick (Butch) Philip Price the 2nd Squad Rifle Team Leader. Be ready to pull out at 0600, you will be on the West side to protect the CH-46's while they bring in Marine troops. 3rd Squad leader Ssgt Thomas Kidd and 4th Squad leader Ssgt Harvey Powell will be on the East side to protect the CH-46's while they bring in Marine troops. Our mission is to Kill and drive the PAVN back to the Demilitarized

Zone (DMZ). Those sneaking little son-of-a-bitches have been coming across the DMZ, in which they feel they should not be constrained by the Demilitarized Zone. Commander Rifle Platoon 2ndLt Harry Wilson said: "Well, I got news for those little bastards, cause Company L 3rd Battalion, 9th Marines is going to put a stop to their movement for once and all"

On the morning of 10 September, before Company L 3rd Battalion, the 9th Marines pulled out. A-4 Skyhawks and F-4B Phantoms began bombing and napalming the area that was going to be used for the CH-46's to land. At 0700, 3rd Battalion, 12th Marines Artillery with M177 lightweight howitzers with a maximum effective range of 30 km, began shelling to clear landing areas for the helicopters. At 0800 20 Boeing Vertol CH-46 Sea Knighst which could carry 25 Marines began landing Marine troops on the West and East sides. North and South of the landing zones, 3rd Battalion, 4th Marines, were added for more protection. At first Company L 3rd Battalion, the 9th Marines met no initial resistance, from the PAVN; everything was quiet. We could see some of the landing areas were too small for the operation. If it was not for good pilots, the CH-46s nearly collided and crashed into each other. While a CH-46 was trying to avoid a crash with another CH-46, he hit a tree and lucky for him, he did not crash. Later that day another CH-46 carrying men from 2nd Battalion, 1st Marines was hit by PAVN fire that damaged the collective pitch control. The collective pitch control, or collective lever, is normally located on the left side of the pilot's seat with an adjustable friction control to prevent inadvertent movement. The collective changes the pitch angle of all the main rotor blades collectively all at the same time and independent of their position. Therefore, if a collective input is made, all the blades change equally, and as a result, the helicopter increases or decreases its total lift derived from the rotor. In level flight this would cause a climb or descent, while with the helicopter pitched forward an increase in total lift would produce an acceleration together with a given amount of ascent. The Marine copter pilot was a hell of a helicopter piot,some how kept the helicopter under control, while Platoon Sergeant GySgt Russell Owens gave direct orders for the 1st and 2nd squads of Company L 3rd Battalion, 9th Marines, to counterattack the PAVN position. Within a few minutes we were in a fire fight with the PAVN and killing 28 PAVN. Now the CH-46's Marine pilot kept the copter under control and he could land safely and drop off the Marines.

Company L, 3rd Battalion, 9th Marines, began establishing blocking positions around the landing zones and to keep the PAVN from moving forward. Then all of a sudden Company L was taking fire from all sides, we were in a cross-fire with no possible way to escape. Companies from the 2nd Battalion, 1st Marines heard the firing and came to their recuse. Company K 2nd Battalion, 1st Marines continued on to their objective south of the landing zone, but they were pushed back by PAVN fire as they tried to cross the Ngan River. Company K decided to set up night positions on a hill from the river and start out early the next morning. The PAVN were now aware of the arrival of the 3rd Battalion, 4th Marines, and started firing small arms, machine gun and mortar fire against the Marine Battalion. By 1900, Battalion Cammander, LTC Joseph Benkly radio that his Battalion was surrounded, and needed help. LTC

Joseph Muller Commander of the Company L 3rd Battalion, 9th Marines had us move out for the recuse. But 30 minutes later, artillery and air support were ordered; by the time Company L 3rd Battalion, 9th Marines arrived, the PAVN were retreating, and we were firing as the PAVN was running away. We did our first body count with no killed or wounded Marine; there was 42 PAVN killed.

At 09:50, CH-46s began dropping three Companies of 2nd Battalion, 4th Marines into Landing Zone Peregrine to support the advancing Marine Battalions. Once landed, 2nd Battalion, 4th Marines began moving west towards 3rd Battalion, 4th Marines, but marching was rough by high elephant grass and unjustly inflicting hardship and constraint heat and humidity. One sergeant from the 3rd Battalion, 4th Marines, was heard making this comment: "it is so damn hot I have sweat rolling off my balls. What I would not give for a nice cold glass of butter milk." The 2nd Battalion, 4th Marines were unable to move to assist the 3rd Battalion, 4th Marines, to help set up night positions. They receive orders to abandon their mission and move towards Hill 96 to set up and control the area around the hill. Then Company L 3rd Battalion, 9th Marines receives orders to proceed directly to join 3rd Battalion, 4th Marines, in the morning.

16 September-The PAVN launched mortars rounds right into the 3rd Battalion, 4th Marines, in the morning and kept them pinned down. Commander Rifle Platoon 2ndLt Harry Wilson radio in with coordinance for airstrikes and artillery. Company L 3rd Battalion, 9th Marines was given orders to help Company K 2nd Battalion, 4th Marines to get across the Song Ngan River. Company L, 3rd Battalion, 9th Marines, were able to advance without being pestered, and were left in peace as we advanced towards Company K 2nd Battalion, 4th Marines, to the north and northwest. When we arrived 1st Squad Rifle Team Leader Cpl Robert Dean Tomlin set up his rifle team on the right of Company K 2nd Battalion, 4th Marines. 2nd Squad Rifle Team Leader Cpl Frederick (Butch) Philip Price 2/4 Marines set up his rifle team on the left of Company K 2nd Battalion, 4th Marines. When we were in position, I gave the arm a signal to commence firing. With rifle, machine gun, and M79 rounds directly on the PAVN, they were dropping like flies. After a half hour of steady fire, the PAVN began to retreat and the Company K 2nd Battalion, 4th Marines made it across the Song Ngan River. Body count with no killed or wounded Marine, but 25 PAVN were killed. The 3rd Battalion, 4th Marines's position was engaged with the PAVN several times, calling in close air strikes, before linking up with the 2nd Battalion. 4th Marines, after crossing the river at 14:45. At 19:30 the PAVN again attacked Company K's 3rd Battalion, 4th Marines, after crossing the river and setting up a new position. The PAVN made three attacks that lasted over three and a half hours. The 3rd Battalion, 4th Marines and 2nd Battalion, 4th Marines suffered one dead, and over 40 wounded from grenades thrown by the PAVN at short range. The PAVN managed to dragged away some of their dead, but the Marines's body count was 79 PAVN killed the following morning. After everything had settled down, finally, Company L 3rd Battalion, 9th Marines got to get some rest and chow. Butch said: "Robert these frigging C-Rats are now fit for a pig to eat." Cpl Robert Dean Tomlin said: "shut up and hand me your peanut butter tin for my 4 pack of cigareetes." As Butch smoked and I ate the peanut

butter, we were happy for a few minutes. Then we got the word we were pulling out in the morning to protect the 2nd Battalion, 1st Marines, when they landed at Landing Zone Wren on 18 September.

Higher command decided to deploy 2nd Battalion, 1st Marines on a High Hill that over-looked the DMZ. This would keep the PAVN from coming through the back door with a surprise attack. They were landed into Landing Zone Wren 3 klicks northeast of Landing Zone Peregrine by 30 helicopters. Our mission was to protect the helicopters from PAVN fire as they landed. Company L, 3rd Battalion, 9th Marines, was in position before the helicopters started to land. Then Butch and I saw the damnest thing at 16:00 a platoon of Marines from the 1st Force Reconnaissance Company rappelled from an MAG-16 helicopter onto the High Hill and took position. A couple of hours later, we spotted a PAVN force to their east and 2ndLt Harry Wilson called in artillery fire from the 3rd Battalion, 12th Marines, killing 61 PAVN. Then later that night, Cpl Tomlin and Cpl Price spotted PAVN positions south of the high hill and again 2ndLt Harry Wilson called in further fire on suspected PAVN positions, killing 43 PAVN.

17 September Based on the sightings from the Marines's lookout point, near the landing zones. LTC Joseph Muller had the 2nd Battalion, 1st Marines, redeployed from Landing Zone Wren to the river valley near the High Hill by helicopters of MAG-16 on the morning of 18 September. Now, with all the helicopter landings, the code word was Helicopter Valley. There was contact with the PAVN, and Company L 3rd Battalion, 9th Marines, was called in so that the 3rd Battalion, 4th Marines could push south and to foresee and act in advance of further night attacks. They set up and established a common perimeter with the 2nd Battalion, 4th Marines .LTC Joseph Muller and LTC Joseph Benkly ordered the two Battalions to withdraw to the northeast the following day of 19 September. The 2nd Battalion, 4th Marines was to establish blocking positions below the DMZ, while the 3rd Battalion, 4th Marines would move to the south of the 2nd Battalion, 4th Marines, and then attack south and take the High Hill. On the morning of 20 September, 3rd Battalion, 5th Marines, would be inserted into a small valley 3 klicks south of the Song Ngan. Company L, 3rd Battalion, 9th Marines, was send in to stop the suspected PAVN's pre-positioned equipment storage site where arriving unit personnel, equipment, materiel, and accompanying supplies are reassembled, returned to the control of the PAVN commander, and prepared for onward movement. We were to blow up the PAVN area and prevent a possible escape route for the PAVN retreating from 3rd Battalion, 4th Marines advance on High Hill. Company L, 3rd Battalion, 9th Marines, Squads 1 and 2, blew up all the PAVN supplies, material, and supplies in place. Then we hid and waited for the PAVN to retreat while they tried to make their escape. It was not long when we heard gun fire in the distance from the 2nd Battalion, 4th Marines, and 3rd Battalion, 5th Marines, as they were raining fire upon the PAVN. Then one of our forward scouts signals the PAVN is coming. We waited until the PAVN were within 100 yards of our position. You should have seen the looks on their faces when we open up with rifle, machine gun, and M79 fire. One old sergeant from Alabama was heard making this comment: " those PAVN

bastards were dropping faster then a Blue Jay eating June Bugs on a hot August night in Alabama." The battle lasted for about an hour with no Marines killed and 7 wounded, but the PAVN had 238 killed.

At Landing Zone Peregrine, on the morning of 20 September 2nd Battalion, 4th Marines swept north towards their new positions; the Company L 3rd Battalion, 9th Marines followed, which we reached. Without incident by around 1300. At 14:00, the 3rd Battalion, 5th Marines began to move out; Company L 3rd Battalion, 9th Marines receive new orders to be rearguard to provide security for the Battalion Command Post and the engineers who were tasked with destroying captured ammunition and the one crashed CH-46s. No sooner when the PAVN's ammunition and CH-46 been destroyed at 1600, the PAVN began mortaring our position and then attacked with infantry. One corporal from the Company L 3rd Battalion, 9th Marines 3rd squad, was heard making this comment: " we just filled in these frigging fighting holes, now we have to dig them out again." Forward scout made an estimated 1,000 thousand PAVN coming right towards us for an attack. Company L 3rd Battalion, 9th Marines 1st, 2nd, 3rd and 4th squads took the brunt of the assault and the 4 squads were separated from Battalion Command Post and the engineers as small groups of PAVN moved between us. Battalion Command called in airstrikes with coordinates that were as close as 45 meters from the Company L of the 3rd Battalion, 9th Marines. LTC Joseph Benkly called for Company L to return to the Landing Zone and for 2nd Battalion, 4th Marines to provide support. By 17:00, Company L had arrived at the Landing Zone, and a Company from 2nd Battalion, 4th Marines occupied high ground overlooking the Landing Zone. First Platoon of Company K was able to withdraw but had to leave their dead behind. Platoon Sergeant GySgt Russell Owens assured Company K that Company L 3rd Battalion, 9th Marines we will guard and take care of your dead. By 19:00 2nd Battalion, 4th Marines and 3rd Battalion, 4th Marines had established a common perimeter 1.7 klicks northeast of Landing Zone Peregrine. The 3rd Battalion, 4th Marines had 14 dead and 49 wounded while the PAVN had 178 killed. One sergeant from the 2nd squad was heard making this comment: "somebody miss counted it more like 500 PAVN killed. Company L 3rd Battalion, 9th Marines stay until all the the dead Marines were picked up and taken away.

On 21 September some 3rd Battalion, 4th Marines, were pulled out for rest and the remainder of 3rd Battalion, 4th Marines, were assigned blocking positions, while 2nd Battalion, 4th Marines reorganised for the assault on High Hill. On the morning of 22 September, intense airstrikes were called in, while 2nd Battalion, 4th Marines attacked up High Hill, but found the heavily fortified position abandoned. A corporal from the 3rd squad was heard making this comment: "I ran my ass off to find the frigging PAVN had abanoned this position." The 3rd Battalion, 4th Marines, was pulled out and replaced by the 1st Battalion, 3rd Marines, on 23 September. Company L, 3rd Battalion, 9th Marines, were kept as rear guard in case the PAVN made a counterattack.

On 24 September 1st Battalion, 1st Marines joined 3rd Battalion, 5th Marines in the valley below the Song Ngan, and they met with a light fire fight from small groups of PAVN as they patrolled to the west. 2nd Battalion, 1st Marines, was ordered to deploy and establish blocking positions at the western end of the valley 4 klicks north of the High Hill. On the night of 24 September 2nd Battalion, 1st Marines came under fire across their entire front and with the help of Company L 3rd Battalion, 9th Marines responded with rifle, machine gun, M79, mortar, and artillery fire to break up the attack. The Marines had two dead, while the number of PAVN had 79 killed..

On 26 September a special request was made to Company L 3rd Battalion, 9th Marines, to have them returned to Landing Zone Peregrine to recover the Marines that were killed and left behind on 24 September. We found the bodies of all eight Marines were not interfered with, disturbed, or harmed, and still with their weapons and equipment. On 27 September the other companies of the 2nd Battalion, 1st Marines joined Company J and began patrolling through Landing Zone Valley. During these two days of the operation, Company L 3rd Battalion, 9th Marines, was assigned to search and destroy missions; on 28 September we were fired upon and the point man hit and killed by machine gun fire. At that point, Cpl David Henderson immediately moved forward through the heavy fire and carried the fallen Marine back. On 29 September Company L 3rd Battalion, 9th Marines 3rd Squad was engaged in a heavy fire fight and was pinned down by machine gun fire. 1st Squad Rifle Team Leader Cpl Robert Dean Tomlin and 2nd Squad Rifle Team Leader Cpl Frederick (Butch) Philip Price then advanced and while exposed to intense fire charged the enemy positions. Cpl Tomlin's 1st Squad on the right and Cpl Price's 2nd Squad on the left silenced one enemy position and were advancing towards the second and third PAVN positions. Cpl Tomlin gave the arm signal to the M79 grenade launcher to launch several rounds of anti-personnel rounds right into the PAVN's machine gun positions. With a few minutes the PAVN's machine guns were quiet, and the Marines advanced forward. They found 21 PAVN killed. They destroyed their weapons and equipment and moved on.

On 30 September Company H 3rd Battalion, 5th Marines was setting up a radio relay station on a hill about 7.5 klicks north of the High Hill. As the 2nd Platoon was advancing forward to put defense positions on the hillside, the PAVN opened fire from a concealed bunker. 2nd Platoon radio for help that they were pinned down and could not move. Company L; 3rd Battalion, 9th Marines; Cpl Tomlin's 1st Squad, and Cpl Price's 2nd Squad ran forward with machine guns to lay down a steady steam of fire to cover the retreat of the 2nd Platoon. When the 2nd Platoon was in the clear and retreated to the crest of the hill, when the 1st and 2nd Squads were ready to pull out, Cpl Tomlin, noticed the dead and wounded Marines were left behind. Cpl Tomlin said: "there is no way in hell I am leaving those Marines behind for those frigging PAVN just to cut them apart. As the PAVN moved forward to finish off any surviving Marines. The Marines were keeping the PAVN at bay, until PAVN started dropping mortar fire close and near Company L 3rd Battalion, 9th Marines 1st and 2nd Squads on the crest of the hill. After a hour of exploding mortar rounds, then Cpl Tomlin called in a Marine UH-1E Gunship to silenced them. It was a joyful sight as the UH-1E Gunship started to blow the PAVN to hell. Company L was having a hell of a time getting the wounded and dead Marines from the thick jungle canopy, which made it complicated for the evacuation of wounded. Engineers were called in to cut out an Landing Zone for the helicopters to evacuate the wounded. Company L 3rd Battalion, 9th Marines kept the PAVN at bay while the helicopters were picking up the wounded Marines. The PAVN made several assaults on Company L getting as close to within 5m near the Marines. One sergeant from the 4th Squad was were making comment: "I can hear the PAVN talking and breathing nearby. Let's get these Marines loaded and get the hell out of here." As Company L 3rd Battalion, 9th Marines lay down rifle, machine gun, and M79 fire, the PAVN had pulled out. The Marines suffered 8 dead and 12 wounded; 57 PAVN bodies were found and four prisoners taken. Marine prisoner interrogator told 2ndLt Harry Wilson with the help of chocolate bars and cigars, the PAVN prisoners revealed that the Marines had been attacked by the PAVN 6th Battalion, 812th Regiment. On 1 October, Marine upper brass met at Dong Ha and decided to withdraw the Marine Force due to the difficult terrain for maneuvrers and the lack of Landing Zones for helicopter assaults and have them move south.

On 2 October 1st Battalion, 1st Marines moved south to Cam Lo. 3rd Battalion, 5th Marines continued to sweep to the west and operate north of the High Hill On 3 October 2nd Battalion, 1st Marines moved east towards the High Hill. In Landing Zone Valley, 2nd Battalion, 4th Marines was replaced by 2nd Battalion, 9th Marines on 4 October and on 5 October 1st Battalion, 3rdMarines and 2nd Battalion, 9th Marines and marched south out of the valley. With the withdrawal of the battalions, Company L 3rd Battalion, 9th Marines were still on Reconnaissance patrols and continued to operate in the Operation Green Hell area. On 6 October while on recon patrol Company L 3rd Battalion, 9th Marines spotted 550 to 950 PAVN 5 klicks southwest of High Hill. 2ndLt Harry Wilson called in artillery strikes killing at least 500 PAVN. After the report of this mission Octopuss Patrol was given the name of the recon patrols because you never knew which of the eight arms was going to find the PAVN.

While Operation Green Hell officially ended on 7 October, the action on 7 October was the last major action of the operation, and it appeared that the PAVN 324B Division had crossed back over the DMZ or distributed and spread over a wide area into the jungle to the west. Ssgt Harvey Powell was heard making this comment: " we fought those frigging bastards to the bitter end, they were well-equipped, and aggressive to the point of obsessive enthusiasm. The stupid son-of-a-bitches attacked in massed formations of thousands with no second thought of dieing." Cpl Tomlin said: "Butch will this Green Hell ever end, or do they carry us out in a body bag." Cpl Price replied with: "Robert it looks like we are in for the long haul brother."

Operation Green Hell Casualties
Date September – October 1966
Location Vietamese Demilitarized Zone
Result U.S. Clain victory
Belligerents

United States	North Vietnam North Vietnam

Commanders and leaders

Strength

Units involved

1st Battalion 1stMarines	6th Battalion, 812th Regiment
1stBattalion 3rd Marines	324B Division
2nd Battalion 3rd Marines	
2nd Battalion 4th Marines	
3rd Battalion 3rd Marines	
3rd Battalion 5th Marines	
2nd Battalion, 9th Marines	
3rd Battalion, 9th Marines	

Casualties and losses

United States 78 killed	US body count 1,844 killed
124 wounded	4 captured

CHAPTER NINE

Vietnam War

Operation Tomahawk Base

The Operation Tomahawk Base was fought from January - March 1967 it was to prevent North Vietnamese PAVN from capturing and forcing the surrender of the US Marine Corps base at Camp Rotan.

Key United States Commanders	Key North Vietnam Commanders
LTC Joseph Muller USMC	Colonel Pham Chi PAVN
1stSg Roger L. Lewis USMC	
GySgt Russell Owens USMC	
Ssgt Henry Watson USMC	
Ssgt William Houser USMC	
Cpl Robert Dean Tomlin USMC	
Cpl Frederick (Butch) Philip Price USMC	

Tomahawk Base was intended to be used as a base for backup in cast Canp Rotan Operation Base was attacked. The Tomahawk Base was to prevent infiltration of South Vietnam by PAVN forces from North Vietnam and Laos. The main purpose of the Tomahawk Base is to prevent People's Army of Vietnam (PAVN) infiltration across the DMZ (Vietnamese Demilitarized Zone.) The firebase relates to the gaining of a military advantage because it offered not controlled and restricted views for 9.5 miles east to the coast and north into North Vietnam. It was also very open to attack and damage because it was within range of PAVN artillery north of the DMZ, which was largely from the enemy's indirect fire elements of guns, rocket launchers, artillery and mortars. Then all hell broke loose and the People's Army of Vietnam launched a direct attack on the Marine Base at Tomahawk Base. PAVN started their major shelling of Tomahawk Base , firing 200 artillery and mortar rounds directly at the fire base. As more and more artillery and mortar rounds hit the base. The marines went into action of returning a military attack and counterattack. Tomahawk Basre called in Artillery and Air strikes. Marine artillery fired numerous rounds. US Navy ships fired thousand rounds, and Marine and US Air Force made short, quick attacks and bombed NVA positions. They used Dumb bombs (are unguided bombs), smart bombs (is a guided munition intended to precisely hit a specific target), and Fuel Air Explosives (is a type of explosive that uses oxygen from the surrounding air to generate a high-temperature explosion). Fierce fighting continued through 1968, as Tomahawk went on the defensive.

We were standing in the chow line when the first round of PAVN mortar rounds hit near our camp. Every body scattered for cover, those damn motars were hitting real close to Camp Rotan. Then all of sudden we hear this booming voice: "Tomlin and Price grab your weapons and gear and get your squads and meet me by the back gate." Butch and I were yelling Lima Company, 1st and 2nd Squads get your weapons and gear and fall into formation. Ssgt Henry Watson and Ssgt William Houser, our squad leaders gave the command double time as they were running to the back gate. They gave the command to halt and stand at ease. Then 1stSg Roger L. Lewis said: " there are four PAVN mortar squads on the upper hill side trying to zero on our Hospital Tent and Mess Hall. They are using the M2 Mortars and they can be more then 200 yards away and they are well hidden. We need to locate, close in and destroy that mortar fire with M79 rounds. We need to maneuver and repel the PAVN's assault using two Rifle Squads by using close combat technics. I want Lima Company, 1st and 2nd Squads to blow them little bastards to hell and gone. Ssgt Henry Watson with 1st squad will go to the right of that knob on top of the hill side and destroy PAVN's mortars 1 and 2. Ssgt William Houser with the 2nd squad will go to the left of that knob on top of the hill side and destroy PAVN's mortars 3 and 4. Once you are in position, hit them son-of-bitches with everything you can throw at them. Have your M79s knock out the mortars, and your rifle squads and machine gun to give them cover. Both squads 1 and 2 stay in position to see if they can put in other mortar squads, then knock them out too." Ssgt Henry Watson told Tomlin of the 1st squad to get his M79 grenade launcher in 375 yards from the mortars and start firing anti-personnel rounds to destroy them. Then lay in flechette rounds, which are (pointed steel projectiles with a vaned tail for stable flight) all around that whole area in 360 degrees. Ssgt William Houser told Price of the 2nd squad to get his M79 grenade launcher in 375 yards from the mortars and start firing anti-personnel rounds to destroy them. Then lay in flechette rounds (pointed steel projectile with a vaned tail for stable flight) all around that whole area in 360 degrees. Then, both squad leaders said: "make damn sure your rifle squads and machine gun gives M79 full cover, while he is laying down his rounds. We have to knock out those PAVN's mortar at all cost.

Ssgt Henry Watson said: " Tomlin once you locate the PAVN's mortars, take yur M79 launcher, with one automatic rifle, (M60 machine Gun) and your rifle squad and set up your position. When you are in position radio silence use hand and arm signals to notific me." I said: "Yes Ssgt Watson." Then I told my squad to move out. Ssgt William Houser told Butch the same thing. As our squads moved outside the fence area, I went to the right and Butch went to the left. Then a corporal spotted PAVN's mortars 1 and 2. using hands and arms signals, he gave the enemy in sight, range and direction. Then we started our low crawl up the hill side to make a low profile target for the enemy. I got my squad up about 1 klicks then I spotted this small clearing that had cover on three sides. I did the arm signal to decrease speed, then the arm signal to have the M79 launcher change direction to the right, and the machine gun to the left. I gave the signal enemy in sight; then I held my rifle horizontally with the stock in my shoulder, the muzzle pointing in the direction of the enemy. I held up 3 fingers to tell the M79 launcher the range of the enemy was 300 meters. I held up two fingers to tell the automatic rifle the enemy was 200 meters. I raise my hand to tell the rifle squad to assemble around me. I told the rifle squad to protect and cover the M79 launcher, and machine gun. When every Marine was in position, I gave the arm signal to commence firing. Then all hell broke loose; we all had clear shots on the two mortars on the right. The M79 launcher started lobbing in anti-personnel rounds right on top of the PAVN mortars. Both mortars squads were getting blown to pieces. Then the PAVN soldiers started coming out of the wood works, and firing rounds everywhere. Bullets were whizzing and buzzing all around us; you would have thought we had broken open a hornet's nest. The machine gun and rifle squads started firing at a moderate speed. As more PAVN soldiers were coming forward, I gave the signal to fire faster and the machine gun to change to the next higher rate of fire. By us changing the rate of fire, those PAVN soldiers were dropping like flies getting hit with a fly swatter. Butch was doing the same thing on the left side. Some of the PAVN soldiers were caught in cross-fire and were being shreaded to pieces. You could hear their commander yelling retreat (rút lui) **(1-43)** in their Vietnamese language. I raise my hand to signal a cease-fire. But then I caught a group of PAVN soldiers seeking up on Butch's far left side; they were low crawling in dense bush. I directed the M70 launcher to place some M79 rounds right on top of them. I gave the arm signal to Butch to dismount, down and take cover. If somebody saw me, they would have thought I was trying to fly the way I was flapping my arms with my palms down. The M79 launcher fired about 3 or 4 rounds and the PAVN went screaming and running the other way. I could see Butch giving me the thumbs up and we all went back to our base camp.

1stSg Roger L. Lewis met us at the back gate and said: "Marines job well done" Then he said: I will personnaly see that you have steak and beer for dinner." I looked at Butch and he had the biggest grin on his face, just like a possum eating shit. We went back to our tent to clean up before chow. When we got to the mess tent, there was a special table sat up just for us. That was the biggest steak I ever saw. The mess sergeant said: " I was ordered to give you two beers, but since you save my mess tent I going to give you three beers. When Butch heard 3 beers he was as happy as Bluejay eating June bugs on a hot August afternoon. We ate our steak and drink our beer and headed back to our tent. I wrote letters home to Dad, Mom, Gene, Jimmy, and Connie. I told them the difficult situations we were in and how sneaking and cruel the PAVN soldiers were. I also wrote to Gene and Jimmy about the good old times we had as teenagers and about the time we were walking to the Stand Theater to see Kirk Douglas in Ulysses. We were walking down the sidewalk when I spotted a 20 dollar bill on the side walk and there was a man and women walking towards us about 100 feet in front od us. I was real cool, I walked by the money and then a loud voice I said: "oh, I dropped my money", and walked back and picked up the 20 dollar bill. We hit the gold mine that day; we had money to burn. We went to Colony Burgers, a restaurant near the Stand Theater; we had 2 hamburgers with french fries and cokes a piece. We paid our way into the theater, got popcorn, soda, and candy bars, and still had 15 dollars left. We each got 5 dollars apiece and walked home very happy. In Connie's letters, since she was only 11 years old, I did not write about how cruel the war was. I just wrote in general about the people, country, food, weather, and how she was doing in school.

Then one night, for no unknown reason, I woke up thinking about Kathy, Lucille, and Mieko and how nice it would be to see them again; then reality sunk in when the PAVN's artillery shells started exploding all over our camp. Every Marine jumped to his feet, grabbed their weapons, and we were combat ready to fight. Our platoon sergeants previously had got over the plans for our positions if we were ever under attack by the PAVN. I was to take my squad and cover the North side of the camp. Butch was to take his squad and cover the South side of the camp. As I was getting my men in position I could hear Butch's squad laying down round after round of rifle and machine fire. A group of PAVNs of about 20 or 30 men was moving forward with the RPG-2 "hand-held antitank grenade launcher") is a man-portable, shoulder-fired anti-tank weapon that was designed in the Soviet Union. They were going to blow up the South side of the camp and come through. Butch and his 2nd squad had a different idea; they were laying down all kinds of fire power. After about 20 or so PAVNs were killed, the rest retreated. Then all of a sudden 20 or 30 PAVNs were charging the North side with RPG-2s. We had set up markers that had different ranges in yards marked on them. When the PAVNs were in the 200 yards range, I gave the command to commence firing. The rifle and machine guns were laying down a line of fire that a mosquito could not fly through. Those damn PAVNs were screaming and yelling as our bullets just ripped through their flesh and PAVNs body parts were flying everywhere and hitting the ground. One corporal from the 1st Battalion 9th Marines, was heard making this comment: "that poor bastard PAVN is still sceaming with his intestents hanging out and he his still alive." The corporal put a bullet between his eyes to put him out of his misery. The rest of the PAVNs only moved about 40 or 50 feet when their leader started yelling to retreat. Butch and I sent out a clean up crew to make sure they were dead. We heard a few shots, so a couple must have been alive. Base commander LTC Richard John Schening said: " Marines job well done, go back to your quarters and get some rest." The rest of the night was really quiet; as soon as my head hit the pillow I was asleep. For the next few weeks it was the same old thing over and over shells and mortars exploding all around us, driving us crazy with lack of sleep, was starting to take a toll on some Marines. They were walking around like zombies with dark spots under their eyes, and they became irritable real easy.

1stSg Roger L. Lewis set up night patrols to keep the PAVN's mortars and RPG-2's at a safe striking distance. We could not do anything about the artillery because they were too far in enemy territory, and it would not be worth getting a bunch of Marines killed trying to knock out the PAVN's guns. We just called in air strikes to take care of the PAVN's artillery. Since the M2 mortars had a range of a mile or so, 1stSg Roger L. Lewis had patrols going out about one to 1 ½ miles from base camp to knock out the PAVN's mortars. One night it was my squad's turn to go on mortar patrol; we no sooner were out of the main gate when the mortar explosions started. I gave the hand and arm signal by carrying my hand to my shoulder, fist closed; then I rapidly thrust the fist upward vertically to the full extent of my arm and back to the shoulder several times. This was the signal for my squad to increase gait and speed in the direction of the mortar fire. We were quick double time in the direction of the mortar fire when we were hit by an ambush. Those damn PAVNs set us up to be killed. As the bullets were whizzing by us, I was thinking fast to get my men to cover. I did a hand and arm signal make a quick right, and dismounted, down, and took cover. We got behind this clump of trees and started laying down a barrage of rifle and machine gun fire. Corporal John Hillberg from the 1st Battalion 9th Marines, in his spare time made a special shotgun that was essentially a volley gun with eight single-shot barrels. He made each chambered to fit a 20-gauge 3-inch magnum shell which held about 8 double aught buck shot. He had arranged the barrels in an octagonal fashion around the central axis. He could fire eight individual times like a semi-automatic weapon or all eight barrels at one time. The action ran on a revolver-like rotating striker mechanism. Then you flip a lever and it had a striker mechanism that fired all eight barrels at one time. He made a detachable buttstock and a pistol grip with a double-action trigger to fire single shots, and had a separate foregrip up front for instinctive shooting.

Corporal John Hillberg was standing in front of a large Teak tree when the PAVN, with about 40 men made a full charge. He put the butt of the shotgun against a tree and fired that eight-barrel shot gun all at one time. Even today Butch and I still can not believe what we witnessed that day when the shotgun went off. Those 40 or so PAVN's were just cut to pieces, as their body parts went flying off everywhere in the air. We can still hear their screams as their blood and guts scattered everywhere.

Then the commander of the PAVNs yelled retreat. As we were walking back to camp, I told Corporal John Hillberg that he should make that special shotgun for all squads. I would be asking my Platoon sergeant permission to talk to the 1st Sergeant, then the base commander, about you making that special shotgun for each squad. I told Corporal John Hillberg that special shotgun that you made just saved our asses. He turn to me and said. "Corporal Tomlin I also save my own ass." Then I ask him: "how did you come up with the idea a eight barrel shot gun?" He said: " every time I went rabbit or bird hunting when you had the perfit shot your shotgun was empty. So I thought if I had a shotgun with muli-barrels then I would never miss out on a perfit shot for rabbits or birds. But while I am here in Vietnam the shotgun is perfit in killing the enemy without reloading."

The next day I asked my 1st Squad Leader Ssgt Henry Watson permission to speak to Platoon Sergeant GySgt Russell Owens about the special shotgun. Permission was granted then I asked Platoon Sergeant GySgt Russell Owens permission to speak to Company 1stSg Roger L. Lewis about the shotgun. Permission was granted then I asked 1stSg Roger L. Lewis permission to talk to Base Commander LTC Joseph Muller. The 1st Sergeant said permission was granted and that he would make the arrangements for the meeting. The 1st Sergeant came back in about half an hour, and said: Tomlin, you can see the colonel now." I said: "Thank you First Sergeant" I went to the colonel's office and knocked on his door. He said: "enter." I opened the door and walked in. I stood at attention, rendered a salute and said: " permission to speak SIR." LTC Joseph Muller said: "stand at ease Marine and what do you need to talk to me about." I said: " SIR there is a Cpl John Hillberg who make a special 8 barrel shotgun that save a lot of Marine's lives in the other night patrol when we were confronted with a PAVN charge." The colonel looked up with a surprise look and said: " a eight barrel shotgun." I said: "yes SIR a special shotgun that he made I asking your permission to have him make the shotgun for every rifle squad." The colonel said: "let me talk to the First Sergeant about material cost and how much time involve and I will get back to you." I stood at attention, rendering a salute, and said: "Thank You SIR" He saluted back and said: "dimissed." I did a bout face and walked out of his office. A couple of days later the 1stSg Roger L. Lewis told me, Tomlin the colonel was not going to approve the shotgun build. He said: "it is too expensive and time consuming and he needs Cpl John Hillberg on patrol." I said: "Thank You First Sergeant." Then 1stSg Roger L. Lewis said: " Cpl Tomlin it was a great idea its just to bad the shotgun did not go through." I walked back to our tent and told Butch what had happened with the shotgun build. Butch said: "Robert I was hoping we could have that shotgun in our squads so we could blow the hell out of them PAVN bastards."

Then one night while we were in the Mess Tent them, damn PAVN's shells were exploding all over again. Every body was getting their last bite and running for cover. Butch and I just made it to the bunker when a shell exploded right in front of us. Butch looked at me and said: " Robert if I took another bite of food I would have got my ass blow off." I said: "Butch we got to get the fuck out of this place we are getting shell and mortar every day." For the next couple of weeks the 1st and 2nd squads were going out on night patrols located and destroying the PAVN's mortar units and patrols. One night while on patrol we spotted about 50 or so PAVNs setting up their mortar squads. This time they were only about ¾ of a mile from our camp. I gave the arm a signal of attention, then signaled to make the shift to the right and left. Then I gave the arm a signal forward, and advanced to the right and left. Once all the men were in position, I gave the arm signal to commence firing. Rifles and machine guns were laying down a steady stream of fire. Then the M79 launcher was popping round after round on top of the PAVN. They did not know which way to run. They were getting hit from all sides with no place to go. When the smoke had cleared we had a body count of 28 dead PAVN and 4 M2 mortars destroyed. We could stop and destroy the PAVN's mortars and patrols, but an infantry combat unit; we could not go on patrol to put down the PAVN's artillery. Then one day in May of 1967 1stSg Roger L. Lewis call our unit together and said: " 3rd Battalion, 9th Marines is leaving Camp Rotan to be assign to to take Hill 880 back from the PAVN. Five US Marine forward observers from Hill 860 when to Hill 880 were checking on PAVN strengths, for Russia and China weapons, and equipmen on Hill 880. They saw 10 times as many foxholes and bunkers than 860. Then there radio sllence and could not be contacted because they were ambushed on a hill side, four of whom were killed by gunfire. One Marine managed to low crawl and got away and told what he had observed.

This will be a search and destroy operation in the area around Camp Rotan. Quang Tri Province. Hill 880 will be the first authorized invasion and attack and you will be entering a place and area that is controlled by the PAVN of the Vietnamese Demilitarized Zone (DMZ)." Then he said: " Tomlin and Price step forward." Butch and I stepped forward to the First Sergeant and stood at attention. 1stSg Roger L. Lewis said: " Tomlin and Price you will be promoted to E-5 Sergeants and will be squad leaders of the rifle team when the paper work comes through." Then he said: " in low voice see me after formation." He called out at attention, then dismissed. After formation Butch and I walked over to see the First Sergeant. He shook our hands and said: "congratulations" Then he said " In all my years in the United States Marine Corp I have never see anybody get rank so damn fast. But both of you earned and deserve it, I see the way you handle and take of your men in combat and off duty. I am for sure that your Fathers and Mothers are very proud of you." Then said: " with all that said and none Operation Hickory will be a lot close combat fighting and those damn PAVNs of 324B Division they are tricky and outstanding fighters. Take care of your men and each other and God's Speed we get this war over quick." We are not to salute an NCO (Non- Commissioned Officer) Butch and I stood at attention and said: " 1stSg Roger L. Lewis we are not to salute you, but Price and I as Marines are going to salute you as an outstanding Marine. Butch and I stood at attention render a salute and said: " Thank You First Sergeant." The First Sergeant stood at attention, rendered the salute back, and said: " at ease and you both are dismissed." Butch and I did about face and walked back to our tent with our new sergeant strips to be sewn on when the paper work came through, we packed our gear to get ready to move out.

Operation Tomahawk Base Casualties

Date January -- March 1967
Location Vietamese Demilitarized Zone
Result U.S. Clain victory
Belligerents

United States South Vietnam	North Vietnam North Vietnam

Commanders and leaders
Strength

Units involved

2nd Battalion 3rd Marines	6 NVA battalions
3rd Battalion 3rd Marines	325C Division
3rd Battalion, 9th Marines	

Casualties and losses

United States 1,100 killed	US body count 5,863 killed 119 captured

CHAPTER TEN

Vietnam War

Operation Prairie Dog

The Operation Prairie Dog was a battle during the Vietnam War between the People's Army of Vietnam and United States Marines. Fighting took place on a hill mass with a collection of ridges and saddles, that rose to different elevations from April -- May 1967.

Key United States Commanders	Key North Vietnam Commanders
LTC Joseph Muller USMC	Colonel Tra Dinch PAVN
1stSg Roger L. Lewis USMC	
GySgt Russell Owens USMC	
Ssgt Henry Watson USMC	
Ssgt William Houser USMC	
Cpl Robert Dean Tomlin USMC	
Cpl Frederick (Butch) Philip Price USMC	

It was an on going battle for the Marines to control the hills by Tomahawk Base. 10 April the Marine forces advanced against Prairie Dog Hill South to cover, by the PAVN. As they found later, there were more than 20 times as many foxholes and bunkers than most of the hills around Tomahawk Base. A forward Marine scout on patrol makes the discovery of the entrenched bunkers on Prairie Dog Hill. When he reported what he had found to his Platoon Sergeant, the report went to the First Sergeant and the Base Commander. LTC Joseph Muller told Company L 3rd Battalion, 9th Marines get ready to move out after the Airstrikes were completes. LTC Joseph Muller called in an airstrike to bomb the hell out of Prairie Dog Hill before Company L 3rd Battalion, 9th Marines made an advance to the hill. Since Prairie Dog Hill had so many different elevations, a Marine observer was in radio contact with the Marine pilots telling them when to use 500-pound Mk-82 Snakeye bombs. The Mark 82 was designed as a low level bomb with pop-out fins, that deploy when dropped from the aircraft. These fins will increase the drag on the bomb, slowing it down, allowing the aircraft to escape the area before detonation. The Marine observer told the pilots if they did fly too low when they dropped the Mk-Snakeye bombs, they would not have to worry about exploding shrapnel hitting their planes. The Mark-15 Tail Retarding Device, nicknamed Snakeye, solves this problem. Upon release from the aircraft, the bomb's four folded fins quickly spring into a cruciform (cross) shape that slows the weapon down. This allows time for the aircraft to pass safely over the target before the bomb explodes. After a constant day and night bombardment, Marine forces of 2nd Battalion 3rd Marines, 3rd Battalion 3rd Marines, and 3rd Battalion, 9th Marines managed to take Prairie Dog Hill. It was a hell of a battle which was one of the closest hill masses to Tomahawk Base. When we finally dug into the hill we found over 400 foxholes and 25 bunkers. The bunkers were fortified with 6 ft of earth and logs. Cpl Tomlin told Cpl Price no wonder the Marine A-6 Intruders were having problems not capable of damage to the PAVN bunkers with thier 250- pound bombs. That Mk-82 Snakeeye 500-pound bomb did the trick. I bet you the damn old PAVN crapped their pants when that baby went off. Then Cpl Price said: " those frigging PAVN was dug in like Prairie Dogs."

When Company L 3rd Battalion, 9th Marines were doing mop-ups on Prairie Dog Hill, some of the hill had insufficiently been bombarded. Marine infantry of the 3rd Battalion, 9th Marines found the going even harder than the previous first part of the hill. Squad 1 and 2 were moving up this ridge to get into position to take and destroy the active bunkers. When two bunkers right in front of us open up with machine gun fire. I said: " Butch I through that last bomb run fron the A-6 Intruders had cleared this hill side." Butch and I gave the command to our squads to take cover and dig in. As soon as we were in position and dug in we returned to rifle, machine gun, and M79 fire. After taking fire from the bunkers we were pinned down and could not move. I told Cpl Herman Watson to put a couple of M79 rounds in the openings of the bunkers.

Cpl Herman Watson's father-law was a tool and die maker for a machine shop. So one day Cpl Watson sent him the sights from a M79 launcher, which was a blade and leaf type that folded. He drew up plans for how he wanted the new site to be made by his father-law. In about 3 weeks or so the new sights arrived; he installed the new sight and made a few practice shots to get everything so he could zero in. To fire a weapon the best way is a straight line shot, but with a M79 launcher you have to fire in a high arch and very difficult to hit your target. Cpl Watson's new site also folded into two different directions, which were up and down and side by side. When he pulled up the site, it gave him the distance in yards. The side by side gave him 90 degrees to the left and 90 degrees to the right. For a full view when both sides were unfolded, he had a 180 degree view. A M79 round has a killing radius of 15 meters. Cpl. Watson could put the round within one foot of the target. He called his M79 "Old Reliable" for the simple reason she never missed her target.

He said: "Cpl Tomlin if I could get a sniper with a scope to zero for me I think I can do it. I yelled at Butch and said: "have your rifleman with his scope low crawl to my position and we will cover him." As soon as Cpl David Henderson started low crawling to my position. I gave the command: "to commence firing." Cpl Henderson got to my position without a scatch. I told him to zero in on the openings of the two bunkers and give the coordinates to Cpl Watson. Cpl Henderson took his scope, made some adjustments and zeroed in on the opening of the bunkers. He said: "first bunkers is 380 yards with opening 45 degress to the left and right. The second bunkers is 365 yards with openings 45 degrees to the right and left. Cpl Henderson said: "Cpl Tomlin I can get in position to cover Cpl Watson when he is ready to fire." I told Cpl Watson to fire 6 rounds each from his M79 directly right at the coordinates given. Cpl Henderson had his sniper rifle fix on both bunkers as Cpl Watson lopped 6 rounds each at the bunkers. Butch and I, to our surprise, at least two rounds of M79 got inside the two bunkers. Then all of sudden both bunkers went quiet with out any machine gun fire. The men started to get up and rush to the bunkers. I told the men to stay put it could be a trick. I asked for two volunteers to low crawl and check out the bunkers. Two Marines from my squad low-crawled to the bunkers. When they arrive both gave the hand signal forward, and advance. I looked at Butch and said: " I'll be damn I did not think the M79 rounds would work."

After the Marines had suffered heavy losses on Prairie Dog Hill, a new commander ordered the Marine aircraft to break with tradition and not use 250, and 500- pound bombs. Instead, start using 750, 1000 and 2000-pound bombs on the hills for next heavily-entrenched PAVN forces. Now, with the Hill properly bombarded, Marine forces managed to take Prairie Dog Hill in a couple of days. After beating off a fierce PAVN counterattack on Hills around Tomahawk Base, the Marines could finally claim victory in one of the fierce battles near the DMZ.. We radio back to headquarters that Prairie Dog Hill was taken and securitized. We got a radio message that 2nd Battalion 3rd Marines and 3rd Battalion 3rd Marines, would take over and relieve us, and for the 3rd Battalion, 9th Marines to return back to base camp. I told Butch this frigging hill cost a lot of good Marines.

This will be a search and destroy operation in the area around Tomahawk Base, Quang Tri Province. Prairie Dog Hill will be the first authorized invasion and attack and you will be entering a place and area that is controlled by the PAVN of the Vietnamese Demilitarized Zone (DMZ)." Then he said: "Tomlin and Price step forward." Butch and I stepped forward to the First Sergeant and stood at attention. 1stSg Roger L. Lewis said: " Tomlin and Price have been promoted to E-5 Sergeants and will be squad leaders of the rifle team." Then he said: " in low voice see me after formation." He called out at attention, then dismissed. After the formation Butch and I walked over to see the First Sergeant. He shook our hands and said: "congratulations" Then he said " In all my years in the United States Marine Corp I have never see anybody get rank so damn fast. But both of you earned and deserve it, I see the way you handle and take of your men in combat and off duty. I am for sure that your Fathers and Mothers are very proud of you." Then said: " with all that said and none Operation Purple Smoke will be a lot of close combat fighting and those damn PAVNs of 324B Division they are tricky and outstanding fighters. Take care of your men and each other and God's Speed we get this war over quick." We are not to salute an NCO (Non-Commissioned Officer) Butch and I stood at attention and said: " 1stSg Roger L. Lewis we are not to salute you, but Price and I as Marines are going to salute you as an outstanding Marine.

Butch and I stood at attention render a salute and said: " Thank You First Sergeant." The First Sergeant stood at attention, rendered the salute back, and said: " at ease and you both are dismissed." Butch and I did about face and walked back to our tent to sew on our new sergeant strips and pack our gear to get ready to move out.

Operation Prairie Dog Casualties

Date April – May 1967

Location

Near Camp Rotan, South Vietnam

Result American victory

Belligerents

United States	North Vietnam North Vietnam

Commanders and leaders

Strength

Units involved

2nd Battalion 3rd Marines	6 PAVN battalions
3rd Battalion 3rd Marines	325C Division
3rd Battalion, 9th Marines	

Casualties and losses

United States 135 killed 455 wounded	US body count 1,048 killed 752 missing or wounded

CHAPTER ELEVEN

Vietnam War

Operation Purple Smoke

The Battle of Operation Purple Smoke was fought from 20 May to 30 May 1967 to prevent PAVN 324B Division from blocking the 3rd Battalion, 4th Marines from landing helicopters on the Bến Hải River

Key United States Commanders	Key North Vietnam Commanders
LTC Joseph Muller USMC	LTG Duong Ly Khan PAVN
1stSg Roger L. Lewis USMC	
GySgt Russell Owens USMC	
Ssgt Henry Watson USMC	
Ssgt William Houser USMC	
Sgt Robert Dean Tomlin USMC	
Sgt Frederick (Butch) Philip Price USMC	

On the morning of 20 May, the 3rd Battalion, 9th Marines, was ordered to advanced north from Tomahawk Base to prevent any PAVN forces from blocking the 3rd Battalion, 4th Marines, from landing their helicopters on the Bến Hải River. 1stSg Roger L. Lewis gave direct orders to Lima Company Squad 1 and 2 to advance forward and set up a perimeter around the area where the Marine helicopters were going to land. As we were moving forward our point man stopped and started giving arm and hand signals with the enemy in sight, halt, and ambush ahead. So Butch and I low-crawled up to thepoint man to observe. Right in front of us were two PAVN 324B Battalions in two bunkers and a very long trench. Butch whispered in a very low voice and said: "Robert there has to be 700 hundred to 1000 thousand PAVNs. We had a small company with about 200 hundred men. I told a Private to run a message back to LTC Joseph Muller that we need help and send reinforcements. The company spit into two groups, half with Ssgt Henry Watson in charge to the right. The other half with Ssgt William Houser in charge to the left. We were just staying in position until the reinforcements arrived. We did not have to wait too long when 2nd Battalion, 9th Marines and 2nd Battalion, 26th Marines wer spotted moving forward. I gave the hand and arm signals to change direction for the 2nd Battalion, 9th Marines go right and the 2nd Battalion, 26th Marines go left. When all the units were in position the signal was given commence firing. We try to knock out the bunkers cause our M79 could not penatate the reinforced concrete. We know the regular army of North

Vietnam did not build those bunkers, it was the damn Russians. We fought a military battle that was is a combat between two forces at a fixed location until nightfall. Our 3rd Battalion, 9th Marines lost 1 Marine, the 2nd Battalion, 9th Marines lost 1 Marine and 2nd Battalion, 26th Marines lost 3 Marines with a total of 5 Marines were killed and 142 Marines were wounded. The body count of the PAVN was 81 were killed, and there no estimate of the PAVN that were wounded. After there was a cease fire we finally got a break to rest and eat. I can tell you those C-Rats nevr tasted so good. Smoking lamp was out so I just chew on my cigar.

That night, LTC Joseph Muller called in airstrikes to knock out the bunkers. We got the bad news that radar-controlled airstrikes were called off on the bunkers because the Marines were dug in to close to the bunkers. GySgt Russell Owens said: " that all we need is friendly fire on our Marines." Then, on 21 May, the wrong coordinates were given to artillery to knock out the bunkers; short rounds were fired (an artillery round which falls short of its target) and killing 3 Marines. The 2nd Battalion, the 26th Marines, were so pissed they proceeded to attack the bunker complex on foot. To our surprise the 2nd Battalion, 26th Marines overran the bunker and killed 34 PAVN. Then, as the 3rd Battalion, 9th Marines was moving forward, my squad and Butch's squad met heavy automatic weapons and mortar fire. I called for the radio operator and called for a M48 tank to be moved in. I got hold of the tank commander and gave him the coordinates of where the PAVN machine guns and mortars were located. The tank commander radioed me back and said: " I'll have two more M48s to follow me in." As the M48 got into position and had the PAVN machine guns and mortars in sight, they commence firing 90mm rounds of canisters right on top of the PAVN. Those canisters filled with steel flechettes just cut those PAVN to pieces. The other two M48s tanks were later knocked out by RPG-2 fire from those sneaking PAVN bastards. The 2nd Battalion, 9th Marines were helping the M48 tanks when they suffered 7 Marines killed and 12 Marines wounded.

On 22 May, the 3rd Battalion, 9th Marines Lima Company, was given orders to cover the left flank of the 3rd Battalion, 4th Marines operation to knock out a PAVN bunker complex. We had to knock out the bunker so that the 1st Battalion, 9th Marines and 1st Battalion, 12th Marines could move forward. We had a battle on our hands, that bunker was covering everything in 180 degree direction. We fought and only moved in a few feet trying to knock out that bunker. The fighting lasted into 21 May, losing 26 Marines killed and 59 Marines wounded and claiming the body count of 72 PAVN dead. The Marines Special Landing Force 2nd Battalion, 3rd got into action on 20 May by landing helicopters of Marines northwest of Firebase Gio Linh. They swept the area north to the DMZ, meeting minimal resistance but helping in fighting to knock out the PAVN bunkers and getting the Pavn supplies.

On 25 May, H Company of the 2nd Battalion, 26th Marines, on a route mission engaged a large PAVN Company at the base of Hill 119, 5 Klicks west of Tomahawk Base H Company joined by L Company of the 3rd Battalion, 9th Marines and 3rd

Battalion, 4th Marines. Sgt Tomlin and Sgt Price's 1st and 2nd Squads made repeated charges up the hill against the PAVN, but kept getting push back with heavy machine gun and rifle fire. Sgt Tonlin and Sgt Price told their M79 launchers to lope some smoke rounds in to give the 1st and 2nd Squads cover as they ran up Hill for the fourth time. Then Sgt. Tomlin told the M79 launchers once the squads were in position, just lobbing explosives 360 degrees all around the top of Hill where the PAVN machine guns and PAVN infantry were. When Sgt Tomlin 1st Squad and Sgt Price 2nd Squad were in position, Sgt Tomlin gave the arm signal to M79 launchers to commence firing. Heavy fighting lasted throughout the day and cost 14 Marines and 1 corpsman killed and 92 Marines wounded. The body count for the PAVN was 93 killed and numerous PAVN wounded. The PAVN still had control of Hill. Commander of the 1st Battalion, 9th Marines called in a Marine air strike and had Marine artillery pounded the top of the hill throughout the night. But PAVN machine gun firing from Hill brought down a UH-1E helicopter and injures a Marine commander. So the new assault was planned for the morning of 26 May, was postponed. On the 27th May when E and F Companies, 2nd Battalion, 26th Marines, and 3rd Battalion, 4th Marines rush Hill to help L Company of the 3rd Battalion, 9th Marines to secure the hilltop with little or no resistance. L Company of the 3rd Battalion, 9th Marines, with the help of the ARVN, were in constant contact with the PAVN 31st and 812th Regiments and had a body count of PAVN 342 killed and 30 PAVN captured. The ARVN suffered 22 killed and 122 wounded. .For the remainder of Operation Purple Smoke, the Marines encountered only scattered resistance but discovered and destroyed numerous bunkers, ordnance, and rice. 1stSg Roger L. Lewis was heard making this comment: "let the little bastards starve with out their rice." The 3rd Battalion, 9th Marines finish mopping up Hill; now it's time to move to another battle. We all headed back to base camp for a rest, a hot shower and food. Butch and I wrote our Dads and Moms about the battle without the gory details.

Then a private came into our tent and said: " Sgt Tomlin and Sgt Price 1stSg Roger L. Lewis wants to see you ASAP (As soon as possible) for a special meeting." We said: "Thank you private" Got dressed and doubled time to the meeting. When we got there, all ranking officers and NCOS were walking into the meeting. That seems funny to Butch and I because we were the only E-5 Sergarants that were at the briefing. LTC Joseph Muller was standing at the podium telling us about our next mission. He said: " lets lower our heads in a brief silence say a prayer for our fellow Marines that were killed or wounded in action. Then I want to give each and every one of you congratulations on a great job on taking the Hill. I know the 3rd Battalion, 9th Marines needs a must needed rest after that hard fought battle on the hill. But duty always calls we have orders from the top that our next mission is going to be Security Operations.(operations undertaken by a commander to provide early and accurate warning of enemy operations, to provide the force being protected with time and maneuver space within which to react to the enemy, and to develop the situation to allow the commander to effectively use the protected force). Then to Butch and I came the big surprise, when LTC Joseph Muller said: " Sergeants Tomlin and Price come forward." Butch and I stood up and walked to the podium, stood at attention, rendered a salute, and said: "Tomlin and Price reporting as directed Sir." LTC Joseph Muller returned the salute and said: " stand at ease." Butch and I were standing at ease. LTC Joseph Muller said: " today we have recipients of the bronze star." then LTC Joseph Muller said: this will be the first time in the Marines that we will have a dual recipient of the bronze star "1stSg Roger L. Lewis would you care to say a few words." 1stSg Roger L. Lewis said: " without L company 1st and 2nd squad it would be more difficult to secured and control Hill ." LTC Joseph Muller said: "thank you First Sergeant." Then LTC Joseph Muller said: " this is the first double citation for the Untied States Marine Corps"

Then the citation was read out loud:

For extraordinary acts of valor while under direct enemy fire during ground operations against a superior hostile force in the Republic of Vietnam. They distinguished themselves by their heroic actions while serving as Squad Leaders for Company L on 25 May 1967. That day Company L had maneuvered across a hill in the area around Tomahawk Base, Quảng Trị Province, and had established a defensive position on the hillside of Hill 119 when Company L began to receive heavy machine gun fire. The 1st and 2nd platoons of Company L were positioned approximately 500 meters to the front of UH-1E helicopters and were also receiving hostile machine gun and mortar fire. Sergeants Tomlin and Price scanned the surrounding area and located the enemy machine gun and mortar tube that was viciously pounding the helicopters position. With total disregard for their own safety and braving, intense enemy gunfire maneuvered into a position to direct their 1st and 2nd Squads and themselves to fire down upon the enemy machine gun and mortar site. The enemy gunners were shot which immediately knocked the enemy machine gun and mortar out of service. Their brave actions stopped further machine gun and enemy mortar fire, reducing casualties and saving lives. Sergeant Robert Dean Tomlin and Sergeant Frederick Philip Price, for bravery and professionalism, is in keeping with the highest traditions of military service and reflects great credit upon their selves; Company L, 3rd Battalion, 9th Marines, and the United States Marine Corps. (1-8)

Butch and I stood at attention while receiving our Bronze Star Medals. We rendered a salute; LTC Joseph Muller shook our hands with congratulations. We rendered a salute and said: "Thank You SIR." LTC Joseph Muller returned our salute and said: "dismissed." We did about face march out of the briefing and went back to our tent. LTC Joseph Muller said: So all officers and ranking NCOs stay after this citation and you will be given details." Butch and I were in our tent when 1st Squad Leader Ssgt Henry Watson and 2nd Squad Leader Ssgt William Houser walked in. Ssgt Henry Watson said: " Congratulations, well Marines our next mission is going to be a rough one. Ssgt Watson turn to Sgt Tomlin and said: "you are a brave son of a bitch , but one day you are going to get your ass shot off." Sgt Tomlin tuned too, Ssgt Watson, just like John Wayne did in The Searchers, and said: " That will be the day."

Operation Purple Smoke Casualties

Date 20 – 30 May 1967
Location
Leatherneck Square, Quảng Trị Province
Result inconclusive
Belligerents

United States South Vietnam	North Vietnam North Vietnan

Commanders and leaders

LTC Joseph Muller USMC	LTG Duong Ly Khan PAVN

Units involved

2nd Battalion, 3rd Marines 3rd Battalion, 4th Marines 1st Battalion, 9th Marines 2nd Battalion, 9th Marines 3rd Battalion, 9th Marines 1st Battalion, 12th Marines 2nd Battalion, 26th Marines	324B Division

Casualties and losses

United States 142 killed South Vietnam 22 killed	US body count 536 killed 30 captured

CHAPTER TWELVE

Vietnam War

Operation Water Buffalo

Operation Water Buffalo from 2–14 July 1967, was an operation during the Vietnam War that took place in the southern half of the Demilitarized Zone, around Tomahawk Base.

Key United States Commanders

LTC Joseph Muller USMC
1stSg Roger L. Lewis USMC
GySgt Russell Owens USMC
Ssgt Henry Watson USMC
Ssgt William Houser USMC
Sgt Robert Dean Tomlin USMC
Sgt Frederick (Butch) Philip Price USMC

Key North Vietnam Commanders

Colonel Hoa La Hung PAVN

On the morning of 2 July, Butch and I were heading for the mess tent for breakfast. As we got there and got our food and ready to set down to eat. A private came running and shouted 1st Battalion, 9th Marines just got ambush at Au Kha. Concording to the report, Alpha and Bravo Companies, 1st Battalion, 9th Marines were making their way up north on Highway 561 to secure a crossroad as their first objective. As they went further north between Gia Binh and A Kha, they made contact with four regular battalions, K-4, K-5, K-6 and K-8, all from the PAVN 90th Regiment, numbered about 400 men each. When they were engaged from snipers fired from all sides with rifle and machine fire. The 3rd Platoon of the 1st Battalion, 9th Marines, were caught in a cross-fire. As the 3rd Platoon took cover, enemy fire intensified, and squads 3 and 4 made efforts to suppress it. The platoon Sergeant radioed for help when a Tri-directional ambushes had virtually tried to kill, destroy, or remove a large percentage of company B. When Alpha Company, sent to rescue Company B, they were also ambushed. During the battle, the PAVN used flamethrowers in combat for the first time. They were using Russian Army flamethrowers which were three backpacks which were mounted on tanks. The PAVN using flamethrowers, started setting fire to hedgerows along Highway 561, forcing the Marines out into the open to be like setting ducks on the water. Now the Marines were being exposed to artillery, mortar and small arms fire, causing heavy casualties on the Marines of A and B Companies. With constant firing from the PAVN, this prevented establishing a connection between A and B Companies. B Company Headquarters was wiped out when a single PAVN artillery 130 mm towed field gun M-46 (Russian: 130-мм пушка M-46) round exploded within the command group. The company commander, two platoon leaders, the radio operator, forward observer, and several others Marines were killed.

1stSg Roger L. Lewis told the 3rd Battalion, 9th Marines, to draw weapons and mount up; we were going to rescue the 1st Battalion, 9th Marines before they were all killed. We loaded up and headed to Gia Binh and A-Kha. First Sergeant called in an airstrike to give help to the 1st Battalion, 9th Marines, until we got there. The Marine A-6 Intruders kept dropping bombs to disrupt the PAVN who had completing surrounded 1st and 2nd Platoons. A pilot radioed back to the First Sergeant and said: " they have pop green smoke to indicate there are wounded on the ground and red smoke to mark where the enemy targes are at. When we arrive the PAVN was started to disperse and 1st Platoon and the battered 2nd Platoon were eventually created an establishment connection between the Platoons, Airstrikes disrupted PAVN's attempts to "hug" the 1st Platoon, eventually allowing them to link up. The 1st Battalion, 9th Marines commander, sent out a small rescue force involving C and D Companies supported by four M48A3 Patton Tanks. Using USMC H-34s were fitted with two M60C machine guns and two 19-shot 2.75 inch rocket pods. M48A3 Patton Tanks fire 90mm M41/T139 gun and 50 cal (12.7 mm) machine gun to disperse enemy troops. 3rd Battalion, 9th Marines, we were able to secure a helicopter landing zone for the evacuation of casualties. Then continued to move north under heavy fire to rescue what was left of the two Companies of the 1st Battalion, 9th Marines. Out of nearly 400 Marines, the two Companies A and B suffered 84 killed, 190 wounded and 9 missing. 1stSg Roger L. Lewis was heard making this comment: " this has to be the worst one-day loss for the Marines in Vietnam." We found out after wards that only 27 Marines from Company B 1st Battalion, 9th Marines, and about 90 from Company A 1st Battalion, 9th Marines, were fit for duty after that first day of fighting. They took a rough body count and found that the PAVN suffered 55 killed, with another 88 believed to have been killed, but they could not be unaccounted for.

On 3 July, a USAF Air Observer pilot flying an OV-10 Bronco was slowly flying over an area that spotted more than 100 PAVN soldiers moving south from positions north of Camp Rotan. He radioed Battery E, 3rd Battalion, 12th Marines, who were using 107mm howitzers that were in the area. The pilot directed their fire on the PAVN, killing 75 or more men.

On the morning of 4 July, following 12 hours of carrying out preparations for airstrikes, the 3rd Battalion, 9th Marines was moving towards Marketplace ambush site to recover the bodies of those killed on 2 July. 4 July 3rd Battalion, 9th Marines met heavy resistance from the PAVN southwest of the Marketplace and called in for help. Battalion Landing Team (BLT) is a battalion landing team in an amphibious operation, an infantry battalion normally reinforced by necessary combat and service elements; the basic unit for planning an assault landing. 1st Battalion, 3rd Marines attacked the PAVN and covered the 3rd Battalion, 9th Marines, as they recovered the dead bodies of the fallen Marines. By the end of the day, the 3rd Battalion, 9th Marines had suffered 15 dead and 33 wounded, while the BLT 1st Battalion, 3rd Marines suffered 11 wounded.

On 5 July, Sgt Tomlin's 1st Squad and Sgt Prices's 2nd Squads of the 3rd Battalion, 9th Marines were operating north of Camp Rotan, and came under artillery and mortar fire, as they tried to recover the dead Marines. But they did have little ground contact from the PAVN in which they were to extinguish very quickly. The 3rd Battalion, 9th Marines were able to collect the dead Marines from the 2 July fighting. As we gathered up the dead, there were several Marines that had fallen very close to each other. I call Butch over and say: " those frigging PAVN bastards shot these Marines at point-blank range." A corporal said: :be careful Sgt. Tomlin and Sgt Price some of the bodies had been booby-trapped." We defused the booby-traps and gathered up the dead Marines. Then a private yells at Butch and I, sergeants, you have to see this. When Butch and I walked over and saw those poor butchered Marines. Butch and I both lost it with tears running down our faces. We were throwing up our guts after seeing those Marines that had been mutilated by the PAVN. I am not going to paint a picture of the mutilated Marines; it was to horrible to describe. In my heart I am just glad their parents did not get to see them like this. I just hope that their memories stay in their Mother's hearts and minds when they were babies and growing up. In the afternoon we received word that PAVN soldiers were seen 3 klicks northeast of Camp Rotan. Artillery and tactical air strikes were called in resulting in an estimated 200 PAVN killed. Butch looked at me and said: " Robert I hope them son-of-bitche's bodies were so torn up so bad that their own Fathers and Mothers could not recongize them." I told Butch no matter the outcome of this war, it is going to be hell with a lot of bloodshed on both sides."

On the morning of 6 July, BLT 2nd Battalion, 3rd Marines ran into a PAVN force north of Camp Rotan in a fierce rifle and machine gun battle and killed 35 PAVN. The Marines had a loss of 5 killed and 25 wounded. After a long engage battle with the PAVN Company A, 9th Marines was finally reinforced by Company C and a detachment of the 3rd Reconnaissance Battalion (amphibious and ground reconnaissance) moved northeast of Camp Rotan and established a forward fighting position. As the Marines advance forward by the afternoon 1st Battalion, 3rd Marines, and 2nd Battalion, 3rd Marines were stopped by PAVN artillery fire and an aerial observer in a Cessna L-19/O-1 Bird Dog reported that 400 PAVN soldiers had crossed the Ben Hai River and were heading towards the two Battalions. The PAVN force was unaware of the presence of Company L 3rd Battalion; the 9th Marines were waiting to ambush the PAVN force. Just as the PAVN were in sight the command to commence firing was given, and quickly the PAVN reorganized; they were under attack by Company L. We were able to penetrate their lines and Marine artillery fire effectively boxed in the PAVN. The following morning Company L counted 154 PAVN dead, while suffering only 12 wounded. While the PAVN 90th Regiment force attacked the remainder of 1st Battalion, 3rd Marines, and 2nd Battalion, 3rd Marines achieving so small and unimportant as to be not worth considering continuing with the fight. The commander of the PAVN 90th Regiment broke off the fight at 21:00 and retreated.

On 6 July, LTC Joseph Muller asked for volunteers to go rescue a downed United States Marine pilot who was shot down near the Quang Tri River. Company L, 3rd Battalion, 9th Marines Sgt Tomlin 1st Squad and Sgt Price 2nd Squad were voluntary for the rescue mission. GySgt Russell Owens said: Company L Squads 1 and 2 go to the briefing room ASAP and LTC Muller will give you the details. Butch and I rushed over to the briefing room where LTC Muller was starting his short duration of the rescue mission. LTC Muller said: " the PAVN fired eight SAM-2s (SA-2 is a Soviet-designed, high-altitude air defence system, built around a surface-to-air missile with command guidance) from positions north of the DMZ. The Marine pilots were flying out of Bien Hoa Air Base and conducted close air support in front of 1st Battalion, 3rd Marines 's lines. VMA-311 Tomcat Major Lawence E. Wainwright was south of the Demilitarized Zone when his A-4E Skyhawk was struck by enemy missiles. Major Wainwright radio SOS (radio distress signal) that his Skyhawk became uncontrollable and he was punching out. He ejected successfully while safely on the ground Maj. Wainwright is in hideing and waiting for rescue. He also reported there are a bunch of PAVN patrols out looking for him." LTC Joseph Muller said Company L, 3rd Battalion, 9th Marines Squad 1 and 2 mount up and go rescue the pilot and bring him back home." 1stSg Roger L. Lewis said: "dismissed, we are counting on you Squad 1 and 2."

As we pulled out, it was my turn to be a point man (to take point, walk point, be on point, or be a point man means to assume the first and most exposed position in a combat military formation; that is, the leading soldier or unit advancing through hostile or unsecured territory). A new replacement a private PFC Jerry Wassel said: "Sgt Tomlin you are an E-5 why are you point man." I said: "1stSg Roger L. Lewis always said: Point man is the position that will be rotated among all squads no matter the rank. So my name came up and I am point man today."

I was supposed to be point man on a route patrol and was not feeling well, so Butch volunteered to take my place. Butch was the best point man in our company; he was always taking care to avoid danger and mistakes. A lot of times you never saw him cause he was in the shadows, always advancing, looking for the enemy. We were walking when all of a sudden Butch gave the arm signals to halt, disperse, and take cover. Then within a flash of a second, all hell broke loose, enemy weapon fire all around us; we just walked into an ambush. I could see Butch was hit several times and I ran towards him to get him out of enemy fire, when I felt this sharp pain in my left shoulder. A 7.62 bullet from an AK-47 went right through the fleshy part of my shoulder without hitting any bone. The pain was great and I did not care. I kept going. I had to save my best friend. As I carried Butch, I was looking for a place to escape from the PAVN who were all over the place. I think I was headed south through the tense jungle. Butch was shot up real bad and lost a lot of blood. He started to get real heavy for me to carry. I was wearing down and getting tired and my shoulder was killing me from being shot. Butch kept telling me, "Robert just say UNCLE and let me go and save yourself." I said: " what the hell are you saying, I have never said UNCLE and I am not to start now. I promise your mother I would get you home come hell or high water. Then I saw an opportunity their on the river bank was two dead Water Buffaloes cows (female) with their stomachs facing the river. When I heard the PAVN off in a distance, I put Butch down and started cutting on the buffalos. First a slit the water buffaloes from their thoats to thier rumps, I pull out all the stomachs, lungs, intestines, interal organs, guts, and everyting that I could clean out. Then I dug a giant hole in the soft mud on the river bank and bury everything. I gave Butch two shots of morphine to ease the pain and keep him quiet. I stuff him in the enpty cavity of one of the Water buffalo pulled down the stomach flap and left a vent hole for he would not suffocate and cover the slit with mud. I told him to be quiet because the PAVN was near. I put myself in the other water buffalo and close the stomach flap, then stuck out my hand and cover the slit with mud. Man did this stomach cavity stink I almost threw up a couple of times. Then I heard the PAVN they were looking for us. I was prayimg and hoping Butch did not make amy noise. Then I heard one PAVN soldier tell another soldier to shoot the dead water buffalo (bắn chết trâu nước chết) then all of a sudden 3 AK-47 bullets come ripping through the buffalo I was in and one bullet just nick my right ear. I just lay there not making a sound and I was hoping Butch did not make a sound. After awhile when everything was quiet, I pulled the stomach flap back and got out and looked around for the PAVN. The PAVN had lefted so I got Butch out and Butch kept saying: "Robert what sinks, it smells worse then a skunk." I found a large Haldina (Gáo tròn) tree that Butch and I could sleep in for the night. Even with his help it was a real job getting him up in the tree. I found a nice flat limb that I could observe the PAVN actively and we could sleep on. Then, in the middle of the night, I was waken when I felt a heavy breathing with a hot breath and a sticky tingle sensation on my neck. I looked upward and there was a tiger looking right in my face. He stiffed me a couple of times and back up. I think the stinking smell from the dead water buffalo kept him from killing Butch and I. Butch, who was delirious, coming and going out of consciousness, said: " Robert did I just see a large pussycat." To humor him, I said: "yes Butch that was a huge pussycat." The PAVN was back and one PAVN soldier said: "he heard a noise." They shine their lights all around and the tiger makes a growling noise, then they start shooting at the tiger. He jumped out of the tree right on top of a PAVN soldier. The tiger had the dead grip on the PAVN soldier's head; you could see him sink his fangs right into his skull. The PAVN soldier was screaming and the PAVN Patrol shot and killed the tiger, but it was too late for the PAVN soldier; his head was crushed. I lay as flat as possible and was hoping Butch would be quiet, even thought he was in a lot of pain.

Early the next morning we got down from the tree and headed for our company. It seemed like we had walked for hours when I heard a voice say: "hey these two Marines need help" A Marine Sergeant asked me our names and what unit we were from. I said: "Sergeants Tomlin and Price from the L Company 3rd Battalion, 9th Marines we were on a daily patrol and got ambush. They put us on a helicopter and took us to a field hospital. Butch and I were very lucky we only had flesh wounds and lost a lot of blood. Major Paul Hess field hospital doctor on duty, clean, sew, and bandage our wounds. He had us stay in bed for a week until we were completely heal. The next day he came by to check on process.. Major Hess was talking to Sgt Tomlin and said: "Sgt Tomlin, with your quick thinking, you saved Sgt Price's life by putting on Quick Clot Power and Steri-Strips on his wounds. Kept the infections down to a minimum by bandaging his wounds before sticking him in the dead carcass. Then, Major Paul Hess and I were talking about how we joined the Marine Corp. How his Father and Mother wanted hin and his twin John Hess to apply to the U.S. Naval Academy in Annapolis, Maryland. He told his dad and mom he wanted to get into action while on the ground and not on the water. He took the United States Marine Corp after graduation from U.S. Naval Academy. That his dad and mom were not very happy with his decision. I told Major Hess that my dad and mom wanted me to join the Navy, since all my family members were in the Navy. We both had a good laugh; I stood up and rendered a salute. He returned the salute, and we shook hands and wished each other good luck in our endeavors. One day, while laying in bed, the Battalion Commander came in and gave me a Citations for the Purple Heart, which read.

CITATIONS FOR A PURPLE HEART

TO SERGEANT ROBERT DEAN TOMLIN UNITED STATES MARINE CORPS FOR WOUNDS RECEIVED IN COMBAT AGAINST HOSTILE ENEMY FORCES ON 6 JULY 1967 WHILE SERVING WITH COMPANY L 3rd BATTALION, 9th MARINES IN THE REPUBLIC OF VIRTNAM GIVEN ON THIS 11 DAY OF JULY 1967.

I got out bed and stood attention, render a salute, and said: " Thank You Sir" The Battalion Commander said: " get back in bed sergeant and Thank You for bravery and decation to the Untited States Marine Corp." He return my salute and proceeded to give Butch his citation for a Purple Heart, which read.

TO SERGEANT FREDERICK (BUTCH) PHILIP PRICE UNITED STATES MARINE CORPS FOR WOUNDS RECEIVED IN COMBAT AGAINST HOSTILE ENEMY FORCES ON 6 JULY 1967 WHILE SERVING WITH COMPANY L 3rd BATTALION, 9th MARINES IN THE REPUBLIC OF VIRTNAM GIVEN ON THIS 11 DAY OF JULY 1967.

Butch got out bed and stood attention, render a salute and said: " Thank You Sir" The Battalion Commander said: " get back in bed sergeant and Thank You for bravery and decation to the Untited States Marine Corp." After the week was up, the Major Hess said: "you will be release tomorrow for light duty for a couple of weeks and will be send back to your units. When we got back to our unit 1stSg Roger L. Lewis said " My best two sergeants; I almost gave you Marines up for dead." Butch and I had light duty in the camp for two weeks by doing guard duty for a couple of hours a day. After the two weeks were up, we were right back on patrol duty finding those damn PAVN. Years later, Butch and I still talk about how those sinking water buffalos and tiger (the large pussycat) saved us from being capture or killed.

On our very first morning of active duty with Company L, we were ambushed by a PAVN Battalion with a continuous line forming the boundary that boxed us in. I call in an artillery strike, and the PAVN received a heavy Marine artillery bombardment hit with their bodies flying everywhere. The next day saw minimal ground contact and Company L 3rd Battalion, 9th Marines spent most of the day trying to achieve an accurate PAVN body count. But this proved difficult due to the the flesh of slain PAVN humans caused by the artillery and air strikes. Butch said: " Robert I never saw so many pieces of human bodies scattered everywhere. I said: " How about that PAVN officer, the poor son of a bitch, after they tried several times to piece him together with 5 legs and 6 arms, that was all different." Finally, 1stSg Roger L. Lewis said " just give the best body count you can give." So Butch and I came up with an 180 or so body count of PAVN.

Operation Water Buffalo Casualties

Date 2–30 July 1967
Location Quang Tri Province, South Vietnam
Result US declares victory

Belligerents	
United States	North Vietnam
Commanders and leaders	
Strength	
3,000	1,500
Units involved	
1st Battalion, 9th Marines 3rd Battalion, 9th Marines 1st Battalion, 3rd Marines 2nd Battalion, 3rd Marines	90th Regiiment, 324B Division
Casualties and losses	
	US body count
United States 159 killed 845 wounded 1 missing	1,290 killed, 1 captured 164 bunkers destroyed 15 artillery & rocket positions destroyed 100 weapons recovered

CHAPTER THIRTEEN

Vietnam War

Operation Cardinal

Operation Cardinal was a US Marine Corps operation that took place during the Vietnam War. The operation was carried out in the western part of the DMZ near Camp Rotan, lasting from July -- October 1967.

Key United States Commanders	Key North Vietnam Commanders
LTC Joseph Muller USMC	Colonel Trang Le Duong PAVN
1stSg Roger L. Lewis USMC	Commander Vanh chu Giang PAVN
GySgt Russell Owens USMC	
Ssgt Henry Watson USMC	
Ssgt William Houser USMC	
Sgt Robert Dean Tomlin USMC	
Sgt Frederick (Butch) Philip Price USMC	

On 28 July through 30 July 2nd Battalion, 9th Marines, supported by a platoon of five M-48 tanks (designated with a 90mm Gun), three M50 Ontos (M50 Ontos, Multiple 106 mm, Self-propelled, tank destroyer) and three LVTE (Landing Vehicle Tracked Engineers) moved north along Provincial Route 606. This was a Marine tactical maneuver employed to seriously impair a hostile attack while the enemy was in the process of forming or assembling for an attack into the DMZ. Company L, 3rd Battalion, 9th Marines, were guarding the Forward Observer, who was checking in all directions for any signs of the PAVN. He radioed back to 2nd Battalion, 9th Marines; the area was all cleared that no contact with the PAVN. 2nd Battalion, 9th Marines and 3rd Battalion, 9th Marines set up a night defensive position near the Bến Hải River. That night, Company L had guards in all directions. Sgt. Tomlin told his 1st Squad, who were on guard duty, to keep their eyes peeled and listen ears on. Then he said: "Be on your toes and do a extreme look out, you will hear the wind before you hear those tricky little bastards, they will seek in and cut your throats before you know it." The following morning they mounted up to roll out, as the unit was returning along the same route, some where near by under cover, a PAVN operator detonated a land mine by radio signal. As the land mine land mine exploded wounding 5 Marines from Company A 2nd Battalion, 9th Marines. Before a command was given to halt further down the road to the convoy, hit a a second mine that was detonated. The PAVN then opened fire with small arms and mortar fire and attacked the armored vehicles with

RPG-2 rockets. One good thing it is hard for a RPG-2 to destroy, because it is obsolete against many modern tanks. The RPG-2 is a support weapon for the destruction of vehicles, buildings, and soft targets (transportation systems, and large numbers of soldiers in a group). The PAVN attempted to stop and destroy the US column; air support was called in, and the column broke up into several separate firefights. Company L, 3rd Battalion, 9th Marines Squads 1, 2, 3, and 4 were covering the light vehicles and troops as they were taking cover. Sgt. Tomlin and Sgt Price had their squad in position laying down rifle, machine gun fire. While the M79 launchers were taking care of the RPG-2 PAVN and keeping them at a safe distance. The convoy then retreated; to take cover out of harm's way. Only through the use of napalm support from the Marine A-6 Intriders and A-4E Skyhawks was the Marine convoy saved from a complete a disorderly retreat of defeated Marine troops. The isolated Marine companies set up night defensive positions and were eventually relieved by the 3rd Battalion, 4th Marines, on the morning of 30 July. Marine casualties for the operation were 23 dead and 251 wounded, while 32 PAVN dead were counted by the Marines; Butch and I further believed that 175 PAVN were killed

When the new boots, fresh out of bootcamp, came to Squad 1 and 2 as replacements for the Marines that were wounded or killed, they were always squeamish and nervous. As soon as they walked through the gate at Camp Rotan Ssgt Henry Watson and Ssgt William Houser told them to always listen to your Squad Leaders. Then they would say see your squad leaders to get square away and always be ready for combat. Butch and I would always work and help the new boots get square away to our squads function and operations. We always gave them the Sgt Tomlin and Sgt Price speech. Sgt Price would say: " you will conduct oneself and perform in a specified way set forth by Sgt Tomlin and Sgt Price." Then I would let them have it with both barrels, just like my Drill Sergeant told us. I would say: "In war you cannot afford the luxury of squeamishness. Either you kill or capture, or you will be captured or killed. We've got to be tough to win, and we've got to be ruthless, and tougher, what it boils down too is you have to be tougher and more ruthless than our enemies." Then, Butch said: " just because the enemy is small the little bastard is mighty and tough." We both said: " get your gear stow away and get ready for chow. Tomorrow you will be going on your first patrol. The whole month of August was really quit not much action from the PAVN. In way it was good cause it gave time to work with the new boots. I can not explain it but I started take a real liking to this new private PVT Ben Thompson from Kansas. He was a real fast learner and a Gung-Ho Marine that was always ready for action and never complained. I took him under my wing and started teaching him everything I knew about weapons and combat operations. He was exceptable skill rifleman, M79 Grenade Launcher, and becoming a real weapon expert.

On the morning of 4 September, GySgt Russell Owens called for Company L Squad 1 and 2 to help 3rd Battalion, 4th Marines were engaged by a PAVN force 1.5 klicks south of Camp Rotan. They were trapped by a PAVN force in a cross-fire and radio-in and needed aid. Squad 1 and 2 mounted up and doubled in time to help the

Marines. When we arrived at the battle site, two Companies of Marines were cut off in a cross-fire. I took my squad 1 to the right and set up my position where I could fire without hitting our own men. Butch took Squad 2 and went to the left and set up his position where he could fire without hitting our own men. I gave the arm signal to commence firing, and bullets and tracers and M79 rounds just covered the PAVN 308th Infantry Division with lead and explorations. The battle lasted about 30 minutes or so until the 3rd Battalion, 4th Marines A and B companies gained control and the PAVN started to retreat. The Marines claimed that the PAVN lost 38 killed and 1 captured, while the Marines lost 6 dead and 47 wounded. Company L Squad 1 and 2 did not lose or have a wounded Marine. I told PVT Ben Thompson he handled himself real well under a combat situation. He was firing that M14 like a mad man.

On 7 September we were having chow in the mess tent when a corporal came running in and said: "1stSg Roger L. Lewis wants Company L Squad 1, 2, 3, and 4 to help support 3rd Battalion, 26th Marines that encountered a PAVN force 4.8 km south of Camp Tan. Company L Squad 1, 2, 3, and 4 got into formation and we marched off to help the trouble Marines. When we were about 2 or so klicks away we double time to the battle sight. We came up behind the 3rd Battalion, 26th Marines. I talked to the officer in charge and said: "SIR, where do you want the Squads." He said: " Sergeant make a semi circle around the PAVN and wait for my signal to fire. When we were in position the command of fire was given. Those frigging PAVN were eating Marine lead again. Then all of a sudden the firing stopped and the PAVN were running away. The PAVN lost 51 killed, while the 3rd Battalion, 26th Marines lost 14 killed.

On the evening of 10 September Company L 3rd Battalion, 9th Marines had just finished dinner and we were walking back to our tents. When a corporal came running up and said: " 1stSg Roger L. Lewis want to see you ASAP. We ran up to the First Sergeant tent to report. 1stSg Roger L. Lewis said: " we are going to truck you to help 3rd Battalion, 26th Marines out again. They are engaged a PAVN Regiment 6 km southwest of Camp Rotan. We have received a report that some of the attacking PAVN were alleged to have been wearing USMC helmets and flak jackets. Sgt Tomlin and Sgt Price take extreme care with these PAVN that are fake Marines, do not get your self killed. When we arrived on the battle site, things were getting real heavy with well-supported PAVN mortars and 140mm rockets. We watched an RPG destroy a M67 Flame Thrower Tank, also known as (M67 "Zippo", nicknamed after a popular brand of cigarette lighter) the poor tankers did not stand a change. By the Compmay L Squads 1,2,3, and 4 stopped the PAVN from penetrating the 3rd Battalion, 26th Marines lines. US artillery was called in, and they boxed in the Marines by using mass artillery in line to enable better fire concentration and support, which forced the PAVN to withdraw by 20:30. The following morning the Marines had claimed that 140 PAVN bodies were found around the Marine lines; the Marines had lost 34 dead and 192 wounded. 1stSg Roger L. Lewis said: " the whole 3rd Battalion, 26th Marines would have been killed or wounded if the 3rd Battalion, 9h Marines had not arrive.

It seems like it never fails we are setting down for breakfast on the morning of 13 September, when a PAVN Company attacked the northeastern sector of the Camp Rotan base. I told my men to stay seated and let the 3rd Battalion, 3rd Marines, and 2nd Battalion, 4th Marines handle the situration. The PAVN Company failed to penetrate the base and were forced back by the 3rd Battalion, 3rd Marines, and 2nd Battalion, 4th Marines, small arms and artillery fire.

On 21 September Companies E, F & G, 2nd Battalion, 4th Marines conducted a large sweep east of Camp Rotan, just below the Trace (where everything was cleared away) As the units advanced through the hedgerows (a hedge of wild shrubs and trees, typically bordering a road or field) the companies came under sniper, mortar and then heavy artillery fire. Company F radio back to Camp Rotan for help. The company had later walked right into a pin-wheel (in the form of a revolving wheel) ambush. They were getting fire up on them from 360 degrees. The Marine Commander told a Staff Sergeant to call in again to Camp Rotan for help. He did not know at the time that Company L 3rd Battalion, 9h Marines were on their way. When we arrived I had the 1st Squad set up a perimeter around the base of the PAVN Pin-wheel. Then Butch took the 2nd Squad and set up a perimeter around the top of the PAVN Pin-wheel. The 3rd Squad set up a perimeter around the right side of the PAVN Pin-wheel. The 4th Squad set up a perimeter around the left side of the PAVN Pin-wheel. When we were in position the signal was given to commence firing. We hit those poor bastards with rifle, machine gun, and M79 rounds of fire. By the PAVN were dug in so well that close-quarters fighting continued all day. By the time it started to get dark, the last shot was fired, ending at nightfall. The Marines had lost 16 killed and 118 wounded, while the PAVN had lost 39 killed. At the end of the battle, the Marines left 15 of their dead on the battlefield. Every time we tried to retrieve a dead Marine, the PAVN had snipers waiting to kill anyone who ever tried to get the body. The Marines were unable to retrieve bodies from the site for three weeks. Until on 10 October 2nd Battalion, 4th Marines were able to retrieve bodies from the site. The 3rd Battalion, 9th Marines cover the area for PAVN snipers as the 2nd Battalion, 4th Marines recover their dead Marines.

At 01:25 on 14 October PAVN artillery with 130 MM (The 130 mm towed field gun M-46 (Russian: 130-мм пушка M-46) hit 2nd Battalion 4th Marines position around Washout Bridge between Charlie Company and strongpoint of the Camp Rotan Combat Base. All the Marines on Camp Rotan Base were reported to their companies and squads to be ready for combat. A night LP (Listening Post / Observation Post) reported by radio that he observe a large PAVN unit with 2 companies or more was moving past his position moving, slowing towards the bridge. Then he reported it was too dark to tell what kind of equipment and weapons the PAVN were carrying. It was verified by Marine snipers using Starlight Scopes (A night-vision device) seeing the PAVN assembled into a mass as one body of a fighting unit in front of Company H's position for an attack. The base commander ordered the Marines tanks to open fire first with beehive rounds, (Beehive was a Vietnam War-era anti-personnel round packed with metal flechettes) machine guns, and infantry with rifle fire. Once the Marine started laying fire from all directions and the PAVN was getting shredded from the metal flechettes. This causes the PAVN to attack prematurely and scatter everywhere. The PAVN failed to penetrate the companies wire (referring to the base; a person is inside or outside the wire) withdrew and retreated.

The PAVN did not retreat very far; at 02:30 on 14 October, the PAVN regrouped; and attacked Company G, by destroying 2 machine gun positions with RPGs. A few PAVN threw their bodies on the barb wire while the others stepped on their backs and penetrated the wire and overran the CP (Company Command Post) killing the Company commander, his forward observer, and 3 Platoon leaders. We had three young 2nd lieutenants who had just arrived in the country about two weeks ago. Orders were given to a captain to take over Command of the Company, as he started running to the Command Post, he was killed by PAVN machine gun fire before he could reach the Command Post. Company L and Company F were ordered to support Company G to sweep through the area and drive the PAVN out. Sgt. Tomlin told Squad 1 we are not going to have another Marine killed we have to safe Company G. Sgt Price call in the coordinates for an air strike for the AC-47's gunships The AC-47 Spooky gunships came in real fast and started using their three 7.62 mm General Electric miniguns. When those miniguns started spitting out bullets every square inch, the PAVN was forced to withdraw by 04:30. The Marines had lost 21 dead and 23 wounded. With the body count, the PAVN lost 24 killed and numerous wounded. I told Butch that damn kill ratio is lobe-sided; it should be a hell of a lot more dead PAVN to our dead Marines.

On 25 October 2nd Battalion, 4th Marines began a sweep north along Route 561; there was no enemy contact; but their progress was slowed by heavy undergrowth. A private was heard making this comment: "We are fighting amidst the humid, mosquito choked jungles, walking through dense underbrush, and looking for the damn attacks from the PAVN. I just hope we do not run into any Rock Apes. Then a corporal said: "What the hell are you talking about Rock Apes." Then the private said:" Yes Rock Apes, hairy ape like creature known by various names, such as the Batutut (forest people) or Người rừng (vietnamese forest people), also written as Nguoi Rung, or (jungle people). These "jungle people" are said to be around 6 feet or taller, stout and very muscular, with protruding stomachs and covered in hair ranging from brown to black in color, except for the knees, the soles of the feet, the hands, and the face, which remain bare. The corporal said: "private you are so full of shit your eyes are brown". No sooner then, the corporal said Brown, he was hit in the head by a flying giant rock coming somewhere in the jungle. It was killed instantly, with his skull crushed in. Then right in front of them was a hairy man, about 7 feet tall, screaming, yelling, and throwing rocks at the Marines. The Squad Leader just unloaded a full clip (20 round magazine) of 7.62s on that hairy Rock Ape. A corporal was heard making this comment: "

the sergeant just blew that hairy bastard all to hell." Then everybody in that unit was asking the private all kinds of questions about the Rock Apes. One Sergeant was head making this comment: "Not only do we have to worry about the PAVN now we have the frigging Rock Apes." With no PAVN or Rock Apes in sight and the 2nd Battalion, 4th Marines set up a night position. They posted extra guards for the look out for PAVN and Rock Apes. That night PAVN rockets (102mm Russia 102A3 rockets) hit the 2nd Battalion, 4th Marines position killing the Executive Officer a Major and wounding the commanding officer a Lieutenant Colonel and two others of the command group with severe wounds were evacuated by Sikorsky H-34 helicopter.

The regimental operations officer from Camp Rotan Base, a Lieutenant Colonel, was flown in to take over command of 2nd Battalion, 4th Marines. As soon as the Lieutenant Colonel took command, he

had his staff, ranking NCOs going over the situation and operation of the 2nd Battalion, 4th Marines. Then one staff sergeant said: " SIR the PAVN is not are only problem now we have reports of Rock Apes." The Lieutenant Colonel said: " Now that old myth of Rock Apes again." Then the staff sergeant said: SIR Company A, while on patrol, just shot and killed one." Then the Lieutenant Colonel said: enough of the Rock Apes , it was probably a piss-off Vietnamese villager that the patrol was trespassing on his land. Now lets get back to business on these PAVN that attacked the 2nd Battalion, 4th Marines.

On 26 October, 2nd Battalion, 4th Marines, moved north and secured the objective by 13:00. Orders were given to Company F to remain in night position to guard a stock pile of ammunition. While the rest of the Battalion was moving north after going 5 or so klicks they came under PAVN mortar and small arms fire. A UH-34D helicopter of HMM-363 was part of (Lucky Red Lions) it was shot down as it attempted to pick up casualties, killing the pilot and door gunner who was firing his firing his M60 machine gun to keep the PAVN back. They called in another UH-34 that attempted to land but was heavily damaged and had to pull up and made a forced landing at Charlie 2 Strongpoint and Firebase. Lieutenant Colonel called for reinforcements, and 3rd Battalion, 9th Marines Company L moved north to the Battalion position. Sgt Tomlin and Sgt Price set up their perimeters on the outside of 2nd Battalion, 4th Marines, to keep the PAVN from coming up from the rear. Two Companies from the 3rd Battalion, 3rd Marines moved north from the Charlie 2 Strongpoint and Firebase, arriving at the 2nd Battalion, 4th Marines position at dusk. The PAVN to search into and examine thoroughly the Marines position. Then the PAVN started on the Marine position with direct and indirect fire and ground attacks. Then the PAVN commander questioned closely whether it was feasible to attack the Marines or lose a bunch of his men. The PAVN commander made a decision to withdraw all his men at around 02:00 on 27 October. The following morning the Marines claimed 19 PAVN dead but were unable to police the area due to PAVN mortar and artillery fire. The Marines had lost 8 dead and 45 wounded in the period from 25–27 October.

Operation Cardinal Casualties

Date July -- October 1967

Location

Quảng Trị Province, South Vietnam

Result Both sides claim victory

	Belligerents	
United States		North Vietnam North Vietn
	Commanders and leaders	
LTC Joseph Muller 1stSg Roger L. Lewis GySgt Russell Owens		Colonel Trang Le Duong PAVN Commander Vanh chu Giang PAVN
	Units involved	
3rd Battalion, 3rd Marines 2nd Battalion, 4th Marines 3rd Battalion, 4th Marines 2nd Battalion, 9th Marines 3rd Battalion, 9th Marines 3rd Battalion, 26th Marines		308th Infantry Division 812th Regiment
4,000 - 5,000	Strength	8,000 - 10,000
	Casualties and losses	
United States 340 killed		US body count 1,117 killed 5 captured 1,942 estimated killed 155 weapons recovered

CHAPTER FOURTEEN

Vietnam War

Operation Illinois

Operation Illinois was a multi-battalion operation conducted by the United States Marine Corps in the area south of the DMZ in Quảng Trị Province. This was another operation to secure the Camp Rotan area from the People's Army of Vietnam (PAVN). The operation ran from November 1967 -- March 1968.

Key United States Commanders

LTC Joseph Muller USMC
1stSg Roger L. Lewis USMC
GySgt Russell Owens USMC
Ssgt Henry Watson USMC
Ssgt William Houser USMC
Sgt Robert Dean Tomlin USMC
Sgt Frederick (Butch) Philip Price USMC

Key North Vietnam Commanders

Colonel Hoa La Hung PAVN
Commander Vanh chu Giang PAVN

Company L, 3rd Battalion, 9th Marines, was going out on daily patrols south of the DMZ in Quảng Trị Province looking for PAVN strongholds, bunkers, and trenches. Our main job was to make a clearing all around Camp Rotan Base to keep the PAVN from coming through the wire. On November 8 1stSg Roger L. Lewis called GySgt Russell Owens, Ssgt Henry Watson, Ssgt William Houser, Sgt Robert Dean Tomlin, and Sgt Frederick (Butch) Philip Price in for a meeting. When we all arrived 1stSg Lewis had a map spread out on a table in his office, and he was pointing to a circle on a section of the map. Then he said: "Company L Squads 1,2,3, and 4 of 3rd Battalion, 9th Marines will be on patrol duty until construction of a strongpoint is completed. Your main mission is to keep the damn PAVN interrupting the 1st Combat Engineer Battalion, 4nd Battalion, 12th Marines, 9th Engineer Support Battalion, and 11th Engineer Batttalion from constuction and building." Then stood straight up and said: "any questions about your mission." Everybody said: "no" Then the 1stSg Lewis said: " make sure everybody in your squad does a "Field Strip" and watch and help your "Fobbits" and make damn sure every body is in "Full battle rattle" dismissed mount up and go protect the 1st Combat Engineer Battalion, 4nd Battalion, 12th Marines, 9th Engineer Support Battalion, and 11th Engineer Batttalion Marines." We all walked out to get our squads ready for our new mission.

The 17th Parallel was the dividing line between North and South Vietnam with the Demiltarized Zone that separated the North from the South. The PAVN was always crossing over 17th Parallel Line and seeking across the Demilitarized Zone On November 9 Company L 3rd Battalion, 9th Marines set perimeters all around were the the 1st Combat Engineer Battalion, 4nd Battalion, 12th Marines, 9th Engineer Support Battalion, and 11th Engineer Batttalion Marines where they first cleared traces, minefields, sensors that the PAVN installed or laid down. Day after day the 1st Combat Engineer Battalion, 4nd Battalion, 12th Marines, 9th Engineer Support Battalion, and 11th Engineer Batttalion Marines continued construction of the SPOS (Strong Point Obstacle System). The system would be comprised of 500 meter-wide cleared traces running from the coast west to Gio Linh and then southwest to Camp Rotan and beyond.

The next few days construction went smoothly, without any interference or movements from the PAVN. November 12 as Compnay L Squads 1 and 2 were making their sweeping patrol around the back of the construction. From out no where a small company of PAVN from a bunker was firing on the 1st Combat Engineer Battalion. The Marine Engineers were running to take cover when both the 1st and 2nd Squad of Compnay L, were in full combat fighting with the PAVN 803rd Regiment. Ssgt Henry Watson gave Squad 1 the arm signals range, direction, and commence firing. 1st Squad opens up with rifle and machine fire. I yelled at Cpl Herman Watson to put a few M79 rounds near or in the bunker where the PAVN machine gun is. Cpl Watson set up his special made M79 sights with adjustments and distance and lobe two rounds right in the bunker, just like dunking a basket ball in a hoop. Those PAVN little bastards came running out of that bunker faster then you could say Jack Rabbit. After the battle was over, we noticed where the Combat Engineers had started to make a clearing about 1,500 or so feet wide.

PFC Jerry Wassel came up with a good idea to make this an ambush trap with Claymore mines the next time the PAVN made an attack. The Claymore mine fires steel balls (700 1/8 inch in diameter ball bearings) 100 feet wide out to about 110 yards within a 60° arc in front of the device. PFC Wassel talked to one of the engineers about building a spring-loaded device that would pop up from a pull cord. His idea was, lay the Claymore Mine down on a spring-loaded platform; then when the enemy was coming pull the cord, and the Claymore Mine would spring up in the up-right position to be fired. After the engineers made the spring-loaded platforms, and gave them to PFC Wassel. He assembled all 15 Claymore together with a Daisy chain (is a wiring scheme in which multiple devices are wired together in sequence to fire as one) using a M57 firing device (referred to as the "clacker") with a 3 volt pulse. . Now with 15 Claymores, a special M57 was modified to produce 12 volts to have enough current to fire all 15 blasting caps in the Claymores. PFC Wassel put all 15 Claymore mines on their spring-loaded platforms and wired everyone to a 12-volt M57. The Marine construction team was given orders not to work around the opening that the Combat

Engineers had cleared. He covered everything with dirt and leaves to camouflage all 15 Claymore mines and PFC Wassel kept the special made M57 clacker with him at all times. Now the trap was set and we waited for the PAVN attack.

A forward lookout reported that about 500 hundred of the PAVN 803rd Regiment was headed our way. All the construction battalions took cover and Company L 3rd Battalion, 9th Marines got into positionand PFC Wassel hooked up his M57 clacker and got out of sight. Then, before you knew it, the PAVN 803rd Regiment came charging through the clearing, yelling and carrying on. Platoon Sergeant GySgt Russell Owens gave the order to commence firing and all hell broke loose. PFC Wassel pulled the trip wire and all 15 Claymore mines sprung in the up way position. Then he pushed down on the M57 and all 15 Claymore mines went off at the same time. Those poor PAVN were shredded like hamburgers going through a meat grinder. Body parts of all descriptions were flying through the air followed by blood and guts. I saw PAVN human bodies with their arms, legs, hands, fingers, faces, and pounds of flesh just blow off. We all watched in amazement when none of L company did very little of firing our own weapons. Every PAVN of the 803rd Regiment that was still alive just retreated back into the jungle. We tried to separate body parts of legs, arms, torsos, and heads to get a body count. With the most acute body count we could get with all the PAVN body parts that was all mixed together. Our final count was 138 dead; we estimate the wounded of 200 or more; but some were carried off while others on their own retreated. PFC Jerry Wassel was promoted to E-3 Lance Corporal for his thinking of the ambush and saving Marine lives.

Company L, 3rd Battalion, 9th Marines, kept doing patrols around the construction area to guard and protect the construction battalions who were using bulldozers, power shovels, and scrapers to clear areas of bush, trees, tall grass, and level out the hilly ground. We guard and protect our equipment operators making the ground and surrounding area smooth and level. Then we guarded and protected the construction builders and engineers as they built A-4 and C-4 Fire Support Bases (strong points). Before A-4 and C-4 were finished Company L 3rd Battalion, 9th Marines was called back to Camp Rotan Base for other duties. Other Marine Battalions were guarding and protecting the construction battalions as they were designated to build A-1, A-2. A-3, A-5, A-6, C-1, C-2, and C-3 Fire Support Bases (strong points). The higher command decided to put one additional Marine battalion of the 4th Marine Regiment, 3rd Marine Divsion, with the ARVN 1st and 3rd Divisions would also be stationed at the Marine Combat Base at Dong Ha.

The US Marines would be responsible for Fire Support Bases A-3 through A-6 and base areas C-2 and C-3. The ARVN would be responsible for Fire Support Bases A-1 and A-2 and base area C-1 and C-4. By December 10, 1967 A-4, C-2, and C-4 were finished. Platoon and company-sized PAVN units, often in bunkers, were always trying to ambush the Marines on patrol and guard duty and create difficulties for the battalion of engineers and builders, resulting in delays in construction. The Marines killed 65 PAVN during these encounters. On 29 November 3 Marine Battalions and 2 Battalions from the Army of the Republic of Vietnam (ARVN) 1st Division conducted a clearing operation between Camp Rotan and Gio Linh. On 30 November, during the construction of A-4 Fire Support Base while on patrol Company L 3rd Battalion, the 9th Marines found and overran a PAVN bunker system killing 41 PAVN for the loss of 5 Marines killed and 13 wounded.

On December 8, this period saw relatively little PAVN activity other than harassment fire on the Camp Rotan Base, and the Marines used this relative quiet to continue to improve the strongpoints along the Trace line. On 31 December, Company I of the 3rd Battalion, 4th Marines on a patrol north from Strongpoint A-3 spotted PAVN soldiers in the southern DMZ. Company I of the 3rd Battalion, 4th Marines, started an engagement with the PAVN, and they soon realized that the PAVN occupied a line of bunkers in front of them. Company I platoon sergeant called in for help. A radio operator in Company L 3rd Battalion, 9th Marines intercepted the message and told his Platoon Sergeant GySgt Russell Owens. GySgt Owens told 1st Squad Leader Ssgt Henry Watson and 2nd Squad Leader Ssgt William Houser to get their squads over there in double time. As soon as we arrive a strike was called in for Marine mortars and artillery and two UH-1E Huey gunships they are equipped with rocket launchers, grenade launchers, and machine guns from VMO-6 (nickname Cherry Six) provided supporting fire and Company I 3rd Battalion, 4th Marines with Company L 3rd Battalion, 9th Marines covering their six was able to withdraw sustaining only 4 wounded, while the PAVN had lost at least 35 dead.

Company L, 3rd Battalion, 9th Marines, got back to Camp Rotan Base; a corporal came running and said: "Sgt Tomlin and Cpl Price the first sergeanr wants to see you." We walked up to the First Sergeant's tent and reported that Sgt Tomlin and Sgt Price were here. 1stSg Roger L. Lewis said: " come in and stand at ease." Then he said: " LTC Joseph Muller and I were talking about your process and your combat duties. We both feel that you have always went above and beyond the call of duty and he suggested since the PAVN active is low that I give you both a three day pass in Da Nang." Then he stood back and kind of laughed and said: "if it was me on a three pass, I would drink my ass off and fuck my dick off." Then he just laughed again, and said: well, maybe not fuck your dick off, with some of the venereal diseases going around, your dick will just probably fall off. So if I were you two, you might want to take it easy on the fucking department." He said: "any questions". We both said: "no". The First Sergeant said: "dismissed and go get some rest and relaxation and here are your pass papers. The next supply helicopter is leaving for Da Nang in about two hours." We both said: "thank You first Sergeant." We ran out of his tent to go pack our sea bags and catch the next supply helicopter to Da Nang Air Force Base.

At last Butch and I got a three-furlow from them, damn battle and rice fields. Always on your guard worried about if the next bend in the road would be your last walk because a PAVN bullet had your name on it, would put you under. We were going to Da Nang; the city was home to a major air base that was used by both the

South Vietnamese and United States air forces As we were flying over Camp Rotan Base, looking down on the vast jungle thinking the Old PAVN was not going to get us today. Then I was listening to the song from the chopter blades making this pulsing, oscilating, slapping sound Then my mind started drifting back to my childhood, missing my brother Gene and Jimmy and all the stuff we did as kids. Then I remember the Soap Box Derby that we were going to make with the big idea to win that $3,000.00 thousand dollar prize money. Dad, Gene, Jimmy, and I went to our local Metropolitan Chevrolet Dealership in Springfiedl, Illinois to get the kit to build Soap Box Derby car. The kit included the brake, steering assemblies, and wheels. axles, and building instructions. Each boy was required to construct the car by himself, though he was allowed to seek advice from others. The total cost of the vehicle out of pocket was not to exceed $10. Dad said: "he would only give advice when we started to build assemble the car." We built the car and painted it bright red and I need the gold lettering with the Chevy Dealership name and our names. We took it to Lincoln Park for trail runs. Gene tried first, then Jimmy tried second; then it was my turn. I started down the hill and the steering was feeling kind of funny, then I heard a snap, the steering cables broke. I was pushing on that brake like a mad man, then all of a sudden the car turned a real hard right and I went into the cement curve. Our beautiful red car, the whole front end was smashed and broken off. Gene, Jimmy, and I were all sad as we carried our broken Soap Box Derby car home. Then I thought my brother Jimmy was calling my name Robert. Then I realized it was Butch saying: " Robert hay wake up we are landing at Da Nang Air Force Base."

We were at a bar named the Golden Dragon in Da Nang, setting outside at a table drinking a couple of Buds. Then Butch said: " lets try the local beer called Tiger Beer", but was actually named Biere Larue, and came in a one-liter bottle. After one slip Butch spit it out and said: "this taste like shit." He called the waitress over and ordered another Bud. We were in idle conversation about the war, going home seeing our families again. When this Vietnamese girl about 5 feet tall, weighing about 100 pounds, coal-black hair, and brown eyes, she had a pretty face and was about 21 or 22, approached us and said: "Do you want miso" Well, stupid me said: " do you mean miso soup food." Then she got kind of pissed and said " No Meso Horny, I do you for 5 dollar." Then stupid me again said: "5 dollars for what" By now she is boiling and said: " give you a blow job 5 dollar." Both Butch and I said: "no" She turned around and hiked up her skirt and showed us her bare ass and said: You two must be Đồng Tính Luyến Ái (Who is found loving in the same field. Gay Neutral). **(1-44)** Butch and I just laughed and started saying miso soup; then we would say meso horny. We had a couple more beers and asked for the tap, which was 42,000 VND Vietnam dollars converted to US dollars for a total of $2.10 dollars and 10 cents. Butch left $2.50 dollars and 50 cents, told the waitress to keep the change, then we headed back to our hotel. We got back to the Anna Hotel when to our room, I took a hot shower and Butch took a long hot bath. We went out and got some food from the street vendor, which was Ba Mua, a mixed bowl of frog, chicken, eel, and beef with rice noodles, spring onions and vegetables. It was really tasty compared to those damn C-Rats (C-Rations) we got in the field. Then Butch and I were talking about Vietnamese girl who kept saying Meso Honey. Then Butch said: “Robert we really screw up with that Vietnamese girl maybe she was a real hummer (person who really gives good blow jobs) we just blew our chances.” Then I said: “ Butch she so pissed at us besides she think we were queer and she would not come back even if we gave $10,00 dollars a piece.” Then Butch was being funny; then he said: “ Queer ah give me a kiss baby” We though it was really funny and both just laugh our asses off.

I suggested to Butch after breakfast we could do a little sight seeing only in the areas where the Marines said it was safe. We ate our meal, then we went back to the hotel and hit the racks. Got up early the next morning, went down and had breakfast. I had the Pho is a kind of soup with rice noodles flavored with meat, which could be beef, chicken, or pork, and vegetables. So I ordered the Pho with chicken with coffee and orange juice. Butch ordered Banh Cueo rice flour with ground pork with wood-ear mushrooms wrapped inside thin rice rolls, served with bean sprouts with coffee and orange juice. We had a nice breakfast and conversation and headed out of the hotel to sight-see. The three days went by real fast and the next thing you knew we were on the chopter flying back to Camp Rotan Base. We got to our tent and unpacked our sea bags and headed for the mess tent for chow. The next morning a corporal came by and said: “Sgt Tomlin and Sgt Price the First Sergeant wants to see you first thing this morning.” We said: “ Thank You corporal.” We headed the the first sergeant quarters when we went inside to our surprise along with 1stSg Roger L. Lewis was LTC Joseph Muller, GySgt Russell Owens, Ssgt Henry Watson, and Ssgt William Houser. Butch and I stood attention and rendered a salute to LTC Muller. The LTC Muller returned the salute and told us to stand at ease. LTC Muller said: “it has come to my attenuation that Ssgt Thomas Kidd 3rd Squad Leader and Ssgt Harvey Powell 4th Squad leader are going to be DIs at Camp Pendleton and will be rotated back to states in about two weeks.” then he said: “ 1stSg Roger L. Lewis and GySgt Russell Owens both have agreed to move Ssgt Henry Watson to 3rd Squad Leader and Ssgt William Houser to 4th Squad Leader and I am promoting Sgt Tomlin to Ssgt Robert Dean Tomlin as 1st Squad Leader and Sgt Price to Ssgt Frederick (Butch) Philip Price as 2nd Squad Leader.” We stood attention, rendered a salute, and said: “Thank You SIR, First Sergeant , and Platoon Sergeant. LTC Muller said: “The only reason we are making a switch is for Ssgt Watson to 3rd Squad and Ssgt Houser to 4th Squad. For a simple reason that Ssgt Tomlin knows 1st Squad inside and out and Ssgt Price knows 2nd Squad inside and out. Later you can give the name to the First Sergeant who you want your 1st Squad Rifle Team and 2nd Squad Rifle Team Leaders you want. Any questions.” We all said: “no” Then LTC Muller said: “dismissed and go and let your new strips sew on.” Butch and I both decided that 1st Squad Rifle Team Leader would be Cpl Herman Watson and 2nd Squad Rifle Team Leader would be Cpl John Hillberg.

On the morning of 7 January, while attempting to neutralize a PAVN sniper, two fire teams from Company L 3rd Battalion, 4th Marines, were ambushed. The remainder of Company L and Company K were sent in to help the 1st and 2nd fire to break away from the PAVN sniper but were pinned down and could not move. Staff Sergeant from Company K called in for help from Company L 3rd Battalion, 9th Marines so that they could get their 1st and 2nd Squads out of PAVN sniper fire. His last comment: "we have been into a daylong battle." So Ssgt. Tomlin and Ssgt Price double time with Company L Squads 1 and 2 to eliminate the PAVN snipers. When we arrived both squads were low crawling into position to get clear shots at the PAVN snipers. When we were in position I could see 10 or so PAVN snipers bunch together by a clump of bushes well hidden from the Marine down below. They had 30 or more Marines pinned down where they could even move. I gave an arm signal to 2nd Fire Team Leader Cpl John Hillberg with his 8-barrel shotgun with enemy in sight, change directions go right, range with one finger, commence firing. When that 8 barrel shotgun went off, all you could hear was screaming and yelling and about 9 or so dead PAVN bodies. When it was all over with, by the end of the day, the Marines had lost 6 killed, 36 wounded and 1 missing. Staff Sergeant from Company K said: " with out Company L 3rd Battalion, 9th Marines I could have lost my whole company." Company L, 3rd Battalion, 9th Marines, pick up the dead and wounded Marines and looked all over for the missing Marine and never found him; so we went back to Camp Rotan Base. Companies L and K 3rd Battalion, 4th Marines, went on to finish their mission. When we got back to base I made the report and stated we never found the missing Marine.

On 11 January those dirty rotten bastards PAVN had dragged the body of that poor Marine into the DMZ and were using him as bait to trap and kill US Marines when they came to take his body home. Butch and I were so pissed that we volunteered for Company L 3rd Battalion, 9th Marines alone, with two other companies to mount an operation to recover the body of the Marine missing in the 7 January operation of them, damn PAVN snipers. As the three companies were getting closer to the DMZ, we all stopped. I sent forward 3 scouts to check out the PAVN positions. And where the missing Marine was located. They came back and made the report a corporal said: "Sgt Tomlin they have that poor Marine all exposed in the middle of tall grass with PAVN all around with an ambush ready to fire on us as we go pick up the Marine. Platoon Sergeant GySgt Russell Owens and the other Platoon Sergeants called in Marines air strikes with support from the artillery and ordered the companies to outflanked the PAVN positions, once the bombs and shells strated going off. I told my squad when you hear the first bomb or shell run as fast as you can and recover that dead Marine. Within a few minutes everybody was in position then the explosions started. My 1st squad covered two corporals as they ran after the dead Marine to pick him up. They got him and carry him back to safely In the process the air strikes and artillery destroyed 25 bunkers and killed 75 PAVN for the loss of 2 Marines wounded. Then one corporal was head making this comment: " lets get one of the dead PAVN bodies and stake him out for an ambush." Ssgt Price said: " are you frigging crazy they would let that poor son-of-a-bitch rot before they would come and get him."

On 18 January Company L 3rd Battalion, 4th Marines launched a patrol about 3 klicks northeast of Camp Rotan Base into an area where a lot of Marines were wounded and killed. A corporal from the Company L 3rd Battalion, 9th Marines nicknamed the area Meat Market. The patrol was ambushed by PAVN in well-camouflaged bunkers that spit the company up in several groups. Fire Team squad one, the lead squad was cut off from the rest of the Company, was left out to dry, with no Marine was killed or wounded. They were being used as bait by the PAVN for the rest of the company of Marines to try and rescue them. The PAVN commander had his men in the bunkers to spring the trap for the isolated Marines. Ssgt John West called for back-up from Company L 3rd Battalion, 9th Marines, to come up behind the bunkers and take them by surprise. Ssgt West called in support from Marine gunships and artillery fire. Sgt Robert Dean Tomlin radioed the survivors and dead of the isolated squad to make their way back into the Company perimeter. Company L 3rd Battalion, 9th Marines then moved forward to relieve Company L 3rd Battalion, 4th Marines. Then when Company L 3rd Battalion, 4th Marines and Company L 3rd Battalion ,9th Marines were in position. The Marines hit the PAVN bunkers. with everything but the kitchen sink. Marine losses were 9 dead and 22 wounded, while the PAVN had 100 killed and numerous wounded.

Company L, 3rd Battalion, 9th Marines, was always on call to help or relieve a company of Marines from fire fights, ambushes, and some times United Staes Army support. At 0200 on 2 February the PAVN launched an attack against Combined Action of Marines in Company P and a detachment of United States Army M42 Dusters at headquarters at Cam Lộ. Although the M42 Duster was initially designed for an anti-aircraft role, it proved to be highly effective against unarmored ground forces in Vietnam. M42 was equipped with 2A1 40 mm twin anti-aircraft gun and a 7.62mm M60 machine gun. Since Company L 3rd Battalion, 9th Marines, was close to Cam Lo, we received the radio call for help. The Marines and M42 held off the PAVN attack until relieved by a quick reaction force from Company L 3rd Battalion, 9th Marines. We arrive just as the PAVN makes their final attack on Compay P headquarters. Squads one and two hit them head-on with rifle and machine gun fire. Ssgt Tomlin and Ssgt Price had their M79 men launching M79 rounds directing on the attacking PAVN. Then the M42 cut loose with 40mm rounds into the charging PAVN. With M79 explosions and 40mm rounds firing directing all around the PAVN. The PAVN commander was yelling retreat, but it was too late. The PAVN lost 211 killed and 23 captured while the Marines lost 2 dead and 18 wounded. The United States Army lost 1 killed; he was firing the 7.62mm M60 machine gun outside the tank and was shot by a PAVN sniper.

On 7 February the PAVN ambushed a route patrol platoon of Company K 3rd Battalion, 3rd Marines south of Camp Rotan. The Marines were putting up a hell of a battle until 9 Marines were killed along with the Platoon Commander. Again, Company L 3rd Battalion, 9th Marines was on patrol a few klicks from the ambush.

We got the radio call for support to help Company K 3rd Battalion, 3rd Marines. While we were double time to the ambush, Ssgt Tomlin and Ssgt Price put their two squads into a spear head attack. When we arrived the remainder of Company K moved to reinforce the ambushed platoon and they were ambushed from well-concealed PAVN bunkers. I told my squad to concentrate the PAVN bunkers to the right. Ssgt Price told his squad to concentrate PAVN bunkers to the left. As squads one and two lay down all kinds of fire power, we were too late. Company K, 3rd Battalion, 3rd Marines suffered 18 killed and 10 wounded in the first 5 minutes. The Platoon commanders and their radio operators were also killed. At Company K 3rd Battalion, 3rd Marines operations center their support on Strongpoint A-3. The Battalion Commander ordered Compny L 3rd Battalion, 9th Marines to establish blocking positions while Company M 3rd Battalion, 3rd Marines maneured to relieve Company K 3rd Battalion, 3rd Marines. Company M 3rd Battalion, 3rd Marines, was unable to reach the ambush site before dark, and Company L 3rd Battalion, 3rd Marines returned to Strongpoint A-3. When night came Company K 3rd Battalion, 3rd Marines and Company 3rd Battalion, 3rd Marines M dug in for the night. On the morning of 8 February, the three Marine Companies, an air strike was called in. Gunships supported by tanks, artillery attacked the PAVN bunker complex, killing 239 PAVN, while suffering a another 3 Marines killed. With the defeat of the PAVN at A-3, there was a decline in PAVN activity along the DMZ apart from ongoing artillery, rocket and mortar fire.

The decline in PAVN activity lasted about two weeks and they started all over again. In the two weeks that PAVN did not attack any strongpoint, it made the patrols for Company L 3rd Battalion, 9th Marines, just an easy route out and in of Camp Rotan Base. Then, while on patrol Company L 3rd Battalion, the 9th Marines received a radio call again for support. A scout sent Company L 3rd Battalion, 9th Marines a radio call that the PAVN had a battalion headed straight for A-3 strong point between Camp Rotan and Gio Linh. On 3 March RRT (Radio Reconnaissance Team) contacted Company L, 3rd Battalion, 3rd Marines, occupying an outpost on Hill 28 just north of the A-3, to intercept a PAVN battalion attempting to pass in groups through gaps in the Marine defensive line and the Marine positions. As the PAVN battalion of the 320th Division encircled the Marines, Compny L 3rd Battalion, 9th Marines was called into action again. When we arrived at Hill 28 Company L 3rd Battalion, 9th Marines squads one, two, three, and four were getting into position. The PAVN battalion was getting ready to make their attack, when the PAVN commander gave the command to attack all hell broke loose. Machine guns, rifles, and M79 rounds were firing everywhere. As we were squeezing our fingers off, the company commander had called in an air strike. It was a sight to see the Huey gunship spitting out bullets faster then you could blind an eye at those damn PAVN. They were dropping faster than Meadowlarks eating mosquitoes on a June night. The PAVN were driven back by airstrikes and Compny L 3rd Battalion, 9th Marines fire fight. One Marine was killed and thirteen wounded while killing over 300 PAVN.

On 16 March, Company M, 3rd Battalion, 3rd Marines and Company C, 1st

Battalion, 4th Marines clashed with another battalion-sized PAVN force. The two Marine companies called in artillery and air strikes upon the PAVN, the bulk of which disengaged. But the PAVN commander leaving a company behind to fight, and defensive and delaying fight engaged in by the PAVN's rear guard, as in covering the retreat of its battalion and the evacuation. PAVN artillery from the north of the DMZ answered the American supporting arms with a 400-round barrage of its own on the Marines. Marine casualties were two killed and nine wounded for 183 PAVN killed. For the entire month in Operation Kentucky, 9th Marines reported over 600 enemy dead, while Marine casualties were 37 killed and more than 200 wounded.

Operation ILLinois Casualties

Date November 1967 -- March 1968

Location Camp Rotan, Quảng Trị Province, South Vietnam

Result Allied tactical victory

Belligerents

United States South Vietnam	North Vietnam North Vietnam

Commanders and leaders

LTC Joseph Muller .	Colonel Hoa La Hung PAVN Commander Vanh chu Giang PAVN

Units involved

2nd Battalion, 1st Marines 3rd Battalion, 3rd Marines 1st Battalion, 4th Marines 2nd Battalion, 4th Marines 3rd Battalion, 4th Marines 2nd Battalion, 9th Marine 3rd Battalion, 9th Marines 3rd Battalion, 26th Marines 2nd Battalion, 12th Marines	320th Division 803rd Regiment, 324B Division

Strength

Casualties and losses

United States 520 killed	US body count 3,839 killed 117 captured

CHAPTER FIFTEEN

Vietnam War

Operation Ben Hai River

Operation Ben Hai River was an operation conducted by the United States Marine Corps in the area around Camp Rotan, and Vietnamese Demilitarized Zone from April -- May 1968.

Key United States Commanders	Key North Vietnam Commanders
LTC Joseph Muller USMC	Colonel Trang Le Duong PAVN
1stSg Roger L. Lewis USMC	Commander Vanh chu Giang PAVN
GySgt Russell Owens USMC	
Ssgt Henry Watson USMC	
Ssgt William Houser USMC	
Ssgt Robert Dean Tomlin USMC	
Ssgt Frederick (Butch) Philip Price USMC	

Operation Prairie V started on 20 April as a two regiment search and destroy operation, covering the same area as Operation Prairie IV. The 3rd Battalion, 3rd Marines, and the 3rd Battalion, 9th Marines, were placed in the northwest portion of the area of operations. The 9th Marines, using the 1st Battalion, 4th Marines, and the 1st Battalion, 9th Marines were to cover the vital piedmont area (landform created at the foot of a mountain) in and around Quang Tri City. Initially, the operation confined all units to relatively fixed positions. But now, with the PAVN moving around everywhere, fixed positions were changed to moving positions. LTC Joseph Muller's 3rd Battalion, 9th Marines was a temporary transfer from Camp Rotan Base and was charged with security for Camp Carroll and the Mai Loc Camp. Company L, 3rd Battalion, 9th Marines, was on patrol every day, keeping the PAVN in check. Lt. Col. Gary Wilder's 3rd Battalion, 3rd Marines held the Rockpile and placed companies at Ca Lu Combat Base and Ba Long and was responsible for providing security for the 11th Engineers who kept Route 9 open to Khe Sanh Combat Base. In the 9th Marines area of operations, the 1st Battalion, 9th Marines defended Đông Hà and provided one company for security of Cửa Việt Base. The 1st Battalion, 4th Marines protected the engineers clearing the trace between Firebase Gio Linh and Camp Rotan and provided a company as security for the Gio Linh Composite Artillery battalion.

Although contact with the PAVN was light at the beginning of the operation, with very little fighting. Then one day, LTC Muller received reconnaissance reports that indicated a PAVN buildup northwest of the Rockpile. LTC Muller gave direct orders to 1stSg Roger L. Lewis to have Company L 3rd Battalion, 9th Marines squads one and two to stop the mortar, rocket attacks. LTC Muller said: "the Marines must continued clearing the trace around Camp Rotan and Gio Linh. Tell Ssgt Tomlin and Ssgt Price to put a damn end to those frigging mortar and rocket attacks." Every day Company L 3rd Battalion, 9th Marines squads one and two were in a fire fight destroying PAVN's mortar and rocket sites. Attacks on the positions of the 1st Battalion, 4th Marines and the engineers became almost daily affairs and included not only mortar and rocket fire from the southern half of the DMZ. PAVN artillery attacks with medium and heavy artillery fire from a growing number of fortifications north of the Bến Hải River, to stop the Marine engineers from completing their job. Then a major air strike was called in to eliminate the PAVN's artillery fortifications. F-105 Thunderchief, F-4 Phantom II, and A-4 Skyhawk dropped more bombs and rockets than you could point a stick at. Within 2 or 3 days, after the air strikes, the PAVN artillery fortifications started to disappear. Then the Marine engineers were started to complete their mission. Company L, 3rd Battalion, 9th Marines squads one and two were still out every day knocking out mortar and rocket sites.

On 24 April hill fighting continued on the western sector of the DMZ at Hill 758 near Khe Sanh. Once again, Company L 3rd Battalion, 9th Marines, was called in for a clean-up. This day was a real rough one for squad one and two; the damn PAVN had us in a cross-fire; we were pinned down and could not move. Ssgt Tomlin told 1st Fire Team Leader Cpl Herman Watson to take two men and crawl around to the right of the PAVN crossfire and lobe in several M79 rounds. Ssgt. Price told 2nd Fire Team Leader Cpl John Hillberg to take two men and crawl around to the left of the PAVN crossfire and lobbed in several M79 rounds. Ssgt Tomlin and Ssgt Price told both Fire Team Leaders to use the new phosphorus M79 rounds and burn those PAVN son-of-a-bitches out of there. When the fire teams were in position, Ssgt Tomlin gave the arm signal to commence firing. As soon as those M79 rounds started going off, all you could hear was screaming and yelling from them, poor PAVN bastards, as the phosphorus was burning through their bodies. Within 15 minutes the PAVN crossfires had stopped; the PAVN were gone. We checked the area to make sure it was clear before we moved on. Attacks from PAVN forces cut Route 9 between Cam Lộ Combat Base and Khe Sanh. Now supply trucks could not get troops or supplies to Marine bases. Those damn PAVN repeatedly made an attempt to isolate the Marines on Route 9. Finally Rout 9 was open now another problem was the PAVN attacked Gio Linh, Camp Carroll and Dong Ha with mortars rockets and artillery. On 27/8 April it was like a 4th of July with all the and fire explosions from the PAVN at Gio Linh, Camp Carroll and Dong Ha. The Marines tried mopping up the areas, but not before the PAVN had fired approximately 850 rounds of artillery, plus 200 mortar rounds hit Gio Linh, while more than 50 140mm rockets hit Đông Hà.

Company L, 3rd Battalion, 9th Marines, were sleeping in their tents when, at 03:00 on 8 May, some 300 rounds of mortar and artillery fire hit Camp Rotan as a decoy. So that PAVN Sappers (a PAVN Special Operations Force, who did not care if they lived or died) with Bangalore Torpedoes (is an explosive charge placed within one or several connected tubes) could make a gap in and break through the perimeter wire. Squads one, two three, and four of Company L 3rd Battalion, 9th Marines were racing towards the perimeter wire to stop the PAVN break-through. As soon as we were in position at 04:00 two battalions of the PAVN 812th Regiment armed with flamethrowers were starting to come through the busted wire. Ssgt Tomlin and Ssgt Price told the riflemen to hit the PAVN's flamethrower tanks.. Numerous shots were fired from the M14s and then all of a sudden the whole place lit up like it was day light. Those PAVN flamethrowers tanks of napalm (gelling agents aluminum naphthenate and aluminum salts) blew up after getting hit by 7.62 bullets. The PAVN flamethrowers were on fire screaming and running around like human torches lighting up the whole base camp. Sgt Tomlin and Sgt Price told their riflemen to shoot the poor son-of-a-bitches to put them out of their misery When the PAVN attack started the base was defended by the command element and Company D. 1st Battalion, 4th Marines, that fell primarily on Company D's northern perimeter. Fierce hand-to-hand combat with the PAVN 812th Regiment along the perimeter with the Marines eventually led to repelling the initial attacking forces. Only to be stopped by a relief column from Company A was sent with a M42 Duster, 2 LVT-5s (Landing Vehicle, Tracked, Personnel 5) and 2 quarter ton trucks. The PAVN hit the M42 with an RPG-7; the Marines escaped before the tank was destroyed. Then the PAVN hit one LVT-5 and one half ton trucks were destroyed by flamethrowers and satchel charges. A large number of casualties continuing for an extended period or without interruption by Marines of A Company. By 09:00 the PAVN had withdrawn, leaving 397 killed and 8 prisoners. The Marines had suffered 44 killed and 110 wounded.

Attack after attack on Camp Rotan Base, I think at one point we were taking cover more than going on. Patrol. Butch Said: " Robert I can not hardly sleep with all this frigging mortars and rockets going off."

I said: "I hope the first sergeant send us on a mission to eliminate those frigging mortars and rockets sites." PAVN activity became greater, more serious, and more extreme throughout Leatherneck Square was an area just south of the Vietnamese Demilitarized Zone that separated North Vietnam and South Vietnam.. Every frigging night at Camp Rotan Base the number and volume of artillery attacks increased greatly. Some Marine engineers estimated that more than 4200 mortar, rocket and artillery rounds were fired at Marine positions during the month of May. The PAVN makes unknown and secret information known and is followed up by the Marines intelligence. The PAVN started extent to which something happens and the process and result of becoming knowledgeable of its buildup in the area. On 10 May, a Marine A-4E Skyhawk flying a radar-controlled mission near the southern boundary of the DMZ. As the A-4E Skyhawk approached its target, 3 Russian SAM (surface to air missiles) fired from positions north of the Bến Hải River. CPT Philip Barlow received the signal it was being painted and diverted with turns and speed and caused two SAM missiles to miss him. But at the last minute, when he straightened the plane up from a real hard bank right, one of the SAM missiles hit the A-4E on the right wing. CPT Barlow radio in and said: "Mayday, mayday, mayday." He kept in radio contact giving coordinates near the Ben Hai River until he had to bail. Base Commander LTC Joseph Muller was madder then a wet back hen, and made this comment: "this is the first reported use of PAVN SAMs over South Vietnam." Then he said: Company L 3rd Battalion, 9th Marines squads one and two mount up and take two UH-1 helicopter gunships and go save that pilot at all cost." We were in the air within 15 minutes going to save that pilot before the PAVN got him. As we approached his location we could see him "popping purple smoke" as one helicopter landed to pick him up; the other helicopter circled to give us protection while we were on the ground. We got him in the helicopter, safe and sound. CPT Barlow said: "without you Marines saving my ass I would be in the hands of those damn PAVN and I woud be dead meat by now." We flew back to Camp Rotan Base and CPT Philip Barlow took another helicopter and flew back to his Marine Air Base.

With the PAVN ground activity also increased during the period between 13 and 16 May, while the Marine engineers began clearing Route 561 from Cam Lộ to Camp Rotan, once again Company L 3rd Battalion, 9th Marines were protecting and keeping the engineers safe as they were working on Route 561. The 1st Battalion, 3rd Marines got into a fire fight with a large PAVN force in well-prepared positions south of Camp Rotan. 1st Battalion, 3rd Marines radio for support with the aid of 1st Battalion, 4th Marines, and 1st Battalion, 9th Marines, the PAVN retreated north in to the DMZ after 115 PAVN were killed.

Marine Battalions station below the Vietnamese Demilitarized Zone participating units joined Prairie V sweeping Leatherneck Square and the area southwest of Camp Rotan. On 28 May 1st Battalion, 3rd Marines ran into a bunker complex on Hill 174, 6 klicks southwest of Camp Rotan. Companies M and L attacked the complex but were driven back by small arms, machine guns, 57mm recoilless rifles and 82mm mortars. Marines of Companies M and L 1st Battalion, 3rd Marines charge the PAVN complex again with the loss of 2 Marines killed and 21 wounded. Company M called in an artillery strike; the Marines shelled the hill throughout the night and the next day. Companies M and I attacked the hill, thinking there were only a few PAVN left, without driving the PAVN from the crest of the hill; the Marines suffering 5 KIA (killed in action) and 33 wounded. The Marines 1st Battalion, 3rd Marines Company M and I attacked unsuccessfully again on 30 May suffering 1 killed and 45 wounded. The PAVN abandoned the hill during the night of 30/31 May with 148 killed.

Operation Ben Hai River

April -- May 1968.

Location

Quảng Trị Province, South Vietnam
Resul Both sides claim victory

Belligerents

United States	North Vietnam North Vietnam

Commanders and leaders

LTC Joseph Muller	Colonel Trang Le Duong PAVN Commander Vanh chu Giang PAVN

Units involved

1st Battalion, 4th Marines 1st Battalion, 9th Marines 2nd Battalion, 9th Marines 3rd Battalion, 9th Marines 2nd Battalion, 26th Marines	324B Division

Strength

Casualties and losses

United States 164 killed	US body count 905 killed 9 captured

CHAPTER SIXTEEN

Vietnam War

Operation Purple Martin North and South

Operation Purple Martin North and South was a U.S. Marine Corps operation that took place southeast of Khe Sanh, Quảng Trị Province from 2–19 June 1968.

Key United States Commanders	**Key North Vietnam Commanders**
LTC Joseph Muller USMC	Colonel Tra Dinch PAVN
1stSg Roger L. Lewis USMC	Commander Vanh chu Giang PAVN
GySgt Russell Owens USMC	
Ssgt Henry Watson USMC	
Ssgt William Houser USMC	
Ssgt Robert Dean Tomlin USMC	
Ssgt Frederick (Butch) Philip Price USMC	

Operation Purple Martin North

On 2 June Company L 3rd Battalion, 9th Marines broaded helicopters from Tomahawk Base to Khe Sanh to be Roving Patrols for the the 1st Battalion, 1st Marines that conducted a helicopter assault into Landing Zone Purple Martin 10 km southeast of Khe Sanh. The 1st and 3rd squads of Company L were hiding on the outskirts of the landing zone in case they ran into trouble or conflict with PAVN. The 1st Battalion, 1st Marines, with Company L 2nd and 4th squads, then moved north towards Route 9 in an attempt to push the PAVN towards the 2nd Battalion, 3rd Marines, that were in position as they blocked Route 9. As the PAVN advanced towards 2nd Battalion, 3rd Marines on Route 9 a fire fight erupted. The PAVN was caught in a cross-fire between Company L 3rd Battalion, 9th Marines 1st and 3rd squads on the right side and 1st Battalion, 1st Marines with Company L 2nd and 4th squads on the left side. The PAVN retreated after about half an hour into the fire fight with several casualties. That evening, when the PAVN did not pose a threat and all clear was the radio for the helicopters to land. The 2nd Battalion 4th Marines were lifted from Ca Lu Combat Base to Purple Martin Landing Zone. On the morning of 3 June the 1st Battalion, 4th Marines relieved the 2nd Battalion, 4th Marines at Landing Zone Purple Martin.

The 2nd Battalion 4th Marines boarded helicopters to conduct sudden violent and fierce destructive attacks into Landing Zone Loon was a U.S. Marine Corps base located southeast of Khe Sanh, Quảng Trị Province in central Vietnam. Landing Zone Loon 4 klicks west of Purple Martin and approximately 8 Klicks southeast of Khe Sanh. When the 2nd Battalion 4th Marines landed at Loon on 3 June, they set up their base camp. At 06:00 on 4 June, they were met by the PAVN 88th Regiment with small arms, mortar and artillery fire. Company commander of the 2nd Battalion 4th Marines radio for help and back up. Company L, 3rd Battalion, 9th Marines, received the call we were in bound to help 2nd Battalion 4th Marines. When we arrived, the 2nd Battalion 4th Marines, were pinned down and could not move. Ssgt.Tomlin's 1st squad started putting down rifle and machine gun fire and knocking out small arms and mortar fire with M79 rounds. Ssgt Price called in an air strike to take care of the PAVN artillery fire. That Bell AH-1 SuperCobra came in from no where and started dicing and slicing that PAVN artillery up with its 197 20mm Turret Gun and rockets and just blew the PAVN artillery to pieces. When everything was under control the Company F 2nd Battalion 4th Marines had 2 Marines killed and the PAVN 88th Regiment 54 dead. Company L 3rd Battalion, 9th Marines returned to Camp Rotan Base.

On 5 June Company C 1st Battalion, 1st Marines while on patrol engage in conflict with a PAVN bunker with machine gun and small arms fire 4 klicks south of Route 9. One Platoon Sergeant was heard making this comment: "those little bastards were well dug in it took us until the following afternoon until the battle was over." Then another Platoon Sergeant was heard making this comment: "once we busted into the bunkers, it was like a fox in the hen house then the feathers started flying."

At 06:00 on 6 June, a PAVN Battalion attacked Landing Zone Loon again with machine gun, rifle, and mortar fire. After a 2-hour battle, the 1st Battalion, 1st Marines had the upper hand that resulted in 184 PAVN dead. The only way the PAVN could withdrew and retreat was under cover of mortar and artillery fire. During the afternoon the 1st Battalion, 1st Marines, were extracted by helicopter. As the last HMM-165 CH-46 was ready to lift off from the Loon, it was hit by PAVN anti-aircraft fire and crashed, killing 13 Marines. . The total Marine losses for their 3 days at Loon were 24 dead and 37 wounded and PAVN 197 killed. After several battles and due to the steady pressure on Loon, the upper brass decided to abandon Landing Zone Loon project.

Operation Purple Martin South

On 6 June the 3rd Battalion, 9th Marines conducted a helicopter direct attack against PAVN forces into a landing zone southeast of Purple Martin. They sent a small ground force and were near the eastern end of the PAVN supply road. The Marines found that the road was well constructed, up to 18 ft wide with numerous culverts and the trees overhead tied together to reduce aerial observation. Ssgt Tomlin was heard making this comment: " I did not know those little bastards could built a road so well. Those little son-of-a-bitches tied the trees together to form a living archway of vegetation beneath which troops and vehicles could pass unseen from the air." Ssgt

Price was heard making this comment: " you would not believe what was beside the road they had fighting holes, living bunkers, hospitals, kitchens, and a wealth of equipment, especially tools. There were picks, shovels, wrecking bars, axes, and explosives." CPT Joseph Cotowelski, who commanded Company I, 3d Battalion, 9th Marines, was heard making this comment: " the road was a virtual clone of the Ho Chi Minh Trail." The 3rd Battalion, the 9th Marines, was given orders to move west along the road, and for several days they destroyed PAVN bunkers, hospitals, kitchens and storehouses and facilities as they went down the road.

After several days of interrogating, PAVN prisoners were asked where the major supply area and how the road was built, and none of the prisoners were talking. Platoon Sergeant GySgt Russell Owens came up with a great idea by having interpreters ask the PAVN prisoners if they knew what a Hollywood beating was. The PAVN prisoners did not know what the interpreter was talking about. So the Platoon Sergeant Owens gave a little demonstration with a bar soap in a sock and gave a couple of quick whacks on the PAVN prisoner's back. He started crying and screaming and saying "không còn, không còn" (no more) **(1-45)**. This time Platoon Sergeant Owens put all his force with the next blow right between his should blades, the PAVN prisoner went down like a ton of rocks. He was screaming "họ sẽ giết tôi" (they will kill me) **(1-46)** "nếu tôi nói với bạn" (if I tell you) **(1-47)** . 1st Squad Leader Ssgt Robert Dean Tomlin asked Platoon Sergeant Owens if he could have a go at it. Ssgt Tomlin took the sock with the bar of soap in it and banged it real hard on the floor next to the PAVN prisoner's ear. The PAVN prisoner started screaming and yelling"Tôi sẽ nói cho bạn biết, "Tôi sẽ nói cho bạn biết" (I will tell you) **(1-48)**. He spilled his guts about Lang Hole a Montagnard village south of Landing Zone Loon where a PAVN major supply area was located. Then 2nd Squad Leader Ssgt Frederick (Butch) Philip Price took the sock to the next prisoner and before he banged the sock on the floor, the PAVN prisoner started singing like a canary. The PAVN prisoner said: " that the construction schedule called for the road to reach Hue by 30 July, a task with inspiring fear from Colonel Vương Thừa Vũ who had them pushing the road through the steep jungle terrain at a rate of over one mile-as the crow flies, per day". Then the PAVN prisoner let the cat out of the bag by saying: "PAVN 83rd "tiểu đoàn kỹ sư" (Engineer Battalion) **(1-49)** was helping build the road." LTC Joseph Muller makes arrangements with the 3rd Battalion, 4th Marines, to destroy the road and Company L 3rd Battalion, 9th Marines, to destroy PAVN's major supply area.

On 11 June the 3rd Battalion, 4th Marines with helicopters made a physical attack on the road by blowing up trees, and Douglas A-1 Skyraiders and F-105 Thunderchiefs were dropping bomb after bomb-making craters the size of elephants all over the PAVN's road. A sergeant from the 3rd Battalion, 4th Marines, was heard making this comment: " it will take them damn PAVNS years before anything could move on that road again."

Company L 3rd Battalion, 9th Marines was moving close to Lang Hole a Montagnard village south of Landing Zone Loon. We came up on Montagnard village in the middle of no where. Ssgt Robert Dean Tomlin told the point man to scout ahead and give the signal if every thing is clear. The platoons are staying back under cover, waiting for the signal. It is hotter than hell, and the humidity is so damn high your back is sticky with sweat and your flat jacket feels like it weighed a ton. Then your nose smells, an odor flows upward, out of the open neck of your utility shirt, and you discover with an ugly, twisted expression on your face that the smell is you. The sun pounding down on you like a giant heat wave. Then you are thinking, I need a hot shower and a very cold drink. Butch comes over and says: "Robert this sweat is burning my eyes, flowing along the edge my nose, gathers, then pushes on down to the corner of my mouth, I need a frigging cold beer." Then we get the signal all clear, the two platoons move forward. Me and my M79 launcher, Corporal John Hillberg see a Vietanese villager standing by a hut, giving us a hand signal to come here. We are both hotter then a whore in a whore house when a cattle drive and a bunch of cowboys come to town on Saturday looking for a frig. Our tongues are flicking out from the lack of drink. Hot, tired, smelly and uncomfortable, then we hear the villager's voice: "Cold soda, Marines?" We smile with a big "yes!" He flips off the coke top and pours that wonderful fluid into a paper cup full of chipped ice. Then, with fast thinking about ice, I said: "they have no refrigeration is this village." Jusy before 1st Fire Team Leader Cpl Herman Watson takes a big gulp down a large mouthful of the cold, sweet coke; I knock the cup out of his hand. When the cup hit the ground, small chips of chard glass also hit the ground. Cpl. Hillberg was standing there with a cut lip. If he had drank that coke with glass, his throat would have been chopped up hamburger. Then he would have realized, too late, that slivers of glass would be cutting his stomach from the inside, out. Cpl. Hillberg was so pissed without thinking he put a M79 round right into the stomach of that villager. Lucky for us, the round did not explode. I grabbed Cpl. Hillberg we we ran a long way from the villager. That M79 round hit the villager so hard it turned him inside out, it took his legs and asshole and wrapped them around his shoulders. He looks like a freak in a circus walking around on his hands, saying in Vietnamese, "giết tôi" (kill me) **(1-50)**. Then all of a sudden the M79 round went off and his body parts were scattered all over that village. 3rd Squad Leader Ssgt Henry Watson came running over and said: "what the hell is going on." I explain about the coke with the ice. Then 4th Squad Leader Ssgt William Houser gave direct orders to his squad not, I repeat, do not drink any offered drinks from this village. Ssgt William Houser said: "The games people play in Vietnam are in favor of the PAVN and are deadly." he was telling about a convoy of trucks moving slowly down the highway to Hue. A group of small Vietnamese boys offer loaves of French bread to Marines who ride on the backs of their vehicles. One Marine on a supply truck yelled: "throw me the bread." The trucks, loaded with supplies, suddenly blew into the air; Marines tossed into lifeless shapes, landing in piles on the side of the road. The deadly loaf of bread contained a hand grenade. Ssgt Robert Dean Tomlin and Ssgt Frederick (Butch) Philip Price said: do not accept a frigging thing from these people no matter what it is. Butch and I reminded our teams again; do not accept anything from these people unless you want your asses blow off. We found the PAVN's major supply area under an empty hut buried under the ground. 1st and 2nd squads threw in several satchel charges and blew those PAVN's supplies all to hell. Even today I get cold chills seeing that poor Vietnamese villager with his ass wrapped around his shoulders, walking on his hands, asking to be shot.

On 14 June Company L 3rd Battalion, 9th Marines was getting scouting reports of more PAVN bunkers and stores being found. So the 2nd Battalion, 4th Marines, were lifted by helicopter onto the PAVN road near the Laos border and moved east to link up with the 3rd Battalion, 9th Marines Marines locating and destroying more bunkers and stores as they moved on the PAVN road. They advanced east along the road, toward the 3d Battalion, 9th Marines, which was still moving down the road from the other end. The 2d Battalion found the western portion of the road as well developed as the rest. In one area they found a complex of over 500 bunkers and storage areas containing 400 hundred pounds of ammonium nitrate (to be used as an explosive). The 3d Battalion, 9th Marines took the 400 hundred explosives and set them in the middle of the PAVN's roads and blew it up; that damn hole was so big you could park an aircraft carrier in there. Then a corporal yelled: " you have to see this." There were hand tools, a welding machine, a one-and-one-half-ton truck, and a complete machine shop mounted on a Russian three-ton truck. Ssgt Tomlin and Ssgt Price said: "just blew in place." Unwilling to leave the great prize behind, the Marines wanted to take everything with them. One corporal said: "Ssgt Tomlin and Ssgt Price give us young Marine tinkerers time to dismantled the entire truck and machine shop, then we transferred the pieces to Khe Sanh by helicopter. I through I was being a smart ass and said: " You have four hours or we blew it up." Those young Marines had trucks and machine shops torn apart and loaded on the helicopters with in three hours. When we got back to base camp, they reassembled Russian truck and machine shop and drove along Route 9 to the 3d Marine Division headquarters at Dong Ha. Butch kept on my case for days after that for four hours and he said: " should have told them two hours."

The sun just started coming up on 15 June, when a battalion of the North Vietnamese 88th Regiment, was getting ready to attack the 3d Battalion, 4th Marines, south of Lang Hole. PAVN planned their attack with the beginning of destructive action behind heavy rocket-propelled grenade (RPG) fire. The PAVN infantry penetrated Company M's lines and took over several fighting holes, or fighting positions in United States Marine Corps has a slang is " gun-pits.' North Vietnamese 88th Regiment started setting up a machine gun in what had been the company command post. As the battle turn in to three hours of fighting, the 3d Battalion, 4th Marines and Company L 3d Battalion, 9th Marines counterattacked, driving the North Vietnamese from the perimeter. Helicopter gunships were called in to put multiple gun fire on the enemy attack formations, helping to reduce their excitement to continue the assault. Butch came up to me and said: " we were all feeling the stress of being rushed, overworked, and harassed by the frigging North Vietnamese 88th Regiment Just before 0900, the Marines saw the most enjoyable sight the North Vietnamese fired a "green star cluster" and the attack ended. Ssgt Tomlin's 1st Squad and Ssgt Price's 2nd Squad swept the area, looking for engaged North Vietnamese troops who were willing to fight. We came across a group of North Vietnamese 88th Regiment troops who were scared to death to fire their weapons, when they saw us, they threw their weapons down and gave up as prisoners. Ssgt Tomlin was heard making this comment: " I thought the PAVN troops were tuff little bastards, but these pussies are chicken livers." After the final body count there were 419 PAVN killed and we had captured 31 prisoners, 182 weapons, and 30 field radios . The total lost for the 3d Battalion, 4th Marines, and Company L, 3d Battalion, 9th Marines, is 16 killed and 58 wounded. Company L, 3d Battalion, 9th Marines, had mostly flesh wounds, and no Marine was killed.

As I saw the PAVN casualties the North Vietnamese suffered on 15 June, at the battle near Lang Hole the only words I could think of were inconceivable, incredible, unbelievable, unimaginable, and unthinkable. After all that the PAVN had lost, it appeared, only to wet their appetites for fighting. The very next morning on 16 June at 0215, the 88th and 102nd NAVN Regiments struck LZ (Landing Zone) Torch, a new fire support base was located about 14kn SSE of Khe Sanh and was promptly occupied by C Battery, 1st Battalion, 12th Marines , with Alpha 1st Battalion, 4th Marines and Delta 1st Battalion, 3rd Marines in place as an infantry force. As the 88th and 102nd NAVN Regiments were advancing near the jungle road, which was defended by the 1st Battalion, the 4th Marines, they had a withdrawal from LZ Loon. The 88th NAVN Regiments company charged upon with the continuous line forming the boundary of the Marine base from the south and west. The 102nd NAVN Regiments join in using mortar fire, RPGs, machine guns, and satchel charges to blow the wire and to pave the way for the attack. Now both 88th 102nd PAVN Regiments focused their attention and effort with their physical attack on a small part of the perimeter, and penetrated Company I's lines and advanced on the guns of Battery C, 1st Battalion, 12th Marines. The 1st Battalion, 3rd Marines kept shooting up flares, to give light for the Marine gunners to see. 1st Battalion, 12th Marines cranked down the barrels of their M102, which is the light-towed 105 mm howitzer, and fired round after round of Beehive (an anti-personnel round packed with metal flechettes) ammunition into the attacking PAVN. The PAVN were screaming and yelling as the flechettes cut through their bodies. Some of the PAVN did reach one of Battery C's gun emplacements, but the Beehive rounds proved too much for them and they retreated, running with their tails between their legs. The 88th 102nd NAVN Regiments left 128 dead, and they fell back at 0400. Fourteen Marines died in the physical attack by the PAVN.

The 88th 102nd PAVN Regiments did not get enough of the flechettes and bullets to eat on the 16 June, so they came back on the morning of 18 June for seconds. The PAVN attacked Company K 3rd Battalion, 4th Marines night defensive position in a daylong battle. The Marines called in air and artillery strikes in support that pushed back the PAVN attack resulting in PAVN losing 231 killed. 11 Marines were killed and 30 wounded. Operation Purple Martin was over and the PAVN stopped on 19 June. After all the Marine bases were secuted and new perimeters set up, the 4th Marines returned to Khe Sanh Combat Base.

Operation Purple Martin Casualties

Date 2–19 June 1968
Location
Vietnam Salient, Quảng Trị Province, South Vietnam

Result U.S. claims victory
Belligerents

United States South Vietnam	North Vietnam North Vietnam

Commanders and leaders

LTC Joseph Muller Colonel Hoa La Hung PAVN Commander Vanh chu Giang PAVN	Colonel Tra Dinch PAVN

Strength
Units involved

3rd Marine Division	308th Infantry Division
1st Battalion, 1st Marines 2nd Battalion, 3rd Marines 3rd Battalion, 9th Marines 1st Battalion, 12th Marines 4th Marine Regiment	88th Infantry Regiment 102nd Infantry Regiment

Casualties and losses

United States 65 killed	US body count 1,029 killed 48 captured

CHAPTER SEVENTEEN

Vietnam War

Operation Bulldozer

Operation Bulldozer was a U.S. Marine Corps operation that was a land clearing project from Camp Rotan to Gio Linh from June -- July 1968.

Key United States Commanders	Key North Vietnam Commanders
LTC Joseph Muller USMC	Colonel Pham Chi PAVN
1stSg Roger L. Lewis USMC	Commander Vanh chu Giang PAVN
GySgt Russell Owens USMC	
Ssgt Henry Watson USMC	
Ssgt William Houser USMC	
Ssgt Robert Dean Tomlin USMC	
Ssgt Frederick (Butch) Philip Price USMC	

On 1 June, Operation Bulldozer began at Camp Rotan Base to Gio Linh, making a clearing so that the Marine troops could not be ambushed while on patrol. By clearing all the trees and bush away, the Marine could set up scouting posts to signal ahead when the PAVN were spotted in the area. Company L, 3rd Battalion, 9th Marines, was on patrol everyday protecting the 11th Engineer Battalion who were operating the bull dozers and heavy equipment. 20 June until 2 July Ssgt Tomlin 1st Squad would walk the patrol all around the perimeter where the 11th Engineer Battalion were working. Ssgt Price would have 2nd Squad hiding under cover to see if the engineers got attacked. 21 June 1st and 2nd Squads would switch. Ssgt Price's squad would walk the perimeter and Ssgt Tomlin's squad would hide under cover. That day a scout, Cpl David Henderson for the first squad, came over to Ssgt Tomlin and said: "sergeant there is something funny about the tall grass." Ssgt Tomlin said: "what funny about the tall grass." The corporal said: " the grass is moving and there is no wind blowing." Right away Ssgt Tomlin gave the signal "enemy in sight." Squad 1 and 2 immediately went into combat mode. Ssgt Tomlin gave arm signal range, then held up two fingers, telling 1st Fire Team Leader Cpl Herman Watson with the M79, it was 200 meters. Squads 1 and 2 held their positions until they got the command to fire from their Squad Leaders. When Ssgt Tomlin saw the grass move forward, he gave the command to commence firing. Marine rifles, machine guns, and M79 Launchers going off, you might think it was Fourth of July. As soon as the bullets started flying, the tall grass was really moving and some were on fire. The PAVN had disguised themselves as grass

and were trying to sneak upon the 11th Engineer Battalion and kill them before they could make the clearing. The fire fight lasted about half an hour and then everything went back to normal. Matter of fact, one of the bull dozer operators never heard the weapons fire because of all the noise that the diesel engine was giving off. He just kept pushing over trees while the bullets were whizzing all around him. Butch came over to my position and said: "Robert I counted 15 dead grasses and no trees." I just laughed because I through Butch was funny. Cpl Herman Watson came running over and said: Ssgt Tomlin and Ssgt Price; I have some bad news the frigging grass is back."

This time we had the M79 Launchers put down frechette rounds all around the grass area and above on the hill side. You never heard just screaming and yelling from grass in your life. You could hear the PAVN screaming tôi đang bị cắt thành từng mảnh (I'am being cut to shreds) as they were running away. Ssgt Price was heard making this comment: "that damn grass is bleeding like a stuck hog." Some men on the rifle fire teams were popping the PAVN as they were running away. Then all hell broke loose the PAVN 209th Infantry Regiment with the 165th Infantry Regiment was coming over the hill straight at us. I ordered squads 1 and 2 to get in position and the bulldozer and heavy equipment operators stopped their machines and got in a fighting position with us. I called in an airstrike for help; I knew there was no way in hell these Marines were going to stop a solid human wave of PAVN running at full speed. On my command I gave the signal to commence firing. With rifle, machine gun, hand grenade, and M79 firing. Bullets, hand grenades, M79 rounds cover the air around us right on top of the charging PAVN. Then Butch said: "Robert can you hear that wonderful sound of them Bell Cobra helicopters coming to our rescue." Then I got a radio call from the led helicopter with: "put down red smoke in front of you so we do not have friendly fire." I had two corporals popping red smoke like crazy right in front of us. Then the fire works started; the cobras with their 20 mm belly-mounted gun pods, rockets, and grenade launchers; the PAVN did not stand a chance. They were getting mowed down like a powermore cutting blades of grass. The cobra made another sweep by firing several rounds and the PAVN high tailing out of the grass heading for the hills. This time when we did the body count we had 371 PAVN dead, 10 Marines killed and 31 wounded. I thank the cobra pilots and one Captain Bob Jackson told me: "any time we can be service just give us a call" Then he said: "I will circle a couple of times in case them little bastards come back and want some more lead to eat." Then you could hear him laughing on the radio. I radio back to the captain and thank him again. CPT Jackson radioed me back and said: " anytime Ssgt Tomlin just call me you have my number," you could still hear him laughing as he was headed back to his base. Then Cpt Jackson made this comment: "what a wonderful day to be a Marine."

I was walking towards a bulldozer and just lite up a cigar. When one of the bull dozer operator said: " hey sergeant I am Sgt Alfred Watson 11th Engineer Battalion Bulldozer Operator, but everybody just calls me Big Al." I said: " I am 1st Squad Leader Ssgt Robert Dean Tomlin Company L 3rd Battalion, 9th Marines. Sgt Watson said: "

What a hell of a job your squad did on them frigging PAVN." By that time Ssgt Price was walking up, then I introduced him to Big Al. We exchange idle conversations about the war, our families and home towns. Then Sgt Watson said: " Ssgt Tomlin you would not happen to have another cigar." I said: "yes" So I reached in the vest pocket and pulled out a cuban and handed it to him. Big Al had the biggest smile as he was unwrapping the cigar. I got out my lighter to light his cigar. He said: "no thanks I just chew them", when he put that cigar in his mouth, you would have though he was in heaven. Sgt Watson said: " Thank You Ssgt Tomlin, my God I have not had a cigar in months, I am going chew this baby down to a nub." Butch and I said our fair wells got our squads together and went back on patrol.

22 June 1st and 2nd squads had only light contact with the PAVN. 23 June one of the heavy equipment operators called me over and said: " there something funny about this ground when that I am clearing." The Company L 3rd Battalion, 9th Marines discovered and destroyed several large, abandoned, fortified positions in the area southwest of Camp Rotan. Ssgt Tomlin and Ssgt Price told their men to make a complete sweep within a couple of miles of the fortifications. As the squads were making their sweeps, Cpl John Hillberg let out a yell. He was yelling: "Ssgt Tomlin and Ssgt Price come over here quick." When we arrived at the spot there were numerous of PAVN fresh graves and several supply caches. The supply caches had weapons, ammo, medical and food supplies. A corporal from Squad 2 was heard making this comment: "man we hit a gold mine now them damn little PAVN is really going to starve."

While Operation Bulldozer progressed with the land clearing project from Camp Rotan through Gio Linh to the high water mark on the coast. Company L 3rd Battalion, 9th Marines kept protecting and guarding the 11th Engineer Battalion from PAVN attacks. The Marine engineers widened the previously cleared area to 600 meters for the entire 13.5 kilometers of its length. The 11th Engineer Battalion contributed more than 10,000 thousand man-hours and 4,500 hundred tractor hours to this hazardous effort. During the last days of Operation Bulldozer, a sharp increase in enemy artillery occurred; sometimes the men would be working, then artillery shells would start whizzing in. This one bulldozer operator was heard making this comment: " you push dirt, trees, and bush for a minute or two then the PAVN shells started coming, you stopped jump off the cat take cover for an hour, then it starts all over again." So Big Al said: " Ssgt Tomlin can you call in a air strike on that damn PAVN Artillery, I am too old to be jumping off and getting up on this cat." I call in an airstrike on the PAVN Artillery by the DMZ. The airstrike was successful; the 11th Engineer Battalion went back to work without any interruptions from the PAVN Artillery. Squads from Company L 3rd Battalion, 9th Marines, still had several small but intense engagements between PAVN, who were dug in around Camp Rotan. We always clean up enemy patrols and PAVN that were dug. Ssgt Tomlin was telling Ssgt Price he had a funny feeling that the enemy was preparing for renewed offensive operations in the area. Operation Bulldozer reached completion by 1 July. Company L 3rd Battalion, 9th Marines stayed until 5 July making patrols around the clear area. We did a lot of hole digging and sandbag filling before we left to go back to base camp.

Operation Bulldozer Casualties

Date June – July May 1968
Location
Camp Rotan to Gio Linh
Result inconclusive

Belligerents

United States South Vietnam	North Vietnam North Vietnam

Commanders and leaders

Units involved

3rd Battalion, 9th Marines	209th Infantry Regiment
2nd Battalion, 26th Marines	165th Infantry Regiment
11th Engineer Battalion	

Casualties and losses

United States 10 killed 31 wounded	US body count 386 killed 30 captured

CHAPTER EIGHTEEN

Vietnam War

Operation Ireland

Operation Ireland was a U.S. Marine Corps security operation that took place in northwest Quảng Trị Province from 10 – 20 July 1968

Key United States Commanders	**Key North Vietnam Commanders**
LTC Joseph Muller USMC	Colonel Pham Chi PAVN
1stSg Roger L. Lewis USMC	Commander Vanh chu Giang PAVN
GySgt Russell Owens USMC	
Ssgt Henry Watson USMC	
Ssgt William Houser USMC	
Ssgt Robert Dean Tomlin USMC	
Ssgt Frederick (Butch) Philip Price USMC	

10 July the 3rd Battalion, 9th Marines was taking a much needed break and rest from the last battle of Operation Bulldozer and the frigging on Hill 119. Butch and I saw some good Marines get killed and wounded.. I was laying in my rack thinking, was this frigging war even worth one live of a good Marine. Butch and I were talking the other night, why in the hell do Russia, China, and North Korea have to stick their noses into everybody's affairs. South Vietnam and North Vietnam could have fought their own battle. But Russia, China, and North Korea had to give Noeth Vietnam aid to help them fight this war. This made the war lobsided for South Vietnam, and that's why the Marines are here to help then fight. Butch said: " Robert why can countries fight their own battle with out getting the United States involve." I kind of scratched my head and said: " But the real question behind this War is: What started the Vietnam War? If you look back in history the conflict in Vietnam took root during an independence movement against French colonial rule and evolved into a Cold War confrontation. This Vietnam War is being fought between communist North Vietnam, backed by the frigging Soviet Union, China, and North Korea against South Vietnam. So the United States is to support South Vietnam with South Korea, the Philippines, Australia, Thailand, and other anti-communist allies." Then I kind of laugh and say: " I almost forgot, also with Tomlin, Price and the United States Marine Corp." Butch and I just laughed and carried on.

Then a private came into our tent and said: " Ssgt Tomlin and Sgst Price 1stSg Roger L. Lewis wants to see you ASAP (As soon as possible) for a special meeting."

We said: "Thank you private" Got dressed and doubled time to the meeting. When we got there, all ranking officers and NCOS were walking into the meeting. That seems funny to Butch and I because we were the only E-6 Sergerants that was at the briefing. LTC Joseph Muller was standing at the podium telling us about our next mission. He said: " lets lower our heads in a brief silence say a prayer for our fellow Marines that were killed or wounded in action. Then I want to give each and every one of you congratulations on a great job on taking Hill 117. I know the 3rd Battalion, 9th Marines needs a must needed rest after that hard fought battle on the hill. But duty always calls we have orders from the top that our next mission is going to be Security Operations.(operations undertaken by a commander to provide early and accurate warning of enemy operations, to provide the force being protected with time and maneuver space within which to react to the enemy, and to develop the situation to allow the commander to effectively use the protected force). Then to Butch and I came the big surprise, when LTC Joseph Muller said: " Staff Sergeants Tomlin and Price come forward." Butch and I stood up and walked to the podium; stood at attention, rendering a salute, and said: "Tomlin and Price reporting as directed Sir." LTC Joseph Muller returns the salute and said: "stand at ease." As Butch and I were standing at ease, LTC Joseph Muller said: " today we have recipients of the bronze star." then LTC Joseph Muller said: this will be the first time in the history of the Marine Corps that we will have a dual recipient of the bronze star "1stSg Roger L. Lewis would you care to say a few words." 1stSg Roger L. Lewis said: " without L company 1st and 2nd squad it would be more difficult to secured and control Hill 119." Then LTC Joseph Muller said: "thank you First Sergeant." Then LTC Joseph Muller read the dual citation out loud.

For extraordinary acts of valor while under direct enemy fire during ground operations against a superior hostile force in the Republic of Vietnam. They distinguished themselves by their heroic actions while serving as Squad Leaders for Company L on 27 May 1967. That day Company L had maneuvered across a hill in the area around Tomahawk Base, Quảng Trị Province, and had established a defensive position on the hillside of Hill 119 when Company L began to receive heavy machine gun fire. The 1st and 2nd platoons of Company L were positioned approximately 500 meters to the front of UH-1E helicopters and were also receiving hostile machine gun and mortar fire. Sergeants Tomlin and Price scanned the surrounding area and located the enemy machine gun and mortar tube that was viciously pounding the helicopters position. With total disregard for their own safety and braving, intense enemy gunfire maneuvered into a position to direct their 1st and 2nd Squads and themselves to fire down upon the enemy machine gun and mortar site. The enemy gunners were shot which immediately knocked the enemy machine gun and mortar out of service. Their brave actions stopped further machine gun and enemy mortar fire, reducing casualties and saving lives. Staff Sergeant Robert Dean Tomlin and Staff Sergeant Frederick Philip Price for bravery and professionalism, is in keeping with the highest traditions of military

service and reflects great credit upon themselves; Company L, 3rd Battalion, 9th Marines, and the United States Marine Corps. (1-8)

Butch and I stood at attention while receiving our Bronze Star Medals; we rendered a salute, and LTC Joseph Muller shook our hands with congratulations. We rendered a salute and said: "Thank You SIR." LTC Joseph Muller returned our salute and said: "dismissed." We did about face march out of the briefing and went back to our tent. LTC Joseph Muller said: So all officers and ranking NCOs stay after this citation and you will be given more details."

Butch and I were in our tent when 1st Squad Leader Ssgt Henry Watson and 2nd Squad Leader Ssgt William Houser walked in. Ssgt Henry Watson said: " Congratulations, well Marines our next mission is going to be a rough one." Then Ssgt Henry Watson said: " at 0700 we will be pulling out for Khe Sanh base for Security operations." We told the staff sergeant we would have our equipment and men ready to move out at 0700 in the morning. So that night our squads packed their gear and we torn down our weapons and gave them the JPS (Joseph Peterson Special) lube and made sure the weapons were in good operating condition. We fought out why we were going Khe Sanh base for security operations. We were to prevent the PAVN from attacking Khe Sanh base and the surrounding hills around Khe Sanh. Ssgt Henry Watson said: " 3rd Battalion, 9th Marines were going to be the security force with dayly patrols all around Khe Sanh and the hills." Ssgt William Houser said: "Company L would be point man for every patrol."

Ssgt Henry Watson said: "Some Marine General was send to Khe Sanh base to take control of the forces there to be made up of and consist of the 1st Marine Regiment which was relieving the 26th Marine Regiment, the 1st Battalion, 9th Marines and the 2nd Brigade, 1st Cavalry Division, (Untied States Army) this force would be known as Task Force Stop." Then we found out. The Task Force and Regimental command posts and 2nd Battalion, 1st Marines were located at the Khe Sanh base. 1st Battalion, 1st Marines occupied Hills 558, 861, 881 South and 950. The 2nd Battalion, 3rd Marines provided security along Route 9 and the 3rd Battalion, 4th Marines was deployed to secure Hill 689

The 3rd Battalion, 9th Marines would run security checks every day on Khe Sanh base and all the hill locations. Ssgt William Houser said: "On 16 June 1968, Company A 1st Battalion, 9th Marines began a patrol southwest of Hill 689, when it was ambushed by PAVN soldiers in bunkers concealed in the thick vegetation. Two more companies from 1st Battalion, 9th Marines were dispatched to save them, but they became ensnarled in this confusing battle and were unable to disengage until the early morning of 17 June. Casualties amounted to 38 Marines and 3 Navy Corpsmen killed, 3 missing and 32 wounded. The battalion commander Lieutenant Colonel John Smith was relieved of duty. Ssgt Henry Watson said: " On 19 May the PAVN ambushed a convoy of the 1st Battalion, 11th Marines killing 3 Marines. Following this ambush, 1st Marine Regiment commander Col. Stanley B. Powell kept within certain limits on traffic on Route 9 and formed a Provisional Mechanized Company combining an anti-tank company, 2 infantry platoons, and elements of the 3rd Tank Battalion to improve road security. At the beginning of June BG Carl W. Johnson replaced BG Lawson and the force was briefly designated Task Force Johnson but after the ambush had happened; afterward Task Force Lima based is now the radio callsign."

The 3rd Battalion, 9th Marines was ready to go at 0700 on the morning of 10 July 1968. We had about a 14 mile march through enemy territory. Until, LTC Joseph Muller said: " we are taking trucks to Khe Sanh base and these Marines need a break. So we were getting about 40 Marines into a 5 ton transport truck. The trucks were going in a 5 truck convoy in case they would be attack by the PAVN. My 1st Squad and Butch;s 2ns Squad were on the first 5 truck convoy to pulled out. We made to Khe Sanh base without any problems. When the last truck rolled in we all headed for the mess tent. After chow we were assigned our living quarters. Then LTC Joseph Muller had a meeting telling us we would be on patrol at 0700 in the morning and that 1stSg Roger L. Lewis would give us the sectors to patrol.

At 07:10 a platoon from Company F 2nd Battalion, 1st Marines Marines supported by 2 tanks on a road sweep operation from Khe Sanh base towards Route 9 was ambushed, the Marines attempted to assault the PAVN positions but were repulsed and pinned down. The 3rd Battalion, 9th Marines, was sent to reinforce the platoon, but the Marines of Company L, 3rd and 4th platoons attack was pushed back, and pinned down. 1stSg Roger L. Lewis said: I need Platoons 1st and 2nd to clean up this frigging mess. Now Ssgt Henry Watson and Ssgt William Houser squads 3rd and 4th Company L 3rd Battalion, 9th Marines who were to rescue Company F 2nd Battalion, 1st Marines were under fire and could not move. When the 1st and 2nd squads arrived we could not get any where near Company F and Company L. They were really pinned down by heavy PAVN machine gun and mortar fire. Ssgt Henry Watson radioed me to call in napalm strikes and make sure you get the coordinates right and make sure the pilots drop it is close to the Marine fighting lines. So I radio in the coordinates for the napalm drop zone away from our Marine fighting lines. The F-100D Super Saber pilot, CPT William Lowe had radio contact with me and said: "Ssgt Tomlin I put this sticky jelly babies right on top of them frigging NAVN. About that time the F-100D zoom over and dropped his pay load right on the top of the PAVN forcing them to retreat. We lost 8 Marines while PAVN losses were 113 killed and 3 captured. I told Butch this will increased PAVN activity around Khe Sanh base. After that battle on Route 9 orders were send to keep the 3rd Battalion, 9th Marines as reinforcements units in the area.

The next day, Company G 2nd Battalion, 3rd Marines engaged a PAVN company in bunkers on a ridge overlooking Route 9, 4 klicks southeast of the base known as "Turkey Ridge" Air and artillery strikes were called in on the bunkers, but the Marine attack was pushed back and pinned down and radioed for help. Again, Company L 3rd Battalion, 9th Marines, was called again to help them out. When we arrived 15 Marines had already been killed. Ssgt Henry Watson took his 3rd squad around to the north side and hit the PAVN from behind. Ssgt William Houser took his 4th squad to the south side to get the PAVN in a cross-fire. When 3rd and 4th squad were in position, Ssgt Tomlin's 1st squad and Ssgt Price's 2nd squad they open up with a machine gun, rifle, and M79 rounds. We had them damn PAVN in a vise and was tightening. Then gunships and artillery strikes were called in which allowed the Marines to capture the position by 2000 for the loss of 15 Marines killed, while the PAVN had lost 158 dead. Company G was reinforced by Companies E and F and dug into positions 700m apart along the ridgeline. At 0300 Company L 3rd Battalion, the 9th Marines detected PAVN movement outside their perimeter and artillery strikes were called in. Then the unthinkable happens three PAVN armed with Satchel charges then attacked a listening post killing themselves and 3 Marines. When the explosion went off, this action started a PAVN battalion attack on Company F's positions. Company F radio in for help before being over run with enemy. When the Sergeant radioed me, he said: "get here quick the PAVN is about to take the Company's 60 mm mortar position." My squad was there in 15 minutes and started to lay down rifle, and machine fire. I told the M79 launcher to put some rounds right on the advancing PAVN. By 03:30 Company F was saved and started firing their 60 mm mortar again. Then all of a sudden we were hit by PAVN 130 mm artillery firing about 38 klicks from across the Vietnamese Demilitarized Zone (DMZ). An air strike was called in and a pilot from an F-105 Thunderchief radioed in and said: " I put a AGM-12 Bullpup missile right down the old stove pipe and you can say farewell to the old 130 mm PAVN artillery. At 04:15 an AC-47 Spooky gunship that had been modified by mounting three 7.62 mm General Electric miniguns to fire through two rear window openings and the side cargo door, all on the left (pilot's) side of the aircraft, to provide close air support for ground troops . A C-130 Flareship nick name Blind Bat would strip the enemy of his cover by turning night into day. Gunship and flareship arrived over the battle and were engaged by PAVN antiaircraft fire. Company L 3rd Battalion, 9th Marines Squad 1 and 2 were ordered to knock out PAVN antiaircraft gun. This would clear the way for the AC-47 and C-130 could finish their job on clean up. Ssgt Tomlin took 1st squad to the right of the PAVN antiaircraft gun and Ssgt Price took 2nd squad to the left of PAVN antiaircraft gun. We both open fire with rifle, machine gun, and M79 rounds at the same time and blew the PAVN antiaircraft gun to smithereens.

The PAVN made repeated attacks to try to overrun Company G 2nd Battalion, 3rd Marines positions by continuous firing RPG-2s. At 07:00, a napalm strike was called in against PAVN reinforcements killing over 90 PAVN, and starting a wildfire that forced Company F 2nd Battalion, 1st Marines, from its fighting positions. Company F called for reinforcements to cover them as they evacuated the wildfire. Company L, 3rd Battalion, 9th Marines, double time to cover F 2nd Battalion, 1st Marines as they evacuated from the wildfire to take up a new position. Company F regained its positions as the fire died down and the PAVN began to disengage and move out. At 11:50 when Company E 2nd Battalion, 3rd Marines arrived to reinforce Company F to overran the PAVN RPG position. Company L, 3rd Battalion, 9th Marines, move out to take up new positions. The Marines lost 13 dead, while the PAVN lost 330 killed.

Then the damn PAVN 130 mm artillery firing about 38 klicks from across the Vietnamese Demilitarized Zone (DMZ) had renewed with 40 or more artillery firing on Khe Sanh base. On 15 July,, 4 M107s 175 mm self-propelled guns and 4 M110s 8 inch (203 mm) M110 self-propelled howitzers were deployed to Khe Sanh base from Camp Carroll and were engaged in a 48-hour artillery barrage shooting match against 130mm PAVN artillery positions. None of the Marine guns were hit but the shots from the PAVN 130mm guns were decreasing. At 04:00 on 17 July the PAVN battalion supported by artillery fire attacked Company E 2nd Battalion, 3rd Marines on Turkey Ridge but were beaten back. At 08:50 Company B 1st Battalion, 1st Marines was ambushed as it moved to support Company E 2nd Battalion, 3rd Marines, they were then reinforced by Company G 2nd Battalion, 3rd Marines and Company E 2nd Battalion, 1st Marines who overran the PAVN positions. The Marines lost 32 dead, while the PAVN lost 236 killed. Company L, 3rd Battalion, 9th Marines, was ordered back to Khe Sanh base for rest and food. On 20 July, as we were walking back to base camp Butch Said: " well brother looks like we live and fight another day." I asked Butch how many days have we been on this battle field? He said: " I think about 5 or so months" I looked at him and said" "hell in another month we should get R &R."

Operation Ireland Casualties

Date 10 – 20 July 1968
Location: northwest Quảng Trị Province, South Vietnam

Result U.S. operational success
Belligerents

United States
South Vietnam North Vietnam North Vietnam

Commanders and leaders

LTC Joseph Muller

Colonel Pham Chi PAVN
Commander Vanh chu Giang PAVN

Units involved

1st Battalion, 1st Marines
2nd Battalion, 1st Marines
3d Marine Regiment
4th Marine Regiment
9th Marine Regiment

308th Infantry Division

26th Marine Regiment
3rd Battalion, 9th Marines

Casualties and losses	
United States 43 killed	US body count 769 killed 3 captured

CHAPTER NINETEEN

Vietnam War

Operation Red Dog

Operation Red Dog the PAVN appointed Major General Qu'ach Lam Minh as the local commander for the actions around Khe Sanh to capture or destroy the Marine and Army Special Forces at Lang Vei Special Forces Base from Date July – August 1968.

Key United States Commanders	Key North Vietnam Commanders
LTC Joseph Muller USMC	Major General MG Qu'ach Lam Minh PAVN
1stSg Roger L. Lewis USMC	Commander Vanh chu Giang PAVN
GySgt Russell Owens USMC	Colonel Pham Chi PAVN
Ssgt Henry Watson USMC	
Ssgt William Houser USMC	
Ssgt Robert Dean Tomlin USMC	
Ssgt Frederick (Butch) Philip Price USMC	

Major General Qu'ach Lam Minh assigned the operation to 304th and the 325th Infantry Divisions. MG Qu'ach Lam Minh told the commander of the 325th you will have responsibility for the areas around the north, of Khe Sanh and Lang Vei Then the MG Qu'ach Lam Minh pulled out his sword and pointed it directly at the commander of the 325th gave this little speech: " if you fail your head belongs to my sword rồng nhanh (Swift Dragon) and with one quick wack your head will roll and you will flip around like a beheaded chicken" MG Qu'ach Lam Minh told the commander of the 304th you will have responsibility for the areas around the south, of Khe Sanh and Lang Vei Again MG Qu'ach Lam Minh pulled out his sword and pointed it directly at the commander of the gave the same little speech: " if you fail your head belongs to my sword rồng nhanh (Swift Dragon) and with one quick wack your head will roll and you will flip around like a beheaded chicken" The Marine intelligence was in a pickle in attempting to determine when and where PAVN was going to attack. A special squad of the 26th Marine Regiment had a scouting party out to gather intelligence with information and confirmed where the PAVN was advancing to. The 26th Marine Regiment had gather enough information within a period of a week on the movement of the PAVN divisions. The 325th Division had moved into the vicinity of the new Special Forces Base and two more divisions were within supporting distance. The 324th Division was located in the DMZ area about 15 miles north of Khe Sanh and

Lang Vei. While the 320th Division could be easy be within striking distance to the northeast. PAVN operations dealing with the supply, maintenance, and distribution of equipment and personnel from the nearby Ho Chi Minh Trail (Đường mòn Hồ Chí Minh), was a logistical network of roads and trails that ran from the Democratic Republic of Vietnam (North Vietnam) to the Republic of Vietnam (South Vietnam) through the kingdoms of Laos and Cambodia. With the result of this scouting report LVSFB (Lang Vei Special Forces Base) was reinforced on 23 July by the 1st Battalion, 9th Marine Regiment and 3rd Battalion, 9th Marines. At the time the Marines did not know that the PAVN had in place, within striking distance the 320th, and 324th Infantry Divisions to back up the 304th and the 325th Infantry Divisions. The PAVN had a reserve 270th infantry Regiment with five artillery regiments of the 16th, 45th, 84th, 204th, and 675th. The PAVN had nother three AAA regiments of the 208th, 214th, and 228th four tank companies,; one engineer regiment. one engineer battalion, one signal battalion; and a number of local force units.

LTC Joseph Muller had a special meeting with Compnay L 3rd Battalion, 9th Marines and said: " we know those damn PAVN have some kind of artillery, rocket, and mortar base in Laos that can fire on Lang Vei Special Forces Base." I know as a Marine I am asking my fellow Marines to risk their lives by crossing into Laos to knock out that damn PAVN rocket base. If any Marine does not want to go I will understand. All four squads stood up and shouted at the top of their lungs: "BAMCIS SIR." LTC

Muller said: be ready at 0600 tomorrow, Company L squad 1, 2, 3, and 4 will move out." Then he said: it is very important that damn PAVN base is knock out, we do not want any surprise rockets, shells, or mortar rounds coming on top of the Lang Vei Special Forces and Marines at night. Now get your equipment ready and get some food and rest before 0600 tomorrow. We all said: "yes SIR" and headed for the mess tent because we knew it would be a long time for our next good meal. After chow we all headed back to our tents to check our equipment and got our weapons ready. 25 July Company L 3rd Battalion, 9th Marines was in formation at 0600 ready to move on the PAVN Rocket Base loctated in Laos. Platoon Sergeant GySgt Russell Owens had all the Squad Leaders check their men, equipment, and weapons before we moved out. Cpl David Henderson drew the short straw for point man. Before the squad was ready to move, Cpl Henderson was way in front of us scouting out the areas as Complay L squads were following on the outskirts of Highway 9 to Laos. Squad 1 was moving on the right, Squad 2 was moving on the left, and Squads 3 and 4 were divided moving in the middle. We had gone about 10 klicks when I notice Cpl Henderson giving the arm signal Halt, then raise his hand to change direction to the right. He held his rifle horizontally, with stock in shoulder, the muzzle pointing in the direction od the enemy. Then Cpl Henderson held up his fist then open four fingers telling us the enemy was about 400 hundred meters away. Ssgt Tomlin gave the signal for the 1st Squad to move to the right of Cpl Henderson. Ssgt Price gave the signal for the 2nd Squad to move left of Cpl henderson. Ssgt Watson and Ssgt Houser gave the signal for Squads 3 and 4 to move directly towards Cpl Henderson.

I low crawled up to Cpl Henderson to scout out the PAVN situration, when I got there I could see 270th Infantry Regiment setting around a camp fire eating and drinking. Then I notice both guards were asleep. I gave the arm and hand signal for direction and range to the M79 Launchers. I then Extend the arm in front of the body, hip high, palm down, and move it through a wide horizontal arc several times. With that signal telling the M79's to commence firing. All you could hear is pop, pop, pop and pop as the M79 were fired. Then Squads 1,2,3, and 4 double timed up to Ssgt Tomlin and Cpl Henderson. Those M79 rounds went directly into the middle and all around the sitting PAVN. When the explodsions went off the gauards woke up, but only for a few monmets the rifle fire team had drill them right between the horns. Then Company L open up with machine gun and rifle fire. The PAVN 270th Infantry Regiment did not know what hit them, the ones that survive were running towards Laon. We had 5 Marines wounded with just flesh wounds, the corpsman clean and bandaged their wounds and gave the ok for combat duty. The PAVN had 81 killed and several wounded that high tailed with the rest of the PAVN regiment. Cpl Henderson took off in front of us and Company L Squads 1, 2, 3, and 4 were moving forward to Laos to the PAVN Rocket base. After we had crossed over into Laos now we close to the PAVN's artillery, rocket, and mortar positions. I saw in a distance Cpl Henderson was sneaking and staying under cover back to Company L with vital information. When he got to our position Cpl Henderson said: Ssgt Tomlin they have frigging guards all over that PAVN position. There is no way we are going to take them by surprise." Then I said: " is there anyway we can knock out the guards individually and not alert the PAVN camp." Then Ssgt Price said: " the onlu way is to sneak up on them and cut their throats for they can not scream." I ask Cpl Henderson: "how many guards?' Cpl Henderson said: "staff sergeant there two each in all directions with a total of eight." Ssgt Tomlin, Ssgt Price, Ssgt Watson, and Ssgt Houser took two men each from their squads to knock out the PAVN guards. Ssgt Tomlin said: " two mean from Squad 1 will take the guards station at the North. Two men from Squad 2 will take the guards station at the South. Two men from Squad 3 will take the guards station at the West, Two men from Squad 4 will take the guards station at the East. Remember you will have to work as a team and kill the PAVN guards at the same time." Cpl Henderson took the eight Marine to where the PAVN guards were stationed. The rest of Compnay L followed close behind, then I put the arm signal to tell Company L to halt.

The rest of Company L stay hidden and watch from a safe distance as the two man team knocked out the PAVN guards. Squad 1 grabbed the guards at the same time clamped their hands tigthing over their mouths and cut their throats from ear to ear. LCpl Jerry Wassel was real smart he propped the guards up like they were taking a rest. We all watched as each squad preformed their jobs with out any flaws. When the last guards wer knocked out, Complay L move to get into position. At our position West and North of the Co Roc Mountains not far from Highway 9, across the border in Laos. I could see the PAVN established artillery, rocket, and mortar positions from which to launch attacks by fire on the base and to support its ground operations. The PAVN 130 mm and 152 mm artillery pieces, and 122 mm rockets, had a longer range than the Marine artillery support which consisted of 105 mm and 155 mm howitzers. This gave advansion to the PAVN to avoid counter-battery fire from the Marines. We set up the machine guns, M79 launchers in every directions. I hand signal for the men in Company L to wait for the signal to commence firing. I told Ssgt Watson forget the artillery stirkes the shells will never reach the PAVN's camp, just call in air strikes. Ssgt Watson radio in coordinance for the air strikes and told then to make it fast. We only waited for a few minutes when we heard the most beuifull sound with the A-6's roaring engines flying directly over head. I gave the arm sign to commence firing. With the bombs dropping and explodsions and our machine gun, rifle, and M79 fire we caught the PAVN with thier pants down. The PAVN camp lite up like Roman Candle, Company L and The Marine's A-6s just blew the crap out of that PAVN camp. While Ssgt Watson was in radio contact with the A-6s, Marine pilot CPT Philip Barlow came on and said: "is Sergeant Robert Tomlin down there with you over." Ssgt Warson said: " yes he is, I will get hime for you over." Ssgt Watson handed me the mike and I said: "Ssgt.Tomlin here over." Then CPT Barlow said: "hey Robert it been a long time since we have spoken on the radio since the last airstrike you call in over." I said: "yes SIR it has been awhile over." Ssgt Tomlin said: " CPT Barlow what happen to your A-4E Skyhawk over." CPT Barlow said: " well Ssgt Tomlin the A-6 Intruder has a bigger payload and more armor to stop them damn Russian and Chinese bullets over." Ssgt Tomlin said: "the next time I get to Da Nang Air Force base I will look me up, we will go have a beer over." CPT Barlow said: that sound good, will I better head back to base my fuel pressure is getting low over and out.: Ssgt Tomlin said: "Thanks again SIR over and out". When the smoke had settle, Butch Said: "Robert we do not have to worry about sleeping at night now., we blew the hell out of that PAVN rocket position."I turn to Butch and said: "you can say that again brother." I told the squads to do a body count, I was surprise with the numbers we had 6 Marines killed and 20 wounded. The PAVN had 386 killed, numberous wounded but the PAVN carried them off to safely, so we could not get accrued count on the PAVN wounded. We were given direct order to blow all operating equipment in place. After everyting was blown up we headed back to Lang Vei Special Forces Base.

Within a couple of days Company L 3rd Battalion, 9th Marines were back on patrol again looking for PAVN's bunkers, mortar, rocket, and artillery positions. Then I got a radio call with some some bad news. CPT Philip Barlow was flying a call in airstrike against some T-55 Russian main battle tanks about 15 klicks north of Khe Sanh that 2nd Battalion, 3rd Marines were pinned down. The report was CPT Barlow was making a low sweep with 500-pound Mk-82 Snakeye bombs to knock out the tanks. When he was hit with Russian ZU-23 twin 23 mm anti-aircraft cannon in the front section of his A-6 Intruder. A Marine observer saw only one pilot ejected from the plane, and PAVNs were running toward the ejected pilot. LTC Joseph Muller make a direct radio call to Company L 3rd Battalion, 9th Marines and direct orders: "save that pilot at all cost." Without any hesitation Company L 3rd Battalion, 9th Marines was headed directly on the outskirts of Khe Sanh to save the Marine Pilot. In the back of my mind I was hoping it was CPT Philip Barlow who had save our asses several times. As Company L 3rd Battalion, 9th Marines was geeting close to where the Marine pilot went down. We had several scouts out in front od us checking the area fro PAVN and booty traps. Cpl David Henderson was the best when it came to PAVN's booty traps, he could detect them a mile away. Unlike most mines, many of the PAVN's booby traps were made from bamboo and mine detectors couldn't locate them. Cpl Henderson was an expert when came to PAVN booty traps everyting from all kinds of traps with a spiked mud ball that swung down on its victim after a trip wire release, impaling him. Other impalement devices included bamboo whips and triggered sapling spikes. To bows with poisoned arrows that was used. Cpl Henderson has had some close calls once when he almost walked into an explosive booby traps that was going to be detonated by hidden PAVN. The only thing that saved his butt was, he heard the click which made him step back to the side when the explosive went off. Then the PAVN expose himself and Cpl Henderson put a 7.62 round right between his eyes. The biggest thing Cpl Henderson was noted for was saving 3 helicopters that were hovering by a bunch of trees picking up wounded Marine. When he notice explodsives that was strapped in the the trees, then he saw the PAVN ready to detonate the explodsives. Without thinking and quick reflexes he put his M14 to his shoulder took quick aim and fire a 3 round burst, with all 3 rounds hitting the PAVN in the head. The PAVN's brains was scattered all over the trees with his brain gone that kept the signal to the PAVN's index finger to push the trigger button.

As Cpl Henderson was moving forward, he marking the trail for safe places where we should step. We had gone about 15 klicks when we spotted the down A-6. The co-pilot was recognizable with all his face was shot away.. As the 3rd squad was pulling him out of the A-6. I notice a couple quick flashs of light about 2 klicks to my right. I told the 1st square go directly to the light it must be the pilot signaling us he was still alive. 1st squad came back carring the pilot, he had be wounded when the PAVN's anti-aircraft gun fired on them. I said: "CPT Philip Barlow." CPT Barlow said: "yes and Ssgt Robert Tomlin is that you." I said: "how did you know SIR." Then CPT Barlow said: " I would recognize that voice anywhere." I said: " take it easy SIR we have a helicopter coming in to pick you up and take you to a hospital." Then CPT Barlow said the strangest thing: "I told my self if I was going to be recuse, it would be Ssgt Robert Dean Tomlin, and by God I was right." Then we started to be taking fired all around us, those damn PAVN had laid an ambush for who ever pick up the down pilot. I told 2 corporals to take CPT Barlow behind that tree directly in front of us and stay with him until it was all clear. Squads 1 and 2 low crawl to a small clearing just right of the PAWN's position. Squards 3 and 4 low crawl to a clumb of trees left of the PAWN's position. Ssgt Tomlin. Ssgt Price, Ssgt Watson, and Ssgt Houser waited until the men were in position then all gave the arm signal to commence firing. With machine gun, rifle, and M79 fire directly into the nest of PAVN, all you heard was screaming and yelling. Cpl Herman Watson was firing round after round of phosphorus M79s right on top the PAVN. One PAVN that poor son-of-a-bitch come running out just covered in burning phosphorus all over his whole body. A corporal from the 3rd squad put a bullet in his his head to put hime out of his misery. We were about 20 minutes into battle when I heard the rotars of our helicopter, what a beauiful sound. Now CPT barlow could be air lifted to a hospital. Just has the UH-1H Iroquois poped up over the trees right behind the PAVN's position with another beauiful sound. The left door gunner had a M-60D a 7.62mm caliber weapon with a cyclic rate of fire of 600 to 700 rounds per minute, just mowing down those PAVN just like cutting grass. The UH-1H make a couple of more passes and the battle was over, he landed and pick up CPT Barlow. As they were loading CPT Barlow in the helicopter he gave me the thumbs up and wave good-bye. I wave back with my thumbs up. We did a body count, 7 Marine wounded and 130 PAVN killed. We destroy the PAVN's weapons and equipment and headed back to Lang Vei Special Forces Base. When we got to camp 1stSg Roger L. Lewis greeted us with a job well done and CPT Barlow just had a shoulder wound and would flying again in about 3 weeks. He said: "sad thing about his co-pilot he had only been in Vietnam for about 4 weeks." 1stSg Lewis said: " take a couple days off Company L 3rd Battalion, 9th Marines deserve it, and I will buy the first round of beers."

The Company L 3rd Battalion, 9th Marines had a couple days off without going on patrol. Butch and I notice by the end of July it seem like Army and Marines were really putting in a lot of troops and equipment in Lang Vei Special Forces Base. Then LTC Joseph Muller stepped up our daily patrols around Lang Vei with the PAVN, stepping up daytime patrols and night ambushes around our camp. On 30 July early morning while the camp was sleeping, the PAVN fired mortars into the Lang Vei compound, wounding eight Special Forces. Platoon Sergeant GySgt Russell Owens was yelling get your asses out of bed, grab your weapons, we have some damn PAVN to deal with. GySgt Russell Owens said: " Company L 3rd Battalion, 9th Marines 1st and 2nd squads take out that frigging PAVN mortar position before they blow us to hell. We could see the puffs of smoke form the PAVN's mortars as we ran out of the gate. Squad 1 and 2 would attack using the old famous spear head attack. Squad would split up with part of squad one as the spear tip and rest of squad one and two as the back edges of the spear. As we were advancing forward toward the PAVN's mortar positions, I gave the arm signals to dicrease speed and change directions to the right and left. Ssgt Tomlin gave the arm signal to the M79 launchers the range and commence firing. Ssgt Price gave the arm signal for the machine guns to commence firing. Then Ssgt Price gave the arm signal for the machine guns to fire faster. There were four PAVN mortar positions firing on Lang Vei Special Forces Base. Company L 3rd Battalion, 9th Marines took out or destroy all four PAVN's mortar positions. When the smoke had settle there was 25 PAVN killed with no wounded or killed Marine. As we were walking back through the gate at base camp we all receive a big cheer from the Marines and Army soldiers.

3 August while Company L 3rd Battalion, 9th Marines was on patrol LCpl Jerry Wassel who was point man come running up and said: "Ssgt Tomlin I saw PAVN tanks moving along Highway Road 9, attempting to make a a gap in and break through the barbed wire in front of Special forces Company. Ssgt asked: "Lcpl Wassel what kind of tanks were they." He said: " I do not know sergeant I have never see a tank like that. Cpl John Hillberg who was a tank expert spoke up and said: they look like PT-76 which is a Soviet amphibious light tank, which is a deadly beast with a AU-220M Baikal turret with 57 mm BM-57 autocannon and that Russian baby just keeps firing. We all double time it back to the operations center and described what we had witnessed the Russian tanks. The operation center call in artillery and airstrikes on the PAVN tank formation just in front of Special Forces Company. But before the three PT-76 tanks were knocked by artillery fire from the 8-inch Self-Propelled (SP) Howitzers was the most accurate artillery weapon system use. One sergeant from the artillery unit was heard making this comment: "this 8 inch Howitzers could cut the nuts of a male squerrel so clean, he wouldn't know his nuts was gone." But before the last PT-76 was destroyed it broke through the barbed wire in front of Special Forces Company and the PAVN infantry was rushing in and quickly making their attack. Company L 3rd Battalion, 9th Marines quickly got into motion and rush the PAVN infantry head on. After about half hour of fighting the PAVN retreated back down the road. It was a hell of a battle fighting hand to hand with the so called elite PAVN froce. Let the story be known we litterly kick their PAVN asses. When the dust had settle we had 3 Marines killed and 28 wounded, the PAVN had 79 killed and no count on their wounded. In the end Ssgt Tomlin. Ssgt Price, Ssgt Watson, and Ssgt Houser were covered with PAVN blood from hand to hand combat fighting. Ssgt Price said: we were to damn close to fire our weapons, so we just slit their throats and sunk our bayonets right into their ribs and stomachs. One corporal from the 4th sqaud was heard making this comment: that was the bloodest fight I ever saw or was in." Then Ssgt Watson make this comment: " the only reason we lost 3 Marines is because we were grossly out numbered. But the 28 Marines wounded was only flesh wounds from being cut." Ssgt Tomlin. Ssgt Price, Ssgt Watson, and Ssgt Houser took a long hot shower and burnt their clothes.

It was quiet for a few days and we were always on guard, because you did not know when those PAVN was going to attack. 6 August then all of a sudden those PAVN mortars started again and those damn tanks were back. There was awhole 308th PAVN Division with six PT-76 Russian tanks. A Special Force's scout spotted them about 20 or so klicks advancing directly to the Lang Vei Special Forces Base. The artillery was on alert with the coordinance and the United Staes Air Force was sending a flareship and an AC-119 Shadow gunship. AC-119 Shadow gunship nick name was "Stingers" primarily with two M61 Vulcan 20-mm cannons and they carried in additional fire power with the AC-119G's four GAU-2/A miniguns. When the 308th PAVN Division got within 10 klicks of Lang Vei Special Forces Base all hell broke loose. Those Army 8-inch Self-Propelled (SP) Howitzers started to zero on the PT-76 Russian tanks. The first PT-76 tank that was hit with an 8 inch shell went off like Roman Candle it was hit directly into ammo magazine. The other PT-76 started to pulled back tried to zig and zag looking for cover but it was too late. The other five PT-76 tanks all had direcr hits. Now with their tanks destroyed the 308th PAVN Division started advancing straight at the Lang Vei Special Forces Base. Now it was the AC-119 Shadow gunship turn, the pilot was an ex rodeo Bull riding campion. He took that AC-119 in slow hard right bank with those 20mm Vulcan (God of Fire) and four miniguns just a blasting. You could hear that pilot you would have through he was riding a bucking bull laying down lead faster then you could bink an eye. Pass after pass that AC-119 would hit the PAVN on the right then on the left, get them in the front and back. 1stSg Roger L. Lewis was heard making this comment: "if that pilot don't let up he going to melt those frigging gun barrels." After several passes he radio with: " I have to return back to base I just ran out of ammo." Now it was the Marine's turn to mop up. We hit the rest of that PAVN 308 Division with machine gun, rifle, mortar, and M79 fire. After about a hour of fighting it was over The PAVN was high tailing the other way. Ssgt Tomlin and Ssgt Price looked out over the battle field and saw so many shredded PAVN bodies from the AC-119 firing. Ssgt Price was heard making this comment: " Robert these PAVN bodies acturally look like Swift cheese, these poor bastards have so many holes in them it is not funny." Ssgt Tomlin said: "Butch some of these poor PAVN were hit several times, there are men without arms or legs." After the body count we had 9 Marines Killed and 43 wounded. The best PAVN body count we could get was that the PAVN had 1,176 killed and we do even know the wounded count was.

By 10 August the United States Marines and United Staes Army working as a team manage to hold on to Lang Vei Special Forces Base. After severl more attempts by the PAVN to take the Special Forces Base they gave up and moved on. Company L 3rd Battalion, 9th Marines spend a few more days at the Special Forces Camp waiting for their next assignment. Then one day in the mess tent when Butch and I were eating chow. We over heard 1stSg Roger L. Lewis talking about sending Company L 3rd Battalion, 9th Marines back up to the border of Laos and South Vietnam looking for dead Marines that were missing in action called Operation Cross Bow.

Operation Red Dog Casualties

Date July – August 1968
Location: Lang Vei

Result U.S. operational success
Belligerents

United States	North Vietnam North Vietnam

Commanders and leaders

LTC Joseph Muller	Major General MG Qu'ach Lam Minh PAVN Commander Vanh chu Giang PAVN Commander Vanh chu Giang PAVN

Units involved

1st Battalion, 1st Marines	325th Infantry Division
2nd Battalion, 1st Marines	308th Infantry Division
3d Marine Regiment	304th Infantry Division
4th Marine Regiment	
9th Marine Regiment	
26th Marine Regiment	
3rd Battalion, 9th Marines	
5th Special Forces Group United Staes Army	

Casualties and losses

United States 18 killed 103 wounded	US body count 1,852 killed 7 captured

CHAPTER TWENTY

Vietnam War

Operation Cross Bow

Operation Cross Bow Route Patrol looking for dead Marines that were missing in action from Camp Rotan Base to Cam Lo to Khe Sanh to Lang Vei. Date from August – September 1968.

Key United States Commanders	Key North Vietnam Commanders
LTC Joseph Muller USMC	Commander Vanh chu Giang PAVN
1stSg Roger L. Lewis USMC	Colonel Pham Chi PAVN
GySgt Russell Owens USMC	
Ssgt Henry Watson USMC	
Ssgt William Houser USMC	
Ssgt Robert Dean Tomlin USMC	
Ssgt Frederick (Butch) Philip Price USMC	

On 13 August 1968 1stSg Roger L. Lewis called Compnay L in for a meeting when we all arive for the briefing 1stSg Lewis said: "just receive word a local village reported see bodies of mutilated Marines near Camp Rotan. I have four straws, the two Squad Leaders that draw short straws will be on Route Patrol." So Ssgt Tomlin and Ssgt Price got the luck of the draw with two short straws. GySgt Russell Owens said: " in the morning Squad 1 and 2 will go and investate and find the dead marines and bring them home.": Without final notice thats when Company L Squads 1, 2, 3, and 4 of Company L 3rd Battalion, 9th Marines were put on a Route Patrol looking for dead Marines that were missing in action from Camp Rotan Base to Cam Lo to Khe Sanh to Lang Vei . If we found any dead Marines we would call in a Bell UH-1 Iroquois (Huey served as a utility, attack, and transport helicopter). It could hold 14 troops or up to six medical litters and medical crew).

We were about 6 klicks from where the dead Marines were reported when LCpl Jerry Wassel who was point man come running up at quick double time and when he stopped his face was as white as a ghost. LCpl Wassel said: "Ssgt Tomlin I can not believe there must be 4 or 5 Marines with their body parts scattered everywhere." Squad 1 and 2 followed LCpl Wassel back where he found the dead Marines. When we arrive I also most threw up seeing the mutilated bodies just threw everywhere. Heads, torsos, arms, and legs that were all mixed up and the sad part we could not match them together. The Marines always told us to put a dog tag in your boot in case you were blow up then you could be identified. We had a total of 5 dog tags, we put all the body parts together in one spot. I radio the Bell UH-1 to bring 5 body bags and that all the body parts were mixed up. Within a half hour we could hear the helicopter coming in. It landed and four corpsman that were 3 Petty Officer 3rd Class and 1 Petty Officer 2nd Class jump out with the body bags. Ssgt Tomlin and Ssgt Price was talking to the Petty Officer 2nd about the condition the bodies were in. Petty Officer 2nd said: "all my years as a corpsman I have never seen anything like this. Those son-of-a-bitchs PAVN are worst then animals." Then Cpl Herman Watson said: " when we catch them I am going to cut off their frigging heads." Ssgt Tomlin said: "no we are not going to mutilated their bodies, we are just going to kill the bastards." Ssgt Price said: " I am going to shoot their nuts off and when they scream for mercy, I am going to put a bullet right beween their eyes." When the last Marine body was put in the helicopter and we said our farewells, the helicopter lifted up and flew off back to base. We all had a little meeting about finding those PAVN who were responable for killing the Marines. A corporal pick up on a PAVN trail that was only a couple days old. Cpl John Hillberg said: " if we find the PAVN and they will have 5 M14s then we will have the frigging bastards that killed those Marines. We had got about 20 or so Klicks on the PAVN trail, when LCpl Wassel came back and said:Ssgt Tomlin and Ssgt Price they are camped about 10 klicks for here. We got within 2 klicks from their camp and then we split into 2 groups. 1st Squad took the right side and 2nd Squad took the left side. As I looked down on the PAVN camp with about 60 or 70 men, sure enough there was 5 M14 rifles stack up. I gave the arm signal to change direction for 2nd Squad for half of the squad go right and left. I signal the 1st Squad to move straight forward. Then I gave them the range by keeping my fist tight and opening one finger at a time and holding up 2 fingers which is 200 meters. One the squad were in position I gave the arm signal to commence firing. We had then in a triangle cross fire with no possible way for the PAVN could escape. With machine gun, rifle, and M79 fire, the PAVN were getting pulverize like round chuck going through a meat grinder. Ssgt Tomlin and Ssgt Price told the M79 launchers to use anti-personnel, buckshot, and flechette rounds to make them PAVN assholes to suffer. The first couple of rounds were anti-personnel followed by buckshot, and then flechette rounds. You could hear those poor PAVN bastards screaming when they were being hit with flechettes as the sharp edges just slice through their flesh. After a half hour or so of fighting it was all over, not one Pavn was standing. Ssgt Price kept his promise he found a wounded PAVN officer, put the M14 to his shoulder pulled the trigger and he shot his nuts off. The office screaming and bleeding like a stuck hog he looked up at Ssgt Price and said: anh đã thổi bay hạt của tôi (you blew off my nuts)." Then Ssgt Price said: I will do you one better then that and blew his frigging head off. We did a body count with no Marines killed or wounded, 73 PAVN killed. We destroy their weapons and equipment and headed back to base camp.

When we got back to base camp LTC Joseph Muller called Ssgt Tomlin and Ssgt Price in for a meeting.

We knocked on his door, we heard enter Butch and I stood attention render a salute and said: "Ssgt Tomlin and Ssgt Price reporting as directed SIR." LTC Muller return our salute and told us to stand at ease. Then he said: " it must have been ruff seeing those Marines in that condition." I said: " yes SIR it was very hard trying to piece them together, there was a couple of times I almost threw up. If it had not been for their for their dog tags in their boots there was no way in hell we could have identified them." Then Butch said: " SIR we took real care of the PAVN that were responible, and they will not be chopping up any more Marines." LTC Muller said: " go get some food and rest, I will send squad 3 and 4 on the next Route Patrol. Youe are dismissed." Butch and I stood at attention, render a salute and said: "Thank You SIR" did about face and walked out headed for the mess tent. While we were in the mess tent Butch and I was talking about getting out of the Marines when out tour was up. Butch turn to me and said: "Robert I never want my Mom see like those mutilated Marines. I know for a fact I am not going to reenlist for another 3 years, I just want to go home." I said: "you can say that again Brother."

17 August 1st and 2nd Squad were back at it again on Route Patrol around Cam Lo. As we were making our way through some thick under bush and grass our point man came up and said: "Ssgt.Tomlin and Ssgt Price we might be frigged. There is a battalion of PAVN SAPPERS (are ordinarily thought of as being engineers with tunneling or trenching capability) digging the biggest tunnel I ever saw. They are directly right in front of us about 10 klicks away." I called the squads together and said: "we might be in the fight of our lives, there is a battalion of sappers about 10 klicks in front of use. Lets get into the spear head position and I will call in an airstrike." I had 1st Squad with 7 men at the point of the spear and 5 men on the right and 5 men on the left of the spear point. Ssgt Price spit his 2nd Squad half on the right tail of the spear and half on the left tail of the spear. I called in the airstrike and gave them the coordinance of the PAVN position and tunnel. We had not gone more then 2 klicks when a PAVN scout saw and fired upon us. A rifle man from 2nd Squad took him out in the matter of seconds. We knew we were in for fight of our lives. A mass wave of PAVN sappers was coming directly at us. I told the men steady get ready and commence firing. With all the fire power we were putting down someone might of thought it was World War III starting. We stopped the first and second wave of PAVN sappers, then 6 Bell AH-1 Cobra helicopter show up. Three were taking care of the PAVN ground troops and three were putting rockets into the feashly dug PAVN tunnel. With Squad 1 and 2 firing directly into the on charging PAVN sappers and Cobra fring directly on top of them they were dropping like June Bugs on a hot summer night from a band of Blue Jays on a eating frenzy. The fight lasted over an hour, the Cobras ran out of ammo, but before they pulled out they had completeing seal the front of the PAVN's tunnel. We did a body count with 3 Marines Killed and 21 wounded and 463 PAVN killed and numerous wounded. I signed off to the pilots and Company L Squad 1 and 2 3rd Battalion, 9th Marines headed back to base camp.

19 August Squad 1 and 2 back on Route Patrol close to Khe Sanh, we were looking down pilot flying a A-7 Corsair II. His last radio call he was taking flack from PAVN anti aircraft guns, he was hit in the tail section and could control the plane. He was making observation of the area to land and they lost radio contact. We had to find him to see if he was dead or alive. We were about 10 klicks off of Highway 9 when we started to draw fire from a tree line. Ssgt.Tomlin told squad one to set up position just north of the PAVN's fire. Ssgt Price told squad two to take position on the left side of squad one. Then Cpl Herman Watson said: "Ssgt Tomlin I can see the tail section of the A-7." I turn to Butch and said: " thats why those frigging Pawn are shooting at us, the Marine pilot is still alive." So butch and I had a small conversation what our next move would be. I said: " I will take Cpl Herman Watson, Cpl John Hillberg, LCpl Jerry Wassel, and my radio man Cpl Ronald S. Baxton and try to circle around the PAVN in the the tree line. Wait for my signal which will be one long push on the radio mike, then give us a minute until we are in position. Have everybody put all your fire power into that tree line." Ssgt Price took squad two and the rest of squad one and got then into position. While I took my small squad and low crawl along a small ditch cover with tall grass to the back side of the kine of trees. We must of low crawl for about 2 or so klicks then I spotted an opening to the tree line. We got up behind the PAVN and saw the down A-7, I could see inside the cockpit and the Marine pilot was dead. He looked like he had been shot several times. I arm signal Cpl Baxton to to push the mike button, as we got into position. Squad two and and rest of my squad one was laying down machine gun, rifle amd M79 fire like no body business. The PAVN were in total surprise and started to scattered everywhere. As they ran in front of us we started firing directly upon on them. The fight lasted about 15 minutes and then it was over. We got to the dead pilot and took him out of the cockpit. We figure he was still alive when the plane landed and the PAVN shot him while he was still strapped in. I radio the helicopter with the coordinance to pick him up. We did a body count no Marines killed or wounded , 57 PAVN killed. We destroyed the PAVN weapons and equipment and blew up the A-7 for the PAVN could not use any parts from it. After the helicopter pick up the the dead Marine pilot, we headed back to base camp.

Everything was quiet for a couple of days so Butch and I wrote letters home. I wrote Dad and Mom that I was not going to reenlist, my three years in the United Staes Marine Corps was going to end in September 1968. Writing about my Platoon Sergeant GySgt Russell Owens wants me to relist, he is always saying your a good Marine and the Marine Corps needs you. My 1stSg Roger L. Lewis is saying the same thing, but has added with the rate of moving up in rank, you are going you will E-7 Gunnery Sergeant before you know it. Then I wrote about, now the Base Commander LTC Joseph Muller is on the band wagon telling me with you will not regret your reenlistment back in the Marine Corps, then to put the icing on the cake with I know you will make E-9 Sergeant Major. I finish writing my letters and headed for the mess tent. So while Butch and I were talking about not relisting GySgt Owens walks by and makes the same comment" Ssgt Tomlin and Ssgt Price the year will be up before your know it, I can draw up those enlistment papers early." We both said: "we will think about it

SIR" Butch said: " do not tell me they are hounded you ass about reenlistment too." Then Butch said: " Platoon Sergeant GySgt Russell Owens, 1stSg Roger L. Lewis, and Base Commander LTC Joseph Muller has been after me for about two weeks and I still have a month or so until my next enlistment is due." I told Butch that I am not going to reenlist I want to go home, go back to school and get a good paying job. Butch said: " you can say that again Brother." Then I said: " I never want my Dad and Mom ever see me in a body bag. I know it would break my Mom heart." Then butch said: " you can say that again Brother. "

21 August GySgt Russell Owens said: " in a couple of weeks company L 3rd Battalion, 9th Marines will be off Route Patrol at the most in three weeks. Now with that said we have another down pilot near Lang Vei. With reports coming in they think he is still alive and the damn PAVN are using him for bate. This one is going to be tricky we know the PAVN are setting up the ambush." Then GySgt Owens said: " here are the coordinance with an arerial view of the down McDonnell Douglas F-4 Phantom II. There is a lot trees, over grown bush and high grass, and those damn PAVN will have alot of hiding places. Further more they wanted me to send Squad 3 and 4, and I said "no" I an sending the best 1st Squad Leader Ssgt Robert Dean Tomlin and 2nd Squad Leader Ssgt Frederick (Butch) Philip Price if any body can get that pilot out alive it will be Squad 1 and 2." GySgt Owens stood back and said: "any questions." Butch and I said: "no Platoon Sergeant." 1stSg Roger L. Lewis said: " you will carrying extra rations, ammo, and water, you could be out there for a few days. Then he said:"LTC Joseph Muller wants the pilot brought back alive and hopefully with God's speed you have no casualties." Butch and I said: "1stSg Lewis we will do our best to complete our mission." We grab the map and pictures and headed for our tent. We call Squad 1 and 2 for special briefing about next mission. We had everybody check their weapons and equipment and be ready to move out at 0600 in the morning.

LCpl Jerry Wassel was point man we gave him a nick name "Bird Dog" he had a certain way about spotting PAVNs that no body in squad 1 and 2 could. As we were moving in a steady pace and about 15 klicks from the coordinance where the Marine pilot was at. When we saw old Bird Dog running at a fast pace giving us arm signals with decrease your speed, change direction, go right, and enemy in sight. I gave the arm signal to halt, then move right, with enemy in sight. Cpl Wassel said: "Ssgt Tomlin and Sggt Price The PAVN camp is about 8 klicks dieectly in front of us. Them damn PAVN bastards have the Marine pilot staked out in the middle of their camp like a piece of meat with four guards with rifles pointed directly at him. If we try to rush them the Marine pilot is dead for sure." Ssgt Tomlin and Ssgt Price got squad 1 and 2 into a meeting about the possibility and what could happen if they rush the camp. Then Cpl John Hillberg came up with a good idea with four snippers firing at the same time with head shots on the guards before they could pull their triggers to kill the Marine pilot. I looked at Butch and said: "what do you think." Butch said: " I think it will work if the snippers fired with in less then a second of each other." So then we had to figure out who was the four best marksmen in squads 1 and 2 . I said: "to make it fair I will pick two, and Butch will pick two. Ssgt Tomlin picked LCpl Jerry Wassel and Cpl Herman Watson they were both very good at firing the M14. Ssgt Price picked Cpl John Hillberg and Cpl David Henderson who were also good at firing the M14.

We had our shooters and we were worked out a plan. When all shooters were in good firing positions they would arm signal with I am ready. When Ssgt Price see each shooters give the signal they are ready then he will give the arm signal commence firing. Squad 1 amd 2 would wait until the PAVN guards are shot then move forward at double time with weapons a blazing. Ssgt Price went with the four shooters to signal when to fire. As each shooters gone into position and gave the signal I am ready. Lcpl Wassel was in the north corner, Cpl Watson was in in the south corner, Cpl Hillberg was in the west corner, and Cpl Henderson was in the east corner. As each shooter gave the signal to Ssgt Price I am ready. Ssgt Price waited a minute or two to make sure all snippers had a good bead on their targets. Then Ssgt Price gave the arm signal commence firing. It was a sight to see, each PAVN guard had their brains blow out with in a second for all four shots. When the last guard hit the ground the Marine pilot ran for cover by a fallen tree. Then squad 1 and 2 open fire on the whole camp, those damn PAVn did not know what hit them or where the shots were coming from. The whole fight lasted maybe ten minutes with several PAVNs killed while the other retreated. I walked over to the pilot and said: "Sir I am Ssgt Robert Dean Tomlin. The pilot said: sergeant Tomlin I am CPT William Johnson and thank you and your men for saving me." I said: "no problem SIR , I'll call in a helicopter to pick you up and take you back to your base." CPT Johnson said: "Ssgt Tomlin you wouldn't have some spare food and water, I am so damn thirty and hungry. Those damn PAVN would not give me any water or food." I said: " sure thing SIR." I handed him my canteen and a package of C-Rats. He drank down that water faster then you could say water. CPT Johnson said: "sergeant do have a P38." I open his cans of meat loaf, peaches, and peanut butter for the simple reason I did not want to loose my P38. He ate like like a starve dog and said: "Thank you I needed that my stomach was completely empty." The helicopter flew in to pick him up, we said our goodbyes and I threw him anther C-Rats before they lifted off. We did our body count no Marines killed, 3 Marines wounded with flesh wounds, 36 PAVN killed. We destroyed their weapns and equipment and headed back to base camp.

For the next week all Butch and I heard "its not to late to relist", and we kept saying the same thing no we are going home. 28 August I just knew we would be on Route Patrol until our tour was up on 15 September, 1968. 29 August Compnay L 3rd Battalion, 9th Marines we called up on to recuse a couple of M551 Sheridan light tanks that gone off course and were buttoned down from a trap the PAVN had set. Now the tanks were boxed in at the Demilitarized Zone near the Ben Hai River. 1stSg Roger L. Lewis gave us the coordinance and said: " those damn PAVN have set up another anbush again. Be careful, we have to free those tanks and give them cover until they can move out from the PAVN's guns. Be ready to move out at 0600 tomorrow morning. Company L Squads 1, 2, 3, and 4 went back to thier tents check their weapon and equipment and was ready to move out at 0600 in the morning. By reading the coordinance we were only about 6 klicks away when we came upon this clearing. Cpl David Henderson was point man, we saw him coming back towards us then he said: " the tanks are up in mud and every time they try to move they are fired upon by the hidden PAVN. I said: "Cpl Henderson take a couple of men back with you and pin point where that firing is comming from." I gave him a corporal from my 1st Squad and Butch gave him a corporal from his 2nd Squad. So squad 1, 2, 3, 4, stay hidden until the scouting team came back. An hour a or so went by then we spotted the scouting team comming out of the bush in front of us. Cpl Henderson said: " we are frigged the PAVN have RGP-2s point directly at the tanks, if we rush in there those Marines will be roasted marshmallows. Ssgt Tomlin said: " lets all the platoon sergeant get together and come up with a plan, to save the men and their tanks." 3rd Squad Leader Ssgt Henry Watson said: " if have to find a way to sneak up on the RPG-2s and cut their throats before they fire their weapons." 4th Squad Leader Ssgt William Houser said: " we will never get that close to them without being detected." 2nd Squad Leader Ssgt Frederick (Butch) Philip Price said: " what we really need is Marine Scout Snipers they are highly skilled in fieldcraft and marksmanship, who can deliver long-range precision fire on selected targets, from concealed positions in support of combat operations." 1st Squad Leader Ssgt Robert Dean Tomlin said: "Ssgt Price hit the nail on the head with the Marine Scout Snipers, they can shoot fast and quick with head shots, then Complay L can rush the PAVN."

Platoon Sergeant GySgt Russell Owens said: " there is a company of Marine Scout Snipers at Camp Rotan Base, I will radio to have the a couple of squads to help us to take out the RPG-2s." Ssgt Tomlin said: there is only one wat this can work, if the PAVN have the RPG's shouldered or near bye. If they have then at port arms we are frigged there is no way we can get off a head shot without them pulling the triggers." Ssgt Price said: " there is no way the PAVN will holding a RPG at port arms all day the weapon weight over ten pounds." I said: "get Cpl Henderson up here and we will asked him how the PANN is holding their RPGs. When Cpl Henderson came up from the rear, he said a direct question how was the PAVN holding their RPGs. Cpl Henderson said: " some had them by their sides while others had them rested against a tree." GySgt Owens said: " I will radio the Marine Scout Snipers to come to this coordinance, then we can set the plan in motion." It was several hours before the company of Marine Scout Snipers reached us. Platoon Sergeant GySgt William Bean of the Marine Scout Snipers reported GySgt Owens and said: "Gunny Sergarant I have 12 Scout Snipers at your disposal." GySgt Owens said: " we have a problem if we rush to free the tanks the PAVN have men with RPGs that will fire directly on the tanks. We have to killed the PAVN before thy fire the RPGs."

GySgt Bean said: "how many RPGs?" GySgt Ownes said: " they have four, a couple are by their sides and a couple resting on a tree near them." GySgt said: "great we will do head shots and if have to we will blow off their damn hands. With my men the PAVN will not get off a shot. They will be firing the Remington Model 700 is a bolt-action centerfire rifle with a 5-round internal magazine that has a hinged floor-plate for quick unloading and fires a .300 Winchester Magnum. Every one of my men can hit a target at 2,000 thousand meters. GySgt Ownes said: " GySgt Bean put two shooters on each of the PAVN with RPGs and I will put four of your Scout Snipers in front when we make our charge." GySgt Bean told his Scout Snipers as soon as they knock out the RPGs that Company L will be charging. He added pop as many PAVN as you can to save the lives of Company L when they make their charge.

Everybody was in position waiting for the PAVN RPGs to be knocked out. Then all of a sudden the first Marine rifle shot rang out, and there stood number one PAVN without his head. When the .300 magnum hit his head it just exploded. Then just like clock work number two, number three, and number four all without heads. The Scout Snipers were watching the RPG Launchers very closely, then every time a PAVN reached for the RPG launchers his head was gone. Company L rush the rest of the PAVN camped with machine guns, rifls and M79 just a blasting. The four Scout Snipers in our front were knocking off the PAVN that gave us the greatest threat, as we charged their front line. With all four PAVN RPGs knock out and their following preceders, the 8 other Scout Snipers started knocking off other PAVNs that were fighting Company L 3rd Battalion, 9th Marines. The battle lasted about 45 minutes, then as usual the PAVN started to high tail it back to thier Demilitarized Zone. By now all 12 Scout Snipers were picking them off as they treated. GySgt Ownes thanked GySgt Bean and said: " Gunny I think I own you a beer or two." Company L all shook hands with the Scout Snipers and thank them for all their help and actions. Then we heard the tank firing up their engines and to get the hell out of the mud hole. The Tank commander stopped his lead tank and popped the hatch and said: "Thanks alot Marines it was getting hotter then a whore house on Saturday night inside this tank." He added if you ever need help just call on us and thanks again. The tanks were headed south with treads clanking and smoke rolling and before you knew it they were out of sight. We did a body count no Marines killed and only 6 wounded with flesh wounds, the PAVN had 87 killed. We destroyed PAVN weapons and equipment and headed back to camp to wait for our next mission.

31August Butch and I were counted the days until we got out of the Marine Corps that morning we had 14 days and a wake up. then it was back on Route Patrol again looking for dead and missing Marines. This time we were making a large swept aroud Khe Sanh and Lang Vei areas and making damn sure we were not walking into an ambush or booty traps. We were looking around the area of Khe Sanh checking for PAVN and missing Marines when Cpl Herman Watson come running up and said: Ssgt Tomlin and Ssgt Price there something strange in the clearing about 3 klicks in front of us." I said: " what so strange about it." Cpl said: sergeant you are not going to believe what I am about to tell you."

Cpl Herman Watson was point man for today and he was straining every sense he had to keep watch for the enemy. Everything was quiet until around 13:30 when he heard a human voice screaming. That's when CPL Watson of Complany L 3rd Battalion, 9th Marines saw an odd shape in the light of day.

Cpl Watson saw the shape of a giant form with the wings of a bat, but then it got closer. He could see that it had the body of a naked woman, with flowing long hair and totally purple skin . Cpl Watson said: "My God even her tits and pussy were purple. She slow down the beat of her wings which was attached to her arms as she came closer to him. When she came within 7 feet away from him with blood dripping from her flangs and mouth. She ran her long finger nails down the side of his face, she had a gleam in her eyes that said I want you big boy. By then he was so damn scared, he pissed his pants. He could make out the faint sound of her wings flapping as she hover over him before flying off towards the trees" Cpl Watson said: " Ssgt Tomlin and Ssgt Price after she flew off it just got damn quiet not a bird or anything moving. I throgh for sure I was a goner."

Ssgt Tomlin and Ssgt Price looked at Cpt Watson and both said: " are you frigging high on drugs." Then Cpl Watson said; "no, I will take you back there and show you the blood." Company L followed Cpl Watson in the direction as he walked in front of us. We had gone about 3 klicks and sure enough there was blood all over the place and a trail of blood going into the tree line. Cpl Watson turn to us and said: "I told I was not on drugs. What do you make of it sergeants." Butch and I scatch our heads and said: " there is no sign of a body, but on the other hand there is a lot of blood." Butch said: "do you think it is another PAVN's trick?" I said: "lets go and ask the local villagers, to see if they know anything." We travel another 6 or 7 klicks and saw a small village. Compnay L posted guard, as ten us walked into the village and asked about some Purple Bat Women.

One of the local villager told us about the legends of these creatures and how they usually carry off people to feast on. The villager said: " your corporal is very lucky she must of like him or he would be a puddle of blood in the jungle." As soon as he said that Cpl Watson broke out in a cold sweet. Cpl Watson turn and said: "not only would I have been fucked to death by the Purple Bat Woman, but the bitch would have eaten me." While in Vietnam Cpl Watson never talked about the event again. But years later Cpl Herman Watson was reported to make this comment: " she was naked with purple skin and had knockers that would stop a clock and she flew with wings. She flew right up to my face with a gleam in her eyes that said I like and I want you. He always through is it possibile of a new species in the world?" After all, why would a battle-hardened Marine lie about such a thing? We left the village and headed back to camp. I make the report to Platoon Sergeant GySgt Russell Owens about Cpl Watson and the Purple Bat Women. The first thing GySgt Owens said: " his that boy high on drugs" I said: "no, we saw a lot of bood in the jungle with no evidence of a body. We asked the local villagers and they told the story of a winged creature that feast on humans."

GySgt Owens said: " ok Ssgt Tomlin I will give the report to 1stSg Roger L. Lewis and you know he is going to laugh his ass off." GySgt Owens said: " you are dismissed." I walked back to my tent to write letters to home telling Dad and Mom I will be home soon. Butch came in and said: " what did GySgt Owens think." I said: " he thinks Cpl Watson was on drugs and through it was funny."

2 September Butch and I are still counting the days until we get out of the Marine Corps, we have 12 days and a wake up. When a corporal came into our tent and said: "First Sergeant wants to see Ssgt Tomlin and Ssgt Price first thing after breakfast." We said: "thank You corporal." Butch and I headed for the mess tent. After breakfast we finished our meal and sat around talking about what we were going to say to the First Sergeant about relistment. Butch came up with a good idea and said: " to make everybody happy lets delay our rotaion out of the Marine Corps for two months." I said: " great idea that should make our First and Platoon Sergeants happy that we will stay an extra two months." Butch and I reported to the First Sergeant and told him of our plans staying in the Marine an extra two months. 1stSg Roger L. Lewis though it was a great idea and he would tell LTC Joseph Muller the great news. Then he said: " I can shuttle the paper work around for a couple more months before you have to leave." Why don't you Ssgt Tomlin and Ssgt Price. take off a couple of days from Route Patrol duty and rest up, relax, and have some fun before your next mission. You are dismissed." We both said: Thank You, First Sergeant and headed back to our tent.

Operation Cross Bow Casualties

Date August – September 1968
Location: Camp Rotan Base, Cam Lo, t Khe Sanh, and Lang Vei

Result U.S. operational success
Belligerents

United States	North Vietnam North Vietnam

Commanders and leaders

LTC Joseph Muller	Commander Vanh chu Giang PAVN
Colonel Pham Chi PAVN	

Units involved

3rd Battalion, 9thMarines	812th Regiment PAVN
	716th Regiment PAVN

Casualties and losses

United States 3 killed	US body count 716 killed
30 wounded	

CHAPTER TWENTY ONE

Vietnam War

Operation Prone Horn Antelope

Operation Prone Horn Antelope Route Patrol looking for dead Marines that were missing in action during Vietnam War that took place in the southern half of the Demilitarized Zone, around Camp Rotan and a hill somewhere in Laos. Date from September – November 1968.

Key United States Commanders	Key North Vietnam Commanders
LTC Joseph Muller USMC	Commander Vanh chu Giang PAVN
1stSg Roger L. Lewis USMC	Colonel Pham Chi PAVN
GySgt Russell Owens USMC	
Ssgt Henry Watson USMC	
Ssgt William Houser USMC	
Ssgt Robert Dean Tomlin USMC	
Ssgt Frederick (Butch) Philip Price USMC	

5 September Butch and I had 68 days and a wake up before we rotated back to the states. We had just finish breakfast when we got the alert called from our Paltoon Sergeant to get ready and movd out. He said: " Alpha and Bravo Companies, 1st Battalion, 9th Marines was making their way up north on Highway 463 and secured a crossroad as their first objective. When they got ambush and Company L Squad 1,2, 3, and 4 was being send out to rescue them." As our squad got together to move out. Ssgt Price said " my God that is north between Demilitarized Zone and Ben Hai River, near a place called The Death Trap. We better hurry before the 1st Battalion, 9th Marines are wipped out. As we arrive we could see Alpha and Bravo Companies, 1st Battalion, 9th Marines were pinned down with PAVN cross fire. I had squad 1 set up position to make contact with the elements of the PAVN 90th Regiment to draw their fire away from A company 1st Battalion, 9th Marines. When we were spotted PAVN sniper fire began to break out, to stop our effords to help Compabny A 1st Battalion, 9th Marines. I told Cpl Herman Watson to intensified M79 rounds on top of the PAVN snipers to drive them back. Cpl Watson lopped about 4 rounds all around the PAVN snipers with killing about 5 or six the the rest retreated out of range of the M79. As efforts were made by the 1st and 2nd squads of Compmay L 3rd Battalion, 9th Marines to suppress the ambush. Company L 3rd Battalion, 9th Marines had kill, destroy, and remove a large percentage and part of PAVN ambush. If Alpha Company

free, they went to rescue Company B that was ambushed. As we were cleaning up Ssgt Tomlin notice during the battle the PAVN were going to used flamethrowers setting fire to hedgerows along Highway 463 forcing the Marines out into the open. Ssgt Tomlin send in his rifle squad to blow the flamethrowers tanks in place. You would have through it was 4th of July when those PAVN gas tanks exploded. Those PAVN were burning, running, and sceaming as their whole bodies were on fire. The 1st rifle saud felt sorry for them and shot them as they ran to put them out of their misery. Now we had to deal with artillery and mortar fire causing casualties on A and B Companies and prevented them from joining with and connect up. I called in an artillery strike to stop the PAVN artillery and mortars. With in a couple of minutes you could hear the whistle of the M109 self-propelled 155mm howitzer putting shells right on top the the PAVN artillery and mortars. The PAVN artillery and mortars stop, then Company A move right in to help Company B. We did body count with 31 Marines killed and 211 PAVN killed. Company L 3rd Battalion, 9th Marines was ordered to stay as guards while Comapies A and B 1st Battalion, 9th Marines gather up their dead. We posted men all four corners to protect the Marines from an ambush when they when out to get the dead Marines. When the last helicopter pick up the last four dead Marines, we headed back to camp. 1stSg Roger L. Lewis met us at the front gate and said: " I guess it was real ruff out there." Ssgt Tomlin said: "First Sergeant I saw a lot of good Marines get killed today." 1stSg lewis said: Compnay L get some food and rest; I 'll make the report to LTC Joseph Muller about the mission was completed and a job well done."

The fighting never stopped; there was some kind of fighting and battles every day in Vietnam. There was always one thing for sure you were fighting or helping some one to fight or battle. You would think with your days off you could get some rest and peace, but you never did. As soon as you went to sleep there was always some kind of commotion with rifle, machine gun, mortar, and artillery fire all around you that always woke you up. I was having a really rough couple of nights not sleeping, then finally I dozed off to be woken by Butch telling me to get up. I said: " what the hell I just got to sleep"Butch said: "the First Sergeant wants to see us right away." I jumped up, got dressed, and headed for the First Sergeant's tent. When we got there Platoon Sergeant GySgt Russell Owens, 3rd Squad Leader Ssgt Henry Watson, and 4th Squad Leader Ssgt William Houser were waiting for us. Then 1stSg Roger L. Lewis said: "sorry Ssgt Tomlin I know you have not been sleeping well, but I just receive this report. The frigging PAVN are coming from Laon on Highway 9, attacking all Marine Bases along the way. So we need to stop the PAVN coming from Laod before they get into Vietnam." I asked a question, do we stop them in Laos or Vietnam. The 1stSg Lewis said: "good question, we stopped the son-of-a-bitches in Laos before they cross over to Vietnam." Then 1stSg Lewis said: " LTC Joseph Muller wants to say a few words." LTC Muller said: "men we always had rough assignment and missions, this one is going to test you to the core. In the morning at 0600 Companies A,B,D, and L of the 3rd Battalion, 9th Marines will move out to a hill just across the border in Laos and set up positions to stop, destroy, and push back the PAVN from crossing over into Vietnam.

You could be there for two or more weeks, so take plenty of food, water, and ammo and you be fighting a long hard battle. Get your rest have a good meal, check your weapons and equipment and you are dismissed. We all said SIR yes SIR and walked out to the mess tent.

8 September After the mess hall Butch and I walked back to our tent, to check our weapons and equipment and try to get some rest. O600 came real early,; all companies were in formation ready to move out. We were loaded into helicopters and flown to Lang Vei and from there it was about 5 or so klicks to the hill to get into position. We were going to use an old fish hook position from the Civil War to catch the PAVN in a trap while they were moving from Laos to Vietnam. The eye of the hook was Squads 1,2,3, and 4 of Company A, the shank of the hook was Squads 1 and 2 of Company B, the bent of the hook was Squads 3 and 4 of Company B, the barb of the hook was Squads 1 and 2 of Company D, the point and throat of the hook was Squads 3 and 4 of Company D, and the the Gap of the hook was Squads 1,2, 3, and 4 of Company L. We set up machine guns, mortars, and M79 in all positions. Cpl Herman Watson put out markers every 100 meters to give the mortars and M79 launched a better degree of accuracy for distance. We sent out 3 scouts on the right, center, and left sides of our positions to warn of an approaching PAVN. We started digging fox holes, filling sand bags, and stacking the sand bags around us. We were eating C-Rats when a scout from our left side came back and said: Ssgt. Tomlin the Pavn is about 3 klicks out heading straight towards. I gave the arm signal enemy in sight; then I flash three fingers, machine gun style, telling the men the enemy is 3 klicks away. With all men in position, we just waited until the PAVN was in firing distance. Waiting did not take long; there was a whole battalion of PAVN coming up the hill in our sight. All the Marine Squad Leaders gave arm signals to commence firing. Those damn PAVN did not what hit them. They were getting blasted with rifle, machine gun, mortar, and M79 rounds from all angles of the fish hook positions. They could not run right, left, or in the center without being fired upon. One corporal from Squad One of Company A was heard making this comment: " those damn Pavn were dropping faster then a fly hatch being eaten by Rainbow Trout on the Colorado River." At one time there were dead or wounded PAVN all over the hill side. The battle lasted about three hours when the PAVN commander yelled rút lui, rút lui (retreat) **(1-53)** and they all ran back down the hill. As the PAVN were running down the hill you could hear them say: "những thủy quân lục chiến chết tiệt (those frigging Marines) **(1-54)**." We did a body count, 2 Marine killed and 5 wounded and 187 PAVN killed, and they took their wounded with them. I call in a helicopter to pick up the dead and wounded Marines. Then we waited for the next PAVN wave of attack. We sent out the scouts again to give us a warning of the next PAVN attack. We just settled in for a rest when the second wave of PAVN attacked, only this time there were a thousand coming straight at us. The only thing I was thankful for was that we had brought extra ammo.

As we were moving down the hill making sure there were no live PAVN soldiers, a corporal came running up and said: : Ssgt Tomlin there, a live PAVN about 100 feet down on the left." When we got there we found the PAVN with an arm wound. The interpreter asked him the name of his unit and how many men. The PAVN would not talk; he kept saying: "Tôi cần bác sĩ "(I need a doctor) **(1-55)**. The interpreter asked him again, but this time he grabbed him by his wounded arm and held a knife to his neck and asked him again the name of his unit and number of men. The PAVN kept saying: "đừng làm tổn thương tôi" (do not hurt me) **(1-56)**. This went on for two more hours and PAVN was not talking. We had a corporal named Jake Brown who was 6 foot 5 inches tall and weighed about 240 pounds. I had an idea, if the PAVN saw old Jake standing over him, he would spill the beans and talk like a pissed off parrot when he did not get his food. Jake walked up and stood over the prisoner and in a husky voice said: " you frigging PAVN you are going to talk." Then somebody behind Jake yelled, sat on that son-of-a-bitch, he would talk. Ssgt Price said: "Jake burk that bastard." Jake turned to Ssgt Price and said: "burk what that." Then, Ssgt Price said:" Sit on his damn chest until he talks or dies." So Jake sat right down on the PAVN chest and the PAVN was moving around trying to catch his breath as big Jake just sat there. Then corporal Brown said: " talk you frigging DFB, or I will crush the life out of you." Ssgt Price said: " now what in the the hell is DFB?" Corporal Brown turned to Ssgt Price and said: "well Sergeant, DFB is (Dick For Brains)." Finally the PAVN was yelling: "đưa con voi đó ra khỏi" (get that elephant off) **(1-57)**. He kept screaming "tôi sẽ nói với bạn rằng tôi không thể thở" (I will tell you I can not breath) **(1-58)**. So when big Jake stood up that PAVN sang like a song bird. He told the unit's name and how many men were going to attack us. Ssgt Tomlin turned to Ssgt Price and said: "Butch I guess the burking really works. That frigging PAVN had about 3 or 4 minutes left before he would suffocated to death."

9 Setember We had just finished setting the fish hook again with all the Marines in position, when a scout came running to us yelling: "get ready here they come." I looked down and all I saw human waves of PAVN coming right up hill screaming and yelling tất cả thủy quân lục chiến phải chết (all Marines must died) **(1-59)**. Ssgt. Tomlin, Ssgt Price, Ssgt Watson, and Ssgt Houser told their squads to hold your fire until they hit the first marker. The first wave of PAVN, about 3 hundred or so, crossed the first marker, and they were getting hit with everything but the kitchen sink. One corporal from the 3rd Squad was heard making this comment: " my God they are getting shreaded like a meat through a grinder and they keep on coming." As the PAVN were stacking on top of each other from being killed or wounded, some the of the stacks were 4 to 5 feet tall. There were human bodies with all kinds of arms, legs, torsos, and heads that were missing from the explosions of our mortars amd M79 rounds. It did not stop them; they just kept coming. One machine gunner yelled at me and said. "Ssgt Tomlin my frigging gun barrell is really getting hot and its turning a bright orange and red." I yelled back: "use your canteen and pour water on it to cool it down." Just as the corporal was pouring water on the gun barrel, the second wave stopped. Company L was fighting for a solid two hours. A corporal from the 4th Squad was heard making this comment: " thank God they stopped my trigger finger was getting score cramping up

and I could hardly squeeze the trigger; I got a blister the size of Texas." Now we have 4 Marines killed and 8 wounded and 259 PAVN killed. I radio in for replacements and a lot of ammo, food , water, and pick up our dead and wounded Marines. Within a half hour the helicopters were coming in with supplies; and pick up the dead and wounded Marines. We placed guards all around the helicopters as they were landing just in case the PAVN wanted to shoot them down.

Our Company Commander Maj. Ronald Jefferson was wounded in the second wave attack and 2ndLt Harry Wilson was taking command until we got a replacement. Ssgt Jerry Harris, who was in command of the M2 mortar crew, was wounded. He kept saying: "do not medial vac me out, it is only a surface wound." The corpman said: " I can see your ribs its more then a surface wound, you are going to the field hospital" Ssgt Harris was cussing and telling the corpman: " you were shitting your diapers when I was a Marine in the Korea War." The corpman said: "Ok sergeant my Dad was a Marine in the Korea War also, that does not change a thing you are still going to the field hospital." Then Ssgt Harris said: " only because you Dad was a Marine that I am going to the hospital." We got our replacements of 20 Marines, C-Rats, water, 7.62 ammo for the M14's and M60's, 60 mm round for M2 mortars and40×46mm grenades for the M79 launchers. 2ndLt Harry Wilson had a meeting with all the sergeants about getting ready for the third wave attack from the PAVN. 2NdLt Wilson said: " those crazy bastards do not give a rat's ass if they live or died. They are going to rush us with everything they have with all their efford to wipe us off from this hill and to kill us all." Then he said: " I have a trick up my sleeve with using the fish hook with a little twist by using a double barb. The left barb will still be the same position of rifles and machine guns. The added right barb will have mortars and M79s. The next time the PAVN rush up the hill they will have a steady diet of 60 mm rounds and 40×46mm grenades. Ssgt made a comment: " SIR with the right barb that means we will cut off their main attacking force." 2NdLt Wilson said: " you hit the nail on the head sergeant, the PAVN will not exspec the mortars and M79s there." Ssgt Price said: " SIR a better trick is camouflage the whole area around the right barb and the frigging PAVN will never know what hit them." 2NdLt Wilson said: " lets get to work and you are dismissed." Everybody said: "SIR yes Sir" All the squads got busy camouflaging and setting up new positions with men and weapons and waited for the third wave of attack.

10 September We just finished our new fish hook when a scout came running up and said: "get ready they are coming and its looks like a whole battalion." I looked out at all the charging PAVNs; you could see the front of the PAVN with no ending of the mass of men in the rear. The wave hit the first marker and all hell broke loose bullets from our rifles, machine guns, and rounds of mortars, and M79 were firing faster than a bunch of pigs eating slop at their feeding troughs. With bullets buzzing and whizzing all around and explosion after explosion for the mortars and M79. One corporal from the 2nd Squad was heard making this comment: " you think those dumb son-of-a-bitches would learn from the prevision attacks with their stacking up

dead bodies with missing body parts." 2NdLt Wilson ordered Ssgt Tomlin to call in an air strike. 2NdLt Wilson said: " Ssgt Tomlin get those gun ships in here quick before they over run us." I radio in the air strike with the coordinance of the attacking PAVN. In a matter of minutes you could hear the rotation of the helicopters blades and the sound of machine guns of 7.62mm and 40mm grenade launchers firing directly into the attacking PAVN. There were four attacking AH-1 Huey Cobras just blasting the hell out of the attacking PAVN. You could see rows of PAVNs going down and getting destroyed at the same time. After the 4th or 5th passes with AH-1s, the PAVN started to retreat back into the jungle. 2NdLt Wilson said: " said maybe we can get some kind of sleep tonight." After all that fighting we had 3 Marines killed and 4 wounded; the PAVN had 411 PAVN killed. I radio a helicopter to pick up the dead and wounded. The AH-1 gun ship stayed around until the UH-1 Huey helicopter came in to pick up the dead and wounded.

11 September Finally Butch and I got to sit down to rest and eat some C-Rats and have a cup of coffee. We talked about going home and what our future plans were going to be. Then we cleaned and checked our weapons and tried to rest and get some sleep before the next wave of PAVN coming up that frigging hill. I just got to sleep when 2NdLt Wilson shook me and said: "Ssgt Tomlin its too damn quiet out there. Do you think the PAVN is up to something?" I said: " SIR there only one way to find out shoot a couple of flares in the air." 2NdLt Wilson said: " use the flare gun with a longer barrel and have them fire parachute flares. A corporal shot a couple of parachute flares straight in the air and the sky lite up like day light. 2NdLt Wilson and Ssgt Tomlin looked over and down the hill and could not beliece their eyes. There was two hundred PAVN low crawing up the hill toward our positions. I started firing my M14 directly right at the PAVN, killing several of them. My shots woke everybody up and the rest of the companies started firing their weapons. The low crawing PAVN mever make it pass the first ground marker, they were getting cut to pieces. Only 10 or 15 PAVN that was still alive retreated back to the jungle. I turn to 2NdLt Wilson and said: "SIR you saved our asses, by you thinking it was so quiet, we could have lost a lot of men." 2NdLt Wilson said: " do not give me all the credit, it was you to use the flares." 2NdLt Wilson said: " double the guard tonight and make damn sure they stay awake." I said: "yes SIR" I got the guard detailed together and set up their guard posts. Then I finally went back to my fox hole to get some sleep. The next morning Butch was shaking me and telling me to get up sleeping-head. I said: "please Butch get me a cup of coffee and a cigar." I took my first sip of good hot coffee and un-wrapped and chewed on my cigar; I did not light it because I did not want a PAVN snipper to zero on me while I was smoking. All day long we did not have one PAVN attack. We were thinking maybe those tricking bastards were building up with several battalions to attack, overrun, and kill us.

13 September The next morning Platoon Sergeant GySgt Russell Owens was talking to all the Squad Leaders about keeping our men and us on our toes in case there is one giant wave of a PAVN attack. Again, all day long there was no PAVN attack. Butch

said: “Robert do you think those PAVN went back to Laos?” I said: “ no I think those little bastards are waiting us out to see if we make a mistake and pull out. Then they will attack when we are our of position and unorganized.” It was 3 straight days with no action from the PAVN not even coming close to the hill. On the fourth day, a scout came running back yelling: “ there are more PAVN coming then you can shake a stick at.” The fish hook was set again with camouflage, six mortars and 8 M79s on the right barb of the hook. The PAVN will be caught in total surprise while running up the hill as they get their asses blown off. I looked out from my fox hole and all I saw was one giant PAVN wave coming straight at us. Everybody held their fire until the PAVN hit the first marker. The PAVN were yelling giết tất cả người Mỹ (kill all Amerians) **(1-60)** as they were running up to the first marker. About 100 or 150 hit the first marker; within 15 seconds; they no longer existed; they were all dead from all the fire power of the Marines. I could hear the machine gunners yelling need ammo; I am running low. When an ammo runner was bringing ammo to the machine gunner who was running low of Squad 2 of Company A was heard making this comment: “ private you better get your ass in gear and Improvise, adapt, and overcome. Or we will be the ones getting their asses shot off, now run back and get more ammo.” The battle was going on for over 5 hours with no end in sight. Not only did we have ammo runners, we had water runners bringing water to the machine gunners, mortarmen, and M79 Launchers. The PAVN had dead and wounded bodies stacking up all over the hill, and they just kept coming with no end in sight. After an 8 hour battle, finally the PAVN retreated back into the jungle. We had 11 Marines killed and 31 wounded; the PAVN had 526 killed. The only difference in the kill ratio is that the Marines were under cover and the PAVN were exposed and in the open. 2NdLt Wilson radio in the helicopters to pick up the dead and wounded Marines, and bring more food, water, and ammo. Within half an hour 4 helicopters came in, 3 to pick up the dead and wounded and 11 with supplies. We loaded the dead and wounded and took off our supplies and watch as the last helicopter lifted off.

14 September 2NdLt Wilson said: “check your weapons and equipment and make sure they are in good operating condition before the next attack. Get some food, water, and try to get some rest.” Platoon Sergeant and Squad Leaders said: “Sir yes SIR.” Then we headed back, checking on our men before we went to our fox holes for food, water and rest. Butch said: “Robert is this frigging battle ever going to end, or we just stuck here forever.” I said: “ Butch with that last wave the PAVN are running low on men to make to a lot of attacks.” Butch said: “ no the bastards will wait for reinforcements and keep making attacks up this frigging hill.” In the back of my mind I was hoping Butch was wrong. The next couple of days all was quiet without a single attack. The scouts kept coming back with reports, no PAVN in sight. I told Butch: “ I think we are all free and clear and the PAVN have finally retreated. We still kept scout out and men pulling guard duty. I finally got some sleep and wrote letters home. The Squad Leaders made sure all weapon position had plenty of stored ammo with out the use of a runner. 2NdLt Wilson said: “ place all ammo runners in fighting positions.”

17 September, when every body though in a couple of days we would be moving back to base camp. The PAVN started dropping artillery rounds on top of us and all around us. Lucky for us, we dug the fox holes deeper and stacked sand bags higher. The shells were exploding, and our position was held with how many casualties. 2NdLt Wilson had a spotter get the coordinates of the PAVN artillery and where all the artillery was coming from. 2NdLt Wilson called in an airstrike and told the pilots to use napalm to clear the forest in front to give us a clearer view of the attacking PAVN. Before you could wet your lips and whistle, the A-6 Intruders, F-4 Phantom, and F-105 Thunderchiefs were diving bombing with napalm on PAVN gun inplacements and setting the jungle on fire. Then all of a sudden, screaming PAVN came running out of the jungle on fire. We were shooting the poor bastards to put them out of their misery.With in an hour or so the PAVN artillery stopped. We were just waiting for that last wave of PAVN attacks on the hill. It seemed like we waited and waited with no sign of an attack. For the next couple of days we all ate and rested in peace. 2NdLt Wilson called in for a spotter plane to check the surrounding areas around the hill for PAVN activity. The next day a Cessna 0-1 Bird Dog radio 2NdLt Wilson with all clear all around within 60 miles of your hill. 2NdLt Wilson radioed LTC Muller and said: "SIR we are all clear and that we will be coming back to base camp." LTC Muller said: " 2NdLt Wilson will send in the helicopters at 0600 tomorrow to pick you up." 2NdLt Wilson said: " ok men break it down we will move out at 0600 tomorrow back to base camp." We packed up all our weapons and equipment to be ready at 0600 the next day. We double the guards again just in case the PAVN changes their minds and makes another attack.

20 September the helicopters came in to pick us up. Complany L Squad 1 and 2 were the last to lift off and head back to base camp. As we flew out, Butch and I looked down on the jungle with all those burnt dead bodies of the PAVN from the napalm attack and they looked like roasted marshmallons. As we were the last helicopter to touch down at Tomahawk Base, it sure was nice to be off that frigging hill. I told Butch to take a hot shower, meal, and smoke a cigar tonight. Butch turned to me and said: "Robert do not forget the beer, I am getting drunk as a skunk tonight." Butch and I just rested, ate like pigs, and took it easy for the next couple of days. But it all ended to soon when we were asked to report to the First Sergeant. Butch and I entered the First Sergeant's tent and reported as directed. The First Sergeant said: "Ssgt Tomlin and Ssgt Price you will be on Route Patrol looking for missing dead Marines around Demilitarized Zone and the hills around Tomahawk Base. Then 1stSg Lewis said: " I will make this promise that you will be on light duty after this patrol. Get your men squared away and be ready to move out in a couple of days. At the most this mission will last a week or more, then you will be on light duty until you rotate back to the states." Butch and I went back to our tent and had a meeting with our squads about our next mission. We told them to get their weapons and equipment ready and inspected and be ready to move out at 0600 on the 25 September. I lite up a cigar and was thinking about home and seeing old friends again. Butch said: " Robert why don't

you think about moving to Colorado with me and getting a good job. I said: " no I think I will stay in Springfield, Illinois and get a job there." Butch was always funny and said: " what ever blow your skirt up." The next day GySgt Owens had a meeting with Company L Squads 1, 2, 3, and 4 3rd Battalion, 9th Marines. He started off by saying: "this mission could be a ruff one, those damn PAVN are every where and looking for an opportunity to ambush you. Make damn sure you keep your eyes and ears open and put out your best point men. You are dismissed get a good hot meal and some rest, it might be a long time for a good meal and rest." We all headed back to our tents to get ready for another damn Route Patrol.

Operation Prone Horn Antelope

Date September – November 1968
Location: Demilitarized Zone, around Camp Rotan and Laos

Result U.S. operational success

Belligerents

United States	North Vietnam North Vietnam

Commanders and leaders

LTC Joseph Muller	

Units involved

3rd Battalion, 9th Marines	325th Infantry Division

Casualties and losses

United States 51 killed	US body count 1,994 killed
	48 wounded

CHAPTER TWENTY TWO

Vietnam War

Robert and Butch Go Home

Robert and Butch Go Home Route Patrol looking for dead Marines that were missing in action during Vietnam War that took place around the Demilitarized Zone, and Camp Rotan Base. Date from September – November 1968.

Key United States Commanders **Key North Vietnam Commanders**

LTC Joseph Muller USMC
1stSg Roger L. Lewis USMC
GySgt Russell Owens USMC
Ssgt Henry Watson USMC
Ssgt William Houser USMC
Ssgt Robert Dean Tomlin USMC
Ssgt Frederick (Butch) Philip Price USMC

24 September: We got reports of dead Marine that were spotted by local villagers at the DMZ. We were making our search south around the Demilitarized Zone and several small villages. Just finish walking through tall elephant grass headed for this clearing of a large group of Teak Trees. We just came to a complete stop when they heard a bunch of rifle and machine guns firing in the distance. Little did we know that LCpl Jerry Wassel my best point man for Squad 1, had run right into a PAVN regiment ambush and he was fighting for his life. Then I spotted LCpl Jerry Wassel running as fast as he could, yelling take cover its an amabush. Then all of a sudden RPD (Russian Degtyaryov hand-held machine gun), AK-47 rifle (known as the Russian Avtomat Kalashnikova), Degtyaryov DP-27/DP-28 (Russian Light Machine Gun), and PK Machine Gun (Russian belt-fed general-purpose machine gun) were firing directly at us with 7.62 bullets whizzing and bussing over our heads and all around us. It was like someone had knocked down a hornet's nest and 7.62 bullets were mad hornets buzzing around us. Then the frigging mortars started with the 82-pm-41 (Russian: 82-Полевой Миномёт-41) exploding all around us. Ssgt Tomlin and Ssgt Price's squad were in direct fire of the mortars. Squad 1 and 2 were scrambling all over the open field looking for cover. As the mortar rounds were exploding in front of us. I yelled fall back and get the hell out of that damn mortar's range.

No sooner than I said that when a mortar shell landed right next to LCpl Jerry Wassel. The M82 mortar explosion blew the lower half of his body away. LCpl Wassel was screaming and yelling Ssgt Tomlin help me. I ran over to him; I had tears in my eyes when I picked up his upper half of his body and held him in the center of my body, and I tried like hell to keep him from looking down. Blood was pouring out of his body like a water fall; to my amazement he was still alive. Blood just kept pouring out of his upper torso and I could not stop the bleeding. I kept yelling corpsman, corpsman. LCpl Wassel said:" Ssgt Tomlin do not let me die here and my legs hurt like hell. Ssgt Tomlin could you rub my hurting legs." So I just pretended to be rubbing his legs. Then, he said: " keep rubbing that feels good and the hurt is going away." The hurt was going away because he was slowing starting to turn pale white, and the color of his blue eyes were turning gray and he was dying in my arms. The corpsman ran up and whispered: " Ssgt Tomlin he is too far got, I can give him some morphine to make him comfortable." I told the corpman to give him as much as possible to take the pain away. Then my tears really started to flow from my eyes when LCpl Wassel said: " Ssgt Tomlin do not let my Mom and Dad see me like this." Then he just dropped his head and I knew he was dead; I told the corpsman it was too late he is gone.

I was as mad as hell when I laid him gentlly down. I pick up my M14 and yelled at my squad: "charge those dirty no good PAVN bastards and kill them all." I told 1st Fire Team Leader Cpl Herman Watson to zero in on that mortar M82 and knock it out or destroy it. Cpl Watson fired four M79 rounds directly on the M82 mortar squads knocking out both M82 mortars and killing the PAVN squads. Butch's 2nd Squad set up a defensive perimeter in front of the tree line of Teak Trees. Two of Squad 1st rifle teams joined in and stopped the advancing PAVN squads. The fire fight lasted about an hour or so, and the PAVN broke it off after losing 78 of its men compared to one dead Marine and 7 wounded Marines. I call in a MedEvac helicopter, the Bell UH-1, to pick them up. Within 15 or so minutes the copter was landing to pick up the wounded and LCpl Jerry Wassel. We looked for Lcpl Wassel's lower body half and never did find it. We figure when the mortar round went off, it must have shreded his lower body half and threw bits and pieces everywhere. I personally carried his upper body to the copter and gave one of his dog tags to the corpsman. As the corpsman took his body from my arms, the corpsman said: "I got him sergeant I will take care of him." I just stood there covered in LCpl Wassel blood as the copter flew away to take his body back to Camp Rotan Base.

After returning back to Camp Rotan Base I talked to Platoon Sergeant GySgt Russell Owens about putting LCpl Jerry Wassel in for the Silver Star. GySgt Russell Owens said: "with the silver star he will elible to be bury in Arlington National Cemetery. There is a lot of good Marine bury there. Ssgt Tomlin do you want to write the citation or should I." I said: " I will write it and I want to write his Father and Mother." When I got back to my tent. I wrote up the combat report about the fire fight with the PAVN, that we killed 78 PAVN with our lost of 1 Marine killed and 7 wounded. Then I wrote the Silver Star Citation for a **Silver Star (Posthumously) to Lance Corporal Jerry Wassel, United States Marine Corps, who display exceptional valor while engaged in military combat operations against an enemy force while serving as a Rifleman**

with Company L, Third Battalion, Ninth Marines, in the Republic of Vietnam. Then I wrote the letter, no parents should ever receive about the death of their child. I stated in the letter to Mr and Mrs. Wassel in my deepest regret I write this letter that your brave son Jerry was killed in action while saving the lives of 78 fellow Marine while under continuous enemy fire. For his outstanding bravely I his 1st Squad Leader Ssgt Robert Dean Tomlin I am putting him in Posthumously for the Silver Star and he will be buried at Arlington National Cemetery in full military honor.

The next day 1stSg Roger L. Lewis called Butch and I to his tent and said: "Ssgt Tomlin and Ssgt Price you are flying back to the states for Burial Detail at Arlington National Cemetery for LCpl Jerry Wassel Posthumously Silver Star recipient." You are dismissed and see Base Commander LTC Joseph Muller, who will have a few words and instructions. We knocked on LTC Joseph Muller's door and we heard him say enter. Butch and I entered and stood attention and rendered a salute and said: " Ssgt Tomlin and Ssgt Price reporting as directed SIR. " LTC Muller returned the salute and said: "stand at ease." Then, he said: "ever been on burial detail before?" We both said: "no" LTC Muller said: "Ssgt Tomlin and Ssgt Price you will be with the casket and it will be your responiabily to guard and protect that casket at all times and never let it out of your sight. The only time and I mean the only time is when you turn the casket over to the burial detail Arlington National Cemetery. They are known as "The Last to Let You Down." They are the Body Bearers, an elite unit that carries Marines to their final resting place at Arlington National Cemetery, and the caskets they lift can weigh up to 800 pounds." LTC Muller said: " Please escort the fallen hero LCpl Jerry Wassel's parents to and from the grave sight. Any questions we both said "no." LTC Muller said: "one more thing Ssgt Tomlin and Ssgt Price I know you have 50 some days and a wake up before you rotate back to the states." I am personally going to cut the Burial Detail at Arlington National Cemetery, and your discharge orders and paper work, that both of you will release from the United Staes Marine Corps. After burial detail at Arlington National Cemetery, take your discharge orders and paper work to the United States Marine Corps office in Washington DC; they will proceed you out of the United Staes Marine Corps. I just want to thank you for doing an outstanding job as a fellow Marine. You have demonstrated outstanding leadership, bravely, and are truly a great Marine. I just want to shake your hand for keeping a lot of Marines alive. LTC Muller stuck out his hand and gave Ssgt Tomlin and Ssgt Price the firmest hand shake ever. We stood attention rendering a salute. LTC Muller returned our salute and said: "you are dismissed and take LCpl Jerry Wassel home." We did about face and walked out of LTC Muller's office. We went back to our tent and packed our sea bags with our dress blues and the rest of our stuff.

27 September We headed to the copter to fly the casket to Da Nang Air Force Base. From Da Nang Air Force Base to Kadena Air force Base in Okinawa. From Kadena Air force Base to Travis Air Force Base near San Francisco. From Travis Air Force Base to Andrews Air Force Base Washington DC. When we landed at Andrews Air Force

Base, Marine Body Bearers took the casket and gave us a time frame for when the burial would be held. Marine Burial Detail made arrangements for Butch and I to have quarters on Andrews Air Force Base. We got to our room, unpacked and waited for a call from the Marine Burial Detail. We were setting around and talking when the phone rang. I answered the phone and said: "hello Ssgt Tomlin speaking." The voice at the other end was Mr. Wassel, and he said: "His Mother and I have change our minds we don't want Jerry to be buried at Arlington National Cemetery, we want him bury at the family plot in Kansas." I said: " yes SIR I will have to call and make different arangement, but I will see that he gets bury at home." As soon as I hung up the phone Butch said: "what was that all about." I said: " Mr. and Mrs. Wassel they want their son bury in the family plot at home." I called the office of Executive Director, Army National Military Cemeteries, Arlington National Cemetery, and told them that Mr. and Mrs. Wassel wanted their son to be buried at home in the family plot. The Executive Director said: "they would make arangements for Butch and I to fly the casket to Atwood, Kansas." While Butch and I were in Vietnam we got news that Drill Instructor SSgt Robert Johnson had been killed in action at Khe Sanh and was awarded the Metal of Honor and buried at Arlington National Cemetery.

I told Butch lets get up early in the morning and visit SSgt Robert Johnson's grave. We were looking for the grave of SSgt Robert Johnson and reminiscing about the hell he put us through in Boot Camp. As we were trying to find his grave, I was telling Butch that Drill Instructor SSgt Robert Johnson was a real Marine. Butch said: "I think I would have followed that Marine to hell." Then I felt a hand on my shoulder and a voice said: "friend or family" I turned around there was this older gentleman standing in his Marine uniform with more ribbons, medals, service and combat strips you could shake a stick at. I said: "Sir a friend, he was our Drill Instructor at Camp Pendleton and one of the best Marine that you ever want to know." Then the Marine said: "I am Sergeant Major Ben Johnson and Robert was my son, ever since he was a little boy he always wanted to be a Marine just like his Dad and Grand Father. Now all I have is just fond memories of him when he was just a boy, teenager, man, and great Marine." Butch and I said: " we are sorry for your lost Sergeant Major." Then Sergeant Major turned to Butch and I and said: "no sons do not be sorry just be good Marines and keep the honor of the Corp." He stood back with small tears trickling out of the corner of his eyes, standing attention, rendering a salute to his son's grave. Then, in a small tone in his voice, he said: "I miss you son, now you can spend time with your Grand Father." Then Butch and I stood attention render a salute to Drill Instructor SSgt Robert Johnson's grave. We are not suppose to salute NCOs but it was an honor to salute SSgt Robert Johnson Father Sergeant Major Ben Johnson. Butch and I said: "Good bye and God Bless to the Sergeant Major."

We did about face and went back to our quarters to pack and get ready to fly LCpl Jerry Wassel's body back home to Atwood, Kansas. Butch said: " what about our discharge orders and paper work." I called the Marine Washington Office and told them the situation we were in. They said: "come by the office today and we will have everything straigten out before we leave to Kansas." Butch and I got a cab to Marine office before we walked up to the doors a Marine Corporal had our papers ready and handed them to us and said: "officially you will be out of the United States Marine Corps when the funnel is over in Kansas. We took another cab and when we arrive at Travis Air Force Base they had prepared LCpl Jerry Wassel casket and loaded it on the tramsport plane for McConnell Air Force Base Wichita, Kansas. From McConnell Air Force Base then we had to get a Private Jet to Atwood-Rawlins County City-County Airport. When we arrive at the Atwood Airport there was a hearse from Jackson Mortuary waiting for us. They loaded the casket and the driver said: " The funeral will be at 1400 hundred tomorrow at Jackson Funeral Home; then we go to Atwood Fairview Cemetery at the Wassel Family's Plot. I told the driver that the body of LCpl Jerry Wassel is the responsibility Ssgt Tomlin and Ssgt Price of the Untied States Marine Corps, and we have to ride with you to the funeral home. The hearse driver said: "no sweat off my nose jump in." The drive to the funeral home was only two miles from the airport. When we arrived Butch, I helped get the casket out of the hearse and took it in the funeral home so they could get everything for. viewing.

The Funeral Director approached Butch and I and said: " I contact the United States Marine Corps to request an Official Burial Detail. The United States Marine Corps Burial Detail send one additional Active Duty Marine for Bugler Ssgt Tomlin and Ssgt Price you will fold the Flag and you will be the final detail who attends the final burial at the cemetery." Then, he said: "do not worry Ssgt Tomlin and Ssgt Price I have special instructions from United States Marine Corps Burial Detail and we will take good care of LCpl Jerry Wassel. I have made arrangements for you to stay at our local motel until after the funeral. I can have the driver take you there now." Butch and I said: "Thank You SIR." Shook his hand and left for the motel.

The next morning we were up by 0600, had a good breakfast went back to our room to get dressed for the funeral. Butch and I shave our faces real close without taking our skin off. Then we got dressed in our Blue Dress "A" with a midnight blue coat with standing collar, seven gilt buttons and red trim; a white web belt, white peaked cap (known as a "barracks cover"); blue trousers, white gloves, and black dress shoes and socks. Butch check me out, said: "Ssgt Tomlin you are one good looking Marine." Then I checked Butch out and I said: " Ssgt Price you are also one good looking Marine." We both put the last buff shine on our black shoes and headed for the funeral home. We arrived at Jackson Funeral Home at about 1100 to get ready for LCpl Jerry Wassel burial details. As we walked in we were greeted by Funeral Director and he said: " everything is ready to go and arrangements have been made for Marine Corps League (MCL) Then Funeral Director said: "I gave you a lot of details did I leave anything out." I said: " This is the first burial detail that Butch and I have been on, the only request that we have is that Butch and I stand at each end of the casket as it is in the viewing stage." They brought out the casket and pulled it in the middle of the viewing room; I was on the right end and Butch was on the left end of the casket.

They opened the lid for full viewing, and there lay LCpl Jerry Wassel in his dress blues, and they put some apparatus on his lower half to show that he had legs. As I was looking down on him, I remember holding him with out any legs, as his life was being stuffed out, from the lost of blood. I felt small tears fall from my eyes. Then I heard Butch saying Robert pull yourself together, people are starting to come in. As we were at parade rest, a little boy approached us and said: "mister are you a real Marine like my Daddy." I looked down and said: "yes son I am a real Marine just like your Father." He went running back to his Mother yelling: "Mommie he is a real Marine just like Daddy." Every body in the funeral parlor through it was funny and you could hear people laughing and saying: "is he a cute little boy." Then Mr. and Mrs. Wassel came up to view their son; they both just stood there for a moment, both in complete silience. Mrs Wassel bent over to kiss her son on the cheek; then she just grabbed him and started crying uncontrollable and saying why, why did God take my only son. Then I was thinking of my poor Mom when my baby brother Kenny died, she just cried and sopped for days. She would tell Dad he was just a baby; couldn't God let him be. Then Dad who was also suffering, would say its God's will and Kenny is in heaven now. I help Mrs Wassel back to her seat.

Then the pastor said: " lets bow our heads and say a prayer Almighty God, into your hands we commend your son LCpl Jerry Wassel, in sure and certain hope of resurrection to eternal life through Jesus Christ our Lord. Amen. Then he begin with Oh God take your son home to heaven and Dear God praying for peace to bring comfort, courage to face the days ahead and loving memories to forever hold in your heart. LCpl Jerry Wassel will remain in our hearts forever. May you be comforted by the outpouring of love and support." All the while I was biting my lower lip and trying not to cry when I saw his Mother wailing and other family members crying. I noticed Butch was having a hard time trying to keep it together.

After the service was over Butch and I placed the United States Flag over the casket, and the pallbearers picked up the casket and carried it and put it in the hearse. Once the casket was loaded in the hearse, Butch and I rode in the hearse to the cemetery; this was our final ride with LCpl Jerry Wassel. I remember how green he was when he arrived in Vietnam and then turned into a damn good real Marine. I surely lost a good friend and a good Marine that day from that damn ambush from the PAVN. I keep thinking if only I could have stopped the bleeding. The hearse arrived at the grave site and stopped; the pallbearers carried the casket to the grave. In the old days when caskets were made of wood, they used to be lowered by two guys using ropes to slowly lower the casket into the grave. These days, given the weight of metal caskets, which are so heavy, a sort of lift is used to lower the casket. When the family is ready to proceed, the Funeral Director signals the pallbearers to withdraw the casket from the hearse and carry it to the grave. The pallbearers pulled the casket on the lift and stepped back and went to their seats. Butch and I stood by the casket as the pastor said a prayer.

The bugler and firing party are already at their gravesite positions. The casket arrives and is within immediate view of the gravesite; the Commander will give the following commands; DETAIL ATTENTION, at which time the Commander will give the following command; PRESENT ARMS! When the casket is in place, the Commander will give the following commands, ORDER ARMS, followed by the command, PARADE REST. When the religious service is completed, the clergy or the funeral director will ask the mourners to stand for the rendering of the Ceremonial Volley. Ssgt Tomlin and Ssgt Price will pick up the Flag and extend it over the casket. The Commander will give the following commands: Members of the Detail will execute the following sequence of three movements: The Commander will give the commands A. ATTENTION! B. HALF RIGHT – FACE C.. PORT ARMS (3-step movement) Move the right foot (Left always anchored), 12 inches to the right. The legs are kept straight so the weight of the body rests equally on both feet. Followed by the command READY UNLOCK The Commander will now give the command, AIM FIRE, three times When the command "AIM" is given, each rifleman will raise their rifle to a position of 45 degrees from the horizontal. On the command "Fire", each rifleman will squeeze the trigger quickly and lower the rifle to the position of port arms. After the three commands, AIM, FIRE, have been given, the Commander will give the command CEASE FIRE-LOCK. At this point the detail will bring their feet back together (smartly) and finger lock their rifle. Then, on command HALF LEFT, the detail will bring the heel of their right foot smartly against the heel of the left foot, completing the left face. From this position, the detail Commander gives the command "PRESENT ARMS." Taps are now played. Upon completion of Taps, the Commander gives the command, "ORDER ARMS." The detail will remain at attention after Taps is played, and the flag is folded, and Ssgt Tomlin and Ssgt Price will present the flag to LCpl Jerry Wassel's family. Upon completion of Taps, the Commander will give the command, PARADE REST. After the ceremony, (memorial service) is over, the family lays flowers on the casket. I The Funeral Director will make the closing announcements. The Commander will give the command, DETAIL DISMISSED, (one step back) Police, all brass. The detail Commander will give the Funeral Director the spent cartridges which he will distribute among the immediate family members. The detail Commander will now pay his respects to the immediate members of the family and present them with his Detail business card and Tribute coin. The detail Commander requested that Ssgt Tomlin and Ssgt Price give the Tribute coin when appropriate. (Tribute Coin to be distributed only to the families of Marines) The detail will leave the grounds with their rifle at Trail Arms.

When the Marine Corps League did their Honor Guard Ceremonial all the time Ssgt Tomlin and Ssgt Price were standing attention throughout the entire ceremonial. When the rifle team was called attention and fired their weapons, Ssgt Tomlin, and Ssgt Price rendered a salute and held it until the last shot was fired. Butch and I walked over to the casket and folded the United States Flag and presented it to Mr. and Mrs. Wassel, then gave them the Silver Star Medal. Mr Wassel took the Silver Star and made this comment: "My only son was killed for this." I said: "no SIR your son died for the honor of his country and saving the lifes of 78 Marines." Then, Mrs. Wassel said: " would please talk to me after the funeral is over." I said: " yes Ma'am" Butch and I waited until everybody had left the grave site, then headed for the hearse for a ride back to the motel. As we were walking Mrs. Wassel caught up with us and said:" Ssgt Tomlin were you with my son when he died." I said: "yes Ma'am" Then she said: "what was his last words before he died." I said: "Ma'am he said tell my Father and Mother that I missed them and love them, and tell them I want to be bury next to Grand Father John." Mrs Wassel just cried and said: " we did bury him next to my Father." She hug Butch and I and said: " God Bless and may God keep you out of Harms Way when you go back to Vietnam." I looked at Butch and said: "I hope we never put our Mothers through that." Butch said: " no Mother should ever loose a son or daughter in war."

We went back to the motel, packed our bags to catch an early flight tomorrow out of McConnell Air Force Base Wichita, Kansas. Butch and I talked for several hours about we were officially out of the Marine Corps. I told Butch tomorrow when we fly out of McConnell Air Force to fly home, this will be the last time we wear the Untited States Marine Corps uniform. I will be flying home to Springfield, Illinois and Butch will be flying home to St. Louis, Missouri. Just before we turned in I received a phone call from the Funeral Director. He said: "The burial detail went great everybody was please and happy. Mr. and Mrs Wassel was very please that you Ssgt Tomlin and Ssgt Price brought their son Home." Mr. Wassel said: " tell the young Marines I am sorry the wait I acted about the Silver Star. Please tell Ssgt Tomlin I put the Silver Star with my son's picture that will be setting on the mantle above the fire place." The next morning, Butch and I arrived at McConnell Air Force to catch our flights home. As we stood in front of each other, we gave each other a big hug and said: " I love you Brother." We shook hands, stood attention and rendered a salute and said our farewells. As we were going to our airplanes, a Sergeant from the Air Force said:" Ssgt Tomlin since you call each other brothers, is Ssgt Price really your brother." I turned to the Sergeant and said: " not in blood he is not my brother, but in God's eyes and in my heart he will always be my brother." We were on different airplanes flying back home. As my plane lifted off the runway, I was thinking it would be nice going home to my family, Mom's home cooking, and sleeping in a warm safe bed tonight.

As the years went by Butch and I lost contact with each other. Butch's Mom wrote to my Mom one day and said: " Butch quit his job at the ice cream factory in St. Louis and moved to Denver, Colorado to work for Martin Marietta in the space program. Then years later I moved to Denver, Colorado. Then in 1984 I got a job at Martin Marietta. Then my first day while I was driving to work, I notice a truck was broke down on the side of the road with steam and water pouring out of the radiator. I pulled over and said: "do you need help." When the man pulled his head out from under the hood and said: " I could use a lift to work." I could not believe my eyes, there was Butch, my old Marine buddy. I jumped out of my truck and ran over and grabbed him and said: " Butch where in the hell have you been." Butch just stood there like he was frozen and finally said: " you got to be kidding me Robert my old friend." We got in the truck and headed for work. What was kind of funny, we both work in the same department at Martin Marietta with the same boss. As we were driving to work, we talked about old and lost times. The good and bad times that we had together. As we got out of the truck to go into work, Butch made this comment: "Robert the only Green Hell we have to worry about now is these damn dandelions growing everywhere." We just stood there for a moment and laughed and went into work. Still, after all those years that have passed we are still the best friends in the whole world.

CPSIA information can be obtained
at www.ICGtesting.com
Printed in the USA
BVHW060736121022
649159BV00005B/248

9 781977 256713